HERETIC'S WAR

SARAH MACKLIN

MVmedia, LLC
Fayetteville, GA

MVmedia, LLC
PO Box 143052
Fayetteville, GA 30214
www.mvmediaatl.com

Publisher's Note: This is a work of fiction. Names, characters, places, and incidents are a product of the author's imagination. Locales and public names are sometimes used for atmospheric purposes. Any resemblance to actual people, living or dead, or to businesses, companies, events, institutions, or locales is completely coincidental.

Ordering Information:
Quantity sales. Special discounts are available on quantity purchases by corporations, associations, and others. For details, contact the "Special Sales Department" at the address above.

Heretic's War/ Sarah Macklin. -- 1st ed.
ISBN 979-8-9857336-9-3

Contents

Evil as well as good both operate to advance the Great Plan.

—Egyptian Proverb

Chapter One

It was hard to sing when one's feet hurt. Erenemo raised his rich baritone and ignored the throbbing in his heels. Behind him stretched the column of mourners, nearly all Nsongo's populace, and ahead warriors carried the body of his niece and leader. It was usually a joyous affair, a dara joining the ranks of their ancestors, but not this time. To have such a young leader taken away so soon after being chosen casted a damper on the city's spirits. So many had been lost in the war against the northern Ega and Ashaki had put an end to it, surrendering before their army was completely wiped out. Now she was gone.

Ashaki's reign was a salve on the raw wound of occupation, a tiny sliver of hope that the people of Nsongo's lives wouldn't be completely crushed under their new masters. With her death, they found themselves in a state of limbo once again. They couldn't understand how she, a warrior fit and still in her prime, could have suddenly succumbed. Erenemo looked at the shrouded body ahead of him, knowing of the twisted face underneath. Her death had a quite simple explanation. Poison. It was the least she deserved.

He grimaced as he stepped on a rock that stabbed his foot despite the leather of his sandal. He was going to make this quick. There were far more important things he and the council needed to speak on. The sight of his family mausoleum filled him with relief and he struggled to keep his face straight. The great column stretched high above them, a towering monument to the impressive warriors of their line. Nearly a hundred names were already inscribed on it and soon Ashaki's name would be as well. The procession stopped before it and Erenemo craned his head upward to look at the memorial. In his lifetime he'd already seen his father, his brother, all six of his nephews and several of their spouses have their names engraved. He looked around at the rest of the graveyard, family spires thrusting up toward the heavens, demanding the gods' notice. There were so many names carved over the last thirteen years. It was heartbreaking.

A gentle hand on his arm brought him back to his task. The warriors were carrying the body down into the mausoleum. Eerenemo nodded his thanks to his assistant then cleared his throat. Desperately wishing for a bit to drink, he started singing a different song. A different rhythm, a more upbeat one, commanding the attention of the mourners and reminding them that this was a time of celebration. Other voices joined in and as the tomb was resealed, dancers began their part in front of it. The song rose in fervor until the very air was filled with it. The song was a plea as much as a command. See our great leader. See how much we love them. See their great works and welcome them to their eternal home.

As the song ended the last of the bricks was laid and clay smeared over to seal them. Erenemo heard wailing behind him and knew the cry of his wife immediately. He had to resist a sigh. She and Ashaki had been close, almost a second mother to her. Erenemo looked over to her as she came forward, assisted by their son. Normally there would be a host of relatives to gather around after the committal, but now there were three.

People began to come up to pay their respects, Ashaki's in-laws at the front. The couple was solemn, holding hands as if they would fall if they let each other go. Erenemo bowed his head. They gave him a warrior's greeting.

"Has anyone heard anything about Masola?" the husband, Kekame, asked quietly as their wives hugged. They'd been devastated by their granddaughter's disappearance.

"Not a word," he responded. Hopefully, she'd been taken care of by brigands by now. "She completely disappeared. I can't understand why she would run away."

"If something was wrong, she knows she could have come to us."

Erenemo nodded, remembering the night he'd told his great-niece to leave Nsongo.

"I've sent men to look for her. A girl alone in the city or, worse yet, on the road. Anything could happen to her. I pray we find her every day."

"As do we."

They moved on, leaving Erenemo relieved that he didn't have to keep up this facade of concern about his grandniece. Her absence today was surely noted and the fact that she'd disappeared the night her mother died had been the source of a host of rumors. It was as it should be. He went through the motions of accepting and thanking the other mourners for their concern and blessings on his house. There were the heads of the other great households of Nsongo. Behind them came daras from other, lesser cities. He bristled at having to bow, even slightly, to them. He looked about for the daras of the other principal cities of the south but he didn't see them in their proper place in the procession. Erenemo frowned but shook off the feeling. Surely, they'd been delayed by travel and were near the back.

"High Priest Erenemo," purred a voice. A woman decked in a long trio of pearl necklaces bowed before him, flanked by two other men. One wore heavy iron bracelets and an iron choker. The other had a necklace of intricately carved wooden beads depicting forest scenes. Erenemo checked his frown as he nodded to them. The woman gave a subdued smile.

"I am Yasuliba, envoy of Amakari."

"Envoy?" he snapped.

The woman stared back at him, unmoved. "Envoy."

"And I am Bajemi, envoy of Lonki," said the man with the iron bracelets.

The man with the carved necklace nodded again. "My name is Ika and I have been sent from Ofolubaru."

Erenemo worked hard to school the enraged scowl starting to form. Amakari, Lonki, and Ofolubaru. The three other cities that could dare rival Nsongo and they sent envoys to such an occasion. He drew himself up to his full height, ignoring the cracking of his back.

"I find it odd that the daras of such prestigious cities could not find their way here to celebrate the passing on of their Great Dara." His voice rose slightly involuntarily and he could feel the eyes of his son and wife lock on him.

The envoy from Ofolubaru held his hands out in a plea for

peace. "I do not presume to know why my dara did not come. Her decisions are hers alone. I am merely a servant."

The woman sniffed. "My dara, on the other hand, feels that he's done more than enough to honor the traitor of Nsongo."

The air was suddenly charged as if lighting were about to strike. Erenemo took several deep breaths to try to calm himself down. His wife put a hand on his arm. He put one over hers to let her know that he wasn't about to strike. Although, he was sorely tempted.

"How dare you?" his son roared.

Erenemo held up his hand for silence. He looked between the envoys who appeared to share the sentiment voiced by the woman.

"You tell your daras," he said working to keep his voice even, "that the title of Great Dara still rests comfortably on Nsongo's shoulders and they'd do well to remember that."

The envoy from Amakari tilted her head up slightly and smiled, looking more like a viper ready to strike.

"Considering what a whore for the northerners this city has become; we'll see how long that lasts." She bowed again and the others followed suit. "High priest," she said and walked away.

Erenemo watched them, his face hot as if he'd been slapped. It might as well have been a physical assault. It was a momentous event, the funeral of the Great Dara, the de facto leader of the southern cities. No other dara had held the title since ages before. Nsongo had been the center politically and economically for untold years. If the other cities thought they had even half a chance of claiming the title things had grown grimmer than he'd thought.

He endured the rest of the funeral, going through the motions. It had grown hotter as they went along and he wished to join his wife under her protective canopy but he wanted to show he was a different sort of priest. He wouldn't be considered soft. His mind ran back to the smug envoys. Neither would his city.

"Father," his son began, coming to his side, "we can't let this insult stand. We must make them pay."

"This isn't the old days of bickering kings," his wife said calmly.

"We need a new dara," Erenemo said lowly. "And quickly. This city needs strong leadership and a strong one to navigate this new era . . . under the Ega." The last word tasted bitter. "We will just have to pray that council choses well." Seeing that he was through talking, his family left him in his furious silence for the rest of the trip.

~

Erenemo had waited long enough. He made his way along the colonnades that led to the council room. His sandals slapped against the mud brick floors. The sound of his rustling robes filled the empty area. He'd allowed the council to have two days of uninterrupted deliberation. They hadn't chosen a dara yet which was an obvious sign that they were deadlocked. He was sure several were trying to maneuver their family members into the position. Erenemo's lips spread into a humorless smile. It had been held by his family for seven generations —an unprecedented feat! —and would remain in their line. One way or another.

Under his arm was the series of papers that he'd done countless hours of research for. Accounts of the previous daras were lovingly written across the bark paper, preserved in the city's archive. Only once before had a priest held the title of dara, an unremarkable man who'd accomplished little in his reign. It would be easy to do better than that. He was a son of the line of Yundasha. Leadership was his by blood. And if not him then the title must go to his son.

Erenemo frowned at the thought. His son was a good warrior, third in command over Nsongo's military. He was an excellent commander and well loved by the warriors he led. But as far as leadership of an entire city? No. The young man was ill suited for it. He had little comprehension of the day-to-day governance of a city and a region. As much as Erenemo was loathe to admit it, Ashaki had surpassed his son in that aspect. Even if she were the dara that delivered them into bondage. But he'd endure his son's reign before he'd see another sit on the ivory chair of Nsongo.

The servants at the doors to the council chamber bowed low

to him as he approached. They stepped aside, not even asking his business as he made his way inside. The council members looked up, surprised. He smiled genially and gave the elders the slightest bow. Silence hung over the room for a moment, several of the elders shifting uncomfortably on their cushioned stools.

"Erenemo," the oldest man in the room said slowly. His beard was thick, the white mass resting on his chest. "What are you doing here?"

"Elder Okepeli, honored council members, I've come to assist you in choosing the dara."

A handful of the elders eyed him with suspicion. A woman stretched her hands, knuckles gnarled from years of swinging a sword. She regarded him with a deep frown. This woman he knew well. Oshala had as much hate for Ashaki as he did. He was sure that she was jostling for one of her granddaughters to become dara. Her daughter was already the war minister. Getting a granddaughter into the daraship would secure her own dynasty. The old bat. Her mind hadn't dulled in her old age and she would be one of his greatest opponents in this fight.

"Priest Erenemo," she began, "we are perfectly able to choose the dara on our own."

His smile didn't waver as several other council members nodded.

"But I may bring some insight into the process and the choices for my niece's successor. Seeing as you're obviously deadlocked."

There was grumbling but he was waved over to an empty stool to the side of the room. Erenemo took his seat, pleased to be in the council room at last.

An elder with an angular tattoo on his forehead turned to him. "We were just discussing some of the names from Ashaki's list, may she dance with the ancestors."

"Her list?" he asked, trying to hide his utter surprise. He didn't miss the smug smile from Oshala.

"Yes. Before she passed from this world, Ashaki had started making her list of possible abodaras."

"And a good list it is," chimed in a portly man with heavy iron bands going up his forearms. Erenemo held in a sneer.

Hafulo was a banker, from a family that had bought their way into nobility, and the priest couldn't stand him. "It's obvious that she'd put some time and thought into who may become her successor."

Erenemo stopped himself from sucking his teeth. "But it was just a list of those she was considering. Surely those would be too young to take the title now. We must choose someone of age and experience."

"We were discussing just that before you came in," added another elder. "Did you have anyone that you would like to suggest? Perhaps we overlooked them in our days of deliberation."

Erenemo raised an eyebrow at the slight. "If we're having an issue choosing the dara, perhaps we can choose a temporary one. Just to see to running the city. In the meantime, you all could continue your search. I know you all would want to take your time since the last decision was unfortunately rushed."

The council bristled under his comment, but they knew the truth in it. Choosing Ashaki as the dara was done in haste, a panicked decision made after all other candidates had been slain in battle. He knew at least half of this council regretted the choice. Now they had a chance to correct it. He could only hope that they'd take it.

"Did you have someone in mind?" Oshala asked incredulously.

"I was very close to my niece in her day-to-day workings. I tried to steer her into the path my great brother forged as dara. I could easily step into the role until someone was chosen."

Sounds of disbelief and scorn echoed across the room. Oshala stabbed a bony finger at him.

"You've been waiting for this chance. I'm surprised you didn't nominate your own son."

Erenemo fixed her with a calm smile. "Now, General Oshala," he began giving her the honor of her old title, "I'm sure many of us have relatives in mind for this position. But no, I have no plans on nominating my son. His place is among his warriors."

The doors of the council room flew open before anyone could make another comment. Erenemo and the council frowned as a man swished in. He was dressed in the light fabrics of the Ega, the perfume they favored invading the room.

"Why was I not invited to this most important meeting? Surely I am to be privy to the choosing of your next dara."

The man's accent grated on Erenemo's nerves. His mere presence was a poison in the air. The eldest council member took a deep breath.

"Magistrate Hotempkhar," he said between clenched teeth. "This is an Nsongan matter. We didn't see a need to involve you."

"Well, you should have," the man said with a dismissive wave of his lanky hand. His eyes searched the room for a seat, but no one offered their position. "Anything that involves the ruling of Nsongo involves me. *I* am the envoy of the netkoleh himself, voice of the gods. You are his subjects. While you've been given the blessing of keeping your ruler, you should remember who truly rules here." He looked around again. "Is there not a seat?"

Not a body moved for a moment. Then, Hafulo stood with a regretful look on his face. Erenemo dared him to meet anyone's eyes. Let him feel the shame of conceding to this perfumed fool. Hotempkhar sat, making a face as he tried to make himself comfortable.

"I hear you've been deliberating for days. Surely this can't be normal."

"Choosing a dara must be done with great consideration, magistrate," said a councilwoman near him.

"Oh, yes. You don't choose by blood." He sighed as one would with unreasonable children. "Did your Ashaki have a successor?"

"Not yet," Oshala responded.

"Well, wasn't she useless."

"Uncalled for," the tattooed elder blurted out.

Hotempkhar ignored him. "Well, have you any candidates? I won't see you fall into chaos because a handful of old people can't make up their mind."

Erenemo cooled his anger by imagining a knife sliding into the foreign magistrate's soft throat.

"I beg for your patience," he said evenly. "I do believe we may have solution to this problem soon." He looked around the room and people reluctantly nodded in agreement.

Hotempkhar stood. "Good. Inform me of your decision the moment you make it. I will be in my compound." Without another word, he swished from the room.

Oshala spat on the clay floor. "Strutting crane."

The elders watched the door, their faces a mixture of sneers and frowns. Erenemo waited for a moment, then cleared his throat.

"This is why we should choose an interim dara immediately."

The other elders looked to each other. Their expression didn't fill him with much hope. He settled into a comfortable position on his stool and let the discussion continue.

~

Hotemkhar looked up from his lunch at the sound of a servant running down the hall. He stuffed the piece of roasted bird in his mouth, chewing angrily. Meeting with those incompetent Nsongans this morning had put him in a foul mood and he cursed anyone else who might bring him disappointing news. It was past time for the council to choose a leader. How hard could that possibly be? They valued their warriors so damned much. Just choose their best one and be done with it. That way there could be no accusations that he was letting the city slide into chaos. He scowled. They'd better get themselves together or he'd be forced to step in.

The servant ran into the room, stopping at a respectable distance before his table. The man bowed, panting, and held a letter out. Hotemkhar's nearest attendant took it, bringing it to the table.

"You're dismissed," he said, waving the sweating creature away.

Hotemkhar set down his knife to examine the letter, realizing that it was actually two messages. He opened the first, reading it intently and prayed it was the news he'd been anticipating for weeks. But no. His eyebrows shot up when he got halfway through and he had to reread from the beginning. The netkoleh, his leader and voice of the great god Koleh, had declared that there were no gods and all religion was to be immediately banned. It would be up to him to make sure that all temples were stripped of all religious trappings and all priests disbanded. He picked up his cup, drinking deeply from the wine. This was blasphemy. Utter blasphemy. What would they do if the gods responded to this? But the netkoleh *was* the voice of the gods, in fact their body on earth. If anyone would know of the gods' presence, it would be him.

He downed another gulp of wine and motioned for his attendant to refill the cup. He took a moment to contemplate a future without the favor of the gods. It was frightening and repugnant but he had to obey. The gods, be they there or not, may be over his soul in the afterlife but his ruler held the power over him in this life. He had to go along with this and pray for the best outcome. No, he would make sure he had the best outcome.

Hotemkhar set aside that letter, making sure it was folded closed so his servant couldn't see what was written. He picked up the second letter, truly praying that this was the news he wanted. This one was from one of the high commanders of the military in the capital. Hotemkhar's heart swelled with relief. He would have his troops to invade the forest across the Bangi River. He looked at the number and blinked. It was only a third of what he'd asked for.

Further reading revealed that the commander couldn't send the requested number because Metkara was preparing to go to war. Troops were being pulled from other parts of the empire to subdue the rebellion of Wiluru. Hotemkhar set down his cup, reading that line again. Wiluru, the proud kingdom on the northern coast, had been part of the empire for ages. Their line had intermingled with the imperial line since their subjugation. The idea of them rebelling now was inconceivable. And they had no army to speak of. They were a naval power. What could their king be thinking?

He tapped the letter on the table. He hoped that this rebellion would be put down quickly. He had plans. The lands across the Bangi had to be conquered. The people, those little selfish gold hoarders, had retreated to their thick forest and homes, taking with them the treasure that made this region so rich. The empire would have that gold. He would have that gold. His legacy, as the magistrate that tamed the rowdy southerners, would be secured. Surely, the netko — the emperor —would promote him to an even higher position back in the capital. He took a drink from his cup. But it would only happen if they had enough troops.

Hotempkhar rose, pushing his plate to the side to be collected. His attendant jumped to perform his task. He took one last drink of wine before setting out for another compound in the city. He was loathe to speak with the military commander stationed here, but it was necessary to find out just how an invasion would fare with the numbers they had. There were monsters across the Bangi, horrible monsters used by the people there to keep out outsiders. There was only one survivor from the band they'd sent to scout the forest and he was a babbling mess. Only the barest details had been gleaned from him since. An army was needed and an army was what he'd have.

He walked out in the streets of Nsongo, regretting not bringing along a servant to hold a shade. The sun was punishing today and he felt beads of sweat rise on the back of his neck. Luckily, the compound the commander was using as his base of operations wasn't far. The soldiers stationed there paid him little attention when he came into the courtyard. He stood to his full height, doing his best to look dignified.

"You there," he said, pointing at a soldier leaning against a wall. "Take me to Commander Tutahmen."

The soldier frowned but stood up and led him inside. Hotemkhar looked about in disgust. The area the soldiers stayed in was just as trashed as the last time he visited. Surely the commander had better control on these men. They entered the small room Tutahmen used as his office. He scowled at the short haired man, reading over a series of reports. The soldier didn't announce him so Hotemkhar cleared his throat dramatically.

The commander stilled, then looked up.

"Magistrate," he said, a tired look in his eyes. He waved the soldier off.

"I have news from the capital."

"Very good." He looked back to his reports.

Hotemkhar sneered. "Five hundred men are being sent to assist in the invasion of the forest."

"What?" Tutahmen's head snapped up. "Why only five hundred? I thought you asked for thrice that."

"It appears that the empire is going to war with Wiluru. The northerners have rebelled." Hotemkhar watched the man as he sat with the news. He couldn't imagine what thoughts could be going through his head. "Surely, that amount will still be enough. Even with the jungle people's monsters."

Tutahmen locked eyes with him. "Do you even understand what those monsters were?" Hotemkhar had only taken the breath to respond when the commander continued. "One of my men were able to get a full description from the Nsongans. They were beasts taller than a man, with snouts full of teeth that shined like metal. Claws that looked like knives. They were swift and could remain unseen." He paused. "And they spoke. The Nsongans that we sent begged their permission to leave and the things let them. Only Turo came back from our men and you know what kind of state he's in."

Hotemkhar pursed his lips, thinking of the shaking, babbling soldier they'd pulled from the river.

"Five hundred more soldiers will have to be enough. With the men you have here that would constitute a force of a thousand."

"Are you daft?" he asked flatly.

"How dare you!"

"I would send eight hundred at the absolute most. I won't leave this city ripe for rebellion."

"Then pull from the other cities, Afolobaru, Amakari. I'm sure they have soldiers to spare. Their leaders have been more compliant with us so I'm sure a lesser Egan presence can be tolerated."

"You little noble weasel. You don't understand the first thing about —"

"How many times do we have to have this conversation?" Hotemkhar shouted. "You may be the military commander of the southern conquests but I have been placed as magistrate. I am the law and you will do as I say. Take troops from the other major cities. And come up with a battle plan at once. I want to have the jungle people's gold as soon as possible. If the empire is going to war, it will need money and we need to give it to them." He paused, drinking in the seething anger from the other man. "I expect a plan within the next few days. This is our priority, commander."

He turned toward the door, then stopped. "Succeed in this and we'll see both of our stars rise." Without another word he left the room, pleased when he heard something hit a wall and shatter in the commander's office.

Chapter Two

Izriamat took her time walking through the palace, taking in the sights and sound that seemed lost to her for so long. Every day she woke up and realized that she wasn't in the imperial capital was a blessing. Wiluru spread out in every direction, surrounding her in the warm embrace of home. Home. That was a word that she didn't think she'd use with fondness ever again. Seven years she'd been away in the imperial capital of Metkara. Seven years a captive of the Ega and their ruler. She pushed aside the thoughts of her husband—her former husband. There was no need to think of him. None.

She turned down a series of gray stone hallways, nodding to the servants she passed. She reminded herself to make the symbol of Yutuu's blessing over their heads. She was back in her god's favor. No, she reminded herself, she'd never left it. This was her place, in Wiluru amid her people, Yutuu be praised. She gave a blessing over another set of servants who passed. Nothing but death would drag her away from her proper place again.

Her path took her to the section of the palace where her parents' rooms were. One of the attending guards bowed deeply when she came up to him.

"Princess Izriamat, I'm sorry but your parents are at a council meeting."

Izriamat's eyebrows raised. "So early?"

"Yes, my princess. They left shortly after daybreak."

"Thank you." She made the sign of blessing over him and continued walking. The guards at the council room weren't so accommodating and didn't move when she approached. Izriamat stopped, looking up to them with puzzlement on her face.

"We're sorry, princess, but the council is currently in session," one addressed her with a slight nod of his head.

She looked past them to the thick doors that barred her passage. On them was a depiction of crashing waves surrounding a whirlpool, a symbol of Yutuu.

"Am I not allowed?" she asked gently. She raised an amused eyebrow to let the guards know she wasn't angry with them.

The guards passed a nervous look between them. "No one is allowed in once a council meeting is in session."

"Then that will have to be changed just this once." Izriamat stepped past them, placing her hands on the cool doors before pushing. Behind her, the guards stood stunned before calling out that she couldn't. Izriamat ignored them and stepped forward, entering the council room. They didn't understand her place in all of this. The situation surely being discussed by her parents and the council was of her doing and she had a right to speak her mind about what they would do from here on.

A councilor, an elderly man with a ring of gray curly hair from ear to ear was in the middle of speaking when they all noticed her approach. Her father had his head down, chin cupped in his hand as he thought, but he looked up sharply at the sound of her sandals whispering against the stone floor. Her mother's eyes widened until Izriamat could see nearly all the whites.

"Izriamat," her mother breathed, stunned.

"What are you doing here?" her father hissed.

His tone stung her. He'd never spoken to her in such a fashion, never even raised his voice to her. The burning contempt in his eyes was painful to see but she took a breath, steeling herself.

"I wish to speak in my defense." The council members, all nobility, looked to each other then their king. Her father's eyes narrowed. "I'm sure I've been a topic of discussion this morning."

She saw the red grow under her father's brown skin and knew she'd infuriated him.

"You deliberately disobeyed me. You provoked the emperor into declaring war after I explicitly said that we would negotiate with him. You have doomed this country."

From her place beside him, her mother placed a hand on his arm to calm him. The deep disappointment in her mother's eyes hurt more than her father's wrath.

"Do you have anything to say for yourself?"

Izriamat closed her eyes for a moment, concentrating on Yutuu's presence within her. "Father, Mother, honored councilors, I know that you all wished for a continued peace but, as I warned you, there is no peace with the leader of the Ega." She pressed her lips together, a moment of doubt passing through. Her next words would have to be carefully crafted. "I have spoken with Yutuu and he wishes for his chosen people to regain their place in the world. There will have to be war because that is the only language the Ega understand."

She took another breath, thinking of her former husband. "I have lived under them directly, in the fetid heart of this empire. They know only of brutality and subjugation. Negotiation would have only led to another form of captivity for us."

It was her father's turn to take a breath. "But now you doom us to annihilation. Because you feel that you spoke to Yutuu."

"Have you no faith, father?" she asked, genuinely hurt. "You delivered me to the temple yourself, your first child to be dedicated to our highest god just like your elder brother. Why wouldn't I be able to commune with our god as he does?"

The silence that fell on the room was thick like soured milk. Finally, a councilman spoke lowly. "High priest Munabis is still pure."

"You are out of line," her mother snapped.

"I will not tolerate such talk," her father added, his eyes carrying the threat to the councilor.

"But you think it," she said quietly. She let her words settle onto the room before she continued. "Yes, I have been… used by the ruler of the Ega." She still couldn't bring herself to say his name. "Again. And again. And again. Until I was forced to give birth to his son. You, who sit here in your grand palace, so far away from our enemy, know nothing of surviving their brutality. Now, you want to turn over and offer your belly to them again."

"Daughter," the king called, a slight warning in his tone. "That is not at all what I intend."

"Who will be the sacrifice this time? Will you send Umakaal back with me this time? The one who was supposed to be his wife to make up for the disappointment I was." Her father tried to make a response but she cut him off. "How many daughters will it take to assuage them? How many of us are you willing to sacrifice?"

"But you have started a *war*," her father countered. "So many will die because of your stubbornness."

"And so many will live free after it. A free Wiluru, father. You will be the king of a free Wiluru." She turned to look over the councilors. "The majority of the governors are on board with this. My siblings and I made sure of it. We have not gone into this without careful thought and the guidance of Yutuu."

She finally returned her eyes to her parents, sitting aghast at the front of the room. "We no longer have time to speculate about what to do if war comes. War is here and with the gods behind us, we will win." She stood, back straight, waiting for an answer.

Her father's anger clouded his face, then melted into contempt. "You will return to your rooms. You'll not leave unless I have given permission. The guards will make sure of that."

He signaled with a wave of his hand and a pair of guards who'd been at the far walls of the rooms rushed over to flank her. Izriamat stiffened, her resolve wavering for just a moment. "Leave us."

Struggling to keep her face straight, she bowed to her parents and the council. Without another word, she turned on her heel and left the council chamber. She paid no attention to the questioning glances from servants and others on business at the palace. She was the messenger of Yutuu himself. He spoke to her directly. There could be nothing on this earth that could deter her from the path her god had laid out before her. She rolled her shoulders back, raising her chin. Even her own flesh and blood couldn't move her from it. They would understand eventually.

~

Umakaal marched into her older sister's wing of the palace in a fury. She'd finished her watch today, incised those members of the palace guard—that she'd been put in charge of—were moved without her notice or say so. She understood that her father had the ultimate authority over them, but he'd at least give her notice of any decisions. She hadn't even taken off her armor before heading straight here. Izriamat had some explaining to do.

She was shocked to see the two guards standing outside the eldest princess' private chamber. They looked like they were about to not let her pass, but the glare she gave them made them think twice. Umakaal threw open the door.

"What have you done?" she barked at her sister.

Izriamat was looking out of the thin windows of her room, the sea breeze teasing her braids. She looked like the high priestess she was supposed to be at that moment and Umakaal hesitated for a half a second before stomping over. Izriamat turned to her, an utterly serene smile on her face.

"It is good to see you, little sister."

"How can you be so calm? Father's basically placed you under arrest. He's taken direct control of some of my guards. Now I'm hearing rumors that you went to the council meeting? What did you do?"

Izriamat stared at her as if she were a little child challenging her bedtime. Her older sister folded her hands in her lap.

"Uma," she said and her sweet tone grated Umakaal's soul. "I had to go. They were speaking about the upcoming war and I felt I should have been involved."

Umakaal struggled for words. This woman, her sister, had thrown their plans to the abyss. When she arrived from the capital with news of the netkoleh's rejection of the gods, the siblings knew they had the chance—no, the right—to rebel against the Ega at last. When he eventually arrived at Wiluru's gates to survey the kingdom and retrieve Izriamat they would refuse him entry, using her as a hostage to stay his hand. Not only had her sister come to the gates, against their plans, but directly provoked the man. Rage burned anew within her. The man was already unstable. Who knew what he'd do.

"You should have waited until you were called. They haven't even called for me yet."

"It's too late to deliberate." Izriamat stood, coming to her sister. "We have to prepare for war."

Umakaal looked her sister over, not liking this serene latest version of her. "What's happened to you?"

"What do you mean?"

"You've . . . changed." The younger woman remembered her sister's haunted expression when she'd finally returned from being the emperor's second queen. She was angry, shaky, a shell of the sister Umakaal remembered from her childhood. Now, suddenly, she was confident with a serene, faraway attitude that was honestly disturbing.

"What's wrong with you?"

Her sister sighed. "Is it so strange that I should be happy? Yutuu has given me back my peace." She took her hands in hers. "Wouldn't that make you beyond joyful? I can't even express how it feels to regain myself. To . . . to be made whole again."

"You weren't in pieces," Umakaal said firmly.

At this statement, Izriamat's face fell and Umakaal could see some of the sorrow from her return. "But I was broken," she said quietly. "Very, very broken. I don't know if I would have been better without the direct hand of our god." Her smile returned. "And now he's chosen me to be his hand."

Umakaal narrowed her eyes. She wasn't sure she liked the sound of that.

"What do you mean, his hand?"

"Yutuu's hand on earth. He has chosen me to speak for him." She took Umakaal's hands again. "But keep this between us. People wouldn't understand."

Umakaal stared at her sister for a moment. She wasn't sure she understood.

"Izri, please don't do anything else that would make mother and father angry. We've already worked against them. We need to convince them to come to our side, not push them farther away." Her sister didn't answer at first and she could see the conflict in her eyes. At last, she nodded.

"I'm going to write Yutuuan to tell him what's happened. Apparently, there's a small conflict on the eastern border."

"It will be taken care of."

The surety made Umakaal pause again. "Are you sure about the all-out war you started as well? What does Yutuu tell you about when the emperor comes back?"

"Your tone isn't appreciated."

"Then I would appreciate you telling me how you think this is going to go with an enraged man at the helm of the empire's entire army?"

She sighed again, in that annoyed mother way. "It will take him time to build an army. Most of the empire's might is still in the deep South. In that time, we will build ours. We have our people who will be more than willing to set themselves free after ages of captivity. They just need to be shown that it's possible."

Umakaal scoffed. "It must be nice to talk to the gods and know the future."

"I don't know the future," her sister said gently. "However, I can feel that there is hope in the future and I know Yutuu wouldn't lead me in the wrong direction. I trust him utterly and you should too."

The younger woman nodded. "Just don't start anything else with mother and father."

"Very well, little sister." Izriamat gave her a loving smile. "If it will soothe your spirit."

Umakaal gave her a tight hug and left the rooms. She nodded to the guards as she left.

"Tell me if she leaves her rooms," she said lowly to them. There was a hesitation she didn't like, but they nodded.

She returned to her own chambers, sliding out of her armor, and leaving it where it fell. She buried a face in one of her pillows, yelling out her frustrations. Ever since the day at the gates, she knew the consequences of their actions were coming. She and her siblings had committed treason. She understood that. But it was with their kingdom in mind.

How long had Wiluru been under the heel of the Ega and the netkoleh? She frowned. No, their leader had thrown off the title of the hand of their gods and was now the emperor. She punched the pillow at the thought of that horrible man. If she's been a little older, she would have been the one wed to him instead of Izriamat. The very thought of it made her nauseous. She would marry for children eventually, but the idea of never being with another woman again, with her dear Ladawi again made her stomach ache. To lie with the man who subjugated her people again and again . . .

Umakaal shook her head, dispelling the thoughts. On the one hand, she could understand her sister's anger. On the other hand, she'd made things increasingly difficult. They had planned to ease their father into the idea of war, presenting the careful steps they'd taken to ensure the governors' support. Now, they had to overcome his anger as well as his reluctance.

She lifted herself from her bed, heading to the small room that served as her seldom used office. The desk was carved from fused driftwood, fitted together to form swirling waters. It was a small room with only two windows that were latticed to keep out the wildlife. It looked very official even though her main business was with her guard.

She took out paper and quill, addressing the letter to her brother. She wrote out everything that had happened, explaining how Father was furious with them and the whole council now knew of how they'd gone behind his back to speak with the governors. She tried her best to keep her own anger out of the letter, but her mood was clear from her writing. She assured him that she would do her best to smooth things out but the emperor would return with his army soon. Perhaps a word from the heir would convince their father to commit to this war. He needed to return soon, border skirmish or not.

Umakaal sealed the letter, wrote her brother's name on the outside, and took it to the headquarters of the palace's messengers herself. The clerk was surprised to see her, but the small woman recovered and bowed quickly. The princess passed over the letter.

"See that this gets to my brother as fast as travel will allow."

"Of course, my princess." She passed the letter off then reached for another one. "This letter came in for the heir this morning. Would you like it or did you want me to pass it along as well?"

Umakaal sighed heavily. "I'll take it. I'm handling everything else. What's one more matter?"

She took the letter, heading back to her room as she read it. The youngest princess often had to deal with palace correspondence. It was probably a letter from an adoring noble young woman or some other high official wanting her brother's blessing on a matter. She had only gotten halfway through it before she stopped dead in her tracks. She read the last line again, her hand starting to crumple the paper.

A child. No, a bastard. She finished the letter growing increasingly disgusted at the apologies and the repeated referrals to the throne's heir as "my love." She wadded the letter in her hand at reading the Egan name at the bottom. That complete and utter fool. First Izriamat mouthed off at the council and now Yutuuan leaves this mess behind to fall in her lap. Umakaal punched the wall as she passed. The oldest to the priesthood, the second to the throne. That was the way of Wiluru. It looked like the third's job was to clean up the messes of the older two.

~

The morning chill settled on Yutuuan's shoulders as he crawled on his belly up the hill. Underbrush scratched him through his shirt in the places his light armor didn't cover. This was dangerous, the throne's heir going on a scouting mission, but he didn't want to put his soldiers through anything he wasn't willing to do himself. His bodyguard may think he was reckless but it helped to bond him with his people, build their trust. And what kind of commander would he be if he didn't have the trust of his men?

In the low light of dawn, he could just make out the campfires of their new enemy. Rather, an old friend that was proving to be a new enemy. Their ships were gathered just off the coast. A host of smaller ships dotted the shore, ready to take the sailors back to the ragtag fleet. There were more than he'd expected. The attack on their eastern port a month ago had been bad enough. If this force had been the one who attacked Tilizaa he wasn't sure they would have won.

Next to him, his bodyguard grimaced and looked to him. He was thinking the same thing. Yutuuan made a quick count of the campfires, estimating their numbers on the ground and what it would take to maintain the ships. He nodded to Naret and they scrambled backwards down the hill. It was a long journey back to their horses, running hunched over in the shadow of the hill.

The other scouts were waiting for them, having spied from other points around the enemy encampment. Without a word, they mounted their horses and rode off into the west.

It left the prince with plenty of time to contemplate his country's situation. An attack from their distant neighbors to the east was the last thing Wiluru needed. They were about to go to war with the greater empire. It would be the greatest battle the country had seen since their capture. Now, Rahaban had attacked them and he still couldn't figure out why. They had been trading partners for ages. Even their people who had immigrated from the nearby country couldn't figure out why an attack had come. It was a mystery that he wished hadn't presented itself.

The scouting party reached Tilizaa by full on morning, their grim expressions giving the gate guards pause. They didn't stop until they'd reached the building they were using for headquarters. The governor had been generous enough to commandeer it for them and he was grateful. He didn't want to push the limits of her hospitality any longer.

"That was worse than I thought it would be," said one of the scouts as their horses were taken. "Their ships must be packed to overflow with warriors."

"At least fourteen hundred on shore," Yutuuan ground out. He worked his shoulder, trying to rid himself of the stiffness that had settled in with the morning cold.

Naret leaned closer. "Should I summon the healers?" he asked, always the worrier.

"No, no," the prince said, stretching it slightly. He managed to keep the surprise from his face that it wouldn't extend as far as it used to. "It's only bothering me a little bit. I'll be fine."

Naret nodded and they entered the building. Yutuuan was thankful that he didn't inquire further. The injury from the attack still hurt every so often. He didn't want to give into fear, but he wasn't sure if it would ever be the same again.

Some of his soldiers saluted as he came farther inside. They voiced their gratefulness that he'd returned safely and Yutuuan tried his best to greet them all. He was sorry his mood wasn't better. The news he had wasn't what they'd wanted to find out. The other commanders of Wiluru's military that had arrived so far gathered in a small room near the back of the building. Three men looked up in relief when he entered. All of them saluted, fists across their chests.

"I'm sorry, but I have unpleasant news." Behind him Naret closed the door, standing guard as usual. "Our scouting mission was successful but I'm afraid this isn't just a case of pirates. This is a full-on attack."

One of the captains, a gruff man with a scruffy, salt-and-pepper beard, frowned deeply. "How many warriors have they brought?"

"By my estimation, there were at least fourteen hundred. Plus, the crew left on the ships. No telling if they left a skeleton crew or if a substantial number remained." He sighed, running a hand over his short curly hair.

"Then let us estimate a thousand more," added another captain. "Just to be safe."

"And prepare for more to reinforce them when the full attack is underway," said the last captain present.

Just then, the door opened and another captain walked in. Yutuuan forced himself not to grimace. Luunja of Asfara strode into the room as if she alone came to save the day. She nodded to the other captains and they saluted in deference to her rank in the hierarchy. Yutuuan forced himself to smile slightly to his future wife.

"Luunja," he said as respectfully as possible, "I'm glad to see that you've made it."

"My prince," she said bowing and he didn't miss the smoldering look she gave him through her lashes. "When news came of the attack, I had my ship prepared immediately. I and my sailors are prepared to defend our great kingdom."

He saluted her as a show of respect. "I'm glad to have you and your people here and ready. Was the Asfaran fleet able to spare any other ships?"

She kept her face business-like as she addressed him and the other captains. "The Breath of Yutuu and the Tempest's Roar were given instructions to come as soon as they return to port. They should be setting sail for Tilizaa within the next few days."

"That won't be soon enough," Yutuuan said, truly worried.

"The enemy is half a day's ride to the east."

"Bold bastards, aren't they?" She laughed.

"We'll need every sailor you have."

She bowed again. "Of course, my prince."

Yutuuan turned from her, uneasy, and addressed the other lesser captains. "Have your warriors prepared for an imminent attack. We can't let them take this city and we won't let them make it past this city either."

The three captains saluted and filed out to fulfill their duties.

"A moment of your time, Prince Yutuuan," Luunja purred once the rest had left. She tilted her head toward Naret.

"Naret," he started, reluctantly, "leave us for a moment." His bodyguard saluted and did so, but Yutuuan didn't miss the little amused smile on the man's lips. "What did you need?" He asked her, all seriousness.

She moved closer to him, the perfumed oils she used in her braids wafting toward him. "My father told me that he and you agreed to our marriage."

Yutuuan cleared his throat. "Yes, he presented the advantages of it and I agreed. I hope we'll have a very long and happy marriage."

She chuckled lowly but didn't step back. "Oh, my prince, I plan on being a most attentive queen." She moved even closer to him. "I will make you forget about all of those women you've had before."

"What women?" he asked, trying to remain in control of the conversation.

"People talk, Yutuuan. Your reputation as an . . . amorous prince has even reached Asfara. I look forward to the day I get to be the center of your attention." She pressed against him. "And you the center of mine."

He smiled as best as he could. "Dearest Luunja, I look forward to it."

"Shall we seal this arrangement with a kiss?" She breathed.

No thank you, was his gut answer. Instead, he put on his most debonair smile. "It would be my pleasure." He swept her into his arms, kissing her, all the while pretending she was his dear Talekh, back at her temple in Wiluru. But it was a poor illusion.

Luunja was all muscle and sinew beneath his arms, a sailor's perfect physique. Talekh was a study in curves and a backside that his hands sunk into the meat of. He felt himself growing aroused at the memory and ended the kiss abruptly.

"Oh my, Prince Yutuuan," she chuckled as he took a step away, embarrassed. "I didn't realize you looked forward to our union that much." She neared him again and, to his horror, grabbed his manhood firmly. He felt his face flush as his body responded against his will. "I just might be willing to help you with your attraction." She took a dramatic step back, saluting before leaving the room.

Yutuuan leaned against the only table in the room. Was this what he would have to deal with for the rest of his life? He took a few moments to steady himself and calm his erection. He didn't need this. He had an attack to get ready for, enemies from both east and south to fend off. He ran a hand over his face. First the war . . . and then the wedding.

Chapter Three

Waves of heat rose off the grassland turning the world into one giant illusion. The edges blurred into a smear of green, brown, and finally the blue of the sky. The heat sharpened every scent and the Egan army was surrounded by the smells of man and horse. Bakari ignored the phantoms of water and creatures that played at the boundary of his vision. There was only one thing he was focused on: his rage.

His second wife had stood atop the gates of Wiluru and refused him entry. Him. The emperor of all Ega, including her family's tiny northern kingdom. Izriamat, he growled under his breath. He'd trusted that woman to be his right hand in this world, to move through this world as one of the people who carried his voice in the places he could not be. That woman knew her place in this world and had finally submitted to it. Now, that bitch dared betray him. Her defiant face danced in the forefront of his mind, mocking him. She looked down on him physically and figuratively. He looked like a powerless fool in front of his entire retinue. For that she would pay dearly. Her and her beloved kingdom.

A cruel smile stretched his lips as he imagined dragging her back to the capital. No, he wouldn't kill her. She would watch her family tortured and executed. Then she would be returned to the capital to fulfill her duties as his second wife. She would bear him as many sons as he could get out of her until she was too old to have them or she died. She would learn the true meaning of obedience.

Bakari was snatched from his thoughts by the blaring of horns announcing his return to the scholarly city of Djelebe. He took in the high walls and the tall university that was the center of the city. He was halfway home and halfway to beginning war anew with Wiluru.

A host of spectators lined the streets as his large party entered. Most of the caravan would stay outside of the city, ready to depart at a moment's notice. Bakari didn't even pay attention to the crowds who called out accolades and well wishes for his health. A lion had no reason to pay attention to mice. Bakari set his sights on the modest governor's palace that rose up in the northwestern part of the city. There he could rest while his caravan resupplied. Then they would be on their way.

The balding, timid governor was already in a deep bow as Bakari dismounted his horse in the palace's courtyard. Thankfully, his ugly family was nowhere to be seen and he wouldn't have to suffer their appearance.

"My most high and esteemed emperor," Governor Mgobe said as he finally rose. "It is the highest honor to have you grace our city again. We . . . we weren't expecting you back so soon."

Bakari felt himself sneer despite trying to look only mildly displeased. "I am tired and thirsty from my trip. Do you have a proper reception ready?"

Mgobe flinched. "O-of course, my netko —. My emperor. Please, right this way."

Bakari didn't miss the slip of his old title. Emperor had better become as familiar to their lips as their own name. He was no longer the netkoleh. That title was dead, just like the gods he was supposed to be the voice of. No, he corrected himself. The gods weren't dead. They never were.

A proper spread of finger foods and cool drinks were in the parlor the governor took him to. At least the trembling man knew how to provide proper hospitality. Servants stood at the far corners of the room, waiting nervously to fulfill his every need. Mgobe motioned for him to take a low chair with plush cushions. He plopped into it, eyeing one of the servants and motioning to his empty cup. His mouth was sticky and dry from his ride.

"The empire is going to war," he said as the servant scrambled to please him.

Mgobe fell into his chair, gawking. "I'm sorry, my emperor?"

"We're going to war against Wiluru. They have rebelled against the empire and must be crushed."

The silence that hung in the air was heavy but the tension in the room could have sliced through it.

"My emperor," the governor began hesitantly, "may I ask what happened in Wiluru?"

"I told you that they rebelled," he snapped back. "That's all you need to understand." Bakari eyed the man lest he come up with another asinine question. "Have you seen to the library and university yet? My tour was short on my last visit."

There was a nervous hesitation the emperor didn't like.

"I've instructed the institutions to remove all religious iconography."

"That's not an answer," Bakari said, putting his glass down. "Did you destroy all instances of the gods in your city?"

"We . . . did, my emperor."

Another telling hesitation. He stood, his anger a spearhead pointed toward the shorter man.

"Show me."

Mgobe stood after a moment of difficulty getting out of the low chair. "Yes, of course, my emperor." He turned to a servant. "Let the library know that I'll be bringing the emperor there shortly."

"No. Don't let them know," Bakari called out before the servant could take a full step. "I'd not like to give them a chance to prepare for my arrival."

Mgobe swallowed heavily. "As you wish, my emperor." The governor led him out of the room and back into the outside heat. His guards rushed to fall in step behind them. Bakari glanced to Mgobe, his mood smoldering. He knew when someone was hiding something from him and this man was. The governor had best have done what he'd instructed him to do. His temper was looking for a convenient victim and a portly, balding, out-of-the-way governor was the nearest choice.

Luckily, the city's grand library was only a short walk from the governor's palace. The clerks just beyond the entrance looked panicked when they realized who was visiting. They scrambled to come from behind their desks and bow fully. One, a woman with pulled back locs and a wide pleasant face was the first to rise. The other, an older man, took a moment, a hand clutching his hip.

Bakari neared her. Her robes concealed her figure but she

was more than pretty enough. A shame for such a treasure to be trapped in a dusty library.

"Are you married?" he asked, tipping her chin up. She had pretty eyes as well.

"No, my n–, my emperor." The nervous tremor in her voice was alluring. "I have dedicated myself to knowledge."

"Have you known a man?"

Mgobe looked aghast out of the corner of his eye. "Emperor," he gasped.

Bakari silenced him with a look. He turned his attention back to this woman. "Have you?"

She licked her lips nervously. "I . . . have."

"Good." He examined her face for a moment longer before letting her go. "Accompany us. Your governor is giving us a tour."

She nodded meekly and fell in line as they walked on. Bakari looked around intently. He didn't see anything that invoked the gods or any aspect of religion on the surface. Other scholars scurried out of their way as Bakari walked deeper into the building. A stale smell hung about them emanating from shelves and shelves of books and scrolls. He scrunched up his nose. He couldn't imagine being stuck here hour after dreary hour reading.

"Have the books concerning religion been destroyed?" he asked after a few minutes of walking around.

When Mgobe hesitated, he looked to the woman scholar. She jumped under his gaze.

"Not all of them, my emperor," she answered with a look of regret to her governor. "But they were personal accounts of important persons from history. Even if they are concerning certain aspects of religion, we felt they were paramount in understanding these figures."

"*You* felt?" Bakari asked, looking to Mgobe. "It was not your decision to make, Governor Mgobe. Your emperor told you to destroy all mentions and records of religion. You failed me, Mgobe."

The governor bowed his head lowly. "My deepest apologies, my emperor."

Bakari looked around the library again. Who knew how many texts were held here? And how many of them held the poisonous influence of the gods?

"You scholars will go through and purge your city of any and every text that contains references to the gods. In any form. Do it or I will send people here to do it for you."

"Yes, my emperor," Mgobe said, head still lowered.

"Also, I'll need this city to host soldiers for the war. Make your people ready. I may need some of your people to serve in the army as well."

"Our people aren't warriors, emperor. We left those ways behind generations ago."

"You have magicians, don't you?"

Mgobe's mouth worked for a moment before answering. "Mostly in theory, but–."

"Then see that it's more than theory by the time I return."

Without another word, Bakari turned and began to head to the entrance of the library. Once he was near the doors, he turned to the woman walking with them.

"What is your name?"

She looked panicked to be the focus of his attention again. "Yalara, emperor."

"How long have you been a scholar?"

"Thirteen years, my emperor."

He sucked his teeth. "A waste. You will go and pack your belongings. Be ready to travel with us in two days."

"I'm . . . sorry, my emperor?"

"You are too beautiful to waste away in a library. I will have you come to the capital." He tipped her chin up. "Be glad. You'll be a concubine of the emperor. Please me well enough and I may make you a wife." Bakari turned and walked away from the distasteful place, brushing away the dust he knew surely clinging to him.

~

Sept'ha had only seen the palace from afar in her life. She'd barely set foot in much of the capital. Now the palace of the netkoleh—no, the *emperor*—rose before her, a mountain of white in the patchwork colors of the city. Her heart thumped in her chest as she looked over the walls. The bases were being polished; all evidence of the recent heresy being covered up completely.

She took a breath as she thought of what their leader had done. In the past months, all evidence of the gods was erased from the city and, from what she understood, from all the empire. For the life of her, she couldn't understand how one could proclaim the gods nonexistent. *But not everyone has seen a god like you*, she reminded herself.

Sept'ha took an unsure step forward, not certain what she was supposed to do. Two days ago, the goddess of war gave her a decree to go to the palace and help the emperor with his endeavors. Not a single instruction on how, exactly, she was supposed to go about it. But when Met, devourer of nations, mother of leopards, wrath of the heavens, told you to do something you did it. Her parents hadn't been happy about her leaving home. She'd given them the semi-lie of going to find work to save them money and her father objected to his daughter working for someone else. Her brother insinuated that she was going end up a sex slave and she was sorely tempted to give him another black eye to match the first she'd given him.

Now she stood before the incredible walls of the royal palace with a goal and not a single idea of how to achieve it. Sept'ha looked around at traffic heading back and forth before the front entrance. It was like a great river within the city with its own eddies and currents. After a moment's observation, she noticed a trickle of traffic heading off to a small opening to the side of the walls. The people entering there rushed in and out, some carrying baskets on their heads or bundles under their arms. A few looked to be hauling scrolls. She nodded, gaining a little bit of confidence. She knew servants when she saw them.

Sept'ha weaved through the river of traffic to the servant's entrance. She tried unsuccessfully to get the attention of a few.

"Excuse me," she said, catching one woman by the sleeve.

She was a young woman, not much older than Sept'ha if any older at all. She steadied the basket on her head and looked over, confused.

"Yeah?" she said stepping out of the flow of other servants.

"How can I get a job in the palace?"

The woman looked at her then laughed. After a moment, she stopped cold. "You're serious?" Sept'ha nodded. "You . . . don't want to work here."

"I do. I need to send money back home. I thought the palace would be the best place."

"The work is hard."

"I'm not afraid of hard work."

The woman hesitated. "What's your name?"

"Sept'ha."

The woman considered her, shifting her basket again. She looked up and down the line of workers. "Come with me. If anybody asks, you're an old neighborhood friend."

Sept'ha brightened up earnestly. "Thank you. Thank you so much."

The woman nodded and led her inside. Sept'ha rushed to keep up with her pace at first but found the rhythm soon enough. It was more difficult to weave about the other servants. She had more than a few near collisions as they walked. Quite a few curses were snarled at her.

"I'm Hamnen, by the way," the woman said over her shoulder.

"Nice to meet you."

"The head of the maids was looking for more people to clean the inner chambers since. . .well, a lot of people were, uh, killed by the emperor a couple of months ago and people aren't too eager to step in."

Sept'ha almost missed a step. "Why were they killed?"

"An assassin got in. Do you remember those priests who were hung outside the front of the palace for treason?" Sept'ha nodded. "Well, they had hired them. A few guards were beheaded too." Hamnen glanced back. "But the emperor's gone on the south and won't be back for a while so we have nothing to worry about."

"What is the Great Royal Wife like?"

"Not too bad. As long as we clean up good, she doesn't really pay attention to us." Hamnen threw a little smile over her shoulder. "Still want to work here? I can get you out of a side door."

Sept'ha shook her head vigorously. "No, I do. Thank you."

"You're welcome." They turned a corner and headed into a hallway that was, thankfully, not so crowded. "If you work hard, you can make a life here. Maybe even catch a husband who'll get you out of here." Sept'ha made a face at that remark which made Hamnen laugh.

After a dizzying turn of hallways and stairs that led them higher in the palace, Hamnen took her to a room with servant women coming in and out. They were all clothed in simple dresses with various, rather plain hairstyles. When a pair of women left, Hamnen led the way inside. An older woman with the presence of a mountain stood before a chalk drawn schedule on the wall.

"Tikat," Hamnen called, almost playfully. "I have someone to help with the inner chambers."

The woman glanced over. She had the kind of face that looked like it was made for frowning. A stark white streak of hair ran back from her right temple.

"Who is this?" she asked, poison in her tone.

"A friend of mine from my neighborhood. Sept'ha."

Tikat rolled her eyes. "I need more maids and you bring me one of your little friends."

Sept'ha stepped forward. "I'm a hard worker. I swear it. I'll do everything that's asked of me."

Tikat's eyes slid from her to Hamnen, displeasure dripping. She turned back to her schedule. "Fine, she's hired. Since she's so eager, I need someone to clean the chancellor's rooms."

Hamnen took a step forward. "Tikat, you can't start her out like that."

"And you can show her what needs to be done."

Sept'ha looked to her new co-worker in confusion. The other young woman stood, mouth agape. The older woman looked over to her. An eyebrow raised in slow challenge. Hamnen's mouth slammed shut.

"Come on, Sept'ha. I'll get you started."

When they left the room and had put a little distance between them and the head maid's room, Sept'ha asked, "What's wrong with the chancellor?"

"He's particular," she whispered back. "An ass really. He's dismissed so many maids for poor performance." She frowned. "But at least he hasn't had anyone executed."

Sept'ha swallowed. That was disheartening. She sent up a prayer to Met. May her path be clear to her goal and may her life not be the price to be paid for this mission.

~

Cleaning the chancellor's chambers wasn't as bad as Sept'ha thought it would be. The clothes she had to wear were another matter. Hamnen managed to come up with a pair of dresses that served as a sort of uniform and brushed her hair out into a bushy ponytail. She'd never felt more exposed and uncomfortable. The thin material did little to protect her against the cool of the palace and she just knew her figure was showing prominently. She would give anything for a band to tie around her chest.

Sept'ha followed Hamnen around, listening intently but letting the thoughts about her situation swirl in the back of her mind. The emperor was gone. She'd completely forgotten about his trip. She'd gotten into the inner areas of the palace but what good was that when the reason for being here was gone.

"Please put everything back exactly where you found it," Hamnen said as they dusted in his office. "He's picky about that. He doesn't like when people touch his things, so we have to make it look like we didn't."

"If he's that picky, maybe he should clean it himself."

Hamnen grabbed her by the arm, squeezing. "Don't. Say. Things. Like. That. You'll get us both thrown out."

Sept'ha rubbed her arm when the other woman finally let go. "Sorry. I'll be careful."

They resumed cleaning vigorously as the sound of footsteps came down the hall. Hamnen stiffened when a man came in, looking at a thick book. Sept'ha spared a glance. He was not a tall man, very average, but there was something that reminded her of the emperor. He walked around the room comfortably and she realized that this must be the chancellor. He looked at her, and she whipped her head back to her cleaning.

"You're not one of the regular maids," he said after a moment. His voice was even, oddly so. "Who is this?"

Hamnen turned to bow to the chancellor. Sept'ha followed suit, keeping her head low. "This is Sept'ha, Chancellor Hatsaf. She started this afternoon."

Sept'ha watched his sandaled feet come into view. He didn't say anything for a moment, and she faltered for the correct actions. "An honor to meet you, Chancellor," she said. Hamnen's quick intake of breath told her she'd made a grave mistake.

He didn't speak for another excruciating moment and Sept'ha was frightened that he'd hit her.

"Wait for her outside," he commanded. Hamnen immediately obeyed, leaving the palace's newest maid alone. "Raise your head," he said evenly.

Sept'ha did so and looked him in his eyes. There was a tempest behind them. She could almost feel it. A raging swirl of emotions that ranged from disappointment to pure anger. There was even pain.

"You're a bold one," he said, interrupting what she felt from him. "Looking a superior in the eyes."

"How will I interpret your true wishes if I can't see your face, Chancellor? People tell a lot through their eyes."

He raised an eyebrow then stepped closer to her, dangerously close. Sept'ha didn't move, didn't even flinch.

"What gutter produced you?"

"No gutter. I was raised in the southern central part of Metkara. My family isn't the richest, but I never went hungry."

He frowned, narrowing his eyes at her. "Do you have an answer to everything?" He practically growled.

"No, Chancellor. I was taught that only a fool pretends to know everything." At this, the chancellor blinked, clearly caught off guard. He stepped back from her, studying her. She felt something rub against her leg, something leopard sized and took comfort in it.

"Why are you here as a maid?" he asked, still frowning. "Clearly you've had some education."

Her mind raced for a reason. "My father only considers some

professions acceptable for women. I thought that if I had to choose something like a maid, I would be a maid in the best place possible."

"Profession?" He chuckled.

Sept'ha bristled at the condescending tone. "Yes, profession. The type of work that a person plans to spend their life doing." She knew that her snide remark would get her in trouble, but he'd pricked her pride.

"Can you read?"

"Very well."

"So, your father wasted education on a daughter even though he thought you were rightfully good for only a few occupations." He chuckled again. "You must be an only child."

Hamnen was right. This man was an absolute ass. "I have an older brother."

"Even more of a waste."

She decided to test her limit. "I'm sorry, Chancellor. I don't understand exactly what you mean by that."

He considered her for another moment, then a cruel smile tugged at the corner of his lips. "You're a woman. Only put on this earth to serve or breed. That your father wasted time and money on educating you when you had a brother proves that your father is a fool and you've been given an over inflated sense of self."

Sept'ha took a shallow breath. "If my father was a fool or a loving man is not important right now. I am educated. An educated woman who sees that you don't like women which, in my lowly opinion, is very foolish." The back of her mind screamed at her. She was going to get herself killed. "If our service is to cook, clean, raise children, please men, manage their households, and birth their offspring, then what is it that men are doing that outweighs that?"

The chancellor stared at her in shock, but it quickly melted into indignation. "Men run the country, the entire empire. We protect you from dangers that you couldn't possibly handle."

"And without the work of women behind you, most of you would live in filth and starve to death."

"I should have you thrown out."

"And it wouldn't change the truth."

The chancellor narrowed his eyes at her again. He might just have her thrown out and her time in the palace would be a short one. He might have her beaten for being insolent. Very well. But she would be damned to an eternity in a void than give in to this man. Moments passed, neither of them breaking their stare.

"Finish cleaning," he commanded and turned to his desk.

Sept'ha bowed lowly, keeping her eyes on him. Curses flew towards him from her mind. Woman hater. Inhospitable ass. She quickly rubbed the dust from the books and items on the shelves. She made sure to place each item exactly where she found them, using the dust rings to guide her. Behind her, Hetsaf took a seat and began reading through a stack of papers on his desk. The temptation to throw some of these items at the back of his head was great and she actually tested the weight of a few before deciding against it.

When she was finally through, she walked to his desk, bowed curtly, and started to walk out.

"Wait," he called out. She stopped just before the door and was surprised when he caught her arm roughly. Sept'ha instinctually tried to jerk away but he tugged her along. She bit her lip as he went meticulously through the room, inspecting every inch of his shelves with her in tow. His fingers dug into the flesh of her bicep, and she suddenly noticed the muscles of his arms. Some of her anger quelled at the thought of how easily he could hurt her.

"Not a speck of dust or an item out of place," he said with the barest hint of surprise.

He let her go and she took a step away from him. "Am I allowed to go?" she asked as meekly as she could manage at the moment.

"For now. You are to report to my quarters tomorrow morning. Tell the head maid of the inner chambers that I want you, and only you, to clean my rooms from now on." He nodded a dismissal, and she bowed again before fleeing the room.

Hamnen was waiting for her outside the chancellor's wing. She rushed to Sept'ha the moment she saw her.

"Are you okay?"

Sept'ha examined her arm and saw the slight bruise forming. "I'm okay. He grabbed my arm but that's all." She shook her head slowly. "He wants me to be his personal maid."

"By Koleh," Hamnen breathed then looked around. "Are you sure you want to do that? It could be . . . well, I've never heard of him taking a woman."

"No, I don't think it's anything like that. I think he actually was impressed with my work." She looked up to Hamnen with a little smile. "I think I'll be okay."

They started their walk back to report to the head maid. Sept'ha looked ahead as she saw a leopard walk by from another hall. It paused, nodded at her once, and continued on. She took a breath and smiled, pleased with herself.

Chapter Four

Efah sat in one of the small courtyards of Garemba, surrounded by a group of children. The sun shone down through the ruined walls of the abandoned city and she knew she'd have to stop her story soon to let them go for dinner. Forest sounds permeated her tale. Monkeys, also curious to what the group of humans were doing, gathered, and chattered in the overgrown branches. The story was one she remembered from her childhood, in the happy times before her family died. One of the greatest warriors known to the city of Ofolobaru led his forces against the warriors of Nsongo. He didn't win, but he made his enemies revere his name in the end.

The story ended with a great cheer from the children. Overhead, the monkeys hooted along with them. She guessed they wanted to feel included. Just behind the group Efah noticed a man standing patiently, arms held behind his back. He was in dark robes in the style of the northerners, far too hot for the southern forests. But at least he didn't have his weapons on him. Efah corrected herself. At least he didn't have any visible weapons on him. Who knew what he had hidden in the folds of his robes?

"Well," she said standing and dusting off her hands dramatically, "I think that's enough stories for today." The children protested loudly, and she had to laugh. "No, no. I'm sure your families are almost ready for dinner, and you should be there. Go on."

She waved as they ran off amazed that they did so without fear. Not long ago, no child would have dared run off into the innermost parts of Garemba without an adult. A number of horrors would have waited for them. Now, they hadn't a care in the world. They trusted in her to protect them.

The dark clad man came forward once the children had gone, being careful to keep his distance from them. He immediately dropped to one knee once he was in front of her.

"My lady."

"Newa, please get up," she begged. She squirmed under the supplication of a man so much her senior.

He did, looking uncomfortable not to be in a submissive posture. "My lady, I've been thinking. There is something that I've been avoiding telling you as you might find it . . . disturbing."

Efah tilted her head. Since his arrival in Garemba, Newa had been an open book to her, his reverence to her position absolute from the moment he saw her. She was the avatar of the god of death. He was a follower of the god Gu'un, the death god's direct subordinate. Their relationship had established itself as naturally as the one between their deities. Now the assassin priest had been keeping secrets.

"What is it?" she asked at last.

"It's the reason why I was sent out from our headquarters. A few months ago, after the death of the Great Royal Son, the netkoleh declared that there are no gods. He ordered the majority of the priesthood dismantled and all mentions of gods destroyed across the empire. He had the palace scrubbed of the religious murals and statues immediately and commanded everyone to call him emperor."

Efah stared, blinking slowly. Her deity told her a great evil was coming but she had no idea it was something so horrible.

"So, you were sent out to warn others of this?"

He looked aside and she hadn't seen the man look so guilty.

"Yes . . . and no. I was to warn the others of my sect. Our leader made a deal with the netkoleh and his brother, the chancellor. We would be allowed to continue while the other sects were abolished if we were to serve him. I was sent to tell other temples of our leader's plan." His eyes pleaded for her forgiveness. "He was my master when I was an acolyte. I was more than happy to obey him."

When Newa stumbled over next his words, Efah put a gentle hand on his arm.

"It was a good thing you were sent out. It led you here. You helped save these people and found out the truth. You know what your purpose in this life is supposed to be. I'm glad your path brought you here."

"I'm not so sure I know what my path is . . . beside serving you, my lady."

"Serve your god as best as you can. That's how you'll serve me but, more importantly, you'll serve him." He still looked unsure so she moved so she could look him in his eyes. "Newa, maybe you should take some time to think about it. You live your life now."

He nodded slowly. He started to drop to the knee but caught himself and bowed instead.

"I'll do that. Thank you, my lady." He turned and left.

Efah let out a breath. At least he didn't wait to be dismissed this time. She began to wander about the city, marveling at how peaceful it had become in such a brief time. People had started to come to her as a new leader, forgetting their fear of the former one who'd been a terror for so long. Ayodele was still in the city, as far as she knew. She'd occasionally see his second in command skulking about, sending scowls her way. Those in the city loyal to the former "king" of Garemba hadn't caused any trouble to her people since the attack from Ofolobaru. Many had even become followers.

It was so odd that people had come to follow her despite who she served. The god's name wasn't even spoken by most for fear of death visiting their kin. But Efah was their savior and leader. She'd led them in battle against their enemies here and from the outside. She'd performed works of magic unlike any the people here had ever seen. In this crumbling, near forgotten city in the forest, she'd gone from an orphaned grave robber to a great lady. It was beyond her wildest dreams.

The sounds of quiet laughing and yips caught her attention. Efah made her way to a room that had only three and a half walls. The rest opened to the forest. She found her favorite companions playing, chasing butterflies. Nesi and Usi were the size of rhinos, but the two giant hyenas played like pups. Watching them both sat her deity. Death looked on with milky white eyes that soon turned to her. The low light of the forest fled from his gray tinged skin. His thick cape of vulture feathers waved weakly in the breeze.

Efah dropped into a bow. She felt him wanting her to rise and did so, making her way closer.

"You have a good servant in the priest," he said. His white, pale eyes slid away from her familiars to her. "My subordinate was right to send him here. He will be invaluable to your mission."

"He said that the netkoleh declared there are no gods?" She didn't even want to speak the words, especially in the presence of one.

"This man from the north has done so and wishes to leave all people without our presence. This is the evil that comes, for there are some who are more than willing to go along with his plan. But . . . I'm afraid there is more." Efah started to worry. She'd never seen him hesitant.

"There are stirrings in the heavens. Grumblings. And others may move against us for their own purposes. Standfast Efah Abujolou. You have endured many challenges to date, but greater ones are on your horizon."

She blinked and he was gone. Usi and Nesi came to her side, nuzzling against her cheeks. She'd hoped that she could live peacefully now, but deep down a part of her knew better. Peace hadn't been a part of her life for a very long time.

~

Newa was a stranger to Garemba, and he felt it with every wrong turn and wary glance from the populace. He was so far from home, at the farthest edge of the empire, in a long dead city inhabited by poor refugees. It had taken some adjustment to live here. He was born and raised in the vast capital of Metkara, on its streets. He'd forgotten what it was like to lack plumbing and rooms free from the elements. A part of him mused that his life in the order had left him spoiled but he refused to admit it. Joining the Arak'guun made him the man that he was. Even if he had grown used to some amenities.

He made his way to the back of the city, where the damage to the building was worst. They called Garemba a city, but it was more of an immense palace. He wondered who would build such in the middle of the thickest forest but all he could get from the residents were stories of old kings. He took a seat on one of the broken outcroppings that overlooked the drop down to the Bangi River. Whoever they were, they definitely appreciated a pleasant view.

The sun turned the world golden, and animals of the forest made their last calls for the day or awoke for the evening. It was so different from his life in the city, especially in the quiet of the temple. His mind ran to his old room, spare in its decorations like all the priests. He lamented all the weapons he'd left behind, thinking that he'd return.

A thought crossed his mind. Would the capital's temple think he'd died? Would they think he'd deserted? How long would it be before the other temples rebelled against their leader, the Hand of Gu'un, after learning of the imperial decree? For the first time in ages, he said a prayer to one of the gods other than his patron. He knew the Hand was wrong in helping the netkoleh, but that was still his master. The man who'd taken the feral boy he'd found on the streets of Metkara and made into one of the best priests of the order. It was hard to think of his current path as anything but a betrayal.

"'Scuse me," someone said behind him.

Newa turned and saw an older man making his way forward. He was dark and Newa could barely make him out from the shadows of the building for a moment. The man moved cautiously, like he didn't trust the floor to hold him. Newa didn't blame him. Half of the city was unstable.

"Can I help you, elder?" He said getting up.

"You're a priest, right? That's what people are whispering."

Newa studied his face. No, he didn't know this man, but that wasn't surprising. There had to be hundreds of people in the nooks and crannies of this place.

"I am, but not a normal one. I serve Gu'un. Your people call him . . . Takiri."

To his surprise, the man nodded. "You follow the lord of a merciful, just death."

Newa grimaced. "That's not . . . I didn't realize our beliefs differed so much."

"You are Ega." He laughed, showing a pair of missing teeth. "I forgot." He came a little closer, testing each step. "The others are talking about how you fought when Ofolobaru attacked us. They say you were a monster."

"I don't see how they were able to notice my fighting. I came in at the back of the force."

"Yes, but they were pinned between you and Lady Efah. From what I understand, you turned the tide of battle."

For the first time, Newa was embarrassed by praise of his killing skill. "I've been taught to be a very efficient killer."

"Yet you don't seem proud of yourself."

Newa looked to the forest. He didn't feel proud of himself anymore. He wasn't sure what he felt.

"That's all I've known since I was a boy. I've served Gu'un for most of my life, but I don't know if the way I've served him has been the right way." He shook his head. "I don't know what I should do anymore."

"Young man, sometimes we lose our way. Sometimes our cart is upturned, and we don't know which way is up. All you can do is wait for directions." He put a hand on Newa's shoulder, and he was surprised at the old man's strength. "You're a priest. You have a higher power to ask for direction. Why not try them?"

Newa chuckled. "I don't think Gu'un would speak to me directly."

"Why not? The death god speaks with Lady Efah. Do you think yourself too lowly to speak to him?" Newa nodded. "Then your humility is exactly why your god would."

The old man patted his shoulder again and began making his way back into the city. Newa stared after him.

"What is your name?" He called after him.

"Oh, it doesn't matter," he answered. "Old man will do."

Newa wanted to ask further but the man was already inside. He turned back to the cliff and the river far below. He took his seat, the man's words ringing in his head. When was the last time he'd tried to commune with his god? He thought of all his teachings and such things weren't pressed into him. It was generally considered the foolishness of other sects. The Arak'guun was beyond such. They communed through their killing. Newa took a breath, clearing his mind.

It took him a moment before he could allow the noise of the forest surrounding him to blend into the background. The sound of the river became a soothing blanket of steady rhythm. Newa fell into himself, concentrating on the swift blade of Gu'un and his absolute justice. He thought of how he'd learned that his deity wasn't equal to the god of death but worked for him and his will. It was so obvious. He didn't know why he didn't realize it before. Now, he would be the servant of the lady of death, and he was more than happy to do it. He'd never seen someone so in tune with their deity before. She was glorious to behold.

Newa pushed the thought aside, refocusing on the aspects of his deity. He focused on his duty as a priest of Gu'un and slowly, his mind began to turn to what he could do to better serve him. He fell deeper into himself, and images began to form. He saw the image of Gu'un, no, of Takiri, a tall, proud man with twin swords. Skin such a deep brown to be almost black glistened in the sun. He was facing Newa, his eyes burning suns themselves. With one sword, he pointed out and Newa was suddenly facing a great city with tall, gold topped towers. A blackness that came from the north and west was consuming the city. Newa looked down and realized he was walking toward it.

The image changed in a blink, and he was in another city. This one was obviously Egan and he could smell the hint of sea air. Then he smelled smoke. Newa turned to see the city behind him ablaze, tall flames reaching for the sky. He walked as people screamed and ran around him, their bodies hazy and in slow motion to him. He made it to the center of the city and saw a group assembled. They were black, smoky monsters that cut down people as they tried to escape. Newa's eyes shot open when he noticed their weapons. Each of them carried Arak'guun blades. In the center, directing them all and speaking out in an unintelligible voice, was a person, blacker than the others.

Newa came closer. This person had the symbol of Gu'un emblazoned in silver on his chest, but it was not quite right. No, it was very wrong. This was all wrong. These people were not Arak'guun. He looked to this person with a sudden hate and disgust, realizing immediately what was happening. They were pretending.

Newa gasped as reality rushed back to him. He leaned over, placing a hand down to steady himself. The forest was too close and too loud. The stone under him was cold and uncomfortably hard. He took a few deep breaths, trying to calm himself. There was a pretender out there. Someone was causing chaos in the name of Gu'un, and his deity wanted them killed. Newa took one last deep breath. No, his god wanted them brought to a swift justice. He stood, hurrying inside. He would see to the plans of his lady, but, eventually, he had his own mission to fulfill.

~

Tekhamun's blade hadn't tasted blood in days and for the one sent by Gu'un, that just wouldn't do. He paced in his commandeered room, wondering where his disciples were. Surely they'd learned the layout of the city by now. The fifteen of them had arrived here two days ago and Karatel persuaded him to wait before they made their proclamation of the will of Gu'un. The man made sense. If city peacekeepers caught them unaware, they would have to kill more people than he wanted to and it would just make more trouble for them. It wouldn't do to have an entire city after them. They had a very important mission.

At that moment, Moon came in carrying a tray of food. She lowered her head to him in an awkward bit of reverence.

"I brought you food, master."

"I'm not hungry," he said walking to the window, looking down to the street, and then resuming his pacing.

"You should eat." She set it down. "You need to keep up your strength so that you can spread your message."

Tekhamun twisted his lips, reluctant to stop his pacing. Moon was the one of his first followers that cared the most about him. She was always inquiring about his health. If women had been allowed in the sect, he was sure she would have been a dedicated priestess. It was a good thing he didn't care about gender. He submitted to her beckoning and sat down to eat.

The food was delicious, and he wondered if one of his followers cooked it or did they find someone to force to cook.

"Thank you . . . Moon," he said awkwardly.

She beamed under his gratitude, her bad eye scrunching up

oddly as she smiled. "Of course, Master."

Tekhamun kept glancing toward the window. The sun was starting to go down. "When will they be back?"

"I'm sure they'll be back soon," the stocky woman replied. "In fact, I think I hear voices downstairs."

He strained his hearing and there was the noise of extra people downstairs. He leapt to his feet, heading to the door. Moon called after him to finish eating but he ignored her. Karatel had a lot to answer for keeping him waiting this long.

"Where have you been?" he asked the moment he came into the central room of the house.

"Master," Karatel called cheerfully. He had his arms wide as if he were the master of this stolen house welcoming a guest. The rest of his band, who had made up Tekhamun's first followers, were around him. "Sorry that we've kept you waiting. We wanted to make sure that we had a good idea of what this city is like before we reported back to you."

Tekhamun folded his thin arms. "Well?"

His follower bowed. "Yes, Master. We walked as close as we could to the local temples. They haven't been disbanded yet. We couldn't get inside. I don't think that they liked the way we looked."

Mjoma, the largest of the group in height and width, spoke up next. "The peacekeepers are lazy. They spend most of the day strolling around, harassing people, and asking for bribes."

"A disgrace," Tekhamun grumbled. "They'll have to be cleaved with the other heathens. What are the people like?"

"Oh, very sinful, Master," Karatel jumped in. "We found several households, whole neighborhoods even, that live in luxury while their brothers live in the dirt. And among those who live poorly, many do not give the gods their proper due. The temples looked ill kept and we saw few going to leave tribute."

"Did you find the temple of Gu'un?" Tekhamun asked.

Karatel made a regretful face before glancing to his group. "We . . . didn't find one."

"What?!" The others jumped at his shrill tone. "How can there be no temple to Gu'un? No hand of the Arak'guun here? That can't be. Surely this is a place that lives in the same blasphemous way as the netkoleh, may his soul never reach ascension."

"Master," called Moon's quiet, raspy voice behind him. "Calm down."

Karatel came up to him, a concerned look on his face. "Yes, Master. Don't let these filthy people get to you. We'll take care of them." He put a hand on Tekhamun's shoulder. "Rest yourself. I know that our god will give you the best plan for what to do to this city."

Tekhamun tried his best to cool his anger. His hands twitched, wanting his weapons and to shed blood. How he wanted to shed blood. He looked around to the rest of his inner band, those who had given their lives to his cause and had followed him without question. A small smile began to form on his face and he hoped it was encouraging.

"You're right. I will rest and speak with Gu'un. He will lead us in the right path." He turned to see Moon's concerned look. "And I will eat," he sputtered before retreating upstairs.

Once his meal was complete, Tekhamun sat on his bed to commune with his god. It was hard to concentrate with his hatred of the people of this city growing by the minute. How dare they not have a temple to the one god who was truly interested in justice in this world? He knew that people were often uncomfortable about his profession. His old life had proven that time and time again. People who shunned him in the streets or were reluctant to sell to him at market all because he was devoted to his calling. It didn't matter now. They were all dead. They didn't want to heed the call of Gu'un so they were cleaved away from this world. The same fate would fall to the people of this city as well unless they followed him. They must fight against the netkoleh's blasphemy.

The heavy meal lulled Tekhamun to sleep as his mind fixated on the slaying of the filth of the city. In his dreams, he walked the streets of the city. It was night but the sky was pitch black like a bottle of ink had been spilled over the sky. "Tekhamun," he heard behind him.

He swiveled around, mouth agape. His god stood, tall as a building, in front of him. Dark skin covered in veined muscle made up his body. His eyes burned orange like a furnace, the heat of them nearly searing Tekhamun's skin. The god's arms ended in two sharp, curved blades instead of hands and light shown from them.

"My lord Gu'un!" he gasped, throwing himself to the ground.

"The people of this city are evil," rumbled the deity before him. "They would side with the fallen netkoleh against you. They must be punished."

Tekhamun answered, face still in the dirt. "Yes, my lord. I will punish all who would turn away from the gods."

"This city shall be yours. It shall be a holy city by your hand. Do not stop until every soul that can be is brought to a true, devoted worship of the gods."

"Yes, my lord. I swear it shall be done."

Tekhamun awoke slowly but his mind snapped to alertness when he remembered his dream. He looked around the moonlit room, excited to tell the others of the wonderful dream he'd received. Then he remembered he was alone. He threw open his door and shouted down the short hall.

"Everyone! Everyone wake up!"

Slowly doors opened and his sleepy followers came out. They weren't nearly as excited as he was to be awake at this hour.

"What is it, Master?" Moon asked, smiling at him even though she was clearly still half asleep.

"Gu'un has given me a wonderous dream." He grinned from ear to ear, hands twitching in anticipation of holding his sickle like twin blades. "We are to cleave away every soul that doesn't want to follow our path and after that this city shall be ours. A holy city that we will lead into a glorious future." From their doors, his group grinned eagerly, none more than Karatel.

Chapter Five

Erenemo's study was littered with papers. Papers that held everything from tallies from the city's treasury to details of the daily lives of the council of elders. The last category particularly held his interest. He had to turn the council in his favor. If he had to resort to spies and bribes, then so be it. He was the only suitable candidate for Great Dara. He just had to make them see it.

He picked up one of the reports from his informants. They followed Elder Pemaji for three days, making notes of all her habits. Erenemo smiled. They'd noted a few of her vices as well. She had a love of Amakarian wines and spent a large amount of coins to have them brought from the western city. She also had a love of younger men and a couple of them were witnessed coming from her house at odd hours of the night.

Erenemo placed that to the side and picked up another. Elder Hafulo was a user of yeta. A stimulant often consumed by the warrior caste, use of it by others was frowned on in Nsongo. He had no other obvious vices.

So, he had two elders, one with a love of expensive wines and pretty men and one with a love of forbidden fruits. How easy it would be to buy them. If he convinced five more to vote for him, he'd have a majority and that would sway those ibisu fools more than anything.

He was about to move onto the next reports when he heard his son calling him.

"I'm in my study, Ofemu," he called out, shuffling some of the more incriminating papers underneath the reports.

His son came in, face frozen in the same tight browed look he'd had often as a boy. Erenemo stopped himself from giving an amused sigh. His son was about to discuss something important with him and that meant it was probably foolishness.

"Baba, I have something to talk with you about."

"Of course, son," he said with a smile. "But does your father not get a greeting? I haven't seen you in days." Ofemu came to him, kissing him on the cheek as he hugged him. "That's better. Now, what is it that has you looking so serious?"

Ofemu stepped back, his eyes sliding to the floor for a moment. "Baba, I've been thinking of my marriage. I'm ready to do it."

Erenemo was genuinely surprised. His son hadn't even hinted at wanting to marry. "Well, well," he said with a big smile. "It's about time. You're far past marrying age. Did you have someone in mind?"

His son looked a bit embarrassed. "I do, actually."

The priest laughed. "Who is it? There are a host of warriors about your age that would look good beside you. What about General Lishyala's second? What was his name? Soto! He's a nice looking one and it would be good to tie our family to his."

"No, it's not Soto." Ofemu hesitated and Erenemo felt the spear tip coming. His son raised himself up to his full height, his shoulders back. "I would like to have your blessing to marry Barabi."

Erenemo's face fell into a frown. "No."

"Baba, please."

The old priest turned back to his papers. "No," he reiterated. "I will have no other."

Erenemo looked up to his son and saw his face set in determination.

"Barabi is your *direct* subordinate. I will not have my only son entering into such a taboo."

"Barabi and I are an arrow and bow. We are paint and brush. I can't move in this world without him."

"How long has this been going on? You know it's wrong because you've kept it so hidden, I didn't even get a hint that you had someone."

Ofemu glanced at his feet before bringing his defiant stare back up. "Since the end of the war."

Erenemo sucked his teeth. "No."

"How can you say no to me?" Ofemu moved right beside him. "I love Barabi. I love him with all my heart. All my soul. I . . . I can't live without him. If I can just get your blessing, baba, it will smooth over everyone's misgivings about the match." He got down on his knee, lowering his head and raising his clasped hands to him. "I beg you, baba. Please."

Erenemo considered his son, down and pleading before him. His son, pleading to enter a marriage with his subordinate. His *direct* subordinate. That was practically like marrying family. How could he do this when there were so many other, more appropriate candidates to choose from?

"No. You will not have my blessing in this."

Ofemu raised his head and the pain in his eyes stabbed Erenemo. His son stood, kissed him on the cheek, and left the room without a word. Erenemo rubbed between his eyes. Why did they decide that one child would be enough? His entire legacy rested on that boy, that foolish, foolish boy. He was useless without a conflict to throw himself into. Now, when he finally wanted to make a marriage pact, he picks the worst possible choice.

Erenemo pushed his son from his mind and turned back to his task. He could arrange a meeting with the more malleable council members. Buy them some of their favorite pleasures and see if they might change their mind about him becoming interim Great Dara. The longer the city remained without a leader, the closer Nsongo came to losing its place in the south. He would die before he saw that happen.

His wife hurried into the room, taking off the head wrap she'd put on for her trip to the market.

"What's going on with Ofemu?" Patya said coming over. She draped the fabric over her arm and tiptoed up to kiss him. "He was storming out of the house just as I returned. He could barely speak he was so angry."

He sighed. "Our son has asked to marry."

"Well, that's wonderful!"

Erenemo chuckled wryly. "He wants to marry Barabi."

He was humored as his wife looked like she choked on her elation.

"His second?" She squeaked. Erenemo just nodded. "He can't. Wait, when did they start this? He hasn't told *me* anything about it."

"When has any young person told their parents about who they were seeing?"

"If they were upstanding, they would."

He snorted at the notion. "He came here to get my blessing and I refused."

Patya began folding her head wrap. "Good. He can just find someone else."

"He says he loves Barabi. They are an arrow and bow."

"Yes," she huffed, "and that is how they should be in battle. Not united in life." She shook her head. "Not everyone can have love in their marriage."

He brought her hand to his lips. "We were lucky," he said kissing her fingers lightly.

Patya stroked his cheek. "Very lucky. But that doesn't mean that there wasn't a plan involved."

He raised his eyebrows, like he hadn't heard this tale before. "Oh really?"

"Do you think it was an accident that the house of Yameba was united with yours? If I couldn't get you, I was going to try for one of your brothers." She shrugged for effect. "You were the most handsome however."

Erenemo wrapped his arms around her, taking in the face he'd looked into for over forty years. "So, I was just a pawn in your scheme to rise higher." He clucked his tongue. "Shameful, shameful woman." He moved in to kiss her on the neck but she pulled away from him.

"I need to make sure the cook has started on tonight's meal." She walked to the door, throwing a coquettish look over her shoulder. "We can always discuss how shameful I am later."

Erenemo chuckled to himself and returned to his scheming. He might have to take her up on her offer.

~

Servants in the Yira compound didn't impede Ofemu's progress through the halls. Everyone, including the elders of the family, knew why he was here and who would question one of Nsongo's top commanders from speaking with his second in command? Ofemu didn't even stop to acknowledge anyone, only briefly pausing to ask where the other soldier was.

He found Barabi in one of the courtyards. Ofemu halted at the sight of him, bare from the waist up, practicing with his bow. He took a moment to appreciate the movement of the muscles of his second's arms, how they worked in concert with his perfectly sculpted back. His eyes traced along the scar running across one shoulder. He remembered when Barabi received that wound. He'd sewed it up himself. It was the day that he realized his feelings for Barabi were more than a passing emotion.

Barabi took a shot, hitting the strawman target in the chest, just left of the heart. He made a disapproving grunt and reached to grab another arrow. Ofemu smiled. His love was always a perfectionist.

"I know you're there, Ofemu," Barabi said without looking back. "Your overuse of ola oil always announces your presence."

Ofemu ran a hand self-consciously through his braids before coming to stand behind his love. He wrapped his arms around the man's waist, bending his tall frame to rest his shoulders on the other's.

"I missed you."

Barabi chuckled and raised a hand to the side of Ofemu's head. "You miss me when I go to the latrine." He presented his cheek and Ofemu gladly obliged him with a kiss. "But I missed you too."

"How have your nightmares been?" he asked gently.

Barabi shivered slightly. "Less and less. We didn't see half of what the Egans saw, but those monsters were terrifying." He swallowed. "We should have never gone across the river."

"No, you shouldn't have." He squeezed Barabi tight. He'd been so frightened when his love had been chosen to lead a small force across the Bangi River. The Egans were forcing them to break their promise to never go to the home of their neighbors the Batubangi. It was inevitable that tragedy would fall on such an expedition. He was thankful to all the gods that Barabi's cleverness had managed to persuade the monsters to let the Nsongan part of the party go.

"You feel tense," Barabi said, changing the subject.

Ofemu frowned. "I asked father for his blessing today."

The second stepped out of his embrace and notched another arrow.

"And he refused."

Ofemu looked down, suddenly feeling like a failure. "He said we'll never have his blessing."

"I told you." He shot a glance over his shoulder. "I told you to be prepared for disappointment. We shouldn't be together. I'm supposed to watch your back, not present mine to you." He released the arrow with ferocity, the shot hitting in the target's head.

"I begged him, Barabi. I got down on my knees and begged him and he refused me." He came up and hugged his lover again.

Barabi grunted, stiff under his affection. Ofemu knew he hated being interrupted in a task, but he couldn't help it. Barabi tossed his bow down and turned to face him.

"Your father is a hard man and a stickler for tradition. Honestly, did you think he'd approve of anyone he didn't choose himself?"

"Before I told him it was you, he suggested Soto, house of Umo."

Barabi laughed, tossing his long braids over his shoulder. "A nice safe choice. And he has the kind of tight, little ass you like."

"What do you know about it?" Ofemu frowned, making Barabi laugh harder.

"I did have a life before you, my love." When Ofemu pouted, Barabi ran a thumb across his bottom lip. "However, there is no one else that I would have in my life from now until my last day."

Barabi's words touched him, no matter how many times Ofemu heard the sentiment. He leaned in and placed a subdued but passionate kiss on Barabi's lips. He stroked his love's cheek when he finally pulled away. "If I were dara, I'd make a decree to abolish that ridiculous practice. Then I would marry you and you would be the spouse of the Great Dara."

"Ah, but you're not the dara," Barabi said, pushing off him.

Ofemu was about to change the subject, but his mind latched on to their last statements.

"But . . . what if I were the dara?" His mind started swirling with the possibilities. With the power he would hold. Power to make his greatest want a reality.

Barabi looked at him from the stand he laid his bow on. "What are you talking about?"

"What if I were the dara?" He closed the distance between them. "What if *I* were the dara? Then we could marry and it wouldn't matter what anyone would say. We could be happy."

"This is foolishness. You're *not* the dara and I doubt the council would be willing to endure another less than stellar dara. Even if her surrender was a sound decision, the people still think of her as the Traitor of Nsongo."

Ofemu frowned deeply at the mention of his late cousin. "The bitch should have fought until we had no other choice."

Barabi poked him in the chest. "And that is why you shouldn't be the Great Dara. If Dara Ashaki hadn't surrendered, the south would have been destroyed. The Ega would have burned Nsongo to the ground after running over our warriors and you and I wouldn't be standing here having this conversation. We would be dead like the others who fell and propelled us to our current positions."

Ofemu stared at the man he loved in awe. That brilliant, tactical mind linked to a heart that cared about each of the soldiers in his charge was why he'd fallen for him.

"Shit, maybe you should be dara."

Barabi laughed. "Not if all the gods told me and sent my ancestors to haunt me."

"You'd be incredible at it."

He shyly pushed back a few errant braids with an elegant flick. "Do you really think so?"

"You've always been smarter than me."

It was Barabi's turn to frown. "Don't downplay yourself. You're a brilliant commander and people believe in you. I don't have that certain something to command people, but you do. You're great in situations that require on the spot thinking and not too many people can say that." He put a hand on Ofemu's chest. "You're smarter than you give yourself credit for."

Ofemu hadn't been listening to his love. His mind was working again.

"If," he started, still in his workings, "if I became dara and I had you beside me, that might put people at ease. The council knows of your tactical skill from the war. They have to respect that. And once I'm dara, we'll marry."

"I don't want to be the Great Dara's spouse," Barabi said firmly.

"Then don't think about that part. Think about all the good we could do for this city, for all the south. This city needs a strong leader and it needs it now." He bit his lip, not sure if he should tell Barabi about the envoys at the funeral. "The other cities are already vying for the top spot in the region. Their envoys at Ashaki's funeral even insinuated that Nsongo would lose the title of Great Dara."

Barabi sucked in a breath. "They didn't."

"We're wounded and the vultures are circling, my heart. Somebody must do something. Why not us?"

His love looked about, thinking. "All right. I'll do what I can to help you become dara." He held up a long finger and Ofemu resisted the reflex to kiss it. "*But* I will not be happy to be the Great Dara's spouse even though I'll be married to you."

Ofemu swept him into a passionate kiss, savoring the taste and feel of his lips. They were always so soft and full, he had to wonder how anyone had left this man.

"I love you, Barabi," he breathed, lips still brushing his.

Barabi looked around nervously. "I love you too but stop this. My parents may tolerate us but not everyone is neutral about our relationship."

Ofemu still refused to let him go. "Then let's go someplace private where we can behave any way we want in *our* relationship," he said lowly.

The shorter man blushed, but grinned. "Okay. Let's do that."

Ofemu let Barabi lead him back to his rooms. Once they were safely alone, he showed the love of his life just how life would be as his spouse.

~

Hotemkhar didn't like being left out of plans. Especially when those plans could affect his future. Since making it clear that the invasion of the southern jungle would commence soon, General Tutahmen hadn't brought him in to tell him anything about the invasion planning. And Hotemkhar knew that there was planning going on. As he walked about Nsongo, he could see the new troops being told of the great dangers lurking in the jungle. They worked through grueling training sessions. Provisions, most commandeered from the Nsongans, were being stockpiled in anticipation of their deployment. There was a plethora of activity going on and he, the envoy appointed by the chancellor himself, was nowhere near the center of it.

He cursed under his breath and quickened his pace through the city streets. His attendant scurried to keep up with him. He ignored the stares of the native Nsongans as he passed them. Their hatred was as insignificant as the sun that baked their city. A curious people, the Nsongans. Prideful to their detriment but fierce warriors. He hoped they were culled enough to bolster the numbers of troops in the invasion. He was sure they could subdue those jungle people but it was the horrors that concerned him the most. When those . . . things came out, he hoped that they wouldn't run this time.

He walked through the messy yard of the makeshift military headquarters. He cursed the soldiers who still wouldn't give him the appropriate respect. Hotemkhar ignored them too and made his way to the general's rooms. A pair of guards stopped him before he could enter the rear part of the compound.

"The general doesn't want to be disturbed today," one of the guards said curtly, barely looking at him.

"What do you mean, he doesn't want to be disturbed?" He took a step forward and both guards blocked his way.

"We've been given explicit orders. No visitors unless it's urgent, military business."

Hotemkhar burned. "Do you grunts know who I am? I am Magistrate Hotemkhar, son of Kmenti, the man placed in charge of our occupation of this city and all the south." He moved to squeeze past them but they refused to budge.

"Tutahmen," he yelled. "You tell your brutes to let me through. This is a grand insult. I need to speak to you."

After a moment, the general's voice came from a nearby room.

"Soldiers, would you let the magistrate know that I am extremely busy and have no time for his foolishness?"

"How dare you?" Hotemkhar shrieked. "Let me back there, you beasts!"

"Soldiers," Tutahmen's voice came again. "Would you also let the magistrate know that I will be busy for some time because I have an invasion to plan, the invasion he insisted we perform into unknown territory against a dangerous and mysterious enemy?"

The guard who hadn't spoken yet looked to him. "You heard the general," he said with a shrug.

Hotemkhar finally backed away from the guards. His head was abuzz with fury.

"Tutahmen," he yelled, starting to walk away, "I will make you pay for this indignity."

"I'm sure you will," floated the general's voice behind him.

The magistrate ground his teeth together. This was fine. He had more than one commander he could speak to and if one wanted to render himself unusable, then he would go to the other. A few inquiries and a quick walk put him at the door of the compound that housed the commander of the newest soldiers. The Nsongan guards looked over him as he approached but let him go inside, timid attendant in tow.

The newest commander was in the large, rear courtyard standing at a table covered with papers. He was younger than Hotemkhar expected, with an angular, clean-shaven face. The man was rigid in his stance, hands clasped behind his back. Hotemkhar didn't see a chair in sight and had to wonder how long he'd been out here.

"So, you're the commander of the new regiment," he said when he advanced.

The man looked up sharply and gave Hotemkhar a quick, assessing once over before returning to his papers.

"You must be the magistrate. It's Hotemkhar, am I correct?"

"Yes," he replied, trying to sound amicable. "And you are?"

"Kolehem, son of Kolehatun, commander of the Red Spear wing."

"A pleasure." Hotemkhar spared a glance over the papers on the table when the man said nothing further. A few of the documents held drawings of beasts matching the description of the monsters seen in the jungles on their last expedition. Teeth as sharp and long as hunting knives. Claws like hooks on both hands and feet. A muscled body taller than a man. These beasts had torn apart every group they'd sent into the jungle. The only ones who'd survived were the Nsongan squad and the leader of the last Egan group. The poor man was now plagued by terrors and hadn't been able to give them much information when he'd returned.

"May I help you with something?" Kolehem asked. The young commander had tilted his eyes up at Hotemkhar and was waiting.

"Yes," the magistrate said. "As the highest ranked person in the southern area of the empire, I thought I should know who the major players in my city were. Since no formal introduction was done, I took it upon myself to seek you out."

The young man looked a little stricken. He stood up even stiffer.

"My apologies, magistrate. When I arrived, I dove into my work, getting my soldiers prepared for the excursion into the jungle. I wanted to make sure I learned everything I could about the situation. I regret that I didn't make myself known to you. It was disrespectful."

Hotemkhar nodded. Obedient, like a good soldier should.

"Tell me about your experience, commander."

"I joined the army just as the war against the southerners had reached its peak. I was promoted after the battle of Lonki when I assumed the command of my regiment after our leader was killed. We took the enemy general hostage and brought him back to General Matket for execution. After successful operations during other battles in the southwest and the conclusion of the war, I was given command of the Red Spear wing."

Hotemkhar was fond of dealing with this commander so

much more than Tutahmen.

"Have you any aspirations for higher positions?"

"Koleh's will." He immediately winced then lowered his head in Hotemkhar's direction. "Forgive me, magistrate. I know we're not supposed to speak like that anymore. Force of habit."

"All is forgiven." He motioned for the young man to answer his question.

"I have thought about possibly attaining general one day. I hope to learn a lot from General Tutahmen."

Hotemkhar waved his hand dismissively. "The general can be a very uncooperative soul. It's best that you take what he says with a grain of salt."

Kolehem looked surprised for a moment before returning to a neutral expression.

"I will heed your advice, magistrate."

"Very good. Now tell me your thoughts on the excursion."

"I think we have enough soldiers to breach the jungle. Too large of a force would be cumbersome. From the reports I've collected, the jungle people appear to be a simple sort, not even speaking a trade language. They don't appear to have any kind of warrior culture as evidenced by their lack of guards around their gold. They should be easy to subdue."

"And what of these *monsters*?"

Kolehem looked at the depictions, his brows drawing close. "Since we have witnesses, we should be able to assess how they fight and be able to destroy them."

"I like your confidence, commander," Hotemkhar said, nodding again. "And you've given me many reasons to be confident in your abilities."

"Thank you, magistrate." The young man practically beamed under the praise. "I promise you that I will do everything in my abilities to subdue the jungle people and their monsters and bring the empire its gold."

"Very good, young man. And if you make good on your promise, I'll personally make sure general is in your future."

Kolehem beamed more. "Thank you, magistrate."

Hotemkhar nodded and left the room. This was a good meeting. This commander was not only obedient, but malleable, a rising star in the military that was eager to prove himself. He was the perfect replacement for Tutahmen if it came to that. Hotemkhar's attendant raised a canopy as soon as they stepped into the sun. And if that arrogant general didn't come to heel soon, a replacement would be very, very necessary.

Chapter Six

The salt spray was cold on Yutuuan's face this morning. He watched the sun rise from the deck of the *Etainein* and pulled his cloak tighter. The cold was plaguing his bad shoulder and it hurt him to think that he had a bad shoulder at such a young age. However, that was not the heaviest of his thoughts this morning.

Last night two letters from Umakaal arrived. He'd been joyed to see his younger sister's handwriting but once he'd read the contents his heart dropped. The emperor had already arrived and not only had they not gotten to lay out their terms to him, but Izriamat had goaded him into an all-out war. The emperor swore to destroy their country. He was shocked that Izriamat didn't seem repentant at throwing their plan in the trash.

"Are you not cold, my prince?" came Naret's calm voice from behind him.

Yutuuan didn't turn as his bodyguard came to stand beside him. "Yes, I'm cold. But it seemed right. I can't keep my thoughts still."

"I am here if you want to speak on it."

The prince moved a little closer to the man, thankful that he was a friend more than a bodyguard.

"The emperor has declared war against us," he said lowering his voice.

"Is that not what you and your sisters wanted?"

"Well, yes, but Izri was at the wall when he arrived. She goaded him. Made him so angry that he swore to destroy us. Do you remember him?"

Naret nodded. "I was still in training then. Spoiled brat of a man. I can't believe he leads the empire." He suddenly looked to Yutuuan, mouth hanging open. "Oh, shit."

"Yeah. Izri says he's even worse than he was that day. It should have just been a standoff but she turned it into an all-out assault and we'll have even less time to prepare."

Naret didn't say anything but returned to stare out at the sea.

His face moved into several expressions before he spoke.

"And now we're out here, most of our fighting force dedicated to fending off an unknown enemy." He sighed. "The gods are cruel."

Yutuuan gave a bitter laugh knowing how his mother and Izriamat would react to such a statement. He joined Naret in his pensive watching of the sea. He felt better letting someone else know the horrible news from the capital. Yet the silence seemed to make the other subject haunting him bubble up.

"There's something else," he said at last. Naret looked over with a raised eyebrow. "Talekh sent a letter to me at the palace. She's . . . she's pregnant."

Naret threw his head back in a sigh that looked like it would release his soul.

"I told you," he hissed.

"I know."

"I *told* you. If you had urges, you could have come to me. That's why I'm here, to keep things like this from happening."

"I guess I like women too much," he said with a chuckle.

Naret stabbed him with his eyes. "Forgive me, your majesty, but this isn't fucking funny at all." The bodyguard took a breath, regaining his usual composure. "I love women too, but I abstain so that I don't have a host of children in the wild. We both have responsibilities and you just . . ." He stopped, pinching the bridge of his nose. "What do you plan to do?"

"I don't know," Yutuuan replied quietly. "I know it was stupid. We were both stupid. She's left the order. Working in a restaurant near the docks."

"You still care for her?"

"Yes. I do."

"Then you know what you must do."

Yutuuan nodded, feeling gutted. "I have to take care of her . . . of them."

"And give her enough gold to not tell a soul the truth of this, not even her child." Naret looked around quickly then punched Yutuuan in the arm. "I swear I'll have an ulcer before you take the crown."

Yutuuan felt horrible for disappointing his oldest friend. "I'm sorry. I really am." He placed a hand on the man's arm. "In the future, if I am desperate, I'll come to you."

Naret twisted his lips. "Same." Then he gave Yutuuan a cruel smile. "Until you're married." The prince's face showed his complete and utter dismay giving his bodyguard something to laugh about.

"Ships on the horizon!"

Both men looked up at the shout. Yutuuan narrowed his eyes, scanning the far sea. The rising sun made it hard to look that way, but he could just make out a series of dark shapes bobbing in the waves. The captain called out for everyone to ready themselves, and Yutuuan hurried to the nearest mage.

"Send signals to the rest of the fleet. Take a spear formation and attack with fire as soon as they're in range."

"Yes, your majesty."

As the magician sent up the appropriate magical flares, the prince hurried to the captain's side near the wheel. His fingers tapped on his sword hilt impatiently. He'd gotten better at using it with his left hand since his injury, but he truly wished he'd healed faster. Naret stood at his place beside him, all anger pushed aside. It was a long, tense wait to reach the enemy and Yutuuan forced himself to breathe evenly. He was always anxious before battle. But normally, he fought pirates along their trade routes. An enemy that was dead set on attacking his kingdom made for an exciting change.

After what seemed like an eternity the enemy came into range and the magicians across all the ships gathered toward the front of their vessels. Yutuuan's ship crested a small wave and together the mages cast a large fireball at the nearest enemy vessel. The ship tried to evade but the fireball grazed the side. It caught fire briefly before being doused by the sea.

The magical barrage started on other Wiluruan ships and soon the eastern sky was filled with giant fireballs. Some hit their targets dead on, sails catching fire and a good chunk consumed before their magicians could put them out. Yutuuan shielded his eyes from the sun, numbering the opposing ships and their make. As he traced the outlines, he frowned. They weren't any uniform style of ship. While yes, the Wiluruan navy had several different styles of ships, they were all to a certain standard of design. The opposing ships were all different. He saw a few that must have been navy vessels, but others looked like large merchant ships. Some looked a little too ornate for this battle.

"It looks like someone cobbled together a navy," he said to the men at his sides.

The captain raised his eyebrows. "So perhaps this Fahzi empire hasn't gotten itself completely together yet."

"Then hopefully," Naret added, "their sailors are as disjointed as their navy."

"Let's hope so," Yutuuan said. "Because we'll be finding out soon."

The Wiluruan navy finally sailed within the range of the Fahzi magicians and counter spells flew at them. Navy mages tried to enact counter spells, but a few slipped through, setting decks on fire, and sending sailors scrambling to douse them.

"Will we board them?" the captain asked.

Yutuuan's fingers tapped more insistently on his sword. "Yes. Give the signal."

The captain shouted to the mages to signal for boarding and the sailor at the helm aimed the ship toward one of the enemy vessels. It was one of the larger ships, a true battleship with armored sides and windows below decks where magicians could cast spells. Yutuuan spared a look around to see how his fleet fared. One ship lagged behind; its sails ablaze. The others were moving in to attack the enemy. On the Fahzi side, he thought he saw a handful of their ships on fire, but it was hard to see with the lingering smoke around the battle.

"Prepare for boarding," shouted the captain and sailors assembled weapons at the ready on deck.

Yutuuan took out his own sword, itching for battle. The ships reached each other painfully slow. The man at the wheel guided their craft to the side of the enemy ship with expert precision. A few of the enemy sailors tried jumping across before the grappling ladders were secured. A handful fell into the sea, but the majority made it across. Wiluru's sailors swarmed them, taking care of the overeager fighters in no time. The ship shuddered to a stop as it latched on to its enemy. Yutuuan hurried back to the decks, ready to cross. He paused to make sure Naret was at his side, and they ran to the other ship.

There was absolute pandemonium with magicians trying to add to the fight and protect their respective fighters. Smaller spells took down enemies and maimed others. Blood flew, making both decks slippery. An enemy fighter came at Yutuuan, a crude blade in his hand. The prince side stepped his attack, retaliating with a slice across the man's stomach. He dispatched two more fighters before he had to dive out of the way of a spell.

Yutuuan turned his head to see a mage far down the deck. They were preparing another spell by the time he got to his feet.

"Naret!" he yelled, pointing at the mage. The bodyguard stabbed his opponent in the stomach, pushing his sword in to the hilt, and nodded. Both men came together, fighting as a unit to make their way toward the magic user.

The mage had turned their attention to other fighters in the meantime. They cursed when they realized the men were closing in and hurried to prepare another spell. Yutuuan darted forward, slicing for them. They stopped their spell in terror, fleeing. Naret closed the gap between them, kicking aside an enemy fighter, and managed to cut the magician across the back. They recoiled in pain, giving the bodyguard enough time to stab them in the back. Yutuuan gave his friend an approving nod and they rejoined the greater fight.

The prince was exhausted by the time the fighting stopped. He looked up to see a few of Wiluru's ships retreating and the one that was on fire at the start of battle was keeling to one side. However, the Fahzi "navy" was turning and fleeing with far less ships than they'd come with.

He heard the death cries of a man near him and saw Naret finishing off a wounded enemy sailor.

"Don't kill the wounded," Yutuuan called loudly. "We need them for questioning."

"What of the ships, your majesty?" asked a nearby mage.

He looked to the handful of ragtag ships, sitting in the ocean, their crew wounded, dead, or dying.

"Burn them."

~

Umakaal tugged on her armor, checking it for the hundredth time this morning. She smoothed her braids, making sure none of them had come loose from her ponytail. Behind her loomed the ornate doors of the council chamber. Near them, looking as serene as ever, was her sister. She'd tried to be a little kinder to her older sister, giving her the respect of an eldest sibling but it was so hard. She was still furious with her. Now, with a formal summon to stand before the council, Umakaal wasn't sure how much worse her sister could make this.

"When we get inside," she said, "let me do most of the speaking. I know Father is still angry with you."

Izriamat laughed. "Are you afraid that I'll gain the ire of the council? They all think I'm defiled trash. Their anger means nothing to me."

"And that's precisely the problem." She winced, hearing her words echo in the hall. She took a breath and lowered her tone. "Our country is at stake and you're acting like all that matters is this plan that Yutuu has made you privy to and nobody else."

"If we follow Yutuu's will, all will work out for our betterment. That's all we need to do. Follow his will."

"Horse shit," Umakaal snapped. "If you want to be a priestess again, go to the temple. Here we have to think about more things than religion."

The younger princess immediately felt shame at the pained expression on her sister's face. After a moment, Izriamat schooled her expression.

"Yutuu's will permeates every fiber of Wiluru. Even the palace. And it seems that he's needed here more than ever."

The council doors opened, cutting off anything else they had to say. One of the palace guards ushered them in, nodding to Umakaal in respect. Umakaal nodded back, nervous. She said a prayer that things would go smoothly.

The full council was assembled, the old men taking up every seat at both sides of the long, low table. Her mother was seated at her official position, first seat to the right of the king, the only woman allowed on the council. Her father sat, bone straight, in his ornate chair. His gaze was steel as he watched them enter. However, Umakaal noticed a weariness to him. There were dark circles under his eyes and his face seemed pale. She had to wonder how he'd been sleeping.

"My daughters," he said as they came to the appropriate spot before the council. His voice sounded louder than normal and Umakaal felt like she was a nine-year-old again, in trouble for following her brother's foolishness. "You have been called before the council to give a recount of your treasonous actions and for us to decide on a proper punishment."

"Father," Umakaal started, before Izriamat could, "we would like to apologize for —"

"I didn't ask for your apology. Do as your king bid you."

She sucked in a breath. His words cut like a knife.

"After Izriamat returned, she, Yutuuan, and I spoke about her situation and how she didn't want to return to the capital. Yutuuan was infuriated by the emperor's demand that we abandon our gods. He is the one that initially suggested that we refuse the emperor entry into the city."

A few council members gasped, the rest making comments under their breath. Her face burned at the thought of her brother and the problem he'd plopped in her lap. She was still furious with him too.

"Yutuuan and I devised a plan to not just refuse the emperor entry but to use Izriamat as a hostage to stay his hand. After that, my brother went out to secure the support of the other governors to lend aid and warriors to the defense of the kingdom. We have the full support of eleven of the thirteen governors in this. I'm sure the other two would be on board if you proclaimed us at war with the empire, Father."

The look he gave her silenced her for a moment.

"Continue."

Umakaal glanced nervously at her sister. Izriamat looked content to stand there as her sister recounted everything.

"Everything was as we planned until Yutuuan discovered the invasion from the east. We'd planned for him to be at the wall but with him gone, it fell to me. I spoke to the head of the city guard and he agreed to closing the gates to the emperor. But it was at my insistence. I will take full responsibility for that. I went to the gates, but Izriamat joined me and spoke to the emperor herself. He was . . .” She struggled for the right words. “He was less than pleased to see her and our refusal to let him enter made him angry. Now he’s gone back to the capital to rouse the army and attack us.”

“My sister tries to downplay my role in this,” Izriamat said from her side.

Umakaal whipped her head around, panic rising. What was she doing?

“I am merely trying to highlight how we are all equally to blame in this plan.”

“You will not do us any good by painting the truth in gaudy colors. The rain will reveal the ugliness underneath.”

As Umakaal stared daggers at her, she continued.

“I didn’t intend to go to the gates that day. I was called to go there by Yutuu. He guided my steps.” The council murmured again. “I saw a vision. A vision of the so-called emperor burning in his own fires of rage. This fire would not touch Wiluru. This is why I spoke to the emperor the way I did. The sooner he succumbs to his own evil, the sooner Wiluru can be free of him and his people’s influence.” She paused and the room was heavy with silence. “Yutuu wants us to be free, Father. Our captivity has gone on for long enough.”

The silence lasted an eternity. Umakaal stared at her sister. Izriamat had always seemed the wise one, Yutuuan the bold one, and herself the hardheaded one. Now the roles were flipping. She cleared her throat, jumping in to try to soften their message.

“We were only acting in the best interests of Wiluru.”

Their father looked sharply at her. “Do you think I don’t have the best interests of my kingdom in mind? You two, who will never take the throne think you know better?”

“No, father, I would never —.”

“Yes,” Izriamat answered sadly. A gasp passed around the room. Their father failed to find a response. The elder princess closed her eyes. “Yutuu wants to see his chosen people free again. This kingdom was taken through war and it will not shake off the empire’s yoke through begging them for peace. It is not a language they understand so we must speak to them in theirs: war. It's the only way, Father."

Umakaal had never seen such a deep color come to her father's face. Their mother looked to them both, utter disappointment in her eyes. She put a hand on her husband's arm.

"Now that they've confessed, and seem unrepentant, perhaps we should deliberate on punishment."

"We've done nothing wrong, Father," Izriamat said calmly.

"You will be silent," their father snapped.

Umakaal stared at her sister while the council put forth their ideas, her face turning from disbelief to utter hatred. All Izri had to do was let her do the talking. That was all. Umakaal knew she could have smoothed this over and Father might have seen some merit in their plan. Now he was incensed.

"I have decided," the king began after a few minutes. Umakaal's attention snapped ahead, fearful of what was about to come.

"Izriamat, since you have regained your connection to Yutuu, you will go to the temple to serve there."

"My place is here," Izriamat insisted.

"Go willingly or be taken." The finality in his tone made the princess's mouth close. "Umakaal, you will be relieved of active duty as captain of the royal guard until further notice. You are dismissed."

Umakaal felt the floor drop out from under her. Her head felt hollow. Her heart had stopped beating. She wanted to plead with her father to reconsider, to find some other punishment. She'd take anything. Instead, she bowed lowly to him, her mother, and then the council and left the room. Outside, she put a hand to the wall to steady herself. Her armor felt too tight. Not the guard. He couldn't take that away from her.

The doors closed and Izriamat stopped beside her.

"Little sister, I'm sorry that —."

"Don't talk to me," Umakaal spat out. "Don't talk to me at all." She turned and ran back to her rooms before the tears could start falling.

~

Izriamat was surrounded by the presence of Yutuu but had never felt so alone. She sat on her bed in her new room at the temple, knees pulled up to her chest. She could hear the rhythm of the waves nearby lapping at the foot of the building. It was probably high tide and the ocean's waters would be half filling the innermost sanctum of the temple. It should have been a soothing sound to her, a reminder that she was so close to the element of her deity, but it only reminded her of what her coming to the temple truly meant. She wasn't here as a tribute. She was here as an exile.

Izriamat leaned against the wall beside her bed, staring absently at the breakfast brought for her this morning. The porridge, decorated with figs, was cold and congealing in the bowl. Beads of sweat heavily dotted the vessel that now held room temperature water. She was hungry, but her body wouldn't respond beyond sorrow. Her place was in the palace. That was where Yutuu had sent her. She had to guide this kingdom along the right path. How could she do that from here?

A knock at her door dragged her from her despair.

"Come," she said, her voice weak.

A moment later, the door opened and her uncle, the high priest, came into view.

"I came to check on you, dear niece." He put a hand to her forehead like she was a sick child.

"I'm not ill," she said gently pulling her head away.

"I'm making sure." Munabis glanced at the ignored tray on the table. "The priestesses told me that you weren't eating. You will waste away."

"I'm not hungry," she lied. Then her stomach growled quietly.

Munabis nodded and retrieved the bowl of porridge. He plucked a fig out of the cold mush, offering it to her.

"Eat at least a little something."

Izriamat considered the fruit. She looked up to her uncle, who had taught her everything she needed to know about becoming a follower of Yutuu. Reluctantly, she took the fig and placed it in her mouth, chewing slowly. He watched her until she swallowed and then nodded approvingly.

"Thank you," she whispered.

"You're welcome." He handed her another halved fig, watching to make sure she ate it. "You know, this is not a true punishment. I know you're sad to be pushed from the palace, but this is where you would have been had you not gone to Metkara."

"I didn't *go* to Metkara. I was forced."

Munabis nodded. "I apologize. You were forced. I remember when I heard the news that you were to be the netkoleh's wife. I went to the palace and demanded to know how my brother could let that happen." He stroked her braids like he did when she was a child. "You were supposed to replace me when I passed on. I was furious. You were meant for something higher than a wife or princess. But I'm glad you're back where you belong."

She leaned into his hand. She had spent just as much time with her uncle when she was young as she did with her father and feeling his approval pulled her from her despair.

"My place is in the palace."

"How can you say that when Yutuu has restored you?"

Izriamat sat up, finally looking him in the eyes. "Yutuu told me that my place was in the palace. I was needed there. It's like no one believes me."

He nodded and handed her a cup of water. He waited to make sure she drank it before speaking.

"Most people need to see proof before they believe. It's not a fault. It's just how people are naturally. When Yutuu and Inasa crafted us, they made us skeptical so we wouldn't be foolish." He chuckled. "Of course, some of us have a greater portion than others."

She found herself chuckling with him. "But Father forbade me from returning to the palace. How am I supposed to fulfill my purpose away from where Yutuu put me?"

"Sometimes, when we think our paths are straight, they have the curves of a mountain pass." He stood erect, his back cracking. "Come and get some food, Izri. After that, join me on my duties. You might find some purpose in that."

Izriamat considered him, a part of her wanting to give up and waste away in this room. When he extended his hand to her, she took it, the other part of her desperate to find something to focus on. He took her to the kitchen and made sure she ate. The priests and priestesses cooking were overjoyed to have her up and about. Izriamat suddenly felt guilty that she'd made them worry about her so. Many of them had been here when her uncle was training her, and they expressed their happiness to have her return to the temple.

Afterwards, Munabis had her come with him to the various duties. They first went to the infirmary. He had her change bandages and feed those who were too sick to feed themselves while he checked on the priests running it. She was surprised at how much she remembered and fell into an efficient working rhythm.

She came to feed a woman who'd fallen ill after the birth of a daughter and stopped. This woman was no older than her. Her eyes were prominent behind her thin eyelids, and she breathed as if each breath would be her last. Izriamat stopped one of the passing priestesses.

"Is . . . is this woman going to make it?"

The priestess looked over with a pained expression. "We're not sure," she replied in the barest whisper. "We've tried everything. She's in our prayers constantly but nothing is working."

Izriamat nodded and sat on the edge of the bed next to the woman. Her eyes fluttered open, and it took her a moment before she could focus on the princess. Izriamat tried to smile genuinely.

"I'm here to feed you," she said holding up the bowl of broth. "If you're too weak to sit up, I'll help you."

The woman gave the barest nod and Izriamat positioned herself so she could lay against her. She spooned small sips of the broth into the woman's mouth. She couldn't help but think of her own labor. It took days before her son was finally born. At so many moments she swore she would die and here was this woman who might just die because she brought a child into the world. She had to wonder if she even cared for the daughter she might leave behind. She hoped that this woman's baby was conceived in love and would be loved forever. Izriamat closed her eyes for a moment, praying for this woman's recovery.

When she opened her eyes, the woman was falling further

into her sickness. She could feel it. The fact was a heavy weight against her soul. She wanted to push this sickness away from the woman. Then she did feel it, the woman's illness. There was a slimy aura running through the woman's veins as if something had invaded her body. Izriamat sensed that if she reached out, she could touch it.

So, she did.

Her fingertips screamed that she'd been burned and she jerked back. She looked at her hand and it was unscathed, but the sensation lingered. Izriamat thought of this woman and her baby daughter and how a life so young shouldn't be ripped away and reached again. She gritted her teeth against the initial pain. She closed her hand around the sickness, pulling at it with determination. It fought against her. Its tendrils stuck to the woman like a spider's web around an insect.

But she was a priestess of Yutuu. He sent her to help her people. As she thought of her chosen place, the sickness began to loosen its grip until it finally came from the woman. Izriamat's hand no longer burned at touching it and its fire extinguished in her fist. She stared at her hand in disbelief. She could see the purple-black tendrils getting consumed by water in her palm until it was no more.

At her side, the woman groaned, then sat up on her own. Around them, attendants stopped and stared. Izriamat looked to the woman. Her face was full of color, not the pale sickly shade it was when Izriamat arrived. She looked to the princess with clear eyes.

"You . . . you healed me," she croaked in her disused voice.

Izriamat took a breath, thanking her god. "Are you well enough to feed yourself?"

"Yes, priestess."

She handed the bowl of broth to the woman. "Then be well and return to your child." The other priests and priestesses made the sign of Yutuu as she stood. Izriamat looked around the infirmary at the rows of beds in this room with so many that needed help. With a new sense of purpose, she got to work.

Chapter Seven

Arkole, Great Royal Wife and Empress of the Egan empire, couldn't wait for her husband to return home. The horns were already blaring in the city, announcing his approach. She and their daughters gathered in the eastern yard, attendants fanning themselves in the heat, hoping for a quick arrival or a breeze to save them from it. Her brother-in-law, the chancellor, waited stoically in his proper place, face devoid of emotion. The gates to the city proper were open wide and Arkole watched, heart fluttering in anticipation. Her youngest held her hand, her little grip squeezing and unsqueezing. This was the longest she'd ever been without her father and the occasion had her ecstatic.

"Will Father be here soon?" the little one asked, swinging her mother's hand.

"Yes, he will," she answered. "Do you hear how the horns are growing louder? That means they're getting closer."

"Will Father be excited about the baby?"

Arkole put a hand on her slightly round belly.

"He will be."

"If it's a boy," came a low voice from her left.

She shot a stern look to her husband's chancellor before smiling down at her daughter.

"Your father will be happy no matter what the baby is."

The girl seemed to be placated with that answer and went back to watch the open gate. Arkole looked daggers at the chancellor. The man didn't glance at her the entire exchange, and she hated him even more. She could never tell what was going on in that man's head and it left her at a disadvantage.

The horns blared again, this time just outside the palace walls. The youngest princess jumped in excitement and Arkole had to shush her. Soon, the emperor rode around the last bend in the street, his wheat-colored horse at the head of the procession. They came through the gates, stopping just short of the assembly. Arkole put a hand to her chest. Her heart leaped every time she saw him.

He looked displeased when he dismounted, saying less than usual to his attendants. Arkole led her daughters forward, the chancellor at her right side and various attendants and officials gathered behind.

"My husband," she said, reaching up for his cheek.

He leaned into the caress. "Arkole, I —." He stopped, looking down at her stomach. "Arkole, are you with child?"

"Yes, my love. He should come at the beginning of the season of storms." She giggled as he pulled her into a passionate kiss. Behind them, the chancellor cleared his throat.

Bakari pulled away, putting his hand briefly to her belly before taking her hand.

"Welcome, Father," their youngest piped up before her sisters could properly greet their father.

He patted her head. "Thank you little one." The rest of their daughters quickly greeted him and he gifted them with a nod.

"My emperor," the chancellor started, "we were surprised you returned so soon." Arkole saw his eyes flit about the rest of the horses before coming back to Bakari. "I trust the Pilgrimage went well."

Worry birthed anew in Arkole's chest. A look unlike any she'd seen in a long time fell on her husband's face. She gave his hand a gentle squeeze.

"Where is Izriamat?" she asked.

His face grew even darker, and she motioned for the princesses' nanny to come and take them away.

"Hetsaf. Arkole. We need to speak."

Without another word, he led them inside, ignoring the servants scrambling to get out of his way or the other officials welcoming him back. Once they reached one of his private rooms, Arkole felt safe enough to speak again.

"Bakari, my love, what's going on?"

"We are going to war with Wiluru."

Arkole gawked at him. Even the normally calm Hetsaf sucked in a breath. He recovered first.

"Where is the second queen?" he asked hesitantly.

Bakari turned a dangerous look to him. "That bitch can stay

in Wiluru and burn with the rest of it." Arkole and Hetsaf exchanged glances, both in the same confused shock.

Hetsaf took a hesitant step toward his emperor. "What . . . happened?"

"They closed the gates. They dared close the gates to their emperor. Then that bitch stood atop them and told me that I would never enter the city. She dismissed me like some misbehaving child."

Arkole struggled for words. "Surely she knows what kind of punishment would fall on her and Wiluru for this?"

"They knew exactly what they were doing," Hetsaf added. "They want to go to war. The question is, are they insane? Wiluru's might is its navy. They barely have an army."

"I don't care," Bakari snarled. "Wiluru will burn. I will see every member of their royal family piked out on their wall and their people will finally understand that they belong to the Ega."

Hetsaf bowed. "I will start gathering troops from the outermost cities and garrisons."

"Call for warriors from the south as well. I want a force that will be talked about for generations."

Hetsaf bowed again and left the room. Arkole stared at her husband, realizing that he'd be leaving again soon.

"Bakari, are we really going to war against Wiluru? The war against the southerners only ended a few years ago."

"You don't understand the boldness with which they refused me. The boldness of *that bitch*, standing there, looking down her nose at me. Looking at me like she was better than me. *Me*! I made her an empress. I made her mother to a prince of the empire, and she refused me!"

Arkole put her hand on his arm. He was practically snarling.

"Bakari, my love, calm down."

"I will not calm down, Arkole!" he shouted. "You act like this isn't the greatest insult I've ever suffered. And from my wife! When I drag her back here, she'll learn what it means to submit."

She nodded. Izriamat had never been her favorite person. In fact, she hated her, the haughty princess from the north. She remembered how the woman did nothing but cry when she first arrived, as if she'd been punished instead of blessed. But it was hard to imagine her boldly defying their husband. Such was unbelievable. However, it must have been so if it had enraged him so.

She hugged onto him. "Then if you wish it, Wiluru will burn."

He wrapped his arms around her. He sighed, melting down until as much of him touched her as possible.

"How have things been while I was gone?"

"Fine," she said, taking in his scent. "There was a little unrest in the city but I took care of it."

Bakari pulled back, looking at her in surprise. "You did?"

"Of course, I did." She smirked. "Did you doubt me?"

He laughed, the tension falling away from his shoulders. "I never doubted you, my water lily. I'm sure you were brutal in your judgment of them."

Arkole smiled, despite not knowing exactly how their punishment had gone. Hetsaf had taken care of most of it. She'd just given orders.

"I gave mercy where mercy was deserved. But you'll be pleased to know that there hasn't been any problem since then. The people are starting to get used to living without calling on the gods."

"Good." He sat down in a chair heavily, pulling her into his lap. "The other cities I visited fell in line easily. I'm wondering about Djelebe though. The governor seemed reluctant to carry out my orders."

"What do you mean?"

"They took care of their temples, but the university and that blasted library were barely touched."

Arkole rested her chin in her hand. "Then if they're so precious to him, if he won't obey, destroy them."

Bakari smiled and she thought her heart would melt.

"That is why you're my right hand." He placed a hand to her stomach, rubbing the curve. "How is my other son?"

She struggled to keep her face from falling. "Fine and growing the last time I saw him."

"Is Netiri taking good care of him?"

"Do we have to talk about him now?" she asked, trying not to let her annoyance show in her voice. The last thing she wanted to think about was the second wife's son. It would be the son in her womb that would inherit. Not that boy. Not any of the others either.

Bakari's voice took on a dangerous tone again.

"How many times must we have this conversation, Arkole?"

"Why would I be happy to talk about the child that may push mine aside?"

"Arkole," he sighed, exasperated. "Our daughters will be taken care of. And this boy will inherit the empire." He rubbed her belly again, but she folded her arms, defiant. "Don't be so bull headed."

His hand moved from her belly, and he pushed a finger between her closed legs. Arkole yelped at the sudden sensation. He kissed her deeply then moved to bite the side of her neck. She tried to keep the groan building up in her down. With the strength of a true warrior, he lifted her up, turning her and wriggling up their clothing so he could enter her. Arkole cried out happily and let her husband do whatever he wanted with her.

~

Chancellor Hetsaf had a small section of the palace and Sept'ha found it easy enough to clean. He spent most of his day in his office, leaving her plenty of time to meticulously tend to the other rooms. It took her most of the morning to tackle those and by the time she cleaned his office, she still had most of the afternoon to do what she wished. It was a good job and if she hadn't been sent here by the goddess of war, she would have been happy to stay with it. But cleaning wasn't her mission; she was growing worried that she'd never get close to the emperor.

Today, the chancellor had been gone for most of the day and she thought she'd be able to finish cleaning before he returned. Yet halfway through her work, he walked in. Sept'ha bowed deeply but he didn't acknowledge her presence, sitting down at his desk and working. His rudeness didn't bother her anymore. He wouldn't act like she was there until he needed something, and she was fine with it.

Her time here in the palace hadn't been too bad either. The other maids of the inner chambers were jealous of her easy work but not because of who she worked for. Even Hamnen was surprised that the chancellor hadn't fired or berated her yet. They were shocked that he hadn't beaten or treated her roughly. Sept'ha could only shrug at their questions. Once you knew how to handle someone, they weren't that hard to deal with.

She was in the middle of cleaning the floors when the chancellor moved some papers he'd been reading aside. It caused the stack of reports at the side of his desk to flutter out and tumble to the floor. Sept'ha immediately went to pick them up. Her eyes couldn't help but slide to the script on it. It was from the head of a local magistrate. There were a series of murders in his area including one town that was completely dead, no survivors.

Something in her stirred as she read. Anger? Insult? She wasn't sure if it was one emotion or a mix of several. But this was wrong. So, so very wrong. Something had to be done about it.

"I think you should look at this," she said slowly putting the papers back on his table.

Hetsaf looked up at her like he'd forgotten she existed. After a moment he scowled, turning back to his work.

"I forget that you can read."

"Chancellor, I truly think you should look at these reports."

"I have a war to plan. I'll get to local reports later."

Sept'ha frowned at him. "Look," she said pointing to the first of the papers she read. "An entire town was murdered, down to the last child." She pulled out the other papers flipping through them. "Another city saw a madman, dressed as a priest, killing people near one of the city wells. No, not just any priest. An Arak'guun. Another city had several households killed over several nights. And several peacekeepers too."

"Why should I care?"

"Because it must be important if the local magistrate is writing to the capital about it. Plus, how hard is it going to be to gather troops for the emperor's war if people are worried about their families getting slaughtered while they're away?"

He turned his head to her slowly. "Give me those papers."

She handed them over, feeling a little bit of triumph that he was conceding to her request. She waited patiently as he considered the reports. "Hand me that map from the third shelf on the ones by the door."

She quickly did her task. Hetsaf rolled out the map, checking between the reports and the cities to the west of the capital.

"What are you thinking?"

He shushed her and she had to swallow the retort on her lips.

"Did you mix up these reports?"

"No, I didn't. I thought you might have had them arranged by importance or date." She took satisfaction at the shocked look on his face. "However, you might have when you knocked them to the floor."

He frowned and turned back to the map.

"It seems to be a trail. From the first town that was killed to the cities in the following reports. And they said it was an Arak'guun?"

Sept'ha looked back through the papers. "Yes. Two reports say that. He was yelling in the square in one town and by a town well in the other. Wait." She read further. "One says he was yelling about the emperor and his heathen ways. Nobody's seen him since then."

Hetsaf stared at her. "We haven't sent anyone to these towns yet to tell them of the decree. So how did he know?" He looked back to the map, tapping his finger as he thought. Eventually, he motioned to the paper, reed, and ink waiting for him to write correspondence.

"Address a letter to the magistrates from these reports. Inform them that funds will be sent to them to hire more peacekeepers to find this killer. We can't have anything distracting us from the upcoming war."

Sept'ha bowed, surprised but pleased. "Yes, Chancellor." He moved back to his planning, leaving her to write in peace. He'd given her a little bit of trust. It was a small victory, but a victory, nevertheless. After he'd inspected her work and put his seal on the letters, she returned to cleaning the floors.

"Did you need help with anything else, Chancellor?" she asked, trying not to sound winded from scrubbing.

He didn't answer at first and she thought he'd gone back to ignoring her.

"Can you handle writing more of my correspondence? I'll have . . . a lot going out as the war effort ramps up."

Was he asking for actual help? "I can do that for you. And if you need any further help, I'll be happy to be of service. You don't make much of a mess, so I have a lot of free time and I don't like to sit around with nothing to do. It makes me antsy."

Hetsaf looked over, considering her. Had she said too much?

"Your cleaning has been flawless. And your letters were . . . good." Both compliments sounded like they had to be drug out of him. "If you want more work, it can be provided."

"Thank you, Chancellor." She finished her work and quickly left the office. A little closer to her goal. A little closer to influencing the emperor.

Her head snapped up as she suddenly realized someone was coming down the hall. She looked into the face of a man, by his dress, could only be the emperor himself. Sept'ha fell into her lowest bow, nearly dropping her cleaning supplies.

"My emperor," she said as he stopped in front of her.

"Is the chancellor in?" he asked causally.

"Yes, my emperor."

"Really?" His voice sounded utterly surprised. "He doesn't like anyone in his office while he's working. Look at me."

Sept'ha raised her head, keeping her eyes away from the man she'd been sent here to influence but could have her killed if he didn't like the way she breathed. To her surprise, he chuckled and waved her away. She fled down the hall. She didn't stop until she got to her room.

Closer and closer, my servant.

~

It had been months since Bakari had visited his lesser wives. The women who oversaw their care walked beside him, making assurances of their wellbeing, and telling him of how many children had been born in his absence. Just two this time, but that was understandable. He couldn't indulge himself with them as much lately. He could hear the rest of his children playing within their mothers' apartments. It pleased him to hear the voices of so many. His line would continue in all parts of the empire.

After a while, he waved the attendant women away, winding his way to a set of rooms specially set aside. He entered, hearing a toddler fussing and the calm admonitions of his mother. Another baby started babbling, clearly wanting to be part of the conversation. Bakari smiled at the sounds of his sons, especially the youngest. It was good to know his heir was being taken care of.

He found the trio sitting on a mat in a common area that opened to a small, private courtyard. It had started raining this afternoon, a rare shower this time of year, cooling off the room pleasantly. The eldest boy fought to get into his mother's lap, pulling at her clothing in a clear demand to be nursed. She frowned through her struggle to get him to calm down, while keeping the youngest from crawling off the mat. The hungry boy was allowed to latch on, finally stopping his cries.

Bakari chuckled. It was good to see his son demanding what he wanted. This one would be a general one day. He could feel it.

"Netiri," he called softly.

She looked up, surprised, but her face melted into a smile. "My emperor," she said ducking her head. "I apologize. I can't bow at the moment."

"I understand. You're . . . very busy." He stooped down by his youngest son. The boy noticed him, looking up with curious, bark brown eyes. "He's gotten so big," he remarked, reaching out a finger to him. The boy eagerly grabbed it, squeezing and trying to pull him closer." Did the empress name him yet?"

Netiri looked down, rocking her son. "No, my emperor. I haven't seen her in months."

"What?" he snapped.

"I'm sorry, but she hasn't. I've been calling him Enoket. I . . . I thought it would be a good name for now."

Bakari rolled the name around in his mind. Enoket. He liked it. But he was still furious with his wife. With both of his proper wives. He was angry with Arkole for letting her petty rivalry with Izriamat allow her to neglect his son and he was angry with Izriamat for not being a good enough mother to stay here with her son, leaving one of her lessers to name him. That bitch.

His son sat up and reached his hands toward him. Bakari looked to Netiri, confused. She hid a chuckle.

"He wants you to pick him up."

Bakari reached down, placing his hands gently but firmly around the baby's sides. His son squealed in delight as Bakari stood up, propelling him off the floor. Netiri chuckled and got up, making her son stop nursing. He protested with a loud burp. She patiently helped him arrange his arms to hold the boy close. Enoket babbled happily, slapping his hands against Bakari's cheeks.

He knew he should have been angry at being struck, but his son's delight made him laugh.

"Enoket," he said lowly, seeing how the name felt on his tongue. The boy looked directly at him when his name was called, then started bouncing in his grip.

"How is a baby so strong?" he asked, struggling to hold on.

Netiri laughed. "You'd be surprised."

"What is your son's name?" he asked.

She scooped the boy into her arms, tickling his stomach. "Italet, my emperor, after my grandfather." She motioned to Bakari with her head. "Italet, this is your father."

"Fafa!" he shouted.

Bakari smiled. Two strong sons. *And one he lost.* He would really have to count how many he had in case Arkole gave him yet another daughter.

"Are you ready to have more children?" he asked as Enoket put his head down on his chest.

"If the emperor would grace me with enough time to wean the both of them, I'd be more than happy to give you more children."

This woman was so eager to please. That made him more than ecstatic. Enoket reached for her, babbling, "Mama." She took him, holding him on her other hip as naturally as she did her son. It hurt Bakari to his heart that this was the only mother his son had ever known and not the woman who bore him. But eventually he would learn her face, however beaten it was by then. He would know his mother as a traitor and see on her broken body the punishment for treason.

"Does something trouble you, my emperor?" she asked sweetly.

"The second queen has rebelled against the empire along with all of Wiluru." She gasped and he continued, not knowing why he wanted to talk to her about it. "I'll have to go war soon against them."

Netiri looked down, worrying her lip. "But you just arrived. I thought . . . I thought we'd have some time together."

Bakari tipped up her chin, looking into her eyes. So beautiful, so pleasing, and so willing.

"Do you love me, Netiri?" he asked, running a thumb across her lips.

"Yes, my emperor."

And he believed her. He looked to his sons on her hips and could imagine a host of tall boys like Kolehtun running behind her. And he would give them to her.

"I would see you elevated, my dear. For how you seek to serve me before I ask. For how you have taken in my heir as your own son."

She lowered her head. "I would be honored to be your favorite among your lesser wives."

"No, sweet Netiri. I want you to be my second wife."

She gasped, her mouth a perfect oh. She lowered to a knee despite the children on her hips.

"My emperor, I could not possibly hold such a position. It should go to a woman far more worthy than me."

"It will go to whoever I deem is worthy. Stand, Netiri." She put the boys down on the mat and stood back up. He put a hand at her waist and the other stroked her cheek. "I would be more than happy to have you, who obviously loves me so much, to be my second wife. I should have a loving wife after my last betrayed me."

She started tearing up and placed her hand over the one on her cheek.

"I will never betray you. I swear it."

"It would be best if you didn't."

His warning didn't dampen her smile and he appreciated it.

"Would you like to spend the evening here, my emperor?" she asked sweetly.

Bakari glanced at his two sons playing on the mat, being raised by the most capable hands in the palace. "I think I will."

Chapter Eight

There was a weight to the air in Garemba as the sun went down and it crawled across Efah's skin. Since they were surrounded by the forest, darkness crept in faster than it would in a proper city. It gave a surreal feeling to the passage of day and most people retreated to their rooms early, to commune and eat for a few more hours before sleeping. Efah sat in the nest Usa and Nesi made around her. There was no more comfortable place than the space in between them as they snuggled up together. Usa slept peacefully behind her, her hyena's laugh rumbling through her huge chest. Nesi had positioned her head in just the right position to conveniently get scratches behind the ear and Efah wasn't one to keep her familiars waiting.

But even though the scene was peaceful, she couldn't help feeling the extra eeriness to dusk today. Newa ducked his head in the doorway leading to the room she was in.

"My lady, I'm going to check the forest. I feel . . . uneasy."

"Thank you, Newa," she said. "I think I feel something too."

He bowed and left. That put her mind at ease. If anyone would find the source of this, he would. She snuggled back into Usa. The warmth of them had almost lulled her to sleep when she heard screeching overhead.

Efah opened her eyes, coming back to full consciousness. She saw a dark shape in the almost pitch-black window. It took her a moment to realize it was a vulture crying out to her. It took her another moment to realize it was an alarm. She sat up, her hyenas coming alert instantly.

"Come on," she told them and ran out of the room.

When she reached the wide courtyard of the city, she could hear people being ushered inside to Newa's orders. She could just make him out in the low light from nearby campfires. He saw her approaching and rushed to her side.

"My lady," he said going briefly to a knee. "There are forces in the forest. They look to be the same force as before."

"Peacekeepers from Ofolobaru." She shook her head. Hadn't they learned their lesson at the last defeat? How many more warriors did their dara want to lose?

"Could you tell how many?"

He shook his head. "They're cutting through the forest, not taking the path. Do you want me to engage them?"

"Yes, please. I'll stay and protect the people." She put a hand on Usa's side. "Go with him and protect him." Usa rubbed a cheek against hers then came to the assassin priest's side. She lowered herself for him to climb on. Newa glanced to her nervously before mounting the giant beast. With him holding on for dear life, they bounded out of the city.

Efah took a breath then turned to the gathered people. "Go," she shouted. "Bring everyone into this area. We're under attack. It's Ofolobaru again."

While some panicked, most did what she said immediately. They had survived one siege. They knew that they would survive more with her protecting them. Efah took another breath against the fear that was starting to raise up. Nesi nuzzled against her cheek and a host of vultures flew down to rest on the dilapidated walls. Death was with her and if the peacekeepers managed to get into the city, then death is what they would find.

More fires were started, and torches placed in the ancient holders along the outer walls. The people of Garemba were crowded into the space, almost uncomfortably. Probably people straight from the city, come here to escape the tyrannical dara of Ofolobaru like so many here. She wouldn't let a single one fall victim.

The sky grew darker and darker as they waited and Efah estimated that at least two hours had passed. The forest was still full of night sounds and every screech and scream set her people on edge. A guard from the gate ran up to her, stopping to do an awkward bow.

"We haven't seen anything, Lady Efah."

"Keep watching. They might come back to the path, or they might attack through another side." He bowed again and ran back towards his post.

A few minutes later a shriek at the back of the courtyard

caught everyone's attention. Efah looked, adjusting her eyes and saw a small group of warriors coming in from one of the rear entrances. People started running away from them, their panic flowing ahead of them. Efah willed the vultures to attack.

A great column flew down from the walls, slamming into the warriors. She heard their screams just over the commotion from Garemba's people.

"Stay in the center!" she yelled, her voice carrying with authority. "Fighters to the outside. Protect our people."

They did as she told them and Efah was relieved that panic hadn't taken them over completely. Nesi lowered down and she mounted, finding the action coming more naturally to her. The hyena growled, turning toward a hallway. Efah felt it. More warriors. More heartbeats. More threads of life waiting to be cut. She urged Nesi forward and the beast broke into a run. The hallway was dark, and she could barely see except for what little fire light reached in. She closed her eyes. They were useless right now. She felt each of the attacking warriors distinctly.

"Go Nesi," she said quietly and her familiar responded immediately. They worked as one. Efah let her instincts guide Nesi and the hyena acted on those instincts. Warrior after warrior was crunched between Nesi's jaws and Efah felt their lives fading away. When the last one was dying on the ground, she turned the hyena around, rushing back to the main room.

More screams of terror told her that more warriors had arrived. They came in small groups from nearly every hall leading into the courtyard. Some of the fighters among the people were trying to hold them off but what were refugees supposed to do against highly trained forces? Efah led Nesi into battle without a thought for mercy.

When they finally took a moment to assess the battle, most of the attackers were dead. Across the yard, toward the entrance, she could see Usa and Newa finishing off the final few warriors. They were covered in blood, the firelight shining off his blades and her teeth. Around her, the fighters from among Garemba's people were swarming the remaining attackers and Efah urged Nesi on to put a quick end to this.

Newa rode up, sliding off the hyena as gracefully as possible.

Usa padded over, smearing Efah's cheek with blood in her affections.

"There are still a few that are injured but alive, my lady," he said shaking the excess blood off his twin blades. "Do you want me to interrogate one of them?"

Efah shook her head. "There's no need. We know where they came from and who sent them."

She looked at the aftermath of this small battle. She could hear weeping and knew a few of their numbers had fallen. Her people had been wounded and the warriors of Ofolobaru were squandered on an unnecessary battle. The dara had no respect for life. There was no way Efah could let this continue.

"We will bury our dead and burn the others," she called out. She turned her attention to Newa. "Tomorrow, I will have a special job for you to do."

He dropped to a knee. "Whatever you need of me, my lady."

~

Ofolobaru rose in the distance, a great gold capped monstrosity. Newa looked at it warily. He'd reach the city by mid-morning at his current pace and for once he wished he walked slower. Efah asked him to speak to the city's dara and he'd jumped to accept the task. But now, as he walked closer, he wasn't so sure he was up to the task. He was a killer. A priest who worshiped with blades and bloodletting. He was no emissary. Newa straightened his spine, relaxing his shoulders. For his lady and the god of death. Just as his god serves, so would he.

Traffic into the city was light this morning. The guards watching the gate looked bored and barely gave each passerby a look over before waving them in. If the Arak Gu'un standing guard at the entrance of his temple had been so lax, their leader would have them whipped. Newa fell in line behind a wagon carrying rice, obviously on their way to market. Their oxen snorted disapproval at waiting. He nodded in solidarity. He wanted to get back to Garemba as soon as possible.

Newa stopped before the guards when it was his turn. They waved for him to go on without looking and he frowned.

"I'm here to speak with the dara of your city."

One of them blinked, a sleepy looking woman with a long face. "You're what?"

Newa waited until they took in his robes and features, golden, angular, and so obviously Egan, before repeating himself.

"I'm here to speak to your dara on the command of my lady, Efah Aboujale."

The other guard stiffened. He waved for another guard to come over. The guard at the gate nodded to him, very officially.

"Yamma here will take you to the dara's palace. You have a good day." Newa nodded and followed the man deeper into the city. Let them think he was some sort of official. If it would help him in his goal, so be it.

The city was busy as they walked. People hurried back and forth, carrying items, messages, and who knew what else. Newa was impressed. He'd grown up hearing tales of the wild south and their fierce warriors. They were respected for their power on the battlefield, but it was always made clear that they were not as sophisticated as the Egans. They lacked true culture, and it was only through conquest that they would be made closer to a true people. As he looked around it was clear that those stories were lies.

Ofolobaru was as impressive a city as any found in the Egan homeland. The sculpted wooden doors were a wonder. The figures that adorned them stared out at him so lifelike, as if they were ready to leap out and run down the street. The dress of the people was more colorful than most fashions back home and he now knew where most of their patterned materials originated. How the nobles of Metkara would be insulted to know they weren't the height of fashion.

The palace of the dara was a spectacle of itself with the highest gold topped domes and towers. The conscripted guard from the gate was only too glad to drop him off in front of it and be off. Newa looked to the four sets of guards at the closed gates of the palace. He took a moment to inspect them. His eyebrows raised in humor. Three of these people were virtually brand new. Their uniforms were freshly dyed, utterly clean, and without a single fray along the edges. The last guard's uniform was just faded enough to be seen in contrast with the others and there was the smallest stain on the bottom right edge of his tunic. Newa smiled. This was the same uniform of the people who'd attacked Garemba. It did his heart good to see that they'd made enough of a dent in their forces that they were scrambling to replace them.

"I've been sent to speak with your dara," he said coming up to them.

"And you are?" said one of the newer ones.

The more experienced guard shushed him. "Did you have a petition for her? There's quite a line already."

"I've been sent by the Lady of Death, Efah Aboujale, to deliver a message to your leader on behalf of Garemba."

All four of the guards looked surprised at the mention of the so-called "city of thieves." Another of the new ones stepped forward, a little more aggressive than necessary.

"We need to check you for weapons."

Newa nodded and subjected himself to the inspection. He took out his curved twin blades, handing them over.

"These are sacred blades. I expect them to come back to me unharmed."

Another of the guards snorted. "Are you some sort of battle priest?"

"Yes," Newa replied and let the creepiness of his smile settle on him.

Another guard patted him down, not finding his garraut or the various flat knives he had on his body, hidden by padding. The experienced guard nodded his head and pointed inside with his spear.

"Continue to the main doors and speak with the secretary inside. He'll let you know what to do from there."

Newa passed them without any acknowledgement, a messenger too good to deal with common guards. Maybe this attitude would get him in faster. Inside the main doors, Newa was greeted with a long, tall hallway. The arches here were the tallest he'd ever seen, and it took all his training to not look like a country bumpkin. Ahead of him, various people in finery congregated in small groups, waiting. When that guard said there was quite a line, he wasn't lying.

"Can I help you?" asked a tall man with twisted hair. He looked down his nose at Newa and the assassin couldn't help but think of a secretary bird.

"I need to speak with your dara."

"As does everyone here. What is it concerning?"

"I've been sent by my lady with a message from Garemba."

The secretary's eyes widened, and he tensed. "I'll let her know that you're here." He quickly walked off toward the doors at the far end of the hallway. Newa waited patiently for the man to return but another warrior came up. She was the fiercest woman he'd ever seen and carried herself like a jungle cat about to strike.

"The dara doesn't have time to speak to you. She has far more *important* matters to deal with."

"Then I'll wait." Newa looked around then picked an empty spot and sat down. He closed his eyes, placing his hands in his lap. "Let your dara know I'll be ready when she is. Until then, I'll be communing with my god."

The warrior's footsteps didn't recede until a few moments later, all her annoyance showing in her stride. Newa breathed deeply. The dara would hear his lady's message one way or another. He focused on his mission, his service, and his god. Reflexively, he fell into the worship song he'd learned in his training. The humming relaxed his mind and put him in a calmer state to speak with this reluctant dara. Agitated footsteps would come from the dara's chamber every so often, stopping abruptly about ten feet from him before turning around and stalking off. He heard the chatter of the hallway lessen until he was sure that he was the only person remaining.

Steps echoed down the hall toward him stopping closer than the others. They didn't say anything at first and Newa could almost taste their agitation.

"The dara will see you now."

He opened his eyes, looking up to the same warrior woman from before. He raised himself up, stamping out the stiffness in his joints. Suddenly, he was aware of how long he'd been serving the sect. There'd been a time when he could have leaped to his feet.

"Very good. I should follow you I assume?"

"Yes," she practically spat then turned on her heel.

Newa fell in step behind her, hands behind his back. She glanced back every few steps as if she hoped he'd disappeared. He was happy to disappoint her each time. Another set of guards opened the grand doors that led to the dara's audience room. The area was lit with a number of lanterns. He was surprised. He didn't realize that the sun had fallen. No wonder he'd been so stiff.

The dara sat on a raised dais, her throne made of ornate wood and carved ivory. The warrior that led him in went to her side. At the dara's other side was a man with a scared face. Newa smirked as he wondered if this was the work of Usa or Nesi. Around the room were nearly a dozen other guards and he instinctively made a note of each of their positions. Just in case.

"So, you're the messenger from the girl in Garemba," the dara said with a sneer. Her hair was a halo behind her, curls of gray just starting to show through it. She had a sharp face and lips that seemed to permanently smirk. The dara didn't appear to be a warrior but she looked as fierce as her guards. This was a woman not to be trifled with.

Newa bowed, but not with the respect he gave his lady.

"I am Newa and I have been sent by my lady, Efah Aboujale, with a message."

"I don't care what that little gnat has to say. Tell her to surrender her people to me. Most of them are citizens of my city and they owe me my due as their dara."

The insult to his lady washed over him and he felt a sudden calmness.

"May I have your name so I can address you properly?"

The scarred guard to her left jumped in. "This is Dara Ngoli, second of her line."

Newa bowed again. "An honor, Dara Ngoli," he lied. "My lady has sent me to warn you. Leave Garemba alone or you will lose warriors one by one until Ofolobaru is only a city of merchants."

The two peacekeepers at her side bristled at the threat and Newa reached a hand for blades that weren't there. Ngoli looked daggers at him.

"You and your ragged band in the forest dare threaten me?"

"You've already lost twice to us," he said, gesturing casually. From his place across the room, he could see the dara's eye twitch.

She started to speak, but stopped herself, sitting back in her throne. The boiling anger on her face was reduced to a simmer.

"Aren't you Egan?" she asked.

Newa knew that tone. She was working to regain control of the conversation. He would allow it.

"I am. A priest of the Arak'guun from Metkara."

Ngoli's face turned dismissive. "A long way from home, aren't you? Why would you take up residence out in the thickest part of the forest? Surely you'd prefer the comforts of the city."

"My god, the great Gu'un, led me to her. You needn't worry about my comforts. I only live to serve her as my god serves death." He watched her glance to her nearest peacekeepers, noting her unease. Control was back in his hands again. "I have laid out my lady's message. I'm not here to ensure you agree. Come at us again and I will personally make you and your city pay."

Dara Ngoli scowled at him; teeth bared.

"The last time your lady was here she only made it out because of her beasts. You're just one man alone and unarmed. What would your lady say if I sent back the pieces of your body to her precious Garemba?"

Newa started laughing, a rolling sound that started from the pit of his stomach before rising to his chest.

"A brother of the Arak'guun, if ever caught unarmed, will not be unarmed for long. Gu'un is the hand of death, the one sent to bring the unrepentant back to the right way, even if it means the end of their life. You know him as Takiri. My sect doesn't necessarily follow his feelings on mercy."

The guards around the room were a mixture of unease with a tiny sprinkling of fear. He looked at each one before resting his gaze on the dara. She stared back intensely angry that she couldn't use her position to cow him. He could tell.

"You've been warned."

Newa bowed for the last time and turned to leave. He kept his mind alert and ready for a rear attack but none came as he pushed open the doors. He didn't relax until he was off the premises, moon blades back in hand.

The moon was high in the sky and the streets were aglow in its light. He took a breath and began his search for a place to stay for the night. This mission turned out to be easier than he'd thought. He just may be cut out to be an emissary after all.

~

Tekhamun's fingers danced across the hilt of his crescent blades. He couldn't wait to go out today. Karatel had found a group of people that said they were ready to hear his message. This was what he'd been waiting for. People needed to hear him, yet there were so many that refused. It actually hurt him that he had to kill so many. He only wanted to help them see the correct path. It's what Gu'un wanted. That's all he desired so it was all Tekhamun wanted as well.

He ate his dinner with Moon watching dutifully over him, making sure he finished every drop. He'd never been an especially big eater, but with their work had come the spoils of rich people's pantries. Never in his life had he eaten this good and his body had rewarded him with a little more muscle. It was like Gu'un was preparing him for better things. The priest was more than ready to receive them.

The door opened and Karatel came in with an eager smile.

"Master, we're ready if you are."

Tekhamun checked himself over, making sure his robes were as tidy as they could be and every weapon was in the right place.

"You look fine, Master," Moon reassured him. He nodded and followed his chief disciple into the night.

The streets were good and empty. While odd at first, Tekhamun had become accustomed to working under the cover of deep night. It was quiet and almost felt sacred. Perfect for his work. The six of them passed down street after street, picking up the other followers he'd gained in his travels as they moved along. By the time they reached the place that Karatel chose to meet, their group was twenty strong. The building was low and looked ill kept. Tekhamun wrinkled his nose a little at it, not knowing what horrors could be found inside but his duty called and he wouldn't shirk it.

Karatel took the group through a door hidden by a broken wagon. Immediately, the sounds of low talking came to Tekhamun and he wondered just how many people Karatel had assembled. They moved through forgotten merchandise, thoroughly picked through ages ago. Suddenly, they exited what must have been a storeroom and entered a larger room.

Tekhamun stopped short. There were at least fifty or more people gathered. They were rough looking, with haggard braids and clothes but Gu'un had no care of station. If they were here to listen to what he had to say that would be enough.

Karatel gave a short whistle, catching everyone's attention.

"Everyone," he shouted. "This is our master, Tekhamun of the Arak'guun." He motioned to the other four members of his band. "We are his direct disciples. Our master has a message for you and I pray that you'll listen."

He stepped out of the way, giving Tekhamun the floor. The priest swallowed hard, suddenly very aware of every single eye that was on him. He took a step forward, clearing his throat which had suddenly gone very dry. He closed his eyes for a moment and concentrated on his vision from Gu'un.

"I have been sent by Gu'un himself," he called out. "I have been given a vision. The netkoleh has betrayed the gods who put him in his holy position. He's declared the lie that there are no gods and the empire is supposed to believe this too."

A murmur started in the room and Tekhamun faltered momentarily, thinking they didn't believe him. When he suddenly realized that it was the decree that set off the whispering, he continued.

"I have been sent to deal with those who would go along with this blasphemy. They are to be cleaved from this world like fat from meat." He took out one of his swords, holding it above his head. "This sword will strike down the nonbelievers and leave only those with real faith in the city. We will make this city a holy one, ready to welcome all those who believe, whether they're rich or poor, high born or low. Gu'un doesn't care what station you come from. All he asks for is your faith and he will guide you."

The high note of his last statement echoed around the room. It took Tekhamun a moment to realize that there was nothing but silence. Then, a woman stepped forward from the group she was a part of.

"What do we have to do to be one of your followers?" she asked looking over the rest of the group that stood with Tekhamun.

"Profess your belief in the gods before me and I will make sure that you will be part of the number that lead this new holy city."

She bowed down before him, professing her fervent faith in all the gods of the pantheon, calling a few by name. Others began following suit until the entire assembly was bowed before him. Tekhamun breathed deeply, stunned at the sight. These people were his followers. They were the true believers his god knew he'd find in this city. He, Tekhamun, a lowly seventh son from the country, would take these people and mold them into holy warriors. His army of holy warriors.

Gu'un be praised.

Chapter Nine

Yutuuan looked out over the ships gathered at Tilizaa's port, nodding in approval. More of Wiluru's might was gathered at her eastern shore, ready and waiting to take this war to their enemy. After the fleet sent them limping away, his forces were ready to settle this afront to the kingdom. They would set sail this afternoon and hopefully run into what remained of the Fahzi ships at sea. Honestly, he hoped they'd set anchor and the mages could lob spells at them from afar. It would be less danger and he could finally get back to the capital.

"I can't believe you'd leave me," came Luunja's voice from behind.

Yutuuan jumped despite himself. He tried to chuckle, playing it off as a mere scare.

"I must have been deep in thought," he said, putting a hand to his heart.

"Sorry," she said, her smile subdued for the public.

He was thankful that she knew how to keep it professional when people could see them.

"But yes, I want to leave you and your fleet here. I need your people's strength and your cunning in battle to protect the coast in case they slip past us."

"But I was hoping we'd get to spend some time together." She leaned a little closer, lowering her voice to a whisper. "Perhaps we can carve out a few minutes before you set sail this afternoon."

Yutuuan stopped himself from recoiling. "I truly have a lot of work to do before we set out. In fact, I need to talk to the other captains and go over our plan once more." He started walking backwards. "I hope that we'll return soon, and we can talk then."

Without giving her another chance, he fled the area, making his way back to the headquarters. Naret was inside, directing the last of his packing. The bodyguard looked up and nodded. He did a double take at the prince's harried demeanor and smiled. As the last of the couriers left the room, he chuckled lowly.

"Hiding from Luunja?"

"I am not hiding," he said, trying not to sound like he was whining.

"You'd best get used to being around her," Naret said seriously. "It would be suspicious if the king ran away every time the queen neared."

Yutuuan swallowed as the realization hit him. Luunja was going to be his queen. There was no way to wiggle out of it. He did admit that Luunja was beautiful, desirable even. At least physically. But her personality was so, so . . . forceful. She had a way of taking flirting from simmer to boiling in an instant. Not that he didn't appreciate a woman who knew what she wanted, but if she could just come at him a little more calmly, he might be able to tolerate her presence. He would have to when she became queen. He would have to do more with her than just tolerate.

The prince pushed the thoughts aside, throwing himself into his tasks for the day. They didn't have much time to catch the tide and he wanted to be on his way as soon as possible. By the time the sun began its descent, he was safely on his ship and ready for them to pull anchor. The captain of this vessel looked to him for approval and Yutuuan nodded for them to set sail.

A cheer went up from the dock and the ships left behind as they sailed off. Naret stood beside him on deck, the bodyguard unable to keep the eager grin from his face. Yutuuan could feel the excitement of the soldiers around him. They wanted to bring this fight to their enemy and end this conflict. Yutuuan wanted the same. He had to get back to the capital and the real war.

The fleet sailed for two days. They passed the point where the Fahzi fleet had stopped before and even from this far out, Yutuuan could see the remnants of their camp darkening the shore. A few hours later, they passed the remains of a ship, the broken hull sticking out from the shallows. On the night of the third day, the call was made that there were ships on the horizon. Yutuuan was trying to catch a nap below decks but jerked awake at the noise. He rushed to the deck with several of the other sailors.

"What's the report?" he called to the sailor manning the wheel.

"Looks like they've pulled into shore just ahead. They only have a few ships left. The mage in the lookout says that many of their men are ashore."

The captain walked up beside the prince, obviously roused from her sleep. "Then we should be able to destroy the rest of their fleet before they can muster a defense."

Yutuuan nodded and began giving orders on the plan of attack which were quickly conveyed to the other ships. All lights were extinguished, and the mages used their powers to help the ships navigate by moonlight. Naret brought him his sword and Yutuuan happily strapped it on. He doubted it would get much use tonight but he needed to be ready. They moved into formation, curving their line of ships to prevent escape. Even if the Fahzi did manage to pull anchor and try to get away, they would still have to sail through the barrage of spells his navy planned on firing tonight.

The command for attack was about to be given when shouts of alarm went up from the enemy ships. Yutuuan shouted for the attack to begin just as the Fahzi sailors scrambled to put up a defense. Fireballs lit up the night, flying overhead in elegant arcs. The enemy magicians tried to counter by lifting seawater, but it was barely effective. With the opposing ships still, it was like hunting a penned beast. The Wiluruan attacks tore through sails and decks, breaking hulls like kindling. Yutuuan smiled. His people were just as ready to end this as he was.

This Fahzi empire thought they could snipe at their heels, biting off pieces of their kingdom leisurely. It was an insult. Yutuuan didn't tolerate insults to the monarchy lightly. It was the dominion of his forefathers and would be his one day. He wouldn't see it overrun by fleas.

On the shore was utter pandemonium. Enemy sailors scrambled about, some trying to get to the lesser ships to sail for the fleet. A couple of talented mages managed to land fireballs near those ships as well. While they didn't hit them directly, they hit the water with full force, tossing the tiny ships and throwing the crew overboard. His people cheered at the sound of the enemy screams.

More volleys of spells sailed into the ships and two began to sink. A hit just above the waterline sent water into the lower decks of another ship. One more was ablaze, illuminating the destruction further. Yutuuan's fingers tapped the pommel of his sword. This was the battle that would end it all.

In no time, nearly all the ships were incapacitated. He looked to the men on shore with eager, murderous glee. He shouted to the captain, "We need to go ashore. If those men return home, they'll rally the rest of their so-called empire." The command went across the ships and they closed in, surrounding the Fahzi fleet. A few minutes later Yutuuan was on a lesser ship, holding on against the choppy waves. He could hear the panicked shouts of his enemy before him, shouts that he would soon silence. He would end this war tonight.

~

A seagull outside called three times, then twice again. It was a good omen, or at least that's what Izriamat's nanny had told her as a child. She walked the halls of the temple in a good mood for the first time since she'd been sent here. People bowed lowly to her as she passed, making signs of reverence. They wanted to honor their princess but moreover, they wanted to honor the chosen of Yutuu. Izriamat made signs of blessing as she passed, trying to make sure she didn't miss anyone. The other priests and priestesses were starting to treat her less as a disgraced princess and more like the follower of Yutuu she was raised to be. It was nice not be whispered about as she walked the halls of the temple but, also, it was good to be doing her god's good work again.

Her uncle took to the news of her healing that woman better than she'd thought he would. He hadn't questioned it even once even though there hadn't been any mention of a priest using magic to heal a person so completely so quickly in all their history. And he'd looked it up. He even encouraged her to continue. It was clearly a blessing from Yutuu and who was he to impede the will of their god.

"My princess," came a voice just as she made the last turn.

Izriamat looked up to see one of the priests that oversaw the infirmary. He wrung his hands together and she could feel a slight aura of disapproval from him.

"What is it?" she asked.

"There are a . . . host of people waiting for you today." He pressed his lips together until they were a thin line on his face. "They only want you. They're calling you the Touched of Yutuu."

She blinked, surprised at the news. "You say a host. How many are there?"

The priest gave a helpless shrug. "They're clogging the entrance to the infirmary. It's becoming difficult to treat our patients because of them. If you could . . . do something with them?"

"What do you mean?"

"Send them off. Let them know that they'll have to come orderly like everyone else who seeks healing at the temple."

Izriamat blinked again, this time stunned at the callousness of the priest before her. He wanted her to turn desperate people away. People who were probably at their wits end looking for some kind of miracle and she had the power to give it to them.

"I will not," she said firmly. "Yutuu has given me power to help his people and you ask me to shoo them away as if they're a bother. We are here to help people in need and that's what I intend to do."

She slipped past him before he could respond and she was forced to question his faith. How dare he treat Yutuu's people like this. To think there were priests who found the core of their duties so distasteful. She would have to speak to Uncle about this as soon as she could.

The sound of the crowd waiting greeted her before she could even enter the infirmary. She walked in the rear doors to find chaos barely held under control by the temple's workers. The beds were all full and priests hurried between them to tend to the patients. Across the large hall, another group of priests held back a crowd all asking for the Touched One. The moment members of the crowd noticed her, they began begging for her help. Izriamat could feel their desperation, their need to be healed. It washed over her like frigid wind, prickling along her skin and the only way to relive herself of the feeling was to relieve these people of their suffering.

She crossed the room, deftly weaving between the workers.

"Calm yourselves," she called out. Her voice had an immediate effect on the crowd and they became a little less insistent. The priests didn't have to fight them to keep them from over running the infirmary. An older priestess who'd been trying to maintain order, looked up to her with relief.

"I'm so glad you're here, my princess. These people have been here since last night and their numbers have only grown."

Izriamat placed a calming hand on the woman's shoulder and stepped past her. "Then I will give them what they want." She stepped in front of the crowd, a serene smile spreading across her face.

"Oh, my people," she began. The room went silent around her and all eyes moved to her. "I know you've come here seeking healing and Yutuu has heard your cries. But if you will be patient and head back outside, I will see to each of your needs."

As if commanded, the people moved out of the doors orderly without a single protest. Priests around her made the sign of Yutuu in relief and thanked her before returning to their regular duties. The priestess she'd spoken to earlier, put a hand on her arm.

"Do you need any help, princess?"

"No, I doubt I will, but if it comes to it, I'll let you know immediately."

"Yutuu be with you." She nodded and returned to her duties.

Izriamat took a breath and stepped out into the bright morning sunshine. The crowd that had pushed its way inside did nothing to prepare her for the amount of people waiting for her outside. The path leading to the infirmary was packed with people sitting, standing, or leaning against the cliff that overlooked the temple. They were bundled against the cool ocean breeze but looked determined to get a chance to see her. The sight was a bit daunting, and she was tempted to step back into the safety of the infirmary. However, a slight push at the small of her back urged her forward.

She looked over the expectant crowd and saw a little boy in his mother's arms. He was almost too big for her to carry and she struggled to hold him up. He had a bandage and splint around his leg that was stained. Izriamat walked up to her, reaching out to caress the boy's head. It was almost scalding; he was so hot.

"What happened?"

"He broke his leg playing," the mother sobbed. "It was a terrible break. We managed to get it set but he's been feverish ever since. We don't have the money to pay for another doctor and the temple's beds are full."

"You don't have to worry anymore," Izriamat said as soothingly as she could. Her own voice threatened to crack from the pain she could feel from this woman and the suffering of this young boy. His life felt so weak against her senses and the sickness lay like a dark cloak over him. He didn't have much longer if he wasn't helped immediately. She concentrated on this cloak just as she did the woman in the infirmary and pulled. The sickness slid off him. Izriamat felt it burn in her hands like fog in the sun. She stroked the boy's head again and his eyes fluttered open.

"Take him home and let him rest," she said as the woman stared at her son in amazement. "His leg will heal well but most of all, he will live."

The woman clutched her son to her, breaking down in tears. "Thank you, princess. Thank you, chosen one."

Izriamat nodded to her and moved to another in the crowd. She spent her day with the throng moving from one sickness to another, healing illnesses and injuries, even those unseen. Before she knew it, the evening sun was blinding her as she worked. She could feel her strength waning. Never in her life had she wielded such power and it was taking a toll. She wavered and hands caught her before she fell.

"Priestess, you should rest." Izriamat looked to her left to see the woman she'd first healed days ago. "You haven't eaten all day."

"No," the princess replied, despite wanting to sit down more than anything. "People need me."

"You can't heal anyone if you fall dead."

Izriamat looked out at the crowd, feeling their need. She wanted to continue, she needed to continue, but her body was refusing. She pulled herself up as straight as she could.

"I will return tomorrow," she called out, the crowd captivated by her voice. "Please don't worry. I won't rest until I've seen all Yutuu's people free of their afflictions."

The crowd bowed, many making the sign of Yutuu. She made her way back into the infirmary and the temple, the woman at her side. Izriamat was glad for the assistance. Now that she wasn't actively working, exhaustion settled on her like a wet blanket. She sat down heavily in her room and looked to the woman.

"What is your name?"

"Sami, chosen one."

"Thank you for your assistance, Sami."

Sami bowed to her. "I'll see if I can get you some food."

She turned to leave but Izriamat called out to her. "What of your child?"

Sami paused, not quite turning to meet Izriamat's gaze. "My children still have their father and family. I have a better purpose now. To serve you so that you can serve Yutuu." She quickly left.

Izriamat sat back in her chair, letting the day come back to her. So many people needed her. Her mind drifted to the coming war. So, so many people were in danger. They had to know. They had to be ready. And she had to make sure they were. In mind, body, and spirit.

~

Umakaal pulled the hood of her cloak farther over her head. The cool rain poured off the expensive, eel skin leather, splashing around her boots. This was foolish. The streets of Wiluru were almost empty in the early evening shower and Umakaal found herself far from the palace. Alone. With a steadily encroaching night. Her sword was at her hip, ready for an attack that she prayed wouldn't come. She'd never been to this part of the city before. She didn't like it one bit but she had a promise to keep and a mess to clean up.

Umakaal passed a pair of pedestrians who laughed and joked about their winnings. She held her hood securely in place, hoping that they wouldn't recognize their youngest princess. But the pair had their own cloaks pulled over their heads as they rushed by. She breathed out once she was alone again. She had to do this as quickly as possible.

The restaurant she was heading to was already alight with lamps when she turned on the street. Ladawi's directions had been spot on. She would have to question her lover about how she knew where such a lowly restaurant was. It was at the base of a building that was a little recessed from the ones on either side. A large, woven roof had been built to extend the dining area. Even though it seemed like it was going to be a miserable night, patrons still gathered at most of the tables. Umakaal stopped a little closer to the restaurant, looking over the three waitresses serving. As one stood back up from pouring a drink, one could see the gentle swell of her stomach against her dress. That had to be her.

Umakaal took a seat at one of the outer tables of the restaurant. Her cloak protected her from the occasional shift of wind that splattered rain under the overhang. She lifted a hand, signaling to the pregnant waitress that she was ready to order.

The woman came over quickly, a pitcher for refilling drinks in hand.

"What can I get you?" she said with a practiced smile.

"Wine," Umakaal said, trying not to look at the belly that held her brother's bastard. "Honeyed and slightly watered."

"Anything to eat? The goat stew is famous."

"No, no. Nothing to eat."

"All right."

"One last thing though," Umakaal said just as the other woman turned to go inside. "I'm looking for Talekh."

To her credit, the woman didn't flinch or freeze. Now that Umakaal could get a good look at her, she didn't seem like her brother's usual type. There was no flightiness about her. She didn't seem like the type to swoon over a debonair smile from the prince. She studied Umakaal with measured wariness.

"What do you want with her?" she asked evenly.

"I received a message from Yutuuan. I came to talk about his instructions in it." At this, the woman did tense. "I mean no harm. I swear it. I just want to talk."

Another customer called to her and the waitress hurried over to fill their cups. Umakaal watched her carefully as she went inside. From what she could see through the windows, this Talekh didn't make a fuss or even alert anyone of her presence. Good. Talekh came back with her drink quickly, setting it down with the barest hint of annoyance.

"*He* would have come himself," she said looking the princess directly in the eyes. "He wouldn't have sent a servant. So, who are you?"

Umakaal took a sip to drown the retort on her lips.

"I'm his sister," she said coolly. "I don't know if the gossip has reached this part of the city, but my brother is away. Foreigners have attacked Tilizaa."

Talekh's ever present pitcher nearly fell from her hands. "Is he . . ."

Umakaal held up her hand for calm. "He's fine as of the last reports from the front." She paused, her eyes traveling down to Talekh's stomach. "You know, it was foolish to send a letter to the palace. It could have been read by anyone. A servant. An aide. The head of the palace guard."

"He deserves to know," she replied, visibly bristling.

"He deserves to know that the first child of this generation will be a bastard by one of his women?"

This Talekh woman settled a look on her that smoldered with hate. "I am his *only* woman."

Umakaal stopped herself from laughing loudly. The sound instead came out as a choked chuckle.

"His only woman? You must be a fool."

Talekh glanced behind her to make sure none of her other customers needed her. "Did you come all this way just to berate me?"

Berate? That was the word choice of an educated woman.

"I came here because my brother requested that you be taken care of." The words tasted sour on her lips. "You and your . . . child."

"For how long?" Talekh asked.

A prudent question. "He didn't specify. For the rest of your lives, I suppose." Umakaal watched her brother's lover carefully, searching for any sort of joy at the news of steady, royal coins. But she didn't see any happy emotion play across the woman's face. There was a coolness, a calculating look in her eyes that the princess couldn't quite read.

"Very well," she said after several moments. She leaned closer and pointed to a building farther down the street. "I live in that building now, top floor, rear room. You can deliver the money there. But I'm sure that *he* will make sure that our child is brought up in better surroundings."

Umakaal frowned at this shrewd woman. "You should be grateful that my brother is foolish enough to even bother paying you any more attention. Give him time and he'll forget about you just like all the others."

Talekh raised an eyebrow. "It appears that I know your brother better than you do. There have been no other women since we have been together. I know."

The princess chuckled cruelly. "How would you know?"

"You'd be surprised how far your brother's reputation had spread. It's why I was reluctant at first. I can see in your eyes what you think of me and no, I didn't try to seduce him because he was the . . . because of his position. *He* pursued *me*."

Umakaal stared her down, furious at her, Yutuuan, and the entire situation. Furious because this woman hadn't been put in her proper place.

"How in the world did my brother meet someone like you?"

Talekh drew herself up. "In the temple of Koleh. I was working."

"You were a priestess?" she sputtered.

The former priestess motioned to her building again. "Remember, that building, top floor, rear room. When I move, I'll send the location of my new home. Let him know that I'm fine." She looked her up and down. "I trust you'll pay for your drink."

As if on cue, another customer called out to her and she walked off without a second look.

Umakaal sat slack jawed on her chair. That woman was an Egan priestess. They didn't let just anyone enter their priesthood. She had to be a noblewoman. The bastard that woman carried could present a threat to Yutuuan's ascent to the throne. It could even throw question into his loyalties during this war. Umakaal downed the rest of her drink in one long gulp. She threw a few coins down on the table to pay and went back out into the light rain. At the corner, she turned back, watching Talekh chat happily with other patrons, her hand on her stomach. That baby could spell disaster for their family. She cursed under her breath and began the long walk back to the palace. All of this because her brother couldn't bother to keep his sword sheathed.

Chapter Ten

Commander Kolehem was worried. His regiment had been in the godless city of Nsongo for nearly two weeks and there was still no official date on when the invasion of the jungle would happen. His people were ready. More than ready. They itched for the promise of conquering unknown territory and the battle that would ensue. Not to mention the rumors of nuggets of gold that were so plentiful that one could pick up ten and still leave enough for the rest of the wing.

He knew he should be patient. General Tutahmen had been in the south the longest. He knew the people and the terrain. He hadn't given any direct orders to his people so Kolehem knew he should wait. But one had to wonder what was going on. He'd heard the rumors about the terrors across the Bangi River. He'd had to find out himself because the general was scant with the information he'd given. Kolehem collected stories from the native Nsongans and from a few Egan soldiers who claimed to have spoken with the poor fighter that was their lone survivor. From the reports, there was terror, but it sounded like rumors to scare away outsiders. Superstitions. Pure nonsense. That couldn't possibly be why the general hesitated was it?

The thought plagued him and as he sat at his midday meal, he decided to speak to the man himself. Surely, as the third highest ranked officer here, they could come to a more even arrangement. All of this, be it secrecy or withholding, wouldn't do. He pushed aside his plate and left his compound, making his way to where the general was based.

The guards outside let him in with a salute and he saluted them back. He wrinkled his nose at the state of the outer courtyard. It looked like several soldiers were staying here and they'd made themselves a little too much at home for his liking. A couple of questions to soldiers later and he was at the door to the general's office. The guard at the door ducked inside for a moment, announcing his arrival.

"Come in, commander," the general's voice rang out.

Kolehem stepped in the office, bowing with his salute. He didn't miss the middle-aged woman standing off to one side, container of some drink at the ready. Her long braids, streaked with gray reached nearly to her waist, denoting her nobility. He frowned ever so slightly. Was this the lady of the house? He also didn't miss the map on the table in front of Tutahmen showing the curve of the river.

"General Tutahmen, I wanted to speak with you about the invasion."

The older officer looked up. "Calm down, Kolehem. Have a seat. Would you like something to drink?" He motioned to the woman. "Manare, pour the commander something." She stepped up, fetching a cup from a nearby tray.

"No, no, I'm not thirsty," he said sitting in a chair. The woman returned to her position, her face a blank slate the entire time.

"So, you came about the invasion?" Tutahmen asked, clasping his hands on his desk. "What of it?"

Kolehem cleared his throat. "I haven't received much information about it. A firm date beside 'soon.' A launching point. I'd assumed that we'd cross the river here but seeing you looking at that map makes me second guess that assumption. I am the commander of the Red Spear wing and the third highest officer here. I feel like I should have been told more than I have."

Tutahmen blinked slowly. "I've given you the information you needed to know."

"I've had to find out most of what I know on my own." Kolehem knew he was dangerously close to disrespect, but he was feeling exasperated.

"Oh, you have, have you?" The way the general said that chafed Kolehem's skin but he didn't know why. "What exactly have you found out?"

"That perhaps you and your soldiers are hesitant about crossing the river because of local folk tales about monsters roaming the jungle."

"Folk tales," Tutahmen said, his eyes narrowing. Kolehem was about to elaborate on his point but the general suddenly stood. "Come with me," he said leaving the room.

Kolehem got to his feet, confused. "What?"

"I said, come with me."

Still not knowing if he'd insulted the general, Kolehem fell into step behind his superior. They went down an arcade, turning into another hallway. Ahead of them, a healer was coming out of a room, his face grim. Tutahmen stopped just short of the man. The healer bowed deeply on seeing the general.

"Is he awake?" Tutahmen asked curtly.

"Yes, general. He's having a relatively good day. I think he'll be able to talk to you."

"Very good." Tutahmen opened the room's door, motioning for Kolehem to follow.

The room inside was sparse, with only a stool, a chamber pot, and a simple bed. A man sat on the bed; knees drawn up to his chin. His arms were wrapped tightly around them. He stared at the opposite wall, eyes looking unfocused. Tutahmen moved nearby and it wasn't lost on Kolehem that they were just out of arms reach of the man.

"Turo," the general called. The man in the bed twitched but didn't look up. "Turo, it's General Tutahmen."

At this, he slowly turned his head, dragging his eyes away from whatever he'd been focusing on.

"General," he said, almost unsure. He managed a sloppy salute.

Tutahmen motioned to Kolehem. "Turo, I've brought someone to see you. This is Commander Kolehem of the Red Spear wing. He wants to know about the monsters."

Turo's eyes widened, and his hands shot to the sides of his head.

"No, general. I don't want to talk about them."

The general stepped a little closer. "I need you to tell him. It's very important to our mission."

Turo licked his lips, taking a ragged breath. "All right." He closed his eyes, breathing again. "They are bigger than a man. Wider than a man. Thick gray hides, like an elephant. And claws. Oh, the claws. They were like sickles. They moved through the jungle like ghosts. Picking us off one by one. They threw entrails at us like it was a game. I held a man's spine in my hands. I could hear them behind me as I ran. I could feel them getting closer. I could . . . I could . . . No!" His eyes shot open, wide with terror. "They're coming for me. They know where I am. No. No! I see them! I see them!"

Kolehem jumped back when the man screamed, flailing his arms, fighting off some unseen danger. Tutahmen turned, leaving the room just as the healer was running back.

"Should we just leave him like that?" Kolehem asked, glancing back over his shoulder as they took to the hallway.

"There's nothing we could have done for him. The healer will take care of it. Hopefully, he won't shit himself this time."

Kolehem said nothing, following the general down the halls to his office.

"I assume he was among the party that went to the jungle."

"He is the only man I've had survive that went over there. The smaller party we sent? We found their heads in the river. So do you still think my men are frightened of folk tales?"

Kolehem swallowed, his mouth dry. They returned to the office, the general taking his seat.

"Perhaps it's some sort of magic we were unaware of? Some sort of illusion."

Tutahmen leveled a stare at him that reduced his confidence to the size of a mouse.

"Illusions don't rip the heads off soldiers." He took a deep breath. "Look, Commander, I understand that you fought in the south during the war. Made quite a name for yourself. You wouldn't have been given the Red Spear if you hadn't. But you don't understand the dynamics here. You're new to the situation in Nsongo. I've been carving our place here for three years."

"What of Magistrate Hotemkhar?"

Tutahmen frowned. "The magistrate doesn't understand what it takes to subjugate a people. He thinks they have some respect for his position and through that position, he'll make them bow. Fool." The general spat the last word. "His arrogance is why we're in this situation in the first place."

Kolehem weighed asking the obvious question. "What situation?" he asked cautiously.

The general considered him for a moment, then his face fell into resignation. "We have no choice but to invade the jungle and search for the gold mines. The jungle people, the Batubangi they call them, cut off trade with Nsongo because the magistrate revealed that we killed one of their people."

"Why would he do that?"

"Because he's an idiot that can't lie. When confronted about it, he fell like a child's block tower." He folded his hands on the table. "Now, you know everything. Do you doubt our prudence in the invasion?"

Kolehem lowered his head. "No, general. I apologize. I should have never doubted your wisdom in leading your soldiers."

"I don't need an ass kisser, Commander. I need good men with good heads on their shoulders." He turned back to his map. "Then maybe we'll all keep ours."

Kolehem took a step forward, looking at the planning map. "Perhaps I can help with your plans."

"When I need you, I'll call for you."

The general didn't look up with his last statement. Kolehem saluted him, bowing, and walked out of the room. He knew when he was dismissed. That didn't mean it took away the sting anymore.

~

Ofemu had never been so nervous in his life. His wing of the family compound was prepared for his most esteemed guests. He could smell the meal prepared in the kitchen, ready and waiting. He fussed over the low table he'd set out on one of the patios, checking and double checking to make sure everything was perfect. Tonight had to be perfect.

A servant came to him, letting him know that the members of the council had arrived. He tried to will his nerves to be still. What he would have given to have Barabi beside him. He was so much better at things like this. Ofemu stood at the head of the table making himself relax as the elders were brought outside.

"Great elders, I'm so glad you accepted my invitation," he said, putting on his most charming smile.

The first of Nsongo's council members walked in slowly, leaning on a cane, his attendant hovering nearby. His fading eyes took in the scene before him and he raised an eye to the fair younger man.

"I was surprised," he began, making his way to a seat, "that you would suddenly show such hospitality to the council."

"I'm curious too, elder Okepeli," said the woman entering behind the old man. She cast an assessing look at Ofemu. "What might my former field commander be up to this evening?"

"I have an idea," grunted the last council member to enter. The older merchant sported a sour look on his face but took a seat with a nod of thanks.

Ofemu struggled to keep his smile from faltering.

"Councilor Abemisi," he said nodding to the last council member. "Councilor Palia. I only wish to have a talk with you. Please have a seat and I'll have the meal brought out."

He rushed to the nearest door, motioning to his servants to bring the food. The three councilors took in the sights and smells of the meal with questioning looks to each other before beginning to eat. Ofemu smiled brightly as he gave them a chance to enjoy the offering. After taking his own moment to get a few bites in, he looked to Councilor Palia.

"My general, how is your son?"

"He's fine," she chuckled. "Dealing with a host of suitors who wish to be the spouse of a great war hero, so I would say he can't complain."

"That's wonderful to hear. I know his injuries from the war had taken a toll on his spirit. I'm glad to know he's doing better." He turned to Abemisi. "And you, councilor. I hear that your trade with the salt mongers of Amakari is going well."

"Very well," the councilor said around a chicken leg.

"And I wanted to extend my congratulations to you, Councilor Okepeli, on the marriage of your granddaughter. I know you must be exceedingly proud."

Okepeli finished his drink. "You can stop your useless flatteries," he grunted, gesturing for a servant to refill his cup. "We know you've brought us here for a purpose, so what is it?"

Ofemu sat up, stunned at the bluntness of the eldest

councilor. His smile dropped as he took a deep breath to steel his nerves.

"I've brought you here to speak about my father. He is determined to take the Great Dara's seat."

The elders exchanged glances, then laughed. Abemisi snorted.

"Everyone's known that son."

"Your father's been a pain in the council's side for years," Okepeli said, and the other councilors nodded.

Ofemu suppressed a grimace at the sting of being laughed at. He swallowed.

"He might have been just a pain before, but I know he'll be like the sword of an enemy now, trying to hack away at you over and over again." He nodded to himself in approval of his turn of phrase. "He wants it badly. He's becoming obsessed with becoming Great Dara and I know he won't let anything stand between him and the ebony stool."

He took a moment before continuing. His mother always told him he talked too fast. He needed to give his listeners a moment to let his point sink in.

"Nsongo needs to elect a new dara. And my father seems to want to bull his way into it. But what if there were something to stop him? Another choice?" He licked his lips. "Me."

The councilors exchanged glances again and he could see that they thought his idea was ridiculous. Ofemu swallowed the bitter anger that was rising. Palia set down her cup, turning an almost piteous look toward him.

"Ofemu," she started in the tone one used on a child, "you do know that your cousin left a list of abodaras, right? We planned on choosing from there."

He took a moment to think on the revelation. "But they'd all be too young to take the position now, wouldn't they?" After another round of looks, Palia nodded. "Then Nsongo needs something, someone to stand as a barrier between my father and the daraship. I can be that barrier."

Okepeli clicked his tongue, fixing his stare on Ofemu. "How would we know this isn't a plan to pave the way for your father's ascension?"

Ofemu took a sip of his drink, surprised that the question didn't anger him. He took another moment to think.

"My father and I don't see eye to eye on a number of issues and this has been the primary one lately. More than ever, watching my father's obsession with the position, I feel that he is completely unfit for the daraship. Yes, he is the son of a Great Dara, a great warrior, and was raised in that household. I, myself, have dreamed of reaching the fierceness, the grandeur, and the wisdom of my grandfather, may he forever guide his family. But father chose the life of a priest. I mean no slight to priests, but my father has grown soft."

"A Great Dara must be a commander of people and that is one thing that I can proudly say that I am." He was thankful to see Palia nod at the statement.

Abemisi and Okepeli soon nodded to each other. The older councilor looked back to Ofemu.

"I have never heard you speak this passionately outside of the battlefield, Commander Ofemu. If you bring this same fever to city leadership you could be a force to be reckoned with."

"I have already chosen Barabi as my chief adviser." The council members looked surprised but pleased at that.

"Then you have my support," Palia said with a smile. "With Barabi backing you, you would make a fine dara."

Okepeli nodded again. "You have mine as well."

"I suppose I should join in as well." Abemisi chuckled. "You will have my support, but only to stop your father."

Ofemu lowered his head in reverence. "That is all I can ask. But for now, let us eat and talk of more pleasant things."

The dinner progressed well and ended quickly before Ofemu ran out of subjects to speak on. He thanked the council members profusely as his servants walked them out, then dropped back onto his stool, exhausted. He ran a hand over his face. The meeting went better than expected. He looked up at the sound of footsteps approaching from behind him.

"You did well," Barabi said coming up to him.

Ofemu smiled as his lover bent down to kiss him. He ran a hand through Barabi's braids. "What are you doing here?"

"I came to eavesdrop to see how you're doing. I am quite

impressed with how you handled the councilors. You didn't even slander your late cousin once."

Ofemu laced his fingers with Barabi's. "No. I have to convince the councilors on my own on what kind of a dara I will be." He kissed his love's fingers. "And I will have to work to become the type of Great Dara the south needs."

Barabi nodded sagely. "And I will be with you every step of the way." He leaned down and kissed Ofemu again.

~

There was no greater feeling for Erenemo than when a well laid plan came together. His servants were gone, save one. Patya was at a friend's compound for a spirited game of ukara. She wouldn't be back until late into the evening. In the kitchen, his cook had put together a sampling of foods made from the finest ingredients Nsongo had to offer. Their scents wafted down the hallway, making his mouth water. He would need a good meal later. This evening he'd be working in more ways than one.

Unyemi struggled to hold in a groan as he clutched the far end of Erenemo's desk. The priest kept one hand on his acolyte's slim hips as he thrust, the other on the younger man's back, holding him down on the desk. A little celebration was in order. Two of the most manipulatable council members would be here shortly and through them more members would be swayed to choosing him for dara. He was that much closer to his goal.

The high priest finished with as much fervor as his age allowed, slumping over Unyemi. The young man cried out as his own completion came soon after.

"Thank you, master," he moaned.

Erenemo chuckled. He pulled out slowly, enjoying watching Unyemi squirm in pleasure.

"We need to prepare now," he panted, straightening his robes. "Councilmember Pemaji should be coming before the hour is out."

Unyemi stood slowly, stretching his back. "Yes, my master."

Erenemo dropped into his chair to catch his breath. Soon Unyemi had his office desk cleared and cleaned of clutter. He'd placed the last of the plates of food on it when Erenemo heard the distant sound of someone knocking at the compound doors.

He smiled widely. "Let our first guest in."

The acolyte smiled dutifully, turning at once to fulfill his master's wishes. Erenemo tapped a finger against his chin. Unyemi had proved himself a dutiful student, eager and quick of wit. He'd served as a direct acolyte for over five years. It may finally be time to promote him. He would have to think on it.

Unyemi's footsteps were soon heard in the hall, followed by another. Elder Pemaji fixed him with a suspicious stare the moment she turned the corner into his office. Erenemo stood.

"Elder Pemaji, welcome."

"What do you want, High Priest?" Her thick lips were pulled into a sneer. "Your smile tells me that you want something."

"You know me well," he chuckled. *Arrogant hippo.* "Please have a seat. We can have a bit of good food and good drink and speak on a few things."

The elder folded her arms defiantly but sat. "I assume this is about you becoming the Great Dara," she said, popping one of the spiced nuts in her mouth.

"Well, yes." He gave a sheepish grin as if he'd been caught in his scheme. "I know you're still mulling over the possible choices. All this deliberation while our enemies grow stronger. Nsongo bleeds away her influence, and the other cities stand ready to usurp our role." He opened his hand like claws, then closed it. "Like a dog on a lion's forgotten kill."

"Is this supposed to convince me?"

Erenemo nodded to Unyemi who stepped out of the room.

"From what I understand, Pemaji, you have a love of Amakarian palm wine. It's a shame it's not in season."

He watched in satisfaction as she jumped when a cup of the dark liquid was suddenly handed to her from the right. She looked up in confusion into the face of the lone servant working this evening. He was a tall man, young with a frame more like a dancer than a cook. The smile on Erenemo's face grew as she was caught up in the young servant's handsome grin. Pemaji looked back to him then down at the drink. He could practically see her mouth water.

"Please, take a sip. You'll find it to be of exquisite quality." She took not just a sip but downed nearly half the cup. *Lush.* "I have six large thigh tall jars waiting for you and my servant, Siba, would be happy to pour you more, *at home*, if you'd like."

Pemaji's mouth worked as her stare moved between Erenemo and the handsome, young, and willing servant. She took another heavy sip.

"You're . . . you're trying to bribe me." Another sip. "How *dare* you."

At this, Erenemo laughed. "Yes, yes, I am. You may take this as an insult to your integrity, but the bribe still stands." Erenemo motioned and the young man refilled her glass. "It would be a shame to put such goods to waste. Palm wine is so expensive, and one would have to wait until next season to get it . . . if Nsongo is still in Amakari's good graces by then. They may not want to deal with a leaderless city. And Siba here will be quite busy with his kitchen duties." He paused, allowing the decision to weigh on her. "But I can understand if your honor is far more important than Nsongo's future."

"I'll take it," the elder blurted out. He watched the moment of shame play across her face, then be pushed away. "I'll take the wine and your . . . other offer." She narrowed her eyes. "May your soul be lost, sham of a priest."

Erenemo chuckled, the sound low in his chest. "I appreciate your support. Succeed in convincing other councilmembers and I'll keep you in drink for two seasons."

Pemaji scowled even deeper and stood, taking the hand Siba offered to help her up. She stormed out of the room, skirts swishing. Erenemo heard her snap at Unyemi in the halls as her voice trailed away. His acolyte appeared in the doorway a few moments later.

"Elder Hafulo has arrived," he said with a shallow bow.

"Then by all means, bring him in." Erenemo took a moment to snack on a few of the refreshments. One councilor in his bag, one to go.

Hafulo came into the office, a frown on his face. He gave a nod of obligatory reverence.

"What can I do for you, High Priest?"

"Please, Elder Hafulo, sit. Have a bite to eat. We don't need to remain so formal."

The councilor sat, back rigid. "I'd prefer formalities when dealing with you, Priest Erenemo."

"Very well," Erenemo quickly ate a small ball of obuobu, taking a moment to enjoy the savory, tart flavor of the ground nuts. Satisfied, he turned his full attention back to Hafulo. "We must take moments to enjoy the small pleasures in life. Don't you think?"

"Forgive me, but what do you want? It's getting into the night, and I'd prefer to be home."

Erenemo raised an eyebrow. "I want to know what I can do to convince you to support my rise to Great Dara."

"You can be a completely different man."

The priest considered the rude yeta addict before continuing further. He would not be regarded as a lesser man. He'd had quite enough of that as the younger brother of the last true Great Dara. Always being in Ibame's shadow. Always seen as the soft one. Always —. He pulled his thoughts to the present. He forced a smile on his face and said,

"Fortunately, I am who I am which means I have unique insight into what it takes to be a true dara."

He motioned for Unyemi to enter and get a large box from a small table near the wall. Hafulo glanced at the priest warily when the box was handed over. Erenemo ran fingers across the intricately carved battle scenes that adorned the top.

"What is that?" Hafulo asked. He leaned back in his seat as if the box held a snake ready to strike. Erenemo said nothing and lifted the lid, revealing its contents. He looked on, pleased, as Hafulo's eyes widened. The elder took a deep breath, hand gripping the edge of his chair.

"Yeta?"

"A year's worth. Yours for a small price."

Hafulo's lips pulled into a tight line. "To support you." He licked his bottom lip. "How did you get your hands on this much yeta?"

"A small task for an heir to the line of Yundasha," he chuckled. "So, do I have your vote?"

The look of hatred in Hafulo's eyes could have melted iron. "I will give you my support."

"Thank you. I—."

"I'm not sure how much good it will do. From what I hear, you have competition."

Erenemo's face fell. "What are you talking about?"

"You don't know?" Hafulo sat up, his face pulled into a smug smile. "Your boy has entered the competition for dara. He already has supporters too."

"He *what*?"

Hafulo stood, taking the box of yeta from Erenemo's hands. "Looks like you'll have to pull some more favors if you want the ebony stool. At least you have my vote." The older man chuckled. "You have a good night."

Erenemo didn't even watch him leave. Any response was stolen by his building rage. Ofemu was pursuing the daraship. That fool. That overreaching fool. He knew what his place was and now he wanted even more. After he'd been told it was out of the question. This was pure betrayal.

"Master?" Unyemi took a step toward him. "Is there anything I can do for you?"

"Get out," he ground out. At the man's hesitation his ire exploded. "Get out!" Unyemi scrambled from the room leaving Erenemo to fume alone.

Chapter Eleven

Nitiri's hands were magical. Bakari laid back in bed, head in her lap, letting her massage his temples. With each touch the worries of the day melted from him. He could hear the sounds of his sons playing, his heir trying to crawl after his toddling brother. Outside a storm pelted the city with sheets of rain but, thankfully, there was no thunder to frighten the boys. He sighed. If only every day could be like this.

"Does something trouble you, my emperor?" Nitiri asked quietly. Her voice was warm honey.

Bakari opened his eyes and stared up into her loving face. He raised his hand to cup her cheek.

"Lamenting how I must leave you so soon."

Her dark brown face pulled into a frown and the fact that she was still so beautiful pulled at his heart.

"You speak as if you're leaving for some time."

"I have to." He lifted himself up to a sitting position. Nitiri wrapped her arms around his chest.

"I'd expected to be on my way back to Wiluru by now. But Hetsaf keeps speaking to me of the trials of gathering the men necessary for the war. Every day that Wiluru is allowed their rebellion is another day that their will grows stronger. They have to be broken, my pearl."

She squeezed him for a moment. "But surely, breaking the Wiluruans won't take very long. It's not as if they're the southerners."

"No, they're nowhere near the might of the southerners, but they will still fight." He brought one of her hands to his lips, kissing her fingers delicately. "It may take years."

A sudden heavy silence fell on them both. Bakari's mouth set in a grim line. Years. This war may take him away from the capital for years. He would miss seeing the growth of his present heir. He would miss the birth of his true heir from Arkole. A sudden weight filled his chest. But surprisingly, most of all, he would miss the adoration of Nitiri.

He looked over to his sons, the tall, thick son from Nitiri and his heir by his disgraced queen, Izriamat. They had settled against a nest of pillows, speaking in their baby coos to each other. They would grow up as brothers and it seems fitting. As they started to fall asleep, he turned to Nitiri, lying her down. He took his time lavishing affection on every part of her, wanting desperately to remember the smell, the touch, the taste of her. He lost himself to their lovemaking, sighing her name into her ear when he completed.

They kissed their way back down from their high. Bakari rested his head between her ample breasts for a torturous moment before lifting up.

"I should go. I should have already met with Hetsaf."

She looked up at him shyly as he redressed. "I don't want to sound selfish, but will you visit again tonight?"

He choked back a groan. How part of him wanted to say yes.

"I . . . will see. I need to check in on Arkole as well."

"Of course, my emperor," she said bowing her head. "I understand."

He gave her one last, lingering kiss before leaving. He stopped himself from looking back. If he did, then his entire day would be lost. Bakari took to the hallways, ignoring the servants who bowed to him as he passed. He only slowed his pace when he came to the hallway that led to Arkole's rooms. The time for her labor was growing ever closer and he would be away for the war. He'd never been away from her for such a long time either. He frowned. But her growing nagging and neediness would be left behind when he was gone. Perhaps the time away would be good for the both of them. She'd have a son to fuss over and he could delight in breaking the one person he hated most in the world.

The walk to Hetsaf's office was a long one from the wives' quarters. Hetsaf had best have good news about the gathering of troops. He was tired of delay after delay. What else could their able-bodied warriors be caught up with? He opened the door, coming into Hetsaf's office without any announcement. He paused, surprised at the scene.

That same servant woman was there again. She wasn't cleaning this time but looking over Hetsaf's shoulder as he read reports. The space between them was more intimate than he'd seen his brother get with anyone. They both looked up, shocked, as if they'd been caught in the midst of something inappropriate.

The woman took a step away and dropped to the floor in reverence. Hetsaf stood and bowed.

"My emperor." He stepped to the side to offer his seat to Bakari.

The emperor sat, looking from his brother to the woman. She'd risen and stood behind Hetsaf but made no move to leave the room.

"Why is she still here?"

Hetsaf stiffened slightly. "I would prefer her to remain, my emperor. She has . . . been an assistant of sorts to me over these past weeks. I beg your indulgence in this matter."

Bakari stared at his chancellor. He'd never known his brother to make any requests of a personal nature. His attention turned back to the woman. Too thin for his tastes and not exceptionally pretty. Perhaps Hetsaf was telling the truth but he'd hardly let anyone in his office, even to clean.

"Your . . . assistant?" he asked, unbelieving.

"Yes, my emperor."

"Fine. I will allow her to stay even though this is a matter for men." He looked at the small stacks of papers on Hetsaf's desk. "I sincerely hope you have good news for the war preparations."

Hetsaf came closer, handing him a message from a city leader. "Yes. The majority of the eastern cities have contributed all their battle-ready men for the effort. The soldiers from Ixus, Ux, and Imtahera have already arrived. We are still waiting on the force from Karsis but they should be here in a few days."

"The total?"

"Six thousand men. With our own troops here, that brings us to ten thousand."

Bakari leaned on the desk, interlacing his fingers.

"It's not enough. We must have an army large enough to destroy Wiluru. Large enough to stamp out any seeds of rebellion from their people." He looked over to his chancellor. "What about calling soldiers from the south?"

"My emperor, our soldiers are already stretched thin to hold onto the southern cities."

"Fine then," he spat. "What about Djelebe?"

Hetsaf hesitated. "Djelebe wasn't called on," he answered, slight confusion in his voice.

"Why not?" Bakari snapped.

"I thought that the city of scholars wouldn't be considered for a war effort. What could they even contribute but blood for the enemy's swords?"

"They are a part of this empire, aren't they?" Bakari narrowed his eyes when Hetsaf didn't respond immediately.

"Yes, my emperor."

"They will obey the wishes of their emperor! Send the message that they will contribute soldiers, magicians, and supplies to subdue Wiluru as is their duty. I have already made this clear to their governor. Let them know that I'll be expecting them to add to our forces when we arrive there."

Hetsaf blinked, then dipped his head down. "Yes, my emperor."

When the man hesitated again, Bakari's ire grew. "There is another issue, isn't there?"

"There may be a slight delay for your departure." The servant woman handed a scroll to Hetsaf who set it in front of Bakari. "It appears there's a peasant uprising in the east as well. They're having problems getting the supplies we requested out of a few of the cities."

Bakari sneered. "And what do they have to rebel against?"

"Your decree, my emperor."

Bakari's skin felt like fire licked every inch. "Crush them."

Hetsaf inhaled slowly. "That would take away from the coming army forces."

"Djelebe will make up for it."

"I don't think —."

"I haven't asked you to think! You only have to obey!"

Hetsaf blinked twice, very slowly, and just before Bakari yelled again, he answered.

"Any warriors from Djelebe will not be enough for the

invasion force you want."

"Then start conscripting southerners if you have to. It's about time they started contributing more than gold to their empire."

"Can we trust them? Not even a generation has passed since their defeat."

"Then tell them dissenters will be beheaded."

"They may think —."

"I grow tired of your objections, *brother*." Hetsaf straightened his posture a bit but, thankfully, remained silent. Bakari rose from his seat, glaring at Hetsaf and the servant who both bowed. He turned his attention solely to the servant, who'd stayed oddly close to the chancellor throughout the meeting.

"Are you Hetsaf's bedwarmer?"

The woman froze but didn't raise her head even an inch. "Yes, my emperor."

Bakari noticed the unease creeping through his brother's posture.

"Then perhaps you can soothe this objectionable spirit of his."

"Yes, my emperor."

Bakari allowed his glare to burn his brother's way one more time.

"Follow my orders, Hetsaf," he called as he left the room. "Within a half turn of the moon, I expect to be on my way to Wiluru."

~

The future heir to the Egan empire was busy today. Arkole rubbed a hand over her stomach, chuckling at her baby's antics. This would be a son. She knew it. Kolehtun was such an active baby as well. Her mood fell at the thought of her beloved late son.

Had it really been nearly a year since the bright sun in her life had gone out? Her sweet, sweet boy. He'd just begun to take on the traits of a man, becoming more and more the twin of his father. He was bright and fast and the perfect prince. The shining accomplishment of her life as the Great Royal Wife. She had birthed the heir to this empire. She had given Bakari his first true son. *She* had done that.

There should have been more.

The stray thought stabbed her. She didn't want to resent her daughters. They were such a joy to her each and every day. But they weren't sons. They weren't heirs. They would never inherit the throne. They would never ride out to battle and bring glory to the empire. She rubbed her stomach again. A son. Please, please be a son. She needed another son. What was a queen who didn't give the empire an heir?

Arkole rose carefully and began walking to her favorite courtyard. Her attendants fell in line behind her. The water lilies would surely be in bloom with all the rain they'd had and maybe the palace peacocks had decided to spend their day there. She needed something to cheer her up.

She was just about to turn to go down the hall leading to the courtyard when a line of servants caught her attention.

"Is something the matter, my queen?" her lead attendant said from her left shoulder.

"Those servants are heading towards the second queen's chambers. No one should be in there."

Arkole changed course, walking confidently toward the far hallway. More servants passed by, carrying different items. She frowned. No one should be carrying anything *to* that detestable woman's chambers. If anything, it should have been cleared out by now. Arkole weaved past the procession of servants who scrambled to bow to her despite their heavy loads. She burst into the room and halted. That *girl* stood in the middle of the room, directing servants. A stocky toddler held onto her skirts and in her arms was the son of Izriamat.

"What is the meaning of this?" Arkole roared. "What are *you* doing in these rooms?"

This girl, Niriti she believed, bowed as much as she could while holding that baby.

"Great Royal Wife Arkole, I am supposed to be here."

Arkole's anger flared. This innocent act was fooling no one.

"Not a soul is to be in the second queen's rooms."

Niriti handed the children off to a nearby servant woman. Her expression turned apologetic.

"I am the second queen."

Arkole took a step back. Her breath caught in her throat, her mouth forgetting how to form words. She swallowed, freeing her thoughts.

"What did you say?"

This girl had the nerve to smile. "Our Bakari has made me his second queen."

Our Bakari? "There was no ceremony. No announcement. *I* didn't even know."

"It isn't completely official yet. But he made it clear that it will be so before he goes off to war."

Arkole tried to calm her breathing. A maelstrom of hurt and anger swirled within her. Second queen. Second. Queen.

"We will see about this." She picked up her skirts and stormed out of the room.

It took Arkole some time before she found her husband. Bakari was in his private training yard, working with his sword and small shield. He was shirtless and sweat slick, an even more refined version of the young prince she'd fallen in love with. She hated every muscle right now. Arkole marched into the yard, not caring what the dust was doing to her hem.

"Bakari," she called out tersely.

He aborted a sword swing and turned. His face changed from confusion to apprehension.

"What is it, Arkole?" he said, handing his sword to an attendant.

Arkole narrowed her eyes at him. She didn't like his tone or posture.

"How could you?" she hissed.

"How could I what?"

"That woman. No, that *girl*. What is she? Ten years younger than us?"

Bakari sighed heavily, adding fuel to her anger. "What are you talking about? I have work to do."

"That girl you've risen to replace Izriamat. You made her Second Queen? You didn't even ask me."

"Ask you?"

"Ask me. I'm your wife. The Great Royal Wife."

"It was my choice to make, as Emperor. It was the right choice to make. Niriti is a loving mother, a devoted wife, and never questions my decisions." He leveled a look at her that cut to the bone.

"Bakari, you said that you needed me more than ever." She came closer to him. "You said I was to be your voice, your right hand. Why would you do something so important without consulting your right hand?"

"Does the body seek council from the right hand or does the right hand follow the commands of the body?"

Arkole took a few breaths. He was looking at her so coldly.

"I don't like her, Bakari. She's trying to gain your favor. Have you doing whatever she wants. And you made her Second Queen behind my back. How could you do this to me?"

"Do you truly think I elevated Niriti just to slight *you*?" Bakari closed the gap between them, leaning closer. She could feel his breath on her cheeks. "Woman, do you always think only of yourself? Niriti has taken my only true son in as her own. She has nursed him at her breast, made him a brother to her own son. And she is dedicated to her role as my wife." His voice rose with each fact. "Why wouldn't I raise her up? I deserve one wife who doesn't question me."

Tears started to form in the corners of her eyes.

"Bakari, if you truly love me, don't hurt me like this. Send her back to the lesser wives. Choose another. I promise I won't complain."

"Should I consult you on my other decisions so you *won't complain*? Is that the only way I'll be free of your whining?" Arkole stepped away at the force of his voice. "Should I consult you on when I should eat? When I should shit? Who do you think you are to question *anything* I do?"

She cowered, taking another step back. Never, in all their days together, had he spoken to her like this.

"But Bakari, my love, I am your first wife."

"Then act like it!" he bellowed. The sound bounced off the training yard walls. "I chose you to be my Great Royal Wife but, by fire and ash, I will see you replaced if you *ever* question me again."

The tears fell freely down Arkole's face. She picked up her skirts and fled the yard, her attendants scrambling to keep up.

~

Sept'ha had spent more than enough time in the chancellor's bedchamber but never a night. She looked around, noting each detail with new eyes. One lonely bed and two small tables for work were all that furnished a room meant for pleasures. He was the chancellor and the emperor's younger brother. He should have every single one of his desires fulfilled. A room like this was wasted on a man like him. She thought of her room at home or the corner of the servants' quarters she used to sleep in. She would have done a good many things to stay in a room this opulent. She didn't know that pretending to be the chancellor's bedwarmer would be one of them.

The chancellor was nowhere to be found. After his last meeting with the emperor, Hetsaf was working late into the night, doing his best to have provisions and warriors ready to leave on the emperor's timetable. The last time she'd spoken to him, he was on his way to personally speak with military commanders. Who knew what time he'd return?

Sept'ha began unrolling her bedroll and tying up her hair for the evening. At least with this facade, they could speak more freely and plan for longer periods. The war would be a glorious one if Met had her way. But with the emperor's insistent, selfish demands, she wasn't so sure. Reason didn't appeal to him so they would have to find something that did.

"You brought a bedroll?"

Sept'ha jumped at the sound of Hetsaf's voice. She took a moment to compose herself before answering.

"Yes, I will be sleeping here after all."

He shook his head, entering the room and dumping a pile of scrolls onto a table.

"You will sleep in the bed. If any of the other servants want to be nosy, I don't want them to suspect this is a ruse. I know how you all gossip."

The last comment wasn't meant as a jab. She knew him well enough by now. But it stung, nonetheless.

"Are you sure you're comfortable with this?"

He hesitated, jaw working. "No. But I'll adjust. It is a good idea since it appears I've favored you." He glanced at her for the briefest moment. "We have no choice after your confession to the emperor."

She gawked at him. So he was going to place the blame at *her* feet?

"What did you expect me to say?" she hissed. "That I, a woman, am helping you plan the emperor's war? That you, the great Chancellor, need assistance from a cleaning servant?"

He leveled a warning look at her, but his obvious exhaustion had stolen much of its strength.

"I don't *need* help from a woman." His lips twisted as if he tasted something sour. "But your counsel and insight has proven valuable.

Sept'ha watched him as he separated the scrolls. Compliment? This was unprecedented.

"I am happy that you see the value of my advice."

"I truly don't want to hear any of your sarcasm. I'm exhausted." His stomach growled the moment he stopped talking and he looked aside, embarrassed.

Sept'ha resisted the urge to roll her eyes.

"Have you eaten?" she asked gently.

He shuffled his feet. "No. Not since noon."

"Then I'll get you dinner." She gave him a curt bow and walked off toward the kitchens. The chancellor could be a brilliant planner and a fool at the same time. Nothing was so important that one should neglect their body if they didn't have to. Didn't he realize that if he were gone, this empire would surely fall to ruin? And where would that leave her and Met's plans?

Sept'ha paused in the hallway. Met's plans. Why was she even following the whims of a deity that wanted to plunge the land into chaos and war? So many people would die. And why should she be responsible for it? She didn't want that weighing on her soul. This was pure madness.

She picked up a tray of assorted foods from the kitchen staff, who were annoyed to be bothered so late, and returned to her employer's room. He'd moved a stool so he could sit to look over his scrolls.

She sighed, placing the tray on the other table.

"Chancellor, please come eat."

He sighed this time but brought his stool over. "Thank you," he muttered through his first bite.

She nodded, heading to the bed. She watched him eat for a few moments. There could be worse ways to make a living. She could be back at home, waiting on father to choose a husband for her. Now, even if she was shackled to a man, at least it was one that only wanted her mind. If she stayed in his employ, she may never have to worry about the demands of a man her entire life.

"Do you mind if I go to sleep?"

"Do as you wish," Hetsaf said with a yawn. "I will be to bed shortly. And I swear you will remain untouched." The last part was rushed as if he didn't want to bring up the subject.

Sept'ha thanked him, laying down. Her body relaxed instantly. She'd never been in such a plush bed. Her mind responded to the comfort by succumbing to her sleepiness. Yes, there were far worse lives to live.

In no time, she was dreaming. Sept'ha opened her eyes to a battlefield. A dull blue sky presided over a dusty brown field. Warriors in clothing she didn't recognize, filled the landscape. Spears and swords glanced off leather shields. Arrows pierced armor and gouged out eyes. Fighters were trampled by horses, their screams mingling with the shouts of battle, swirling together into one great symphony of chaos. Sept'ha covered her ears, looking for a path to flee but it was too loud to even think. She was drowning in the confusion and she would never escape.

Then she saw her.

Met walked through the battlefield, warriors parting around her like water at a ship's prow. Her gown flowed in the wind, the thin linen barely hiding the perfect, muscled figure underneath. Her leopard walked at her side, ignoring the fighting. She was adorned like a queen but moved with the measured grace of her beast, ready to strike at any moment.

Sept'ha dropped to her knees in awe. This was the woman she wanted to be. A woman who relied on no one, who had power enough to make the world move out of her way. She knew it now. Such a role called to her. Her very soul yearned for it.

"Rise and walk with me, my dear servant," came Met's throaty, smoky voice.

She did as she was told, following the god through the bloody landscape. Sept'ha watched her patron, mesmerized by the power she had in her element. Met swept her arms wide, taking a deep breath and letting it out with a satisfied sigh.

"Look around you. Truly look. What do you see?"

Sept'ha turned as far as she could. The warfare continued around them, but never touched them.

"I see fighting, great Met."

"No, not fighting. Worship." The last word fell from the god's lips with an almost immodest passion. "These people worship me, in heart and spirit. In the truest form, they worship me. Not the empty platitudes of the temples. Not the slain animals, docilely led to the altar. I am not a god of bloodshed. I am god of *war*." Met turned, looking her deep in the eyes. "Do you understand me now?"

Sept'ha looked around again, taking in the scene. A man's hand was severed under the blade of a tall, brawny warrior with wild eyes. A woman ran another man through with her spear, the tip buried halfway in. Her war cry rang out clearly above the din.

"You wish for true worship again."

Met considered her, her head tilting slightly. "No, you still don't understand. I wish for your kind to return to their truest, greatest, and holiest selves. And for that you need to return to war."

"But so many people will die."

Met stroked her cheek gently, like her mother did when she was a child.

"People are always dying. Constantly dying. Constantly churning out more spawn just to die of disease, neglect, or old age. Wouldn't it be better if they were to die with purpose? Peace time has done them no favors." The god sighed, shaking her head. "Your kind have grown complacent, fat from a life of excess. You have time to wallow in your own hubris. You begin to think yourselves greater than you are. You begin to think of yourselves as more than human. And what does a person who's more than a human need with the gods who created them?"

Sept'ha took a quick breath. Her mind immediately turned to the emperor. Most had rebelled against his mandate at first. She'd heard about the all-out riots at some districts of the city. But with time and the royal forces cracking down on them, protests were dying down. Both public and private. How long until the gods acted against being ignored?

Met smiled. "Ah, now you see."

She swallowed. "War makes man humble."

"Exactly." Met swept her arms out again. "How many prayers do you think went up before, during, and after a battle such as this?"

Sept'ha stared around at the seemingly endless battlefield.

"More than I could ever count, great Met."

"That is why I need you, Sept'ha, my chosen. This land rests on the edge of a blade. You will be the one to help it fall on the right side."

"Why . . . why me?"

Met lifted her chin up and Sept'ha was forced to look into those golden eyes. "Because in you I see a warrior's spirit, untested, like a new weapon. With time, you will be a woman who commands the fate of an empire, beholden to no one. Does this please you?"

Just beyond Met, Sept'ha saw a figure. She was dressed in the finery of a noble woman and before her was a force of warriors, kneeling and ready. The woman looked up to Sept'ha and she realized she was staring into her own face. She dropped to her knees.

"Yes, my god."

"Then go and make war."

Sept'ha sat up in bed, heart racing. She looked toward Hetsaf. He turned over, but his breathing remained steady. She ran her hand over her face. The sounds of battle still rang in her ears and she could smell the dust and sweat and blood. A smile spread over her face. War was good.

Chapter Twelve

An odd fog settled on Garemba during the night, holding the first rays of morning sunlight at bay until the last moments. A hush blanketed both city and forest making time seem to stand still. Efah could feel the difference in the air, so much so that it woke her from her slumber. She rose as if called, stepping out onto cool, slightly damp stone. Out of her rooms, out of the palace, onto the edge of the forest itself. Not a single animal protested her approach. Not a single insect hummed in the trees. She looked behind her, expecting Usa and Nesi to be close but they were nowhere to be found.

It was when she felt the chill at her back that she knew why she'd come to the forest. Death walked past her, taking slow, long strides deeper in. Efah fell in line behind him and they continued, not breaking the surrounding silence. They walked until the forest slightly parted, revealing a small cliff overlooking the Bangi. The fog was still persistent and she could only hear the distant churning of the river below. The first rays of sun were just shining through the trees, desperately trying to make way. Where they stood, the light avoided as if his mere presence caused it to die too.

"My servant," he began at last. "I am proud of your efforts thus far. Your following grows. More people will be brought to safety."

He stopped, looking off into the distant horizon. Efah was tempted to say something when she saw the expression on his face. His brows were knitted, his mouth pressed tightly, his jaw clenched. He was concerned.

"The fire grows closer. From without and within." His gaze lowered back down to the fog covering the river. "You must gather as many as you can to save them. So many will be like kindling." He turned his milky white eyes to her. "War walks the earth."

Efah's breath caught, the feeling of dread coming from him

washing over her.

"I'll send Newa out immediately."

"Newa has his own path to walk. *You* will have to go."

Efah froze. Leave Garemba? For how long? This ancient city was the first place that had felt like home since her family died.

"I don't know if I can do that."

Death placed a hand on her shoulder. It was cold but brought her reassurance.

"You have faced your oppressors and sent them scurrying like rats. You have faced your enemy in battle and won. You are my voice on earth. I have not chosen you on a whim. You are more than capable."

Efah's mind was suddenly swept away from the forest. She saw herself on the road, riding one of her hyenas, at the front of a great column of people. She saw herself in a village, speaking to an immense crowd. Then she saw herself in battle once more against the warriors of one of the great cities. Her mind snapped back to her surroundings and she lowered her head, tears threatening to fall.

"Thank you. I . . .I'll go."

"Your path leads you west, my Voice."

When she raised her head, Death was gone. The sound of birds started slowly, followed by the noises of other arboreal creatures, as if the forest was just waking up. Efah took a deep breath, trying to calm her spirit. She had to leave Garemba. Venture to the west, to other villages and cities. Speak with other daras, even the Great Dara to convert them to her cause. She swallowed hard.

And Newa wouldn't be there. She remembered Death's words about him forging his own path. Was he going to leave her side completely? She'd come to rely on him for so much. His presence was almost as much of a comfort as Usa and Nesi. How would she lead without her most fervent follower?

The three of them were at the edge of the city when she returned. Her familiars stood barring Newa's way. The assassin priest had given them plenty of room but looked determined to find a way past. She could hear him bargaining with them, trying to explain that they needed to search for her.

"I'm here," she announced. The hyenas' heads jerked up immediately and they bounded across the distance. Efah laughed as they licked her face. She gently pushed them off as Newa approached. He gave the same deep, nervous bow he always did, his face awash with relief.

"My lady, we were worried. Your hyenas insisted on keeping me here." He glanced at them tightly and she could swear Usa rolled her eyes.

"I was speaking with Death," she replied. "I was safe."

Newa bowed again, unnecessarily. "Of course, my lady."

Efah ran her fingers through Nesi's coarse fur, the visions Death had given her playing in her mind again. The last image, her in battle once again, wouldn't leave her.

"Newa, I need to speak with you. It's about the future of our mission."

"Whatever you need of me I am ready to do." He started to bow again.

"Please stop that," she begged. "Please don't bow to me so much. You are my most loyal follower. I don't want you to act like a servant or a slave. I'd prefer if you thought of us as . . ." She searched for an appropriate term. What did she want them to be? "As friends," she settled on.

Newa's face shifted as he took in her request. "Very well, my lady."

"Please call me Efah."

"Very well, Lady Efah."

She sighed. That would probably be the best she got from him. "Newa, we're going to have to leave Garemba. *I* am going to have to leave."

"I am ready whenever you are, my—, Lady Efah."

"No, I will have to go. You'll have your own path." He frowned for a moment, then nodded. "I have to spread the warning." Silence passed between them. "And I need you to teach me to fight for myself."

Newa looked down to her alarmed.

"Lady Efah, you have Nesi and Usa to protect you."

"What if they're not around? What will I do then?" The hyenas came to her side as if to comfort her. "I need to be able to defend myself.”

“I have people who've volunteered to become my students. I should have several of them ready by the time you decide to leave.”

“They may not be ready in time. I need to learn.”

“My teaching is harsh, my lady. Extremely harsh. It's better I send people with you.”

She came up to him, putting a hand on his arm.

“Newa, why are you dodging my request?”

He looked down, then away before looking her in the eyes. “A fighter must be as prepared for his own death as much as his enemy's. That is why I don't want to teach you. I don't want to see you that close to death.”

He turned away again and Efah turned his face back to hers.

“How can I be any closer to death than I already am?” She looked into his eyes and saw all the pain and sorrow within him. She felt it deep within her as well. She felt how close he had come to walking with death and how much death his blades had dealt. It was then that she understood why he'd been led here. Who else could understand her role in this world but someone like him?

Newa looked to her, defeated. “I will teach you, my—, Lady Efah.”

“Thank you, Newa. This means more to me that you realize.”

~

The sounds of intensive training filled the air and Newa couldn't be happier. He stood, hands behind his back, in full Araakgu'un uniform, watching his latest pupils. They'd broken off into pairs, going over the basic hand-to-hand techniques. He wanted to move to armed arts soon but, until they could find enough blades, he'd made their bodies the deadliest weapons in the South. Newa smiled. It was good to be teaching again.

“Ifisi,” he called out to a young woman who'd fled to Garemba with her mother. “You're relying too much on your right. Remember to work with your left as well.”

She and her partner paused. “Yes, teacher,” she called and they returned to sparing.

Newa began walking up and down the rows of Garemba's future defenders. Giving a tip here. Correcting a stance there. There were nearly forty of them total. Honestly, he was shocked that there were even that many. This was a city of refugees. He'd expected to gain a few veterans of the last war, but there had come parents and caretakers, widows, and widowers along with the war hardened, all ready to defend their home and the Lady of Death. It was all for her.

Newa found himself smiling. Surely the lady would be pleased with the progress they've made. Garemba would be protected. *She* would be protected. And he would be able to sleep soundly. The image of her proud smile came to mind and he sighed. One of his trainees looked over at him. Newa quickly shook his head, moving to the back of the group.

What was wrong with him? This wasn't the first time he'd been lost in thoughts about her. He had to think about her. Serving her was his duty. It was his pleasure to perform any task she asked. It was a pleasure just to be near her. The image of Efah's smile resurfaced and he found himself caught in a wistful smile yet again. He forced a more neutral expression. What was going on? Yes, he enjoyed her company. She was kind, patient, and wise beyond her years. She served her god as faithfully as he did his, if not more. It was something he aspired to. And if she ever approved of his service as much as he wanted her to . . .

Newa's heart beat against his chest and he swore he could hear it. He swallowed, this airy feeling concerning him. He told his class to continue and walked a bit away so he could be alone with his thoughts. He ducked around a half-fallen wall that shadowed him from the afternoon sun.

He took a deep, calming breath. Why was his mind always turning toward Lady Efah? Why did he long for her presence at the mere thought of her? He frowned, concerned even more. Surely, he didn't *desire* her. In all his life he'd never wanted anyone in a physical way. Newa closed his eyes, searching his feelings. No, no, that wasn't it.

Ifisi stepped cautiously around the wall. "Excuse me, teacher, but Lady Efah is here."

Newa's heart leapt, but he willed his expression to remain

calm.

"Thank you, Ifisi. I'll be there in a moment." She nodded and left him. After a series of short breaths, he rejoined the training yard.

Efah waited just beyond the area, watching the group train with intense interest. Newa schooled the smile starting to form and approached her. Someone had cut her hair back down and the style that would have been scandalous in Metkara was absolutely regal on her. She smiled at him when he was closer and he thought his heart would melt.

"Newa," she called happily. "Your class is so good."

He bowed to her. "Many of them may be beginners but with their dedication, they'll be true defenders of Garemba soon enough."

"Might I join the class?" Efah asked.

Newa looked away quickly. "I think it would be better if I taught you privately. I don't think anyone would spar with you but me." He attempted to give her a smile back and even a small chuckle but it came out awkwardly.

"Are you alright?" she asked, putting a hand on his arm.

Her touch was warm against his skin and radiated through his muscles.

"I'm fine, Efah." Saying her name so casually still felt bitter on his tongue. She deserved more respect than this but . . . He pushed down the smile starting to form back down. But she trusted him as a friend. It was the greatest honor he'd ever felt.

They returned to watching his class, him calling out corrections from her side. She glanced his way.

"Do you think we could start after your class ends?"

"There's no discouraging you from this path, is there?"

"No. I told you I have to learn to fight for myself."

He sighed heavily. "Very well. This class is almost through. After they leave, we can begin."

She smiled brightly and he forced himself to focus on the class. When he'd decided they'd had enough training for the day, he released the group. They'd meet again tomorrow in the morning. There wasn't a single protest and it was like a new group of initiates back home. They were eager, hungry to take up their new roles and Newa was glad to see it.

When the last student walked out of the area, he slowly turned to his lady. She was small framed, only coming up to his shoulder. Not that he was very tall himself. She was soft, without any visible muscles on her arms. She had a lot of work to do. He briefly imagined her as a hardened warrior, laden with weapons and ready to kill at moment's notice. It was a repulsive thought. He wanted her to stay just as she was. Kind. Gentle. Compassionate. He sighed again.

"Let us begin."

He took her to the middle of the training yard. He worked with her slowly, moving her into the correct positions. He had her mimic his movements and she picked them up with only a few errors. By the time the sun was moving to the afternoon, he had moved her into a slow sparring session. He actually laughed in approval at how well she'd managed the basics after just hours of teaching. She beamed back at him, her eagerness not breaking her concentration.

When he noticed the slightest bit of sluggishness from her, he called an end to the lesson. Efah stepped back, breathing heavily. He smiled.

"You were an excellent student," he said.

"I had an excellent teacher."

The compliment made his face heat.

"Perhaps we can have another lesson the day after tomorrow."

"Why not tomorrow?" Her smile dropped; her face concerned.

"Then tomorrow," he said hesitantly. Newa assessed her again. Yes, she was tired. She obviously had not worked this hard in a long time, if ever. But she was just as ready as his other students. How could he deny his lady what she wanted? He cursed himself. Who was he to tell Death's Chosen what was best for her? If she wanted to know how to defend herself, then he would give her the best education in it.

"Let me see your hands," he said after a moment. She raised them, her face playfully questioning him.

Newa took them and turned them palm up, inspecting. She

had small hands with relatively short fingers. He took one, running his fingers along the palm. Not the best hands for knives. Perhaps she would be better at the larger ones that didn't require such exact dexterity. But those were a bit heavy. His fingers trailed down her arm. She'd need to build up her muscle.

He was yanked from his thoughts when she pulled her arm away. He looked into her eyes, her confused and concerned eyes, and realized that he'd been touching her more intimately than he should have ever been. She took a step away, holding the arm he'd caressed close to her.

"My lady, I . . .," he stammered, words failing him.

"Tomorrow, then." She hurried out of the yard, leaving him.

Newa stared after her, frozen with mortification. He dropped to his knees, clutching his head in his hands, and let out a frustrated growl. What had he done?

~

Forty. No, forty-five. Fifty if you included his first five followers. Tekhamun smiled, the number astounding him. When he set out on this journey, he didn't think he would be joined by anyone, let alone this many. He gave a quick prayer of thanks to Gu'un. The seventh son, the shunned priest, was now a leader of men. It was more than he could have ever imagined for his life.

In the storage area they'd commandeered, people camped out. They shared meals or told stories. Mjoma passed out weapons they'd taken from the city guards. The big man was meticulous in handing them out, making sure the weights were good for each of the recipients. Netja conducted a class in knifework, his dexterous fingers spinning the blades effortlessly. Even Pta, who was usually glued to Karatel's side, was ensuring that the newly acquired food and clothing were equally distributed.

Tekhamun smiled, pleased. This was how his holy army should be. And when the time came to take the word of the gods to the other areas of the empire, they would be ready. If the people came to their senses and joined his movement or if they had to be cut down, he and his would be ready.

He raised an eyebrow as he noticed a man moving through the crowd, coming his way. He remembered him. The man's hair was nearly white despite being about the same age as the priest. Broad shoulders and a stormy face set him apart from the rest of the new members. In fact, he couldn't remember seeing the man with anyone since he'd joined.

The man neared, not even giving a nod of respect to him.

"Priest Tekhamun," he said. His voice had the rumble of the last, deep note of distant thunder.

Tekhamun drew himself up, trying his best to look like the leader these people needed.

"How may I be of help to you?"

"I came because I want to know when we'll be able to kill more of the enemy."

The statement caught the priest off guard. He was far more used to answering questions of faith or fighting for Gu'un.

"Who is our enemy?" he asked, wanting to know the true intents of this mountain of a man.

He didn't change his expression, but something in his eyes seemed to smolder.

"Nobles."

"Our enemies are not the nobility," Tekhamun chided him. "They are every unbeliever who won't come back to the gods. We must turn people away from the netkoleh's heresy and if they won't turn, then we must send them back to the gods. Do you understand?"

The man didn't speak for a moment and Tekhamun didn't think he'd made himself clear.

"Will it be soon?"

The priest blinked. Why was he so impatient? "What is your name?"

"Nermet."

"There is much anger within you, Nermet," he said, trying to sound sagely. "You must save it for our holy work. I understand you want to do the gods' will, but it will be done in their time. Not ours."

Nermet looked aside, his eyes traveling over the assembled believers.

"I . . . have never learned how to fight. Not properly. Can I learn from you?"

"The master will have to see if he has time." Tekhamun looked over to see Karatel walking over. The younger man smiled warmly at the both of them before turning his sole attention to Nermet. "He is very busy, you see."

Nermet turned back to Tekhamun. "The master can speak for himself."

The priest's soul squirmed. It was as if the air around them had suddenly gone tight. He cleared his throat nervously.

"Karatel, I'm sure that I can find some time to train him. I may have to make time to train even more of you. Everyone needs to be ready."

Karatel's smile seemed frozen. Nermet nodded before glancing darkly at the other man.

"I will wait until you can." Only then did he nod to Tekhamun and walk away.

The priest breathed a sigh of relief, his shoulders slumping. Karatel stepped closer to him, leaning down.

"I don't trust him," he said lowly. "I don't trust several of them. You should be careful, master."

"You speak as if he means to kill me," Tekhamun scoffed.

"We don't know them fully yet. You don't know if they might have other ideas of what this mission is supposed to be."

Tekhamun stared at the man who'd become his right hand and dearest counselor. This wasn't like him, to be so mistrustful. No, no, he was just being protective. He couldn't fault the man for that.

"Karatel," he said kindly, "I doubt that any of the poor people here have such evil notions in their hearts. You should trust people more."

The other man stared at him, then a sheepish smile spread his lips.

"You're right, master. I do need to trust more. Forgive me."

"Nothing to be forgiven. Now I'm going to rest and commune with Gu'un before dinner."

Karatel bowed. "Of course, master."

The priest nodded to the man before leaving the area. He understood how hard it was to trust after being mistreated for so long. It had taken him time to trust Karatel and his band and that had been a mistake. He couldn't ask for a more loyal and devoted core of devotees. He prayed that the younger man's heart would open to the people who would be his brothers and sisters in time. They needed each other if this holy mission was to be a success.

Tekhamun entered his room, changing into something more comfortable. He may be meditating for some time and he didn't need the extra weight of his priestly robes distracting him. He was just about to sit on the floor when his door opened. He expected it to be Moon checking up on him but a different woman came in.

She smiled, braids down to her waist.

"Priest, I brought you a little something to tide you over until dinner." She showed the small plate she carried with an assortment of dried fruits.

"Thank you, uh . . ."

"Hamena, Priest Tekhamun."

He cleared his throat nervously. He'd never been good in the presence of beautiful women. And she was beautiful. Dark, unbelievably dark skin with shapely hips and thighs. Her smile would have entranced any man and her eyes would steal his soul. He swallowed. "Thank you, Hamena. You can set the plate over there."

She put it on the table he indicated and turned back to him. Her gaze unnerved him further.

"Is there anything I can do for you?" she asked sweetly. "Anything I can do to ease your mind? You must carry so many burdens."

Tekhamun nearly bolted when he realized how close she was coming.

"No, I'm fine. Truly." By the gods, she was so close. "Besides, Gu'un fills all my needs."

Hamena tilted her head. "But you have earthly needs too." She took a step closer and if she moved any more, they would be touching. "Let me fill them," she purred.

He was just about to ask what she meant, when she dropped to her knees, raising the fabric of his robes. Tekhamun gasped as she took him into her mouth. She started a slow, torturous rhythm, the priest struggling to keep his knees from giving in. His body responded and she worked more vigorously. His mind was ablaze with euphoric fire. This was a pleasure like no other he'd ever known and just when he could feel the beginnings of completion, she released him.

Tekhamun panted, confused as she stood and pushed him back to his bed, leading him down. Hamena straddled him, settling on his manhood. She placed his hands on her hips as she began to move and he held on for dear life. She put a finger to his lips when his first sounds escaped him. He struggled to obey, but he could barely think. He could only exist.

He writhed in pleasure as he reached his climax, Hamena still moving atop him. Spent, he lay limp on his bed, his breath ragged. She leaned over on his chest. Tekhamun was acutely aware of the pressure from her breasts. As his mind slowly came down, panic began to set in.

What had he done? He was supposed to be dedicated to his god alone. He couldn't give in to such base lust. What kind of creature had he allowed himself to become? Hamena moved, settling herself on his chest like she was about to go to sleep and he longed to know the rhythm of her body again. No, he had to focus on his task.

The door opened, Moon carrying the plates that held his dinner. She opened her mouth to speak but froze at the scene. Hamena sat up, looking coquettishly at the large woman.

Tekhamun tried to sit up but Hamena refused to accommodate him.

"Moon," he began desperately. "It's not what it looks like. Hamena, please get off."

The horrified look in Moon's good eye pained him to his core. She turned without a word, closing the door behind her. Tekhamun looked mortified to Hamena who smiled. The woman slowly rose from his hips, straightening out her dress as she stood. He stared at her, shocked at her casualness, falling deeper into his shame. He didn't move when she leaned in and kissed him on the cheek.

"I am always here for you, Priest Tekhamun. Let me know if there's anything you need."

His breath came labored as his shame overtook him. She smiled down at him and left the room, leaving him to wallow in his failure as a priest.

Chapter Thirteen

Izriamat looked at herself in a mirror for the first time in days. She sat beyond the cursory glance to make sure she was presentable and studied her own face. The years of being the netkoleh's wife had taken their toll on her. She felt she looked older than she should have. In her braids she could already see several strands of gray among the black. She looked in her eyes and smile, however. How long had she looked at herself in the mirror and been disgusted? Disgusted at the tired, used broodmare staring back. The soiled priestess with the painted face. But that image was gone. The haunted look that she'd carried for nearly a decade was replaced by an expression of peace. Izriamat chuckled and arranged her braids for the day. Her people were expecting her.

Sami was waiting for her just outside of her door.

"Have you eaten, princess?" she asked in her matter-of-fact way.

"No," Izriamat responded, suddenly remembering. Sami handed her a small plate with bread and honey. On the side were a few dates and figs. She noticed the woman held a small, sealed jar that must contain water.

"Thank you for the breakfast."

"Of course, princess."

They moved through the hallways, priests, priestesses, and staff bowing to her as she passed. She nodded, not wanting to give out blessings with a full mouth.

"There haven't been any new messages for me, have there?" she asked, popping a date into her mouth.

Sami wrinkled her nose, thinking. "Not to my knowing. No letters either."

Izriamat frowned. No news. She thought that, by now, she'd have gotten word of their brother's return. He was a brilliant military commander who she was sure could outmaneuver any enemy. They needed him here. She chewed slower as worry began to set in. Bakari could return to Wiluru at any time. The bulk of the navy with the bulk of their magicians and soldiers was in the east. They had more than enough people to deal with normal threats but against the rest of the empire? They needed more forces.

Your people are ready.

Izriamat stopped in her tracks. She felt the warm familiarity of Yutuu's touch. Sami came to her side, placing a hand on her arm.

"Are you all right, my princess?"

Izriamat closed her eyes, opened them, then smiled. Her people were ready.

"Hurry, Sami. I know what to do."

The priestess rushed along, the workers of the temple looking to her confused. Izriamat stepped into the courtyard. Her followers gathered in the morning sun and gave her a joyous greeting when she emerged. Sami stopped just behind her.

"Your people love you, princess."

"And I love them."

Izriamat came forward to the edge of the top stairs of the entrance, looking out over the crowd. Their greeting had died down and her heart swelled at their devotion to her and their deity.

"My people," she called out, voice echoing off the stone walls around the wide courtyard. "I know you've heard of the war with the Ega. I know that you may have even heard that I was the cause of it." She let the murmurs in the crowd play out. "And it's true. I was the one who ordered the gates to stay closed when the netkoleh arrived. I am the reason he has declared war on Wiluru. He will come with all the might of the empire. And it is my fault."

The fear of the crowd washed through her and she clutched a hand to her chest. What had she brought to her kingdom's doors? Then a calming sensation, like a gentle wave, touched her. She took a deep breath.

"It is the will of Yutuu that we throw off the yoke of the empire. No more will we bow to the Ega and their blasphemous ways. No more will we watch as they treat us as another bauble to play with. Our warriors are our first defense but we will need more might to combat the Ega. We need as many people as we can gather for this war. It pains my heart to ask this of you, but my people, Yutuu's people, Wiluru needs you to fight."

She expected to hear objections to her request, but the courtyard was silent.

"Wiluru needs you among its warriors. Those who can fight, volunteer to join the military. Those who can't, find a way in which you can support them. Cook if that is your talent. Repair clothing if you know how to sew. If all you are able to do is to lend them your prayers then that is more than enough. But it will take all of us to win this war. And I swear by the will of the great Yutuu, master of the raging waters, that Wiluru will be a free kingdom again."

The crowd burst into cheers. Izriamat felt her eyes water and let the thick tears fall. The courtyard reverberated with cheers for Wiluru, chants of her name, and praises to Yutuu. She closed her eyes, absorbing the sound, her heart filled nearly to bursting. She raised her hand to bid them farewell for the day and turned to go inside, Sami following behind. The first thing she saw in the hallway was her uncle. He stared at her with the anger he only reserved for misbehaving neophytes. He'd never directed such a look at her before.

"Good morning, Uncle," she said nodding toward him.

"You can't do that, Izriamat," he snapped. "Telling those people to join the military. What were you thinking?"

His tone wounded her. "Our warriors are divided between here and the east. Bakari is surely on his way back with an army to raze this city and the rest of the kingdom." She steeled herself against the hurt. "Wiluru needs more people to fight and this is what Yutuu led me to do."

"You are going to get those people killed. If they want to help, they can pray for our warriors' victory."

"The time for prayer is over, Uncle. This is what Yutuu is leading me to do."

Her uncle looked truly angry with her now. "Are you sure this is our god at work or is it your desire for revenge for what was done to you?"

Izriamat's throat clenched. "You cannot understand," she said lowly. "You cannot possibly understand what it means to be truly chosen for Yutuu's will. *I do*." She realized she was shouting and she didn't care. Other priests stopped and watched their conversation but she welcomed their stares. Let them witness this. "He spoke to me. Me. This is his will and how dare you question me."

"Izriamat, I'd hoped you would —."

"You will be silent before the chosen of Yutuu." Her left hand balled into a fist and her uncle's mouth snapped shut. He blinked, taking a step back. Clearly, he wanted to speak but his jaw didn't even twitch. Satisfied, Izriamat stepped past him and took to the hallways of the temple. She prayed she wouldn't have to teach her uncle this lesson again.

~

Umakaal lay in bed, watching the ceiling, listening to the calls of the seabirds outside. She'd been inside for weeks now, reading, training, making love, until boredom finally caught up to her. Relieved of active duty. Sent to languish in her rooms until her father sent word. She sighed. But he hadn't. All this time and not a word from him.

She turned in bed, her eyes following the acrobatic paths of the gulls. Had he truly thrown her away now? The mere thought threatened to bring tears to her eyes. What was she supposed to do now?

The door opened behind her. Umakaal didn't move, even when she heard the soft footprints of Ladawi coming towards the bed.

"Oh, my love," the maid sighed. The princess curled up when she felt her lover's weight shift the bed and soon Ladawi's arms were around her. Umakaal did cry then, all her pain, disappointment, and frustration pouring out. Ladawi cooed sweet reassurances into her ear which she didn't hear.

"My love, I'm so sorry," Ladawi said after a minute, "but you've been summoned to the council chamber. By your father."

Umakaal sniffed, trying to stop her tears. "What?"

"Your father has summoned you. You need to go."

The princess sat up, rubbing her eyes furiously. She tried to speak but it came out in a snot choked cough.

"Help me get ready, please," she said quietly once she could.

Ladawi fetched a bowl of cool water while she struggled to get into proper attire. After a quick face wash and a kiss for luck, Umakaal was on her way. Palace guards still saluted her on her way. The gesture both touched her and stabbed her. She should be here among them, not wallowing in her feelings. A small bit of hope blossomed in her chest. Perhaps her father had decided that she'd been punished enough. Perhaps today would be the day she could resume her duties.

Umakaal nodded to the guards outside the door and one stepped aside to let her in. To her surprise, the room was empty, save her parents. Her mother studied her, an unreadable expression on her face. Her father was a statue of disdain. The lines of his face belonged to a much older man and it pained her to see what recent events had done. Umakaal bowed deeply.

"Come forward," her mother's clear voice echoed around the room.

Umakaal did as she was commanded, bowing again once she reached a respectful distance.

"Father, Mother, how may I be of service to you today?"

Her father looked at her with restrained disdain. "I have spent much time considering your punishment for participating in treason against me and Wiluru. I have even taken into account that your brother and sister were the obvious leaders in your plan. While I will not strip you completely of your duties to the throne, you are immediately removed from leadership of the palace guard. You will now serve as liaison between the palace and the military."

Umakaal struggled to keep her knees from buckling. Her father's words echoed in her head, not a single other thought coming to her. Removed from the palace guard. That was her station, inherited from Yutuuan, as was her birthright. He couldn't do this. She took a deep breath, pulling back the objection threatening to spill forth. Her eyes darted to her mother, looking for some sign of regret in this. Some sliver of hope that her mother would come to her rescue and save her from such an ignoble fate. But the queen of Wiluru sat stoically beside her husband, without a change in her expression.

Umakaal forced herself to take a breath and bowed to them. "Such is the will of my king. In it will I follow." The words tasted foul on her tongue.

"I am glad you have finally learned this lesson," her father responded. "Report to Captain Natkala. I'm sure she has something for you to bring back to us."

Umakaal bowed again, knowing when she was dismissed. She walked through the palace, her feet moving automatically. She stopped at the foot of the main entrance. She slammed a fist against one of the columns flanking the staircase. A messenger. A princess of Wiluru reduced to a lowly messenger! Anger crawled up the back of her neck, pricking into her spine. All she'd ever done; she'd done with the best interests of Wiluru in mind and now she was to be punished for it. Only a coward of a king would roll over at every request of the enemy.

She paused as she walked down the street. The thought that her father might just be that cowardly of a king pained her. It pained her that she would even think that of him. But . . .. She shook her head and the thought away.

Umakaal reached the city docks before she realized it. She slowed her pace as she noticed the crowd gathered in front of the main ship. She could just make out Captain Netkala and several others trying to dismiss the crowd to little success. The princess pushed her way through, people stepping to the side when they realized who she was. Captain Netkala looked almost relieved when she set eyes on her.

"Captain, what's going on here?" Umakaal asked when she reached her.

Netkala pulled back from the crowd, letting her subordinates take charge.

"People coming to join the military, my princess," she said running a hand over her sun reddened short hair. "They've been coming in droves for days. Claiming that Yutuu has declared that they protect the city. Some of them say your sister sent them here."

"What?"

"These people are just going to get themselves killed." She

subtly gestured towards the crowd. "Too old. Too infirm. Too young. We can't allow these people to join in good conscience. I've tried to steer them toward support but most only want to fight." The captain sighed heavily. "I'm afraid that we might have a riot on our hands if something isn't done."

A new anger burst within the princess. Her sister should know better than this.

"I'll talk to Izriamat. Try to get her to settle down her people. But that's all I can do now."

Netkala glanced down before looking her in the eyes again. "I've already been informed of your new position." She lowered her voice. "I'm sorry, my princess."

That tempered her anger. "Thank you," she said, praying the hurt didn't show in her voice. "Are there any pressing messages I need to bring to the palace's attention?"

"Other than this?" The captain gestured to the crowd again. "I'm afraid not. We need people to fight against the Ega, but not this badly."

Umakaal nodded, saluted the captain, and made her way back through the assembled people. She should head straight for the palace, but her gaze moved toward the direction the temple of Yutuu. She turned from the street she was on and made her way along the coast.

The temple residents greeted her warmly when she arrived.

"Were you looking for your sister?" one of the priestesses asked kindly.

Umakaal made sure she didn't look how she felt. "Yes, I wanted to pay her a visit."

"I do believe she's working in the infirmary. I'll be happy to take you there."

"Thank you so much," she answered and fell in line behind the happy priestess.

The infirmary had barely any patients so Umakaal was led inside. She saw her sister tending to a young man with boils covering his arms. Izriamat sat so close to him that Umakaal wanted to recoil. Yet her sister placed a gentle hand on the man, closing her eyes. Within two heartbeats, his boils began to shrink and by the time Umakaal remembered to breathe again, they were gone.

"Now, rest," came her sister's serene voice. "By morning you will be on your way home."

Umakaal stood, unblinking as the priestess when to fetch Izriamat. The elder princess looked up and smiled widely. She excused herself from her patient and quickly came and embraced her sister. Umakaal wrapped her arms around her in response but there was no affection in it.

"Since when can you heal?" she asked her.

Izriamat gave her that content smile that made Umakaal uneasy.

"Since Yutuu blessed me with this power." She hugged her again. "I feel as if I haven't seen you in ages, little sister. How have you been?"

"I'm fine." She pulled back from the embrace. "We need to talk." Umakaal pulled her out of the infirmary into a breezeway that led back to the temple. "Have you been convincing regular people to join the military?"

Izriamat looked at her confused, then a certain coolness settled into her expression.

"Yutuu has led me to tell them to help the war in whatever capacity they can and if that includes fighting for their city and country, then yes."

Umakaal struggled for a response. "Izri, you can't do that."

"Are you telling me to disobey the mandate of our patron god?"

The younger princess winced and glanced around, but they were alone.

"No, that's not it. You can't just —." She released a frustrated breath. Why was her sister being so difficult? "These are *regular* people, Izri. They know nothing of what it takes to be a warrior. Nothing. You have people who are woefully unfit for the military ready to die for your cause."

"Yutuu's cause," Izriamat corrected her. "This is not my cause, but our god's."

"How can you be so sure? How do you know this isn't just you wanting revenge on your husband?"

Izriamat's entire posture changed, eyes narrowing and shoulders stiffening.

"Do you doubt the will of Yutuu?"

"No, sister. I —."

"Then you shouldn't question his messenger." Her voice echoed off the roof of the breezeway.

Umakaal took a step back from her sister. "You're going to get those people killed. They won't be allowed into the military and if they try to fight on their own, the Ega will slaughter them."

"We all must be ready to shed our blood in the name of Wiluru and Yutuu."

"You know I'll bring this up with father."

Izriamat moved to step past her. "Then tell him. But none will stand in the way of the will of Yutuu. Good day, sister." She quickly walked away into the temple, leaving Umakaal at a loss for words.

~

Yutuuan rapped his fingers on the table as he waited for the other captains to assemble for dinner. A table had been brought from one of the ships and set just off the beach in the dunes. There was just enough privacy for this meeting. Food prepared by the best cooks in the force was arriving and a modest but delectable smelling meal was assembling. Yutuuan looked over it, nodding his approval. He prayed a satisfying repast and excellent drink would sway the captains to his latest idea.

After their last battle they'd not seen another sign of the so-called Fahzi invasion force. They had several captives and enough translators to get more information out of them. The prince looked to the east, to the lands that lay just beyond the arid hills surrounding this area. Somewhere out there was the rest of his enemy and beyond that was the Rahaban kingdom. Or maybe what was left of it. They had to find out because this war had to stop. He had an entirely different fight to get to.

He glanced to the west and the setting sun. Wiluru waited for him. The true fight for his people and country waited for him. His fist tightened. His child waited for him. He tried to push the thoughts aside but the idea of Talekh alone, pregnant and alone, made his heart ache. He should be there for her as much as he possibly could. Yutuuan sighed heavily. First this had to be resolved and he had to save Wiluru.

He stood at attention as Naret led the five highest ranked captains to the table. He tried to assess their moods as they approached. Some seemed annoyed, probably by the unusual location. But most merely looked curious. Curious he could work with. Yutuuan smiled brightly.

"Welcome," he said sweeping and arm over the table. "I hope you're hungry."

The last of the dishes was set down just as they began to take their seats and he was sure he heard a stomach growl. He smiled, sitting at the head of the table.

"Eat, drink your fill. I have much I'd like to discuss with you all tonight."

The group watched as Naret ushered the lesser cooks away. Everyone filled their plates in silence until they were sure they were alone. Naret took the seat to his left and nodded that it was safe.

"What have you assembled us for, my prince?" asked the captain to his right before he could begin. Ilniz was an older man, with a nearly bald head. His hair was more salt than pepper. Five gold clips on his ear denoted his rank.

Yutuuan nodded as he finished drinking. He knew Ilniz would bring them right to it.

"I brought you here because we need to discuss solving this war once and for all."

Another captain held up her knife for the chance to speak as she swallowed a bite.

"My prince, I would say we've already done that."

"That is true, Nilhanae." He looked around, making sure he looked everyone in the eyes. "We haven't seen hide nor hair of this Fahzi empire since the last battle. But they must have a home. They must have somewhere they're working from. I don't think a ragtag group of ships would refer to itself as an empire."

"So, you want to root out their nest," concluded another. Tiharzun was always two steps ahead of him.

But not this time. "Not quite. I want to find out how large of an enemy we're facing. If they're as hearty as they'd like us to believe, then they won't stop attacking our border cities." He took another quick sip. "I want to take a ship and sail to the capital of Rahaban. See if they're still on our side."

All five captains stopped and stared at him, some with food halfway to their mouths. Nilhanae swallowed with difficulty.

"My prince," she began, looking at him with doubt filled eyes, "all the way to Ulzimah? What if we're attacked along the way? We're close to needing to refresh our supplies. We can't take a trip like that even if we were to share between ships."

"I don't mean the whole fleet, captain. I mean just one ship that will take me to Ulzimah." The sounds of disbelief and disapproval at the table did nothing to bolster his confidence. "I will speak with their ruler, see if Rahaban is friend or foe. If they're on board with this attack, I'll broker for peace terms. If they're allies, I'll do my best to convince them to aide in getting rid of the upstarts. We can finally put an end to this."

The table was quiet, all eyes on him. Yutuuan sat in his discomfort as they took in his plan. A few of the captains traded glances.

"This is extremely dangerous, my prince," Ilniz rumbled in his deep voice.

"I understand the risks. And I swear, I'll take every precaution while I'm there. But such a negotiation would hold more weight if I come to personally negotiate with their ruler instead of just sending a messenger. And I would never ask any under my command to do a task that I wasn't willing to do myself." There were several reluctant nods but the prince was glad that they were agreeing with him.

"Then let me ask you about these rumors of war with the Ega," came a voice that hadn't spoken yet. Captain Yujaan sat at toward the end of the table, swirling the wine in his cup. At his comment, the rest of the table looked to him pointedly.

"Yes, what of this war?" Ilniz asked. "I've heard that your sister started it?"

Yutuuan glanced to Naret whose face was a stone slate. He took a breath.

"You've all heard various rumors of the war?" There were nods all around. "Yes, war is coming. I was on my way to gain the support of the governor of Tilizaa when the first attack from these forces happened. The netkoleh has decreed that there are no gods and no one is to worship them."

A couple of captains gasped, more than half making gestures of warding.

"I know," he continued. "I know. Blasphemous. My sister, Izriamat, came to warn us of the heresy. He's calling himself the emperor now and has had the palace cleansed of all references of the gods." Yutuuan pressed his lips together, thinking of Umakaal's letter detailing the incident at the gates. "Unfortunately, when he arrived for the pilgrimage, Izriamat had words with him at the closed gates, riling him up to declare war. He swore he would burn Wiluru to the ground.

"My father is still hoping to find a peaceful resolution to this, but I know that this will be a dangerous battle. But it's one that we have to fight. For too long, we've bent to the will of the Ega. Now they want us to give up the blessings that have made Wiluru the prosperous kingdom it is. We must fight this war and we have to win it." He paused, taking time to look into the eyes of everyone gathered. "This is why I'm willing to take this risk to end our present confrontation. We have far greater, far more just battles we need to fight."

Silence fell across the table again. The sound of the sea birds overhead was suddenly sharp and loud. The other captains slowly looked to their superior and the older man turned slowly to the prince.

"We support you in this plan and in ousting the Ega," Ilniz said.

Yutuuan refilled the captain's cup and his own. "Then let us drink to the end of this conflict and to the prospect of a free Wiluru." The table lifted their cups and as the sweet liquid slid down Yutuuan's throat he couldn't help but think that it tasted like hope.

Chapter Fourteen

"High priest, your son is home."

Erenemo slammed down the scroll he was reading and stormed past the servant. He barely noticed anyone in the hallways. He barely saw the halls he was so enraged. Duties had kept him from confronting Ofemu about his betrayal but today he swore he'd catch the boy one way or another.

He threw open the door leading outside. Across the lush courtyard was the quickest way to his son's wing of the compound. He wanted to have this done and set that boy back in his place quickly. Birds and gardeners gave him a wide path as he walked. Erenemo barely slowed his pace when he reached the other side. He almost bowled over the short servant that greeted him.

"Where is my son?" he barked.

"In his lounging room." The servant bowed and looked up apologetically. "But, high priest, he is . . . busy at the moment."

Erenemo side stepped the man, striding down the halls. He threw open the doors to find his son sitting on a plush chair, his lover straddling his lap. The younger men were, thankfully, only topless. Ofemu looked up sharply from where he'd been nuzzling Barabi's neck. Barabi looked daggers at the priest over his shoulder, fingers still entwined in Ofemu's braids. Ofemu sat back, with the nerve to appear annoyed.

"Father," he said coolly.

Erenemo turned his heated glare to Barabi. "Leave us," he snapped.

Barabi raised an eyebrow at Ofemu. The younger men exchanged looks and Ofemu sighed.

"Give us a little while," he said. "Hopefully, this won't take long."

Erenemo stared at his son's second in command as he passed by with all the anger he had in store for Ofemu. Barabi stared back, the same level of hate reflected on his face. This boy didn't know his place either. He would have to remind them. He rounded on his son the moment Barabi left the room.

"You would dare to try to become Great Dara behind my back. I am your father. All support should be swayed toward me. Do you understand me?"

He expected his son to balk at his command, perhaps even ask an asinine question or two. It was his usual response when he was reprimanded. Afterwards, he would cave in then sulk in his rooms. He did none of those things now.

Ofemu blinked slowly several times. "Father," he began, leaning forward in his chair. "Surely you realize how unpopular you are with the entire council. None of them want to vote for you. I gave them a different option."

"How dare you sit there and pretend that you understand the intricacies of politics. I have more support than you know, boy."

"I have support too."

"Who?" Erenemo demanded. He would know the names of the people who were conspiring against him. And he would make them pay.

"I'm not telling you that."

Erenemo ground his teeth. Ofemu got this stubborn streak from his mother.

"This is a foolish endeavor and a waste of the council's time. The city can't afford to continue without a dara. The other cities are breathing down our necks. Now you want to barge in and divide the vote.

"This isn't war, boy. You can't call an attack whenever you feel like it. There's more at play here. A delicate dance. Far more intricate than battle."

"And what would you know of battle?" There was a snarl in Ofemu's voice that stunned him.

"Far more than you know of true leadership. The mere fact that you thought you could even be considered for dara?" Erenemo gave a wry laugh. "Just another one of your stupid ideas and you're too foolish to see it, boy."

Ofemu shot to his feet. "I. Am not. A boy. And I'm no fool." Erenemo scoffed but his son wasn't through. "I know I'm not a politician, but I am a warrior and I know how to lead.

Something you have never done. I am true to my word and those who follow me. Can you say the same, father?"

The priest's throat felt like it would close on him. He sputtered, a response failing to come. Ofemu watched him, calm as a crocodile waiting for its kill to get too close to the water.

"You question *my* loyalty?" Erenemo nearly shrieked. "I have given my life to Nsongo, to the entire land. The council understands this. And you expect them to hand over leadership to an untested man who keeps his second in command in his bed!"

"At least I've been faithful to Barabi. Unlike some."

The pointed look Ofemu gave him made any other points he had disappear. Erenemo stiffened.

"What are you talking about?"

Ofemu tilted his head, the same way he did as a child when he was considering something.

"I," he started slowly, "am not the only one sleeping with a subordinate. I think your little acolyte would count in most people's eyes. I don't think the council would be pleased with a candidate that's carrying on with someone so far beneath him." Ofemu's face lost all expression. "And if mother found out . . ."

Erenemo felt his heart thunder against his ribs. "You wouldn't."

Ofemu didn't respond, staring at him with the kind of expression one would give an enemy.

"If you so desperately want to become Great Dara, I suggest you focus less on me and more on convincing council members."

Erenemo took a step back, shaking his head in disbelief. "You are not the son I raised."

"No, I'm not. But I'm learning how to be more like you every day. You should be proud."

"You will come to regret this." Erenemo turned, storming back to his side of the compound. He knocked over a small table in his sitting room, his anger barely contained. His son, that fool of a boy, was blackmailing him. *Him.* The high priest of Nsongo, second son of Mfone, eldest member of the line of Yundasha. His own father. The absolute gall. He threatened to not only ruin his chance at the daraship. He threatened to ruin his marriage as well.

Erenemo dropped onto a stool, the high of anger wearing off. Patya couldn't find out. The council couldn't either. He picked up a blank scroll and began writing down the names of the next council members he believed he could sway. If this was the game his son wanted to play, he was going to learn what it was to face a master player.

~

The magistrate of Nsongo was up to no good. He paced his room, sandals slapping noisily on the stone floor. His maids stood by nervously, waiting for his commands but wanting to be anywhere else but here. Hotemkhar ground his teeth as he paced. He was the most important person in the entire south and everyone was treating him like he was an afterthought.

He balled his fists, rapping them against his thighs. The city's council still hadn't chosen a new leader for their city. But they were coming close. He knew it. However, every time he sat in on one of their meetings, they were frustratingly close lipped. Their city couldn't continue this way. Surely Amakari and Ofolobaru were inching closer to taking the place of power in the South. He thought to the dried up flow of gold and how he had caused it.

Hotemkhar stopped his pacing, swallowing with difficulty. Admitting it, even just to himself, was arduous. He may have inadvertently insulted the jungle people causing them to cut off the city from the gold supply for at least a decade, but by Koleh, he would rectify the situation. He swallowed again. His very life may depend on it.

They needed to go ahead with the invasion. There had been enough stalling from General Tutahmen. The magistrate tapped his chin. If that old war dog wouldn't go ahead with it, then he could go to someone with enough military influence to force the plan through.

Hotemkhar turned toward the door and snapped his fingers. His primary attendant emerged from beside the door, falling into step behind him. It was raining outside and the steady drops of earlier in the day had evolved into a downpour. The temptation to turn around and do this another time was great, but they needed that gold as soon as they could get it. Muddy sandals aside, he had to do this now.

His servant raised the oiled parasol with expert timing and not a drop fell on his upper body. The streets, however, were another matter. He was thankful that the Nsongans had been clever enough to build their streets with a natural rise that channeled water to the sides. Now if they would have only thought to pave their roads, they'd have proven themselves even more clever.

The bottom of his robes was soaked and sticking to his legs by the time he'd reached the compound Commander Kolehem was using. The soldiers standing guard let him in without protest. He could understand their apathy, standing out here in the rain. A miserable position. It was one of the moments that he knew the life of a soldier was not for him. He was far too used to the comforts of civilized life.

The young commander was in an arcade, practicing with his sword as the rains hammered the open yard to his left. He didn't even notice the magistrate until he cleared his throat loudly.

Kolehem looked up, his face beginning to form an expression before settling on neutrality.

"Magistrate Hotemkhar," he said with a bow of his head, not the full bow the older man expected. "Is there something I can do for you?"

Hotemkhar was thrown off by the cool tone to his voice. The general must have spoken to him. He resisted a frown.

"I'm sure you're sick of waiting to see battle again. Especially with the general dragging his feet about the invasion. Has he set a date yet?"

Kolehem hesitated. "He wishes for us to set out in another month."

"Another month?" Hotemkhar scoffed. "That's another month wasted. Another month that gives those primitives time to hide their gold." He leveled a serious look at the young commander. "Another month before you can prove why you and your wing were sent down here. It's far too long. We need to invade the jungle at once."

"That is not up to me to decide."

"Then ready your wing," Hotemkhar said encouragingly. He didn't need for this powerful young man to falter. "Show him that you can be sent at a moment's notice. Show him that his soldiers are ready to fight for the glory of the empire. Aren't you ready to bring back more gold than this empire has ever seen? Aren't you ready to go down in record as the commander who conquered the southern jungle?" He saw the hunger in the man's eyes at the thought and knew he had him.

"I will speak with the general," Kolehem said, putting aside his sword. "I can't make any promises on what he may do. I . . . am not in his full confidence yet."

Hotemkhar put on his best smile. "I am sure you are more than capable of persuading him."

"I'll do what I can," the young man reiterated.

"Of course, you will." The magistrate nodded to him and left the compound feeling satisfied. Sometimes all it took was a small bug in someone's ear to point them in the right direction.

Just two days later, the army was readying themselves to cross the river. Supplies were being strapped to rafts. Weapons were being checked and gathered for soldiers. It pleased Hotemkhar that everywhere he went, the forces of the Ega were moving with purpose. None of this idle milling about. No more wasting their days bullying the Nsongans. They had true purpose now. Thanks to him. And when they returned victorious, he would be the one credited with starting it all.

He celebrated that night with a small feast, allowing a pair of his servant women to dine with him. It was a high time of the best foods the south had to offer coupled with the best wines from the capital. Afterwards, they took to his bed and spent the rest of the evening enjoying each other until they passed out from an excess of merriment.

It was their screaming that awakened him. Hotemkhar pulled himself to a muddled state of alertness. He heard his servant women as if they were far away. Then hands were on him, dragging him out of bed. His mind jerked awake then. It was still dark, but he could just barely make out several men pulling him along. He fought against them, but their strength was too much. Hotemkhar tried to call for help, but the moment he did, one of the men shoved a cloth in his mouth, gagging him. He could hear the sounds of other people rummaging through his rooms and he grew incensed.

Thieves and murderers. The last part hit him like a stone. He worked to get the gag out of his mouth as they took him outside. He could pay them more money than they'd ever seen. They could live like the highest Metkaran nobles. In the faint light of the setting moon, he made out the slight shine of weapons and armor. Egan weapons and armor. These were soldiers. His surprise caused him to stop fighting. His own people were kidnapping him?

They carried him through the city and to the docks. He could hear the quick movements of troops and materials being moved around. Finally, the kidnapping soldiers set him upright and Hotemkhar came face to face with the general. Tutahmen smiled kindly at him as if he'd just arrived at a party.

Hotemkhar's gag was taken out, but the soldiers to his sides still held him.

"What is the meaning of this?" he demanded.

"You wanted the invasion to happen as soon as possible, didn't you?" The older man swept his arm out, showing the troops loading up rafts with supplies. "You got your wish. I hope you enjoy it."

He nodded and before Hotemkhar could launch any more protests, he was gagged again, his hands and legs quickly bound. The soldiers took him to a nearby boat that had another set of soldiers who tossed him unceremoniously in like cargo.

"Take good care of him, Commander," Tutahmen called out.

Hotemkhar looked up to see a grim faced Kolehem, standing near the front of the vessel. He looked down at the magistrate with anger and disgust. Hotemkhar had never felt himself in so much danger. He lurched as the raft pushed off, leaving the shores of Nsongo, and heading to the jungle.

~

Night fell with a hush on the golden city of Nsongo. The moon rose high, clouds crossing its pale face. Patches of light played in the streets and alleyways, racing across courtyards and down the docks. The shadows deepened, painting the city in sharp swathes of black. And out of the shadows, near the farthest boats, where just two days before a host of soldiers had passed over to the Ibatu'bangi, something large and dark emerged.

Behind it came another, then another and soon a full twenty beasts pulled themselves from the waters of the Bangi. The pale moonlight caught their thick fangs and claws the moment they stepped into the light. The first looked up to the gold capped buildings and its lips parted into what looked like a gruesome smile. A quick jerk of its head and the creatures took off into the streets. Not a single resident realized their city had just been invaded.

The blood thirsty monsters of the Batu'bangi ran through the city, splitting up to find their victims. The interlopers. The disrespectful invaders. They would be torn limb from limb. Their silent screaming heads would tumble down stairwells. The creatures would feast on the blood and terror of their enemy and they would laugh in triumph. The enemy thought themselves untouchable but tonight they would find out how fragile they were.

The first enemy was found atop a lover, the soldier so involved in his task he didn't notice the creature coming in. One, sickle clawed hand grabbed him about the head. The claws found brain nearly immediately, sending the man into a spasm. He was jerked away from the woman the moment she screamed. His body was dragged out of the window and into the street, legs trailing uselessly behind him. The creature flung its prize farther along, snapping the man's neck at a repulsive angle, leaving it for others to find in the morning.

The second prey was walking alone. A bold decision even if there weren't monsters stalking the streets. He didn't get a chance to scream before he was pulled to a roof and his neck slit in one smooth movement. A steady trickle of blood was the only clue to the location of his body. This creature soon found a group of these bold men, walking together as they drunkenly sang. The halting, sharp rhythm of their language was offensive. A sound that had no place in this city and land. They were ripped open and left in various piles in the street.

When the screams of discovery began, the creatures hurried back toward the river, taking fatal swipes at invaders as they retreated. By the time they reached the docks, the sounds of alarm began across the city. The creatures slipped into the waters of the Bangi without a sound or ripple, leaving a panicked Nsongo in their wake.

Chapter Fifteen

Bakari kissed the foreheads of each of his daughters. His youngest daughter sniffed, barely keeping her tears at bay. He kissed his first wife deeply, the kiss of lovers that would be parted for some time.

"I'm counting on you while I'm gone," he said hands on both of her cheeks.

"I will not fail you, my husband," she responded, tears threatening to fall.

"I know that you won't." He released her face, then knelt in the courtyard sand, and kissed her growing belly. "Be strong for me, my son," he whispered and felt the baby move beneath his hand.

Bakari stood and moved to his new second wife. She stood stoically as he kissed the foreheads of her son and Izriamat's. He smiled as he tipped up her chin.

"No tears for me?" he asked lowly.

"Why should I cry when I know you'll return to me?" she replied.

Bakari kissed her, resisting the urge to pull her to him. Why was she so perfect? He took a step back, looking at his first wife and daughters to his right and his second and sons to his left. His legacy. He moved his gaze to all the officials, attendants, and servants gathered to see their ruler off. This was how it should be.

He turned to Hetsaf, who stood at the head of the palace officials.

"I'm counting on you as well, my brother. Be there for my wife as she runs the empire in my stead."

Hetsaf bowed sharply. "As you command, my emperor." He took a step back from his brother. "All praises to Emperor Bakari," Hetsaf shouted, his clear voice carrying across the space. "Long may he reign." The entire assembly echoed him and

Bakari's heart swelled with pride.

He mounted his waiting horse, taking a moment to address them. "I may leave you for a time," he called out. "But when I return, it will be in victory with Wiluru back in its place within the empire."

A cheer rose and he waved one last time before leading the procession out into the streets. Guards and flag bearers flanked his path. People lined the street to watch the emperor as he left for war. Bakari held his head high as they rode through. He had a passing thought that he should have ridden in a chariot for the procession but brushed it aside. Such spectacle wasn't necessary.

Bakari basked in the adoration of the crowd until his eyes caught the stare of a woman farther along in the crowd. He turned his attention and she stared back at him, boldly. Her eyes held a deep hatred. Bakari was caught off guard by her naked contempt. He ignored her as they passed but saw another man in the crowd looking to him with the same hatred. Then he caught sight of another person. The emperor looked around and dispersed in the crowd were several people that refused to cheer and watched him, silent, hateful.

His hand moved to his sword hilt reflexively. Were there still dissenters in the city? Had they grown so bold that they would dare meet the eye of their emperor and the power he wielded? He wanted to shout for these people to be detained but he didn't want the procession disrupted. Bakari focused on the path ahead. No, he wouldn't give them the attention. He held the power here, not these remnants of the disobedient.

The rest of the trek out of the city was without disturbance and he was pleased to be on the way to Wiluru. He amused himself with the idea of the great doors of the city in flames and falling. He daydreamed about dragging that creature that he'd called his wife out of the city by her hair. Her cries for pity or mercy would be ignored and he would enjoy ever tear he caused to fall from her eyes.

The army stopped for the noon meal and Bakari took his just outside of the hustle of the crowd. A stiff breeze was blowing forcefully across the green plains. There may be a roving storm later but he hoped they would miss it. He wanted to reach the northern city as soon as possible. He picked up a bit of meat from the small table beside him and chewed on it thoughtfully. He'd never laid siege to a city before. The southerners' cities were not so fortified since they considered it improper to fight anywhere but a battlefield. Once their forces were broken, the empire's army had marched into the cities to claim them. Some had even simply rolled over from his recollection. He wasn't there for all the negotiations. But this. To reclaim the first lands taken by his ancestor would be a feat he would savor.

A movement in the grass caught his attention. He thought it a bird at first but then he saw the unmistakable markings of a leopard. He stood, ready to call for a weapon in case the beast attacked, but it stayed low in the grass, watching. Bakari stared back at it, nerves on edge. It was in a telltale crouch. The beast should attack, but it remained still except for its tail which switched back and forth casually.

Bakari stood, considering the animal. He could hear one of his childhood tutors schooling him on the symbol of Met, the sign of war. They would have said this was a good sign. A blessing.

"Bring me my sword and shield," he called over his shoulder.

"Excuse me, my emperor," answered his attendant.

"My sword and shield," Bakari snapped. The servant scrambled away at his command. The leopard still watched him, not moving even after he raised his voice. Its tail twitched, almost thoughtfully, as he took sword and shield in and began to approach.

"Come, beast," he said lowly. "Let us see who's greater."

Only when he'd closed the distance between them did the leopard move. It was a subtle difference. Muscles flexed. The tail froze in place. And for the span of half a breath, the world seemed to come to a standstill. Then the leopard attacked.

Bakari brought up his shield, surprised and thrilled by its speed. The first blow, a swipe from the leopard's right paw, staggered him back. He recovered quickly, slicing out with his sword before a second blow could come. The leopard leaped to the side, out of the way of the strike and landed, ready to attack again. Behind Bakari, the servant screamed. Whether in terror or for help, he didn't even have time to discern. He was far too engrossed in the fight to care.

The leopard stalked him, circling to try to get a better vantage point, but Bakari turned with it. When the beast struck again, he planted his feet to meet its strength. He blocked the lunge with his shield and pushed it off. A war cry erupted from his lips as he rushed forward, slicing and stabbing. The leopard jumped away from the blows but each one came closer to finding flesh. The beast snarled in pain when Bakari finally landed a strike. Scarlet blood arced in the air then painted a sickle on the ground.

Bakari moved in to attack but the leopard fled. It retreated to a more than safe distance, looking back at the emperor one last time before disappearing into the tall grass.

"You can neither bless me nor curse me," he yelled, stabbing his sword at the sky. The leopard's blood ran down the blade and onto his hand. "Superstition will never hold power over me again!" He gave another war cry in triumph.

Then he turned and found himself the center of attention for two score of his soldiers. Concern painted most of their faces. Many had weapons ready to help their emperor. But what angered him was the horror in their eyes. Horror at what he'd done.

Bakari's grip tightened on his sword and he pointed it at the onlookers.

"If there is *any* talk of how this is a sign, good or ill, I will find the originator and leave their body for the animals." The men made quick, awkward bows and hurried to disperse. The emperor looked out across the seemingly endless grassland, over his empire. This was a sign. A sign that he and his will was greater than any force of nature.

~

Bakari's absence left a hole in the palace and Arkole felt it acutely. Just when she thought she'd have him for a length of time, war took him away from her again. She rubbed her belly as she watched the artists painting the murals in what would be her new son's bedroom. A scene of her husband subjugating the southerners adorned one wall. His figure was nearly as tall as the ceiling, riding in the royal chariot, sword held high to strike down his enemies. The small, half painted southerners cowered and ran before his horses, some already trampled under the chariot. A fitting scene to play across the new heir's chamber. He would know of the great bloodline he came from and the legacy he'd step into.

She moved closer to Bakari's figure and sighed. It was just like the southern wars again. He was away at war for who knew how long and here she was, alone to struggle through the birth of their newest child. The one time he did manage to slip away from the war, he left her with another pregnancy to deal with alone. She turned from the image. It wasn't fair. Why did life always find a way to pry him away from her?

She left the bedroom to inspect the work on the new prince's courtyard. A couple of servant women bowed to her, stopping their conversation the moment she entered the hallway. She paid them no attention as she moved on but stopped short when she heard them whisper about an uprising. Arkole turned, coming back to them.

"What are you talking about?" she said sharply.

The women bowed again. "Just city gossip, my empress."

"I asked you what you were talking about," she snapped, narrowing her eyes at them. "I heard one of you speak about an uprising. Speak!"

The older of the two pressed her lips together before finally speaking.

"I heard rumors of a rebellion in the west. The city of Ux has been taken over by some force. They've slaughtered whole noble families like animals. Many managed to flee but there are so many trapped there still. And I heard of a whole town killed and left in the streets."

"How do you know of this?" Arkole was furious and her son kicked at the sound of her voice.

The woman flinched. "My cousin's brother-in-law fled from Ux and told her what he'd seen there. Then she told me. We were raised as sisters. She wouldn't lie to me."

Arkole flicked her wrist, dismissing them with a scowl. The women bowed again and rushed away. The empress turned down the hallway, flagging another servant to take her to Hetsaf's office. How could she not know about this? Did he even know that there was unrest happing in the empire? Her scowl deepened. Of course that little weasel knew. He knew everything about the comings and goings about the empire. He purposefully kept her in the dark about this. She knew it. He would pay for this. Brother to her husband or not, he would pay dearly for this insolence.

By the time she reached his office, she was seething and her feet hurt from the walk. Hetsaf stood at his desk looking at a map, a woman looking over his shoulder.

"Why didn't you tell me about the rebellion happening *right now*?" she shouted the moment she entered the room.

The two of them jumped. Hetsaf's face pulled back into a frown when he looked up. The woman stepped back from him and moved to the side.

"Greetings, empress," the chancellor said dispassionately. "What exactly are you talking about?"

Arkole crossed the room and folded her arms over her belly. "The rebellion in the east. The city of Ux being taken over. Why was I not informed of this? I had to find out from the gossip of servants, Hetsaf. Servants!"

"Why are you yelling?" he asked calmly, looking down at her, eyes half closed.

"Because, *once again*, you have failed to give me vital information in the happenings of this empire. I am the empress. I stand above you as my husband's right hand and you are ignoring me."

Hetsaf paused. "Did the emperor not tell you about it? He was aware."

"He . . . has been concerned about Wiluru," she stammered. "I'm sure it slipped his mind."

"Of course."

Arkole's cheeks flushed. How dare he insinuate that Bakari didn't trust her enough to tell her.

"Then it is *your* duty to have told me. Isn't that your duty, chancellor?" She dragged his title across her tongue like a knife. It felt good to take a stab at him. The way he looked at her, like she was a filthy, shit covered beggar that he was forced to speak to, sickened her.

"I didn't feel that you needed to concern yourself with such matters." His eyes flicked downward. "Don't you have more . . . pressing issues to concern yourself with?" Hetsaf casually gestured to the swell of her stomach.

For a moment, Arkole couldn't think. She couldn't form words. Her rage had robbed her of them.

"How. Dare. You," she growled, voice rising with each word. "How dare you? You glorified servant. You forget who you're speaking to. You are to obey me. To serve me. You don't get to decide what I get to know and what gets hidden. With Bakari at war, I am the voice of authority here. I rule here and you will remember it or you will pay dearly for it!" Her shriek echoed around the room.

Suddenly, there was a presence at her side and she turned her head to see Hetsaf's servant near her.

"Please, empress. Calm yourself, for your child's sake," she said softly.

Arkole rounded on the woman, ready to yell again. But the woman held her gaze, concerned but unafraid. Whatever words on her lips fell away. Her breathing calmed with each one until all anger fell away. She suddenly felt spent.

"I . . . should." She looked to Hetsaf, some of her hatred rising back up but not with the same intensity. "You will remember your duty," she said firmly and began to walk out of the room.

The servant woman came to her side. "My empress, please allow me to walk you back to your quarters."

"Uh, yes, of course."

Arkole walked slowly through the halls this time. Her anger had burned through any energy she'd had left. She took a deep breath, trying to find her way back to her hatred of that man. Hetsaf had always been . . . a strange one. But it seemed like he held a particular contempt for her. If he were any other servant, she would have him beaten immediately. Unfortunately, as

Bakari's favored half-brother, he had a special place within the hierarchy of the palace. Arkole frowned. Still, he needed to be punished.

"He shouldn't have held information from you, empress," the servant woman said so quietly, Arkole almost missed it. "Excuse me for speaking out of turn, but you are the empress. You should know as much as he does."

Arkole unclenched her shoulders. "Your master seems to forget that."

"Perhaps I can bring you information if he doesn't see fit to share it with you." Arkole stared at her stunned. The woman didn't return her gaze but kept looking ahead and slightly down as any servant should. "I know how to write. I can copy the letters and papers he gets and bring it to you."

"You would betray your master?"

"In serving you, I serve the emperor who's our true master. And while he's away, he said that you are to be his voice, yes?" Arkole nodded. "Then you are my true master as well."

Arkole continued to stare at this woman. Where on earth did Hetsaf find her? She truly understood how things were to go in this palace. She looked around to make sure they were alone in the hallway.

"Yes, you will bring me copies of whatever Hetsaf is hiding from me," she whispered. "Prove yourself loyal and I will see that you're rewarded."

The woman gave a quick, deep bow. "Thank you, my empress."

Arkole smiled as she and her new spy finished the rest of the walk back to her quarters. Even if Hetsaf chose to disobey her again, she had a way around his insolence. She dismissed the woman, settling into a seat near a window. Her son began to kick again and she placed her hand over the spot, delighted in the sensation. She would prove herself a proper wife and empress and when Bakari returned to her he would see all that she had accomplished. No one else.

~

Sept'ha returned to Hetsaf's office annoyed. That woman

was an airhead. So convinced of her own power that she didn't realize how fragile it really was. She sighed heavily as she made the turn to the door and was cornered the moment she entered.

Hetsaf came from behind his desk, crossing the distance between them faster than she'd ever seen him move.

"I have never seen anyone quell one of her tantrums so quickly." He grabbed her arm, pulling her off to a corner of the room where they were unlikely to be heard by anyone outside. "Not even my brother can quell her moods like that. How did you do it?"

Sept'ha glanced away. How could she explain it to him? At that moment, she knew that this argument was about to morph into something irreparable. She felt the need to calm the situation, felt the ability to do it. Most of all, she felt her god's assurance of the right way to handle it. How did she explain this to a man who'd bought into his brother's heresy completely?

Hetsaf tightened his grip on her arm and shook her roughly. "How did you do it? Are you a magician, a healer and you haven't told me?"

She looked to him, indignation rising. She could hear the growl of a leopard in her ears. Then a hand on her shoulder. *Tell him.*

Sept'ha looked in his eyes, locking his gaze to hers. "I am the chosen of Met, sent here to see her will be done."

Hetsaf let go of her as if she'd burned him. "The gods aren't real," he said, frowning again. "I should have you flogged for saying so."

A growling started up behind her and she saw his eyes grow wide. She reached out her hand and felt the warm fur of Met's symbol. She looked down, running her fingers across its neck and scratching behind its ears. The large leopard rubbed against her leg familiarly. It was so strange. She'd been so terrified of this beast when she'd first seen it. Now it felt like greeting an old friend. A supportive strength came from it and she gave thanks to her god.

Sept'ha turned back to Hetsaf. "The gods are very real, Chancellor Hetsaf. I have seen her myself."

She watched as he struggled with fear and comprehension.

There was no denying that this leopard had to be a sign from Met. How else could it have gotten so far into the palace without anyone noticing? His eyes flicked between her and it, obviously trying to make sense of the scene before him. Finally, he closed his mouth, swallowing hard. He took a breath.

"What . . .what does she want?" he asked carefully.

She smiled. "She is Met. She wants war. She sent me here to help the emperor directly, but you are the key to making sure these wars happen. I'm here to help you."

He didn't respond right away. He took his time forming an answer, something she actually liked about him.

"What about the emperor's decree?"

Sept'ha closed her eyes for an answer and was immediately met with indifference.

"She doesn't care," she said, still petting the now purring divine beast. "War will bring people back to the gods. Back to her."

Hetsaf's eyes flitted back and forth as he thought. He looked back to her and gave a small nod.

"Then let's make war."

The leopard moved from her side and gave him a light rub on the thigh. She smiled truly.

"Good."

Chapter Sixteen

The smells of cooking grains, yams, and spices filled the forest air. Efah grinned, the scent a pleasant distraction as she walked in the grand courtyard of Garemba. A handful of cooking fires were scattered in the area as the city began preparing for dinner. A few wild boars had been hunted down this afternoon, with Nesi and Usa'a help, and a group of women were making short work of butchering them.

Efah moved from fire to fire, greeting people and asking after their wellbeing. People replied to her with bright grins and well wishes. She paused her visitations and took a long look at the people assembled. The sight suddenly hit her. This city was filled. Where before there were people scattered everywhere, now they were out and crowded. She couldn't remember if she'd ever seen so many people in Garemba.

The sound of the massive city doors opening echoed around the courtyard, rippling the surface of the shallow pool in the center. Efah hurried to the city's entrance, curious at what was arriving. No shouts of alarm came so she was glad it wasn't anything threatening. They'd had enough of that for a lifetime.

Her questions were answered by a column of people walking up from the forest path. She could tell by their clothing that they were city people and the trek to reach Garemba had been tiring. Families huddled together, relief on their faces as they took in the walls of the legendary city.

Efah came where she could be seen.

"Welcome to Garemba," she called out to the first of the long line of travelers. "You will be safe here."

An older man came up to her, a man who would have been about her father's age had he lived.

"Are you . . . are you the lady of death?" he asked nervously.

"I am." She smiled, crinkling her eyes at a pair of children nearby. "I am the agent of [NAME] who wishes for all to live well until it is time for him to visit them."

Many uttered their thanks as they passed. Efah tried to count, a nagging feeling growing in her heart. That was at least thirty more. She turned to look at the tall vine covering front of the city. How many were actually in the city?

She walked back inside, counting as she went along. Around each fire were at least fifteen people, all waiting to be fed. She walked through hall after hall, counting. Usa and Nesi eventually found her, nuzzling up to her and lessening her worry. So many people. So many mouths to feed and they were in the middle of a forest.

Her feet led her to the broken courtyard that overlooked the forest and the Bangi River, several stories below. This was the spot where the old thief lord, Ayodele, used to hold "court," but it sat empty now. She had no idea if he or his cronies were even in the city anymore. If they were, she sincerely hoped they changed their ways before Newa found them. If they were gone, good riddance.

She sighed, her shoulders sinking. There were too many people here. They'd managed to clear out small plots beside the city for farming but it would be some time before any of them yielded fruit. The forest itself couldn't produce enough foraging to feed an entire city. And Garemba was becoming a city again. She had to wonder if this resurgence would die just like the old city did.

"I heard more people arrived."

Efah's heart fluttered and she smiled before she realized she did. She turned to see Newa cautiously coming onto the expanse. Nesi and Usa ran up to him, nuzzling him from both sides. She almost laughed watching him accept their affection awkwardly.

"Yes," she said once her hyenas had released him. "About thirty people arrived. City dwellers."

"Probably from Ofolubaru." He came to her side, looking out at the forest scene. "You seem troubled by it."

Efah puffed out a breath. "I think we have too many people here. The city's growing more and more crowded every day."

"I agree." He glanced at her, looking away the moment their eyes met. "I thought it was just my imagination, just me longing for the capital. But I encounter more people in the halls than I have since I came here. More people are hearing of the safety of Garemba. This… is good, my L—Efah. What is exactly worrying you?"

"I don't want us to go back to how things were when Ayodele was in charge. People were barely not starving. I don't think we'll have enough food and eventually we're going to run out of safe spaces. I don't want people having to make their home in spots where the roof could fall on them or the floor could fall out from under them."

Newa slowly moved his gaze around them. "We could always expand into the forest. Make a few wooden buildings to accommodate the influx of people."

She looked at him with raised eyebrows and he smiled apologetically. "To house the number of people coming in."

"I'm just a farm girl, Newa," she chuckled.

"You're far more than that, Efah."

The absolute sincerity of his statement completely lowered her guard and she looked away, cheeks hot.

"I'm afraid it won't be enough space in time. Every day people keep arriving. Garemba's not going to be able to be a safe space for long if we're scrounging around for food and a place to lay our heads."

"So, what do you think we should do?"

She sighed, at a loss. "What do you do in the cities if your family's gotten too big for your house."

Newa's lips pulled into a thin line. "You move."

Efah nodded. His words made it so obvious. As much as she didn't want to, as much as she and so many here had come to think of Garemba as home, they couldn't stay here and survive. It was alright for a few desperate groups but not sustainable for much more.

"Then we move."

"But where?" He looked at her, expression tight.

Efah thought for a moment. Where in the world could they move?

"Ofolubaru," she said, clarity coming to her.

"Ofolubaru? Most of them just came from the city."

She frowned. "It's the only place I can see going. It has food and homes ready. We wouldn't have to work with crumbling walls and the harsh forest."

"I'm not sure," Newa said slowly. He worried his lip and she knew he wanted to say more. She nodded to him encouragingly.

"We would have to deal with that dara again and she wants your blood. You may have to kill her." He grimaced. "And her guard."

Efah ran the thought over in her mind. The though of killing the haughty, blasphemous dara of Ofolubaru didn't bother her at all.

"Then so be it. Death walks with us and if she wants to obey his will, then she will fall to him." Her hand brushed against his and she gently entwined her fingers with his. His hand stiffened, then relaxed against hers.

"I hope you'll follow me in this," she said quietly.

Newa gave her hand a squeeze. "I would follow you until the end of my days, my lady."

Efah nodded once and they watched night fall on the hidden city.

~

If there was one thing Tekhamun couldn't stand, it was his worship being interrupted. His life back home had been lonely, but at least he could commune with Gu'un in peace. The priest opened his eyes, placing his curved blades on the floor beside him. Someone was calling his name and it irked his very soul. He got up and opened the door with an annoyed growl, looking at the follower jogging down the hall. "Yes?" he asked, trying to hide his irritation.

Pta, Karatel's bedwarmer, panted, hands on her knees. "Master, Karatel said that there is an army coming towards the city. Lookouts saw it from the city wall."

Tekhamun sucked in a breath. "An army? Is he sure?"

She nodded. "He wouldn't have sent me running if he wasn't."

The priest moved past her, mumbling an awkward thanks. He hurried downstairs and out of the house they'd taken. The sun was a few hours away from noon and scattered clouds told of a stormy afternoon. Tekhamun reached the outer wall only just out of breath, climbing the stairs at a good pace. Karatel stood, a foot perched in one of the raised sides, staring out toward the horizon.

Tekhamun took a few deep breaths and walked up to him.

"There's an army approaching? Surely, it's just a merchant band."

Karatel didn't look over but continued staring grimly at the road. The priest had never seen his top follower look so serious.

"Merchant bands don't kick up that much dust."

The man pointed out to the distance and Tekhamun followed the line to what he was pointing to. Less than an hour away was a large black dot on the road that led straight to the city. A cloud of dust rose up, obscuring the world behind them. A small seed of panic planted itself in his heart. He could just make out the flashes of light as the sun reflected off their armor.

"Master," Karatel called, snapping him out of his trance. "What are your orders?"

He took another deep breath, stealing his courage. He was a priest who only did his work in the temple. He wasn't prepared for war.

But . . .

But he was chosen of Gu'un. He was prepared for whatever challenges the unbelievers presented. If it was a temple of unworthy priests, he would be ready. If it was an entire army, their god would be with them.

"Gather everyone who can fight," he commanded, not recognizing the sound of his own voice. "Bring them to the gate."

"And then what?" Karatel asked, still grim faced.

Tekhamun stared at him in absolute disbelief. "And then we show them who the gods are with."

He took off down the stairs, heading back to their base. The building they were stockpiling weapons was just next door to where they were staying and the priest happily opened it up, inviting his waiting followers to choose the weapon best for them. He knew he didn't have to worry about his first followers. Each had their own weapons and knew how to fight before they'd come to him. But the newest members of his band he sent up a quick prayer for.

Tekhamun outfitted himself in his full uniform once he left the store house. His fingers trembled as he placed each of his weapons in their proper place. This was a blessing. A chance to prove themselves true believers. He grinned so wide it hurt. Today was going to be glorious and the streets would run red with the blood of the unfaithful.

When he came out to leave, he saw Hamena just opening the door to another room. She looked up, surprise in her eyes. Feelings of shame rose in him as he looked at her, the memories of what they'd done threatening to come back in full force.

"Hamena," he said, voice cracking. "Haven't you heard? There's an army on the way. We have to fight."

She gave him a sad smile, coming closer.

"Master," she said in her husky, syrup sweet voice. "I'm not really a fighter. I thought it would be best if I wait here until everything was over."

The threads of shame snapped at her words. She dared to proclaim herself a devoted follower, cause him to defile himself with her, and now she wanted to hide while he fought for her.

"Everyone who can must fight." He took out one of his own knives, thrusting his hand against her chest as he gave it to her. "Prove yourself a true follower of the gods. Risk your life for our cause."

She took the knife carefully, looking up at him sullenly.

"Yes, master."

Tekhamun stared her down before he walked past her and out of the building.

By the time he returned to the wall, they could hear the rumbling of the footsteps of the army, like a storm in the distance. Below him, just on the city side of the main gate, his people gathered, weapons in hand. There were more than he thought there would be, but most of the newer followers he'd picked up, a ragtag group taught by his first followers and himself, were ready to defend the city.

Moon walked up to him, so quiet despite her size. A sword that almost looked too small was in her right hand.

"Perhaps you should say something to them, Master,"

He nodded, swallowing. Since the unfortunate incident, Moon hadn't stopped her self-imposed duties. She still brought him his meals and made sure he was taking care of himself. However, there was a coolness in her demeanor that he couldn't ignore. Perhaps after today, he could redeem himself in her eyes.

"My people," he called out. Every eye gathered in the main street looked up to him. Tekhamun could feel the rumble of the approaching army and the tingle that ran up from his feet gave him strength. "Agents of the blasphemous netkoleh come to attack us, stop our holy mission. We will not let them. I have been sent by Gu'un himself to rally people against the ungodly decree and you have heeded the call. You are the true warriors of faith. As Gu'un cleaves the wicked from the pure in the afterlife, so shall we cleave the unholy from this earth. Gu'un is with us. We shall not fail."

A cheer went up at his yell, startling him. Tekhamun looked around, his pride and his faith bolstered by their devotion. He spared a glance to Moon and even she had a small smile of pride on her face. She looked to him, giving him the barest nod. Tekhamun came down from the wall and waited for the army with his people.

It was a torturous wait.

Tekhamun stood at the ready, praying his unyielding faith would lend courage to those around. The rumbling of the army's footsteps grew slowly louder and stronger until they stopped just outside of the city's doors.

"Open the gates," he commanded.

Karatel was suddenly at his side. "Are you sure, Master?" He hissed.

"Gu'un demands their deaths." Tekhamun looked over to the man until he backed down with a bowed head.

The gates opened slowly and they saw the army, standing with shields and spears in hand, organized in neat lines. Tekhamun moved so he could look down one of the rows of soldiers and saw that there weren't as many as he feared. He sent up a quick prayer of thanks.

The force's commander rode forward on a dappled horse, one

hand on the reins, the other sitting on his sword's pommel. He sneered at them like he'd opened the door and found fleeing insects.

"Are you the force that's holding this city hostage?"

Tekhamun stepped forward. "We are. I am Tekhamun, son of Tekmanon and priest of the Arak'guun. I have been sent by my god to lead a holy mission against the netkoleh's blasphemous decree. Surrender now to the will of Gu'un and you will be spared. Continue this sinful path and you will be cleaved from this life."

"Surrender?" The commander chuckled. "Just a bunch of zealots. First line, take care of this rabble."

The first line of the force—ten in total—stepped out of formation and came to the city gates. Tekhamun sized them up in a breath. Trained soldiers, yes. As deadly as a member of the Arak'guun, no. The soldiers had to come together to enter the gate and that was the moment he needed. He took out his two moon blades, coming in low.

Two of the soldiers immediately stabbed for him. The first, he parried and evaded. The second cut him across the thigh shallowly. He barely registered the pain, instead blessing the name of Gu'un for this fight. He cut the first soldier across the thighs, the blade cutting to the bone. As he went down, Tekhamun slashed up, cutting the man's throat open. The others gawked as their fellow soldiers went down screaming and that was their mistake.

Tekhamun took down three more before the commander could order his men to attack. The force funneled into the city giving Tekhamun's warriors a chance to fight off just the soldiers that had managed to get inside. The capital's force found themselves surrounded the moment they stepped past the walls and at the mercy of the holy warriors.

The priest of Gu'un laughed as he dipped under spears and around sword strikes. He hadn't moved this well since his training days with his master. His swords dripped with blood and the air was full of the sweet music of unholy agony. Out of the corner of his eye, he saw burly Nermet, sword in hand, chopping a soldier in the shoulder. The man went down, trying to strike with the last of his strength but Nermet chopped him in the head.

To his right, a soldier ran one of his followers through. The woman looked confused at the shaft coming out of her stomach, then convulsed as the soldier ripped it out of her. Tekhamun was on him before she hit the ground. He took both swords, cutting through the throat, the man's spine being the only thing holding his head onto his body.

He could hear the commander shouting orders to his men outside, but it registered to him just barely. Tekhamun's ears were filled with the sound of battle and his own prayers of praise. Bodies began to pile up in front of the gates making it even more difficult for the enemy soldiers to enter. Tekhamun's fighters took advantage of it, waiting for a soldier to get over his fallen comrades' bodies before ganging up on him in pairs or trios. The priest was proud of his people. They were fighting smart.

The sound of a horse caught his attention and he turned just in time to block a blow from the commander. Tekhamun jumped back as the man reared his horse up to stomp down for him.

"You rebellious scum," the man snarled as he took another forceful swing.

Tekhamun twirled to the side, begged Gu'un for forgiveness, and stabbed the horse between the ribs. It was a shame to kill an innocent creature but this battle necessitated it. The warriors on the side of right had to prevail. The commander jumped from his horse as the creature fell to the ground, trying to scream its pain and death.

"Come, agent of the blasphemer," Tekhamun said with a feral smile. "Come and meet your judgement."

The commander howled his fury and attacked the priest with a flurry of sword blows. Most Tekhamun was able to deflect completely but some just barely and before long he was covered with cuts. He waited with the patience of righteousness for the right moment and stabbed in, catching the man in the gut. With a grunt, he brought his razor-sharp sword up, slicing up to the ribs. The commander dropped his sword, unthinkingly grabbing onto Tekhamun's. The edge sliced deep into his fingers.

Tekhamun smiled as he watched life slowly drain from the

man's eyes.

"For Gu'un and all the gods." He slid his blade out, relishing the graceful arc of blood.

Outside of the gate, the gaggle of capital soldiers stared in disbelief at the bloodshed before them. They held their spears loosely as their comrades were piled upon by a motley group of rebels. Tekhamun turned completely from the fighting, stepping on bodies to make his way to the gate.

"Go," he shouted. "Go and tell your master the netkoleh that the gods' will shall be done in this land. Tell him that he will come back to the righteous path or he will face the justice of Gu'un's blade."

It only took the cowardice of one soldier to break the resolve of the last few. They ran back down the road away from the city, leaving their fallen behind. Tekhamun turned his attention back to the fight, helping finish the last of the battles. Before he knew it, they were done, the only sound their heavy breathing. He looked around in disbelief, his expression mirrored on several of his followers' faces. He saw Karatel kneeling beside the body of Pta, his face unreadable. Tekhamun's heart pulled for him. The other bodies strewn about included several of his followers but the bulk of them survived. By Gu'un's favor, they survived.

Tekhamun raised his bloody swords high and let out a war cry.

Chapter Seventeen

The capital of Rahaban was a patchwork of reds and creams, peach, and yellows. A mixture of tiled roofs and flat, mud brick ones soaked up the early afternoon sun. People moved around with purpose, trying to flee the heat. Women under brightly colored parasols, obviously nobility, strolled along the street that ran beside the docks, taking in the sea air and wanting to be seen. In the distance, the palace glittered dazzling white, a series of copper domes its crown. Ulzimah was a city that rivaled Wiluru for its majesty. Even Yutuuan had to admit it. Hopefully, it would rival Wiluru in its hospitality as well.

The prince watched nervously as his small ship docked. Sailors, dock workers, and passersby stared at the foreign warship as it approached. Yutuuan had chosen the least imposing vessel in the fleet. The Nautilus was the smallest ship but the fastest as well. Its captain was more than honored to host the prince on this risky mission. There was no guarantee that he would get to talk to the Lekhem. No certainty that they were even in charge anymore, let alone an ally. Yutuuan swallowed as the ship lurched to a halt. He may barely make it out of the city alive but he had to try.

"My prince," Naret called, coming up to him. Behind his bodyguard was a young sailor. He wore Naret's sash around his waist, the emblem of Wiluru's royal family white against deep blue. "The messenger is ready."

Yutuuan looked him over, then clapped him on the shoulder.

"You look like a true emissary of the crown," he said with an encouraging smile.

"Thank you, my prince," the sailor nervously replied.

Yutuuan nodded and the young man disembarked. A handful of other sailors fell in around him, his escort and protection for the trip to the palace. The prince watched them intently until they disappeared in the streets of Ulzimah. He sighed heavily.

"And now, we wait."

Naret folded his arms, still staring in the direction of the messenger. "I pray this works out in our favor."

"Since when do you pray?" Yutuuan asked with a smirk.

"I pray for the wellbeing of a certain reckless prince constantly. Only the soothing waters of Yutuu could calm my spirit when my prince 'has a plan'."

Yutuuan winced. The man was worse than a nanny.

"This plan will work. Doesn't my name mean Yutuu Is Here? If he is here and *I* am here then there's no chance this could fail."

Naret pressed his lips. "Let us pray."

Prince Yutuuan walked around the deck to pass the time, helping sailors with their tasks and trying to spread good cheer. When he glanced toward the sun, he realized that barely any time had passed. He looked back at the street that his messenger had taken and nervousness began to settle in. His bodyguard must have noticed it because the man put a kind hand on his shoulder. They sparred, played betting games with the crew, and occupied themselves in the prince's cabin but still the messenger hadn't returned.

When the sun was starting to touch the western horizon, the call came that the group had returned. Yutuuan rushed above deck, Naret close on his heels. The group was unharmed to his relief and they were accompanied by even more people. Four warriors in elegant clothing flanked the original group, the leader coming forward.

"I am here to speak directly with the prince of Wiluru," he said in the trade tongue.

Yutuuan stepped forward. "I am he."

The leader bowed lowly. "Our great leader, the lekhem Marlah, sends her greetings and invites you to the palace to speak with her. If you will follow us, we'll take you there."

Yutuuan glanced to Naret, trying to keep the pleased smile from his face. Naret didn't respond.

"We will be happy to come immediately."

He made his final orders to the Nautilus' crew and fell in behind the leader. Yutuuan didn't miss the large, curved swords at the hips of the guards. Or their heavily scarred hands. These men had seen many battles. He was glad he'd remembered to bring his own weapon and that Naret and three other men were at his side. If this was a trap, they'd make the Rahaban regret they'd sprung it.

The streets of Ulzimah were growing lively again as the sun began to set and the temperature lowered with it. People stopped and stared as they passed, gawking at the small procession. Small children were jerked out of the way and hands popped for pointing. Yutuuan gave reassuring smiles to the mothers to try and let them know that all was fine.

They passed narrow streets where elaborately carved lanterns were being lit and squares where vendors were setting up for night markets. The prince was amazed at all the activity. By this time, Wiluru was starting to wind down with only a few places drawing the populace. It seemed that Ulzimah had a second life when the sun set. The adventurous part of him reared up. He'd love to explore it.

By the time they reached the palace, the city was awash in the last golden rays of sunset. The deep purples of the encroaching night attempted to fill the shadows but were held at bay by the army of streetlamps being lit. The palace itself was bright with its own armada of lanterns. Some floated in midair above the vibrant plants of the front courtyard. Flowers he'd only seen in his mother's private courtyard flourished here and fruits he'd only seen dried, fattened on trees. The palace rose up before them and Yutuuan realized that he'd guessed the scale of it all wrong. It was a mountain of white in the heart of the city. The copper domes seemed enormous this close, large enough to be bowls to hold some of the grandest ships of Wiluru's navy.

A thought occurred to him as they passed through the building's ornate gates. Could Wiluru have been this grand if they weren't beholden to the Ega? How much had his kingdom lost by being entangled with the southerners? The idea stoked his ire but it strengthened his resolve. Wiluru had to be a free kingdom again for the good of its people.

The trek inside the palace seemed to take almost as long as the trip to reach its doors. Their footsteps were softened by the elaborately patterned rugs in the halls. A host of hallways led off to each side and servants scurried about, eyes on the floor in front of them. Far to the end of the long hallway was another set of doors, as tall as the entryway to the palace in Wiluru. Gilded flowers and vines covered every space available with blooms as large as his head. It took a trio of servants to open just one of those doors and Yutuuan and his escort were led inside. To an empty throne room. The throne, which sat on a high platform, was vacant. No servants or nobles filled the space. The only movement came from gauzy curtains that moved in the breeze from the open atrium at each side.

The prince looked around in confusion, glancing at Naret who gave a subtle, confused shrug in return. A man in near floor length robes with a golden yellow sash tied at his waist approached them. He bowed; hands clasped.

"Greetings, prince of Wiluru," he said in a reedy, high-pitched voice. "If you will come this way. The lekhem has retreated to the patio."

Yutuuan nodded to his guard and he and Naret followed the man to the side of the wide room. He moved aside the curtain for him and he could see a beautifully tiled patio overlooking another courtyard. This one had an enormous fountain at its center that shot water in the air nearly two stories high. A table and two chairs had been set up near the edge of the tiles and in one of those chairs sat an older woman, casually drinking from a glass cup. Another woman, either a daughter or a high servant, stood by her side.

"Just the prince past this point," the man said.

Yutuuan could feel Naret bristle at the order.

"I am the prince's bodyguard," he said firmly.

The man bowed, hands clasped, again. "I am sorry. You may stay just beyond the curtain."

Yutuuan looked to his friend. "It'll be all right. I'm sure the lakhem presents no danger." Naret pressed his lips together but relaxed and stepped aside. Yutuuan nodded to his friend and protector as he passed, thankful for his diligence.

The woman standing beside the lekhem gestured to the empty seat.

"Welcome, Prince Yutuuan of Wiluru," she said in his

language. Her accent was clipped but he understood her perfectly. "I am Risha, translator for our great lakhem. She is most curious that you're asking for a direct audience when our countries barely contact each other."

Yutuuan bowed deeply to the ruler before taking his seat. The lakhem studied him with deep brown eyes. Her gray hair was pulled back, the curls tucked into a bun decorated with pearls. There was a shrewdness to her expression and the prince could tell this was no fool when it came to negotiations. She was already prepared to get her way.

"Greetings to the honored lakhem," he said and Risha translated. "I come to you, personally, because a threat has presented itself at our eastern border. The Fahzi empire."

When Risha translated the Fahzi, the lakhem scoffed and sat back in her chair. When she spoke, Yutuuan could hear the annoyance.

"The Fahzi are fleas biting at the heels of the empire. A group of rowdy peasants looking to steal power from those the gods have given it to," Risha translated.

"So you've heard of them."

"Yes. They've taken over Masharadi. We let them have it. A small price to pay to rid ourselves of the annoyance of fighting them."

Yutuuan blinked. "I'm sorry. You *let* them take over Masharadi?"

"Yes." The lakhem stared at him, eyebrow raised. "It is just one city on the edge of the empire when I have twenty more just like it or greater. What is there to mourn?"

The prince struggled for his next comment. To hear a ruler so casually shrug off the loss of an entire city to an enemy. Not to mention what the state of the people within that city may be. He didn't understand how she could be so cavalier about it.

"But what of the people? Wiluru usually sees trade from your empire through ships from Masharadi. We haven't seen a single trade ship in over a year. The people there must be cut off from the outside world."

The lakhem rolled her eyes when she heard the meaning of his words.

"Prince Yutuuan, what is it you've come here for? Surely it wasn't to bring me old news."

"No, honored lakhem." Yutuuan's mind was reeling. She didn't even care about her people held hostage by the Fahzi. Basic honor as a ruler wasn't going to appeal to her. His thinking paused. Perhaps her pride as a ruler would.

"But I did want to let you know that we have done your empire a great favor." When she sat up slightly, eyebrow raised, he knew he had her.

"The cobbled together navy the Fahzi had, we've destroyed most of it. Sent the rest running back to their stronghold. I would press into their territory but we have our own conflicts to tend to. And I doubt they'll be able to mount an attack against Wiluru again any time soon, so I think those fleas will be biting at your heels again. I doubt you'll want to devote resources to that when I'm sure your warriors can be more useful elsewhere in the empire."

She pursed her lips, her frown creasing her forehead. "What is it that you want, young man?"

"Since we've sent these upstarts back to Masharadi to lick their wounds, could you do us the favor of crushing them while they're still recovering? It shouldn't be hard for a great and powerful empire such as yours."

"And if we won't?"

Yutuuan's expression hardened.

"If I have to spend time and resources crushing the Fahzi and liberating Masharadi when they're needed elsewhere, then I'll take the city for our kingdom. You care so little for it. I doubt it would harm your pride or reputation as the honored lakhem. We could always use more resources." *Especially with another war breathing down our necks.*

The older woman's eyes narrowed. Risha stared at her ruler in concern. Yutuuan feared he'd gone too far, but he stood by his statements. If he was going to split the nation's military at such a crucial time, then he would have a reward for it. The lakhem sat back again.

"Stay the night, Prince Yutuuan. Enjoy the hospitality of my palace. I will have an answer for you tomorrow for you've given me much to think about."

"Thank you, honored lakhem. A favor for a favor is all I ask."

He stood and bowed to her. She nodded, obviously through with him. Naret fell into step beside him once the prince left the patio. Yutuuan let loose a breath, all bravado leaving him. He let the servant guide him and his escort through the palace to opulent rooms. The servant promised them a meal then left the group alone.

Yutuuan ran a hand down his face.

"I didn't think I was going to reach her," he said quietly. "Who would have thought a ruler would just let a city fall to the enemy?"

Naret was looking pointedly at the door, which worried him. "What is it?"

"Hopefully, the lakhem will keep her word and give you an answer in the morning. If she decides to just string you along, you've just become a hostage. Ready to force Wiluru to clean up the Fahzi mess for her." The bodyguard's face settled into a frown. "I hope she has more honor than pride."

"Let us pray," Yutuuan replied.

~

Yutuuan finished his breakfast, trying to shrug off the weight of anticipation. When servants came into the rooms this morning, he'd hoped he was being summoned before the lakhem. But when they brought in tray after tray of food, his hopes were dashed. He ate slowly, he and his guards silent. Still no word.

With his last bite, Yutuuan looked over to Naret. The bodyguard paced across the room, sparing a glance at the door every few minutes. The man's warning ran through the prince's mind again. This may be a trap. Yutuuan breathed out in frustration. It was a risk he'd taken into account when he'd formed this plan. Having the crown prince in custody would be an easy way to force a kingdom to give you what you wanted. but it was a risk he was willing to take.

Everyone grew restless as time moved on. Finally, when they were nearly ready for the noon meal, the doors opened again. A different servant came in this time, dressed in much finer garb than her earlier counterpart. She stopped just inside the door to the sitting room where they gathered and bowed.

"Prince Yutuuan of Wiluru, the great lakhem wishes for your presence at the midday meal. You may bring your bodyguard but the others must remain here."

Yutuuan looked to each of his warriors. They nodded in turn, Naret holding his gaze for a moment before nodding. His people were ready just in case, and the prince was grateful for every one of them.

He fell in line behind the new servant. Naret was just behind him to his right. The two followed the man through more opulent hallways until they reached a courtyard. It was enormous and the prince had trouble imagining how such a large area was concealed within the palace walls. Servants tended to topiaries, carving the bushes into birds in flight or big cats on the hunt. Several fountains bubbled, catching the midday sun in their droplets. The slight breeze was cooled by them, making the area far more comfortable. Yutuuan tried not to gawk as they were led to the opposite side. It wouldn't do to look like some country farmer, new to the capital. He was a crown prince; he should be used to such riches. Even though he was starting to realize he wasn't.

The scent of the meal prepared for them reached him before he was ten steps from the table. Plates full of food, some completely foreign, some familiar but with different preparation, covered the table before the lakhem. She gestured to a seat near her as she put a stuffed grape in her mouth. Her interpreter stood just behind her.

"Your guard may take a plate and eat over there," said the woman. The lakhem flicked her fingers at a bench a few paces away.

Yutuuan didn't appreciate how dismissive she was with Naret but nodded to him his approval. The men bowed before taking their respective places.

"Thank you for the incredible smelling meal," Yutuuan said, gathering his charm.

The lakhem speared a tiny roasted bird with a golden fork

and brought it to her plate.

"I have never been to Wiluru even though our nations have traded for generations. Tell me of it," she said through her interpreter.

Yutuuan put on his best smile. "Wiluru is a beautiful land. Rolling hills filled with grape vines and low trees. Plenty of land between the cities to farm and raise goats. Our waters are full of fish, crab, octopus, anything you could possibly want. Our ships travel as far as the Outer Isles to bring back turquoise, crystal, and goods from even more distant lands." He saw the lakhem's eyebrows raise slightly at this and decided to gild his description.

"We're the only kingdom the Outer Isles deals with on these coasts since our fleet protects them from pirates."

He took a deliberate pause, taking a sip from his wine. "And we are the gateway for the southern gold. The only gateway, in fact. It would be a shame if the Fahzi disrupted our trade to the east."

The lakhem regarded him for a moment, then returned her attention to her lunch. With her fingers, she pried meat from the breast of the roasted fowl. She lifted it to her lips, a little smirk flashing across her face before she spoke again.

"Tell me of this other conflict you mentioned. The one you needed to get back to?" The lakhem watched him expectantly.

"It's a complicated affair," he began slowly. She motioned for him to continue. "We are about to engage the Ega in war. They have demanded that we stop worshiping gods all together and we refused. My sister, who was sent to Metkara as the netkoleh's bride, warned us of the demand. We were just beginning to gather forces when the so-called Fahzi Empire attacked us."

He sighed, spreading his hands in a sign of helplessness. "If we only could focus on finally throwing the Ega out of Wiluru. We would be able to make trade deals more freely for all our goods, including gold." He tried one of the stuffed grapes. It was good. "We would even be able to freely decide who our main trading partner will be."

The lakhem raised an eyebrow again. "Won't that be a little

difficult with the Ega in control of the southern gold routes?"

Yutuuan thought furiously for a moment. "There are ways to circumvent that." He wasn't sure if the deep south would be willing to trade with them directly but they may just have to try.

The lakhem watched him for a few moments, her mind obviously working behind her light brown eyes.

"Prince Yutuuan, are you proposing a formal alliance of sorts in exchange for eradicating the Fahzi menace?"

Yutuuan swirled his glass, looking up at her through his lashes. "It would be very advantageous to both our kingdoms."

She laughed, setting down the morsel she was about to eat. "Doesn't your father decide such matters?"

"One day I will take the throne and I'd love to have an alliance firmly in place by then."

"And the gold?" She raised an eyebrow at Yutuuan's pause.

"I assume you want a respectable percentage of the gold trade." He cleared his throat. "Would 20 percent be sufficient?"

"Twenty-five sounds better."

The prince swallowed. He was wading farther and farther into territory his father needed to negotiate.

"Twenty-five can be done," he said trying his best to hide his hesitation.

The lakhem ripped the leg from the fowl, pulling off the meat in one bite. She chewed thoughtfully, Yutuuan taking this moment to enjoy more of the meal.

"Very well, Prince of Wiluru," she said at last. "I will send forces to crush the Fahzi and get them out of both of our hair. I'll even send a few ships of our own to aide in your conflict." She smiled but it wasn't what would be called warm. "A show of faith in the success of your war."

Yutuuan blinked at her for a moment. "Thank you, great lakhem. Thank you so much. We —."

"One last thing I'd like to truly seal this agreement." She chewed on a few more of the grapes. "I have two unmarried daughters of appropriate age for you. You may take which ever one you choose for your bride."

His heart halted for a moment, the world halting with it. This was not the sort of agreement he saw coming. He prayed for

Yutuu to soothe the lakhem's heart for telling her the truth.

"I do apologize, great lakhem, but I have to decline your most generous offer. I am unfortunately promised to another."

The lakhem's face fell into a frown. He hid his grimace. "But" he continued desperately, "I have a sister. Nineteen and uncommitted." *Umakaal, forgive me.*

The older woman's face stretched back into a smile. "Even better. My youngest son, twenty, of my least favorite husband. I have yet to find him a wife. You may take him with you for your sister. He has no bastards to make any claims later. I've made sure of that. Take him so he may begin to learn of his new home."

Yutuuan sat, mouth open. This woman would so readily toss aside her own child like another possession. Send him to a foreign kingdom to marry a woman he'd never met, more than likely to never return again. He saw the lakhem's impatient expression and closed his mouth.

"That can be done. We'll be happy to welcome him into our family."

"Excellent," she responded and returned with gusto to her meal. "I trust you'll want to return to Wiluru as soon as possible."

"Yes, great lakhem."

"Then eat your fill and attend to your preparation."

He nodded, numb, and finished eating. He remained silent until he returned to their rooms, only speaking to give the command to get ready to leave.

The gamble had paid off. He'd gotten everything he'd wanted from this trip and more. The Fahzi would be taken care of. Their warriors could focus on the more important war with the Ega. But most importantly, he could return to Talekh and their child. His mind drifted to his sister and the saliva in his mouth tasted sour.

He'd won a victory for Wiluru, but at what cost?

Chapter Eighteen

The deepest room of the temple was hot and Erenemo felt it despite his light robes. Thankfully, the floor where he sat was cool. Countless high priests before him had worn a comfortable dip in the packed earth as they communed with the other world. Erenemo swayed back and forth, singing a song of praise and supplication. It was a song to flatter the ancestors enough to speak to the gods on their behalf. Today, it was specifically on his behalf.

He'd heard nothing from the council. His bribes had been eagerly accepted but there was no word from those stubborn fools. Not a single message even though he knew they'd met every day for weeks. If they were to choose another for Great Dara he was almost to the point where he wished they'd just make it know and be done with it. He pushed his mind back to his worship but it slid away again. What was taking them so long? Hadn't Nsongo been without a dara long enough?

Erenemo paused his song, taking a few breaths. He opened his eyes, looking to the statues of the gods. He rested his gaze on each one, reciting their names and tittles under his breath. If ever there was a time that they could possibly intercede in his favor, it would be now. Determined to move the hearts of both ancestors and deities alike, Erenemo continued to sing.

He was hungry and a find sheen of sweat glistened on his brow when he finally emerged from the altar room. One of the temple compound servants waited for him just outside the door. He raised an eyebrow as he stopped.

"Priest Erenemo," the man said, giving a quick bow. "The council has summoned you."

Erenemo paused in shock. "How long ago?"

"Not long, priest."

He quickly thanked the man, rushing to his rooms within the compound. He changed and washed, trying to keep the eager smile from his face. Surely, this was the day he'd been waiting for. The day all his scheming, all his bribery, all his blackmailing paid off.

The council waited for him, comfortably resting on their stools, a few stretching aching legs out.

"Welcome, High Priest Erenemo," said Okepeli. The elderly man sat at his honored place at the head of the semi-circle of stools. His hands rested, one over the other, on top of his walking cane. He watched Erenemo with the same disapproving stare the priest remembered from his younger days. "We have brought you here because we have come to a decision."

"A long, fraught, torturous decision," Oshala muttered under her breath.

Okepeli ignored the comment and continued. "In light of Nsongo's current state, we have decided to name you the dara of the city, making you Great Dara of the Bangi Shore."

Erenemo couldn't help the smile on his face. "Thank you," he said bowing reverently. "I swear I will live up to the confidence you've placed in me."

"It is only temporary," Palia added hastily. Erenemo stopped himself from giving the younger woman a scowl. "Just until the choice from Ashaki's list of abodaras can be trained up."

The high priest nodded understandingly. "Of course. I will be sure to assist with that process as well."

"Congratulations, Priest Erenemo," the merchant councilman, Abemisi, said, face grim. "May the ancestors watch over us all."

Erenemo let the slight roll off him and bowed to the room. "I am sure they will."

Okepeli nodded his dismissal and the priest left the chamber feeling lighter on his feet than he'd felt in years. Nsongo was finally his. There was no more languishing in his brother's shadow. No more being shoved aside for being a mere priest. No longer would he be his father's *other* son. He was Great Dara and he alone would lead Nsongo back to its former glory.

"Patya," he called out when he returned home. "Patya, we have to celebrate."

There was no answer. He thought she might have gone out until he heard low rustlings coming from the hall that led to his office. Then there was a crash. Erenemo rushed down the hall, stopping in the doorway as his wife threw a clay statuette to the floor.

She looked up, eyes red and filled with angry tears. Around her, his office was in disarray. Books and scrolls were off their shelves and tossed about the floor. Other pieces of his collected art were smashed and lay in shards.

"You wretch," she snarled at him. "You absolute worm."

Erenemo struggled for a response. "My dear, what has gotten into you?"

"My dear?" She laughed bitterly. "How could you do this to me? And with your own acolyte?"

He stiffened for a moment. Erenemo smiled lovingly and came in the room. "Patya, what are you talking about?"

She picked up one of the thicker scrolls, launching it at his head. He ducked just in time. "You! You're fucking your acolyte. All this time you lectured Ofemu about Barabi and you've been doing the same."

His smile wavered then dropped as he decided to abandon the facade of innocence. "Did Ofemu tell you?"

"Oh, ancestors near and far, my son knew?" Her voice cracked at the last word. She gave a laugh again. It was a sound of disbelief and hopelessness. A part of Erenemo was pained but he ignored it to let her finish. "No, my *dear husband*. Ofemu didn't tell me."

Patya walked to his desk, her shoulders shaking. "I was coming in to help tidy up your office. I was even going to leave you a snack for when you returned. I'm so glad that I looked before I wiped away the evidence of your goings on. There are only two people you spend that much time with and I know it wasn't me that you had bent over the desk." She pointed to the edge of the desk where, in the fine layer of dust, were two sets of handprints. One was obviously his thick fingers, wrapped around the edge. The others were Unyemi's long scholar's digits.

Erenemo sighed. There was no use denying it. "Yes, Patya, I've been sleeping with Unyemi."

She rounded on him, throwing the first thing she grabbed off his desk. A book, which he barely dodged.

"How could you embarrass me like this?" she shouted.

"Keep your voice down," he hissed.

"I always knew that you'd take a lover, but your acolyte? Your chosen acolyte? You couldn't have plunged your spear in *anyone* else? He's not even warrior class. Aren't his people artisans?" She came close enough to swing to hit him in the chest. "I welcomed that man into my house and you've been disgracing yourself with him."

She tried to hit him repeatedly, but Erenemo caught her wrists. He frowned as she struggled against him.

"Calm down," he snapped. "What does it matter that I'm fucking Unyemi? Patya, I've been elected Great Dara."

"I don't care, Erenemo," she said, still trying to fight him. "You've shamed our house with your selfishness."

Her words pricked him, bleeding old wounds. "My house," he ground out. She stopped struggling, some of her anger tempered with she saw his face. Erenemo jerked her closer. "This is *my* house. *My* family. *My* lineage. I decide what shames us because not only am I your husband but I am your Great Dara now."

Patya managed to wrench an arm away from him. "Then perhaps I shouldn't be a part of this house until you've come to your senses."

"Perhaps that would be for the best." He let her go and stepped out of the doorway.

Patya stared at him, blinking, mouth open. He watched her face process several emotions before settling on anger. Erenemo didn't try to stop her as she stormed from the room. He didn't even turn as she left. Her angry footfalls grew more distant and he pinched his brow, frustrated. A part of him hurt, but that was quickly devoured by anger and frustration. He picked up the last intact statuette in his office, throwing it against the wall.

~

It was late when the knock came. Ofemu pulled himself awake, wondering what that sound was. He sat up, glancing at Barabi who slumbered peacefully beside him. The man didn't even move. Ofemu smiled. His love had always been a deep sleeper.

The sharp, rapid knocking came again. "Commander Ofemu." He suddenly realized that was a servant's voice. "Commander Ofemu, you have a visitor."

"It's the dead of the night," he hissed, trying not to wake Barabi.

"It's Councilmember Abemisi," the servant responded. "He says it's important."

Ofemu growled, sliding out of bed and into his clothes. He threw open the door, the servant flinching at his expression. "Take me to him."

With a quick bow, the smaller man led Ofemu through the halls to the room where the councilman was waiting. Ofemu tried to erase the annoyance from his face but felt he'd only done so much. Abemisi rocked back and forth on his feet, his clothes slightly disheveled. He gave the warrior a sad smile when he entered.

"Councilmember Abemisi," Ofemu said. "What brings you to my home *so* late at night?" When he was near the man, he paused, crinkling his nose. "You've been drinking."

"Yes, I've been drinking," Abemisi replied. "You will be too after I've said my peace." He sighed. "I have to apologize to you, Ofemu. Your father was elected temporary dara this morning."

The commander took a step back as if he'd just been struck in the chest. "That can't be. I thought we had an agreement."

"We tried." The old salt monger leaned against a wall. His words weren't slurred but there was a weary spirit about him. "We fought hard for you. We truly did but the others were swayed to your father. Some more than others. You father works quickly."

Ofemu sucked in a breath. "He bribed the other members."

"Not all of them. Oshala looked like she'd swallow her tongue when people started voting for your father. Okepeli tried to speak against it but several wouldn't be swayed. Iysha especially. Take that as you will." He licked dry lips and pushed from the wall. "But I had to let you know first. If feel like I've betrayed you, betrayed all Nsongo."

Ofemu put a hand gently on his elder's shoulder. "You haven't betrayed anyone. This is only temporary. What could you have done against such underhanded dealings." He turned his attention to the hallway. "Emi," he called and the servant immediately entered. "Escort Councilmember Abemisi out. Make sure he gets home safely."

"Yes, commander."

Ofemu waited until the man was well outside before running a hand over his face. This was the worst possible outcome. His father just couldn't be great dara. He was just a priest. Nsongo needed a warrior. Did he plan to lead the troops out to the field in the next war? He was too soft from decades of sitting and singing. Ofemu didn't think he'd ever seen his father pick up a weapon his entire life. Moreover, he was far too old. They'd have to choose another dara in just a decade.

If there was anyone left who could live up to his uncle's legacy, it was him. His cousins were gone, Ashaki included. Their children were barely of age and those who were, weren't warriors. It was him alone who could grab the reins of rulership. He didn't care if people thought he wasn't fit. No one who'd become fourth in line for War Minister was a fool and he would make sure people realized it. Grumbling to himself, he walked out of the room.

"What are we going to do about this?"

Ofemu jumped, hand over his heart. "Gods, Barabi, you scared me."

Barabi leaned against the wall, giving a sheepish smile. "I'm sorry, my love. I woke up and reached out for you. When I realized you weren't there, I followed the voices I heard." He sighed. "So, your father's the Great Dara. Gods preserve us."

Ofemu looked around, searching for wandering servants. While his servants should be asleep at this hour, he didn't know who may still be up and this was the family compound. Who knew if any of them would run and tell his father anything they've heard. He put a hand to Barabi's back, ushering him back to his bedroom. He only broke the silence when he'd firmly closed the door.

"We can only talk in here about this," Ofemu said. Barabi

nodded his understanding. Ofemu pinched the bridge of his nose, exhaling in frustration. "This is the worst possible outcome. My father bribed those council members. I know it. I could never imagine him sinking so low. He knew there was no case for his ascension so he resorts to bribery. I can't believe this."

Barabi put a hand on his chest, looking up into his eyes. Ofemu took a breath so he could actually listen to the man who had his heart and his ear.

"This is not the worst outcome. This is only the outcome at the moment. Abemisi said your father was temporary dara. So, we have time. We'll have to make sure that he stays only temporary."

Ofemu nodded, anger and frustration fading. "You're right. I have work to do."

"What work?" Barabi said, looking at him with his strategist face.

That was a cue for Ofemu to start planning. What would he do without this man? He rested his hand on his chin, thinking.

"My father is just as bitter as the rest of us about the defeat so I'm sure he'll want to rectify that somehow. He'll need to do something grand to prove that a priest is worthy to continue being Great Dara."

"So what will you do?"

"I'll have to be patient." He took another breath. Patience was still a struggle for him. "Wait until my father shows his hand. Then I'll sabotage every plan he makes in a way that shows I'm the right candidate for dara."

Barabi looped his arms around Ofemu's waist. "And I'll be there to help, commander."

He smiled, resting his arms over Barabi's shoulders. "You're so wise. Why don't you become Great Dara."

"I'd sooner kill myself," Barabi chuckled and led him back to bed.

~

It was raining in the forest. Again. Hotemkhar stretched swollen, wet toes, and willed the feeling back into them. The cape he'd managed to make out of an old tunic did little to keep out the damp. The trees were damp. The ground was damp. The very air was damp. The only relief was that the frequent showers kept the insects at bay for a time.

Hotemkhar pulled his cape over his head and stared about, miserably, at the rest of the camp. Men gathered around campfires that had just been doused. Curses floated between raindrops. Tonight's dinner would be more rations. He gave a smug smile. At least if he was suffering, they were suffering too. Soldiers hunkered down under their own cloaks. Theirs were oil slicked; his was not. Some attended to comrades who'd grown sick from the rain. Some had contracted some new sickness.

How had his life come to this? He'd always been loyal to the empire. As a child he excelled at his studies and been dutiful to his father. Most of the time. He'd paid his due taxes and gave the appropriate offerings at temple. He'd even married that shrew of a woman his mother had chosen for him and fathered three children from her. Honestly, it was a miracle that he performed the act without putting a bag over her head. He'd done everything he was supposed to in this life but now he found himself here.

Hotemkhar tried to find drier ground under a tree, looking out over the soldiers again. He would give anything to get back to civilization. He'd pay any price. To be back in a warm dry home. He'd even take getting back to his unfortunately faced wife and their children. He looked over the soldiers again. These men were obviously from common families, the army being their best bet at some glory in this life. Surely, they needed gold. They must want to get out of this gods forsaken forest as much as he did. He bit his lip weighing the decision of bribing a soldier to desert their post.

Everyone had their price.

Hotemkhar got up, walking nonchalantly to the nearest gathering of soldiers, and stooping down just outside of it. The men were talking about the rumors of the emperor's decree, those from the capital spreading the news to those that were stationed down here. There were looks of concern and one man outright saying he wouldn't follow it. The netkoleh, or the emperor, or whatever he was calling himself, couldn't stop what he did in his home.

The conversation stopped completely when one of the soldiers finally noticed Hotemkhar. The group one by one turned to scowl at him. The disgraced magistrate sat up as upright as he could underneath his soaked cape. "Good evening," he said, testing their willingness to speak with him. "I was troubled by the decree as well. I only found out very recently."

The group shared glances before one of their number spoke up. "And what did you think of it, magistrate?" His title was added almost as an afterthought.

Hotemkhar shrugged. "I'm not sure what to think. Abandoning the gods is an act that I can hardly fathom. What do you do when the man who is supposed to be the voice of the gods tells you that there are no gods?" He rubbed his cold hands, thinking of ways to endear himself to them. "But you're right. The emperor cannot control what goes on in your homes. And as magistrate, I will guarantee that your personal practices will be overlooked."

"And if you die out here in the jungle?" asked a soldier with a gruff voice.

Hotemkhar sucked in a breath. The thought hadn't crossed his mind. He quickly shut it out. "I know that you soldiers are more than capable of keeping that from happening."

There was a grumbling from the men and Hotemkhar was worried that he'd only succeeded in alienating them.

"So, what did you do to get sent out here?" Asked another man, a younger one.

"Besides being annoying," added the gruff voiced soldier. That got a number of chuckles.

Hotemkhar lifted his chin defiantly. He wouldn't let these common brutes turn him into a source of laughter.

"Your general was hesitant to invade the forest and deal with the tiny, backwards jungle people. I suppose he was too afraid of the tales of monsters to send you all here."

"But the monsters are real," another soldier said quietly. All eyes turned to him. "I saw the heads the fishermen pulled from the river. There's no way those crocodiles could have done that.

Their heads were cut off too cleanly. That was done in one cut by a blade. I've never seen anything like it."

The men were quiet and Hotemkhar cursed inwardly. They'd probably all heard about the severed heads. And everyone knew about the squad that never returned save for one babbling idiot.

"But we've seen no monsters. No terrors by night or day. Only rain and bugs and misery. I wanted to send the army to tend to the jungle people and take the gold mines for the empire. But I see that it was a bad choice." He gestured over to another group where a sick man was being tended to. "This is no way for the proud soldiers of the empire to die."

His group of soldiers looked to the sick man, sweating and writhing in his fever. One looked down glumly then turned a poisoned stare to Hotemkhar. "But this is where we are and until we receive orders to turn around, this is where we'll be." He turned his back on the magistrate and the rest of the group followed suit.

Hotemkhar swallowed, suddenly breathing hard. "I . . . I have money," he said quietly and regretted it. The desperation in his voice made him sound weak. "Get me back to civilization and you'll be richer than all your days in the military."

The gruff voiced soldier stood; fists balled threateningly. "Now you want to bribe us." All around, other soldiers looked up, watching the ruckus. "Get back to your corner, you miserable little bureaucrat."

Hotemkhar quickly left the group, retreating to the tree he'd been sitting next to. The soldiers watched him until it seemed they were sure he'd be no more trouble. He angrily flicked a stick looking bug off his clothes and settled down.

The sick man he'd gestured to earlier, started screaming. He looked out to the jungle past the soldiers, pointing and rambling. "I see them," he screamed. "They're waiting for us. I see them!" His nearby soldiers tried to calm him down but it was no use.

Hotemkhar pulled his cape closer around him, trying to shut out the screaming and the sense of doom closing in. He would not die out here. He would make it back home with his head held high. Another scream broke his concentration. No, he would not die here. By Koleh, he swore it.

Chapter Nineteen

The gates of Djelebe opened and Bakari had never been so happy to see the damned city. After a week of travel, he was eager to stay in proper lodgings. This wasn't like the Pilgrimage, where he'd stopped at every major settlement to assess them. They'd worked to make the trip to Wiluru as short as possible and now the entire army was surely ready for a good rest.

The people lining the streets for his arrival seemed thinner than before, like they'd been roused at the last moment to attend the event. The cheers were halfhearted; he could feel it. It was nothing like the sendoff he received in the capital. He'd have to have a word with Governor Mgobe about that.

The governor and his ugly family were waiting for him again at the end of the main street. Bakari dismounted, walking up to him to get the customary greetings out of the way. The other man bowed, followed by his family and the other officials of the city.

"Greetings most esteemed emperor," Mgobe said. "We welcome you once again to the scholarly city of Djelebe. We hope your stay is a pleasant one."

"I'm on my way to make war, Mgobe," Bakari said with a snarl. "Nothing will be pleasant until I drag my bitch wife back to the capital." The shorter man stumbled in response, raising his ire. "Just lead me to where I'll be staying and we can speak further in the morning. You do remember what we discussed before, correct?" He eyed the governor sharply.

Mgobe swallowed, the bulge in his throat bobbing. "I remember, my emperor."

"Good." Bakari turned his horse over to the grooms and followed Mgobe's servants to the governor's palace. He grimaced again when he saw it. He hated staying at this hovel of a palace, but it was better than a night in his tent again. So he would endure. At least until morning.

Bakari's night was the best night's sleep he'd gotten in

weeks. He had wonderful dreams of Wiluru burning and Izriamat screaming as he dragged her over the rubble by her hair. He stripped her naked in front of her family and the entire army then beat her until his anger cooled.

He awoke the next morning with a smile on his face, eager to be on his way. After breakfast he had the servants fetch Mgobe so that he could collect his new military magicians and be on his way. The governor came in the room in that meek manor Bakari couldn't stand. He bowed, balding head almost the level of his knees.

"Yes, my emperor?"

Bakari didn't offer him a seat. "Have you gathered the magicians I asked of you? How many are there?" he asked, popping the last of this morning's bread in his mouth.

Mgobe hesitated, a sign the emperor didn't like either. "I have counted the most learned magicians in the city and they amount to six hundred. But—."

"But what?" Bakari snapped.

The man flinched. "But they aren't battle ready, my emperor. We are scholars."

Bakari glared at the short, balding, insolent man with all the disdain he could muster. "I told you to have them ready by the time I come back, Mgobe." He growled out the man's name.

"It was barely three months, my emperor. It takes years to fully train a warrior."

"You already know the magics. That's half of the training already."

"We just don't have them, my emperor."

There was a certain finality in his tone that made Bakari pause. Was this weasel trying to tell him what he could and couldn't have?

"And what of the great library?"

Mgobe hesitated but didn't flinch. "What of it, my emperor?"

"Have you destroyed the religious texts?"

The governor took a breath before straightening his back. "No."

"What did you say?" Bakari said after a moment.

"No, we have not destroyed anything. The library contains

the history of this land, its culminated knowledge. We can't destroy that. It would be a . . . an abomination."

Before he knew it, he'd struck the man. Bakari towered over him, breathing hard. Mgobe cowered on the floor trying to scramble away from another blow. The emperor reached down, picking Mgobe up by the front of his tunic.

"You wish to disobey my orders? You wish to disobey your emperor?"

Mgobe's eyes were wide with fear but his voice remained steady.

"There are some things that are even wrong for the emperor to do."

Enraged, Bakari dragged the man out of the room, down the hallway past terrified servants, and out into the streets. People watched him in horror, even his soldiers, as he pulled the city's governor behind him. Mgobe struggled to get free but Bakari's grip was iron.

He didn't let him go until they reached the square in front of the library. He threw him down for just a moment, flexing his hand before grabbing the governor by the throat with the other hand. He jerked the man to his feet, choking him just enough to make it difficult to breath. Around them, people came out of buildings to watch, even some scholars.

"Will you still not destroy the evidence of these nonexistent gods?"

Mgobe struggled in his grip, hands trying to pry Bakari's away. Finally, he relaxed, hands dropping to his sides.

"No, I will not."

Bakari threw him down in anger, taking a few breaths to get himself back in control. He looked up at the towering library, a testament to keeping knowledge of the gods alive. He motioned to a group of soldiers standing nearby. Their leader jogged over immediately.

"Yes, my emperor."

Bakari let his anger settle into a low fire. "Burn it all down."

~

It was storming outside the Metkaran palace and servants

scrambled to keep water from coming in from the wind whipped rain. Arkole sat with her girls snuggled around her, telling them a story. The youngest sat closest to her side, a hand protectively on her mother's stomach, hoping to feel her little brother kick. The others stayed close, too old to admit that the wind and thunder frightened them just as much as the littlest one.

Today's tale was of an ancient warrior, Sek'netep. No one knew where he came from, they just say that he walked out from the grasslands. He slew dragons and many other great beasts, keeping people safe. He wooed a king's daughter and that son, even though he was a bastard, would go on to become the first king of the Ega.

"So Sek'netep was our ancestor?" asked the second youngest.

"These are just stories," Arkole chuckled. "I doubt he was even a real person."

"Tell another one," demanded the youngest.

Arkole gladly obliged. Her girls hung on to her every word and she wished that Bakari was here to enjoy this quiet moment. When he returned, she would have to ask him if he'd spend more time around the girls. She frowned. If he would do it.

As she finished the story and the girls began to entertain themselves, her mind wandered back to one of their last conversations. He'd been so cold to her, so cruel. She remembered his eyes ablaze with anger, anger directed at her. Never in all their days together had Bakari directed his rage in her direction.

It was all that woman Nitiri's fault. She'd entranced Bakari away. No, it was all Izriamat's fault. If she hadn't run away to Wiluru and returned to her duty, none of this would have happened. Yet.... The way Bakari had always looked at her, studying her features, spending so many nights with her and not his first love. She'd rather have that than this new creature trying to hold the emperor's favor hostage. Arkole swore she'd see that Niriti thrown back among the lesser wives.

A wave of fatigue washed over her.

"Girls," she called, "Mother is going back to her rooms. I'm afraid I've gotten a bit tired." The girls complained and whined but she shooed them off to their nannies. She kissed each one of them on the forehead and at another wave of tiredness, she left as quickly as she could.

Her attendants fell into step behind her, but one of them moved a bit closer.

"Are you alright, empress?" She asked lowly. "Should I fetch a physician?"

"No, no, I just need a little rest," she answered. Then a tightness grabbed her abdomen. She slowed, hand to the underside of her belly. It was an uncomfortable sensation, but one she was used to feeling this late in a pregnancy.

They continued walking, making it just outside of her suite. The uncomfortable tightness grew until it slowed her steps to a creep. Wetness slicked her thighs and fell on the floor. Arkole looked at the puddle in disbelief. It wasn't possible.

"It's too early," she breathed. "It's too early."

"My empress?" asked an attendant.

A contraction grabbed her—far too strong, far too early— forcing her to grip the wall to keep herself upright.

"Get," she grunted, "the midwife."

One of the servants ran off immediately. Arkole groaned as another contraction began. This wasn't right. This wasn't right. It wasn't time yet. Tears began to form in her eyes.

"My empress," gasped another voice.

Arkole looked up to see the last person she wanted at this moment. Niriti handed her boy off to her attendant and rushed to her side.

"Not you," Arkole groaned.

Niriti supported her arm, ordering the other attendant to support her other arm. Arkole had no choice but to let them lead her to her rooms.

"Empress, be strong," the younger woman said, guiding her to one of the plush lounges.

"It's too early," Arkole said. "He shouldn't be here yet." Her words were choked by another too strong, too quick contraction. Niriti sucked in a breath, nodding once before calling out orders to the servants.

"I feel him. Where is the midwife," she hissed.

"There may not be time to wait for the midwife," Niriti said solemnly. "There have been children born early that have made it to become fine men. Don't fear. You can do this."

Arkole screamed as the latest contraction ripped through her. This was worse than any of her other births. Something was very wrong. She didn't care what encouragement that woman was giving her. Something was wrong with her son.

Servants rushed over with cloth, water, and other items. Arkole didn't know how much time passed. She felt as if she was being ripped apart, as if her body had forgotten how to do this. Niriti pushed up her skirt and helped her sit on the edge of the lounge. The change in position made Arkole gasp as she felt her child slip down.

"He's coming," she shouted.

Niriti knelt, face one of concentration. "Push, empress," she said firmly. Arkole did but felt no difference. She opened an eye and saw the younger woman frown.

"Something's wrong," she cried.

"No, he just needs a little help. Push again when your body constricts."

She did so and felt a slight tug and twist, then her son fled her body. Arkole wanted to collapse, but a servant was behind her to support. "Is… is it a boy?" She panted.

Niriti cradled her son in her arms, blood and fluid ruining her gown. "It is a boy. Beautiful and broad shouldered like his father."

Jealousy tried to come forth but she didn't have the energy for it.

"Let me hold him." Niriti passed the infant to her and suddenly all her worries about her place in the palace and in Bakari's heart faded. She'd birthed him a son. At long last, the empire had a true heir again.

"Congratulations, empress," Niriti said, bowing her head, "on the birth of the new Great Royal Son. If you need anything, anything at all, from me please ask. I only want to make our husband happy and I know that if you're happy, he'll be happy."

Arkole considered this young woman as she hugged her son. Was she really this devoted?

"Thank you for helping me. Bakari should have been here."

As she started to cry, Niriti put a hand on her knee. "Our

husband is off bringing glory to the empire. Until he returns, all we have is each other and our children." Arkole nodded and held her crying son tighter.

Chapter Twenty

The encampment around Ofolubaru was going well. Efah helped an old woman down to a cushion set out by her daughter and gave her a small bowl of water to drink. She quickly moved on to the next place that she could be of service. Not everyone had been sure of the move when she presented it to all Garemba a week ago, but her old followers talked to the new and soon they agreed. She couldn't blame their hesitation. Who would think to return so quickly to the city they'd just fled? But, as she looked around at the throngs of people gathered, it was clear that she had made the right choice. They couldn't stay in Garmeba and thrive.

Newa came up to her, giving her a shallow bow. "My lady, were you ready to speak with the dara?"

She looked to the high walls of the city and as if responding to her uncertainty, Nesi and Usa jogged up to her sides. She smiled, running hands through their fur.

"I'm ready. Let us hope we get a better reception than our last times."

Newa gathered most of his students, leaving the remainder to defend the populace. They immediately spread out across the green field outside the city, finding a spot to stand watch. Those that were coming along for the trip fell in behind him. Efah climbed onto Nesi's back, giving Newa a small smile. She managed to get a small one in return before his face slid into seriousness.

They came up to the city gates, the guards watching them cautiously as they approached. Garemba's arrival had apparently caused quite the uproar. Merchants on the road fled to the city and hadn't been seen coming out since. More of the city's protectors viewed them from the walls. It was clear that they weren't sure if this was an attack or not.

"Move aside," Efah said calmly. The gate guards

immediately moved to the side, giving them a wide berth. There were advantages to having two giant hyenas under your command.

Efah glanced around the city as she made her way to the palace, Newa leading her. It was hard to believe that it had been only a few months since she'd first come to Ofolubaru. The people that had called her a madwoman and ridiculed her now rushed inside, watching her with fear in their eyes. She frowned, pensive. If the dara had been more evenly fair to her people, she wouldn't be here.

The sun was high in the sky when they reached the golden roofed palace. Efah wrinkled her nose at it. The dara lived with such riches while the people who fled to Garemba had been destitute. The way here had taken them through wealthy neighborhoods, with people who'd obviously never known want in their life. It was disgusting.

As they arrived at the front gates, she noticed the vultures gathering on various perches around the palace. A flock sat on the wall on either side of the gate, staring at the guards. When Efah came up to it, they moved out of the way without a word, their eyes flicking between the hyenas bigger than an ox and the vultures who watched their every move. Efah stopped Nesi and looked down to them.

"Go," she said. "Dedicate your life to the gods and not to a dara who ignores the pain of her people." They fled their posts. As she looked up towards the doorway, she saw Death standing to the side as if he waited to usher them in. He caught her gaze and nodded. It was all the encouragement Efah needed.

The only resistance she experienced was the guards outside the dara's chamber. Efah looked down to him with disdain.

"Tell your dara that the Lady of Death is here to speak with her."

"I'll see if—."

"I didn't ask if she'll see me. Tell her and then I'm entering."

Usa growled lowly and the guard opened the door behind him, shouldering it so it opened wide enough for them to enter.

"My dara," he said hastily coming forward. "The Lady of Death wishes for an audience with you."

Dara Ngoli scowled at her from her throne. They'd obviously interrupted someone else's petition because a couple stared back from before the throne, a mix of confusion and fear. Ngoli waved them off and the scurried to the side.

"Lady of Death," the dara said lazily, "you barge into my city again. What is it that you want?"

Efah felt a great anger rise in her, different and more potent than any she'd felt before.

"Dara Ngoli, we have come with the people of Garemba to ask for your generosity. Garemba can't hold the people who've run from your cruelty so we need a new place that can sustain us." She watched the dara's face carefully. So far it was set in hate. "Give us a quarter in Ofolubaru that we may call home and prosper in."

To her surprise, the dara laughed. "You expect me to just surrender part of my city just because you say so? I won't be commanded by a gaggle of paupers."

"You need to take this seriously, dara Ngoli. You think you're still safe with all your special guards, but I fought my way out of here, Newa fought his way out alone, and your forces were defeated by the people of Garemba when you tried to invade us." She narrowed her eyes at the woman. "Do you really want to have another loss?"

Ngoli shifted in her seat, eyes flicking over the hyenas and over Newa and the other armed people behind them. She pursed her lips then cleared her throat.

"Lady of Death, allow me to think on your proposal. You all are welcome to stay in the city while I deliberate."

"You will give an answer now." Efah's voice echoed around the chamber. The light from the room's high windows was dimmed by the vultures beginning to perch in them. Efah stared at the dara, the anger she felt earlier finding purpose and the subject to be released on. She could see this woman's cruel heart and all she had done in her lifetime. It was filthy. This woman was soiled to the core of her. She had no better nature to appeal to.

"No," Efah continued, "I don't need an answer. I see you for the selfish, violent, cruel creature that you are. You must leave from your position and this place and you must do it now."

Before she knew it, she was on her own feet and walking toward the dara. Around her, the dara's guards jumped into action but were held off by Newa and his students. She rushed up to the dara, placing a hand on her chest. Power flowed through her and into the woman, clutching onto her very soul.

"You are a poison to this city," she said in a voice she barely recognized. "You are a poison to this land and its people. You must go!"

Efah pressed her fingers harder against the dara's chest, holding the other woman's soul tighter with her power. She could feel it as if her hand was touching it. So fragile, so easily broken. She could snap it in two if she wanted to. Efah took in the hollow, frightened look in the woman's eyes. But she would leave her with this experience.

She released her soul, the dara slumping into her chair. Efah took a step back from her.

"Leave," she shouted and the woman fled the room. She turned her enraged gaze to the remaining guards and they dropped their weapons, running to the hallway.

Pleased, the anger left her. Efah stumbled, nearly falling but quick hands kept her upright. She felt the familiar fur of one of her hyenas on the left and Newa's grip on her right. She looked up to him with a smile.

"Bring the people to the palace, Newa," she said, suddenly exhausted. "They will live like they've never lived before. And we'll have a feast to honor the gods."

Newa chuckled and smiled back at her. "As you say, my lady."

~

Something was different today. Newa could feel it in the wind, almost taste it in the air. It had stirred him from his sleep, driving him to head west until he ended up climbing the stairs to the top of the wall. The guards that still watched Olofubaru's border gave him space, finding other, more pressing things to do. Newa looked out at the horizon, slowly growing warm as the sun rose behind him.

The tugging had been plaguing him for days. Nearly since they'd arrived in the city. This constant feeling that he should be elsewhere, that he was needed elsewhere. Every day it grew stronger until he realized what it was at last. It was time for him to leave.

The thought pained him. He didn't want to leave this place, these people he'd come to think of as his. It wasn't that he thought that they couldn't survive without him. He was quite sure they could. He wanted to be present for their every triumph. He wanted to be there to see her triumph.

The pain turned sharp as his mind turned to Efah. He'd miss her like he'd missed nothing but his order. Her smile. Her laugh. How was he supposed to survive without this newfound joy?

"There you are!"

He jumped at the sound of her voice. He turned to see Efah coming up the stairs, grinning widely. He tried to return the smile but he felt it came weakly.

"Good morning," he said, struggling to sound cheerful.

She came up to him still grinning until she looked into his eyes. "Something's wrong."

"No, nothing's wrong." Even though it was to him.

"Please don't lie to me, even to save my feelings."

The look she gave him, trusting and pleading, tore at his heart. Newa sighed heavily.

"I . . . I must leave."

She didn't say anything at first and he thought she was going to cry. Instead, she turned to stare out at the horizon. "I knew this was going to happen one day. I just didn't know it was going to be so soon."

"I should have said something." He turned to the horizon as well, too afraid that she would look him in the eyes.

Efah shook her head. "It's fine. I'm not upset with you." He heard her breath in deeply. "I know your god calls you. Death told me as much." Her hand gently touched his arm and he dared look down at her. Tears were starting to gather at the corners of her eyes. "Just promise me that you'll be back."

Newa dropped to one knee, lowering his head, and bringing the back of her hand to his forehead.

"I swear, I will return. Only death will stop me."

Over his head, she heard him give a sad chuckle. "Somehow, I don't think that will be a problem."

He looked up. She was smiling through her tears, highlighted by the rising sun. She looked like a goddess in her own right. He couldn't help but return her smile. It was infectious. He stood, still holding her hand.

"Then speak with Death on my behalf. Tell him not to visit me on this journey."

"I will."

She rushed in, wrapping her arms around him, knocking a little bit of the air out of him. His eyes stung as tears began to blur his vision. He couldn't remember the last time someone had hugged him. The most affection his memory could conjure up was a pat on the shoulder from his master. Newa slowly raised his arms, putting them around Efah. She smelled of palace soaps over her natural scent. Her afro brushed his chin and he buried his head in it, sorry that he was getting tears in her hair. Sorry that he was leaving her at all.

"I promise I'll come back," he whispered.

Efah turned her head against his chest, looking back at the horizon. She took a shuddering breath before speaking.

"When do you leave?"

Newa searched the nagging feeling. It was urgent. "Today," he said, going with it. "I have to leave today."

She hid her face in his chest again. "Then we need to get your prepared."

They stayed in their embrace for a few more moments before Efah pulled away from him, heading to the stairs. Newa followed, almost in a daze. They made their way back to the palace where he said goodbye to his students who were aghast at his departure. They stopped all protest when he explained that he was sent by his god. The news quickly spread through the others from Garemba and he spent all morning accepting gifts for his journey.

His pack was full by the time he walked to the gates of Olofubaru. Half of the city was there to see him off, Efah at the head of them. Newa was acutely aware of their presence and didn't want to turn around lest he never leave. These people had accepted him in a way that no one else in his life had. The half wild boy from Metkara's slums was far more used to people being afraid of him. This level of acceptance—he dare not say love—was almost too much.

Efah stepped up beside him. He was forced to acknowledge her at last. She gave him that smile that still held a bit of sadness. She took both of his hands, pressing them together and putting her hands over them.

"May the gods watch over you. May Hassa keep your path clear. May Kitabe keep the sun shining on you. May Longe sooth your weary feet. May Death stay far from your side. And may the ancestors remind them of my prayer." She kissed his hands at the spot where the knuckles of his thumbs pressed and then gave him another crushing hug.

He accepted it gladly, trying to memorize this moment, the touch, the scent, the emotion, so that he could keep it close to his heart. After a moment he let her go. He gave a quick wave to the crowd and set off down the road to the west. He would be back, he told himself. By the blades of Gu'un, he would be back.

~

Tekhamun was enjoying having his first student. Nermet was diligent, eager, and quite strong. The priest caught his balance after blocking a blow from the big man, wondering about the condition of his blade after such an attack. Nermet must outweigh him twice over and he attacked with all the ferocity in his spirit. Tekhamun tried to dodge more blows than he parried as they free spared but it was hard when your opponent seemed to truly want to take your head.

"That's enough," Tekhamun called out after he off balanced Nermet.

The burly man seemed to have to take a moment to come back to himself. "Did I do something wrong, master?"

"You attack with too much anger," he responded, trying to remember the words of his own master. "You must think through your moves. You have to remove your emotions from the fight."

Naret kept the same flat face. "But my anger reminds me of why I fight."

Tekhamun didn't know what to say to that. He cleared his throat, covering his pause. "It will cloud your abilities. You must be able to calmly fight. I know you want revenge but fight like a beast and you will get slaughtered." He nodded sagely, proud of his turn of phrase.

Naret looked to the side, taking in the advice. He mulled it over for a moment, then nodded.

"I'd like to go through the forms again." His eyes flicked about. "Please."

The priest smiled. "Then let us go through them calmly."

The went back to the basic forms used by the Arak'guun. Every now and then he'd glance to Naret who was supposed to be mimicking his moves. The man seemed to be concentrating hard on each move but his motions were stiff. Tekhamun stopped to watch him for a moment. His first followers hadn't had so much trouble, but most of them were already good with a blade. He would have to alter his methods for this large man.

He was about to stop Naret to correct him, when Karatel walked into the room where they worked.

"Master, I need to speak with you," he said, without a bow.

The man addressed him with the slightest bit of authority and Tekhamun wasn't sure he liked it. Or the look lurking in Karatel's eyes.

"I'm in the middle of a training session. Can it wait?"

Karatel flicked his eyes to Naret for a moment. "It's rather important. We really should talk. Now."

He really didn't like his follower's tone now. "Alright," he began cautiously. "Naret, continue with the training. I will return in a moment."

Tekhamun followed Karatel outside to the footpath that ran on the side of the building they were in. The sun cast a harsh shadow in the narrow space, saving them from today's brutal sunshine. He took in the other man's angry posture and shrunk a bit. What was it that he wanted? He asked him so.

"We need to abandon this city," he said curtly.

"What? Why?"

Karatel started to make an exasperated growl but swallowed it. "It was different when we were just fighting and killing rich people or some backwater city guard. They're sending the fucking army after us. We should head to another city. Lay low for a while. Start over."

Tekhamun couldn't believe what he was hearing. Start over? "Have you lost faith in our mission, Karatel?"

"It's not about faith. It's simple —." He stopped himself. "Our mission can just as easily be carried out somewhere the army can't find us. We can't do anything if we're dead."

Tekhamun suddenly thought of the sight of Karatel cradling Pta in his lap, her body sprawled on the ground. He put a hand on his first follower's shoulder.

"I understand that your loss in the last battle was great, but she gave her life in the fight to save this land. We will continue fighting to honor her and all that fell."

The look of fury that came over Karatel's face frightened him a bit.

"I have followed you for months now. We have done things your way but it's time for you to listen to someone who actually knows what they're doing. The army is going to come back and this time they're going to take us seriously. They'll bring real numbers and then we're all going to die if we stay here like a bunch of guinea fowl waiting for the slaughter. We're going to leave." He leaned dangerously close to Tekhamun and the priest realized for the first time he was looking into the face of a true cold-blooded murderer. "And if you won't give the order, I will."

"Who are you to give orders?" Naret's voice rumbled through the footpath.

Both men looked back at the giant of a man blocking the entrance. Karatel frowned deeply.

"This doesn't concern you, big man," he said looking over his shoulder.

"It does if you're threatening the master." Naret took a step closer. "You're not, are you?"

Tekhamun felt the tenseness growing in the air. It prickled

along in the air, raising the hairs on his arms. His stomach flip flopped.

"There's no need to come to my defense, Naret," he said, trying to sound in control. "Everything's finished here."

Karatel turned his angry look back on Tekhamun. "Nothing is done here."

"Back away from the master," Naret said a little louder, warning in his voice.

At this Karatel turned fully to the other man. "Who in the deepest pit of the abyss do you think you are to give me an order? Do you want to follow this man until he gets you killed? Cuz his so-called holy mission will. The army is going to come back one day or another." As Karatel started shouting, people came out from other buildings or poked their heads out windows to see what the commotion was. "If you want to be his fool, be my guest. I have to look out for my best interests and my people's. And if he won't do what's necessary, I will."

Naret stepped up to Karatel, rising to his full height. "You don't get to question him or order him around no matter how long you've been with him. Maybe it's you who need to leave."

Tekhamun reached out to turn Karatel to him. "Karatel, we cannot stray from our mission."

"Gods fuck your mission!" The priest recoiled from him. His first follower looked at him with wild eyes. "Your mission cost me Pta. But you don't know anything about that because you couldn't get a woman to fuck your balding ass if you promised to make her the godsdamned empress. Fuck your mission. Fuck your god. And fuck you!"

Tekhamun's blade slid up under the younger man's rib cage, the tip piercing his heart. The priest felt the strongest pangs of regret as Karatel doubled over, crumpling on him. He heard him try to form words as the shock took him over. Tekhamun stepped back, holding Karatel upright as he slid the blade out. Blood began soaking the front of Karatel's shirt, each pulse pushing the dark stain out farther.

Tekhamun looked Karatel in the eyes, his face a mixture of sadness and anger.

"Gu'un cannot forgive such blasphemy and neither can I. I'm

sorry that you allowed yourself to come to a place where I would have to execute his judgement on you."

Karatel started to collapse, hand at his abdomen, with the confused look men get when they start to realize they're dying. He collapsed to the ground. He took a few more breaths, his blood beginning to stain the ground under him. A few moments later, Tekhamun's first follower lay still in the dirt.

Naret knelt beside him, checking his pulse. He looked up to Tekhamun.

"What shall we do with the body?" he asked, face unmoved.

Tekhamun stared at the dark blood covering his moonblade. His emotions were a tempest, each one rising for just a moment before another took its place.

"Take him to one of the fields outside of the city and leave him. He doesn't deserve a proper funeral pyre."

"Very well, master."

The priest watched Naret drag Karatel's body off, suddenly feeling drained. He looked around at all the faces who watched him, the faces of the people he was to lead in this holy mission from his god. Without a word, he went back inside, firmly closing the door behind him.

Chapter Twenty-One

Erenemo sat in his study, trying to ignore the silence of the house. Patya had been gone for days but the ghost of her presence haunted the halls. He swore he could smell her scent at night and hear her voice as he set out for the day. It infuriated him. He shouldn't be this concerned. If she was going to be this stubborn about his lover then she could stay gone until she came to her senses. He was the dara. He had far more important issues to deal with than the tantrums of his wife.

The murders in the night hadn't stopped. Three more Ega bodies had been found this morning. Two more were found by noon because they'd started to stink in the heat of the sun. Gruesome deaths, each one of them. After the council had elected him dara, he made a point of looking at some of them to try to figure out their cause. Rumors were flying of a killer in the city and panic was starting to spread. At least they were only targeting the soldiers of the empire but he wouldn't have such chaos in his city.

He frowned deeply. And then there was the gold issue. That damned woman Ashaki had put too much trust into the decency of the Ega and the behavior of the foreigners had disrupted the gold trade for at least a decade. The cost of everything had risen. The traders from the other primary cities were making a killing off Nsongo's back. Necessities were becoming hard to purchase. Erenemo rested his head in his hand. He had to admit it—he wasn't sure how much longer Nsongo could survive if things kept going this badly.

A cool, night breeze came in from the open door leading out to the courtyard and he took a moment to enjoy it. Perhaps he could use these killings to his advantage somehow. Perhaps, have more of the invaders put themselves in harm's way and eliminate themselves. It would make declaring war on the Ega that much easier.

Erenemo had just returned to his papers when he felt a chill up his spine, like someone was passing too close to him. He turned and stared into the eyes of a beast from his nightmares. It stood two heads above him with shaggy gray-black fur and a mouth full of sharp fangs. It stood on two legs like a man and its hands ended in claws that looked like they were made of metal. It didn't move except to breathe, staring him down.

Only when the priest shot to his feet to try to get away from this creature did he notice the small man standing in front of it. He swallowed his shout of fear as he looked between the Batu'bangi and the monster hulking over him.

"You are the ruler of Nsongo now?" The short man said, halting at every word.

Erenemo forced himself to try to breath regularly. "Yes," he said, hoarse. "I am the Great Dara."

"Good. I am the Beastmaster of the Batu'bangi. I have been sent to speak to you. You have invaded our forest and you must leave. If not, the killings will spread."

"No, not us," the priest countered, regaining some of his composure. "The Egan soldiers are the ones who've invaded. We warned them not to."

"But you are part of this empire now, are you not?" The man cocked his head and Erenemo could just make out the grays sprinkled throughout his hair. This wasn't a young fool and he had to remember that.

"It is a complicated situation, great Beastmaster. We, ourselves, were invaded. We fought a long war and lost so many warriors that our old dara surrendered." Talking about the surrender rubbed at the old wound and made it sting fresh. He pushed the thoughts of his cowardly niece aside. "For the moment, we have to endure the presence of the Ega."

The small man considered him for a moment, the beast eerily staring Erenemo down with its far too intelligent eyes.

"These people belong on your side of the Bangi. Deal with them or we will deal with you. We have already given you the gift of taking care of the force in the forest."

Erenemo's eyes darted about as he thought. "If we push the Ega from our lands, will you trade with us again?"

"You were told we would decide in ten years. Why would

you ask otherwise?"

"I mean no insult," the priest said, bowing as low as he could while keeping an eye on the beast. "But your goods are very precious to us and I know that your people love the items they receive from us as well. Perhaps, if you speak to your leader, we could revisit our agreement sooner for the benefit of both of our peoples."

A shuddering breath came from the monster that had the undertones of a growl. Erenemo backed against his desk. The beast master gave him a shrewd look.

"Remove the invaders from your city and we will speak again."

Erenemo took a chance and bowed to the man. "A chance to make this right is all we ask, great Beastmaster."

He lifted his head and the duo was gone. Erenemo rushed to the door but there was no sign of them in the courtyard. He slumped against the door frame breathing hard with unspent fear.

He went back to his chair, sitting down hard. If they rid themselves of the Ega, the gold would flow again. Erenemo swallowed hard, coming back to himself. He knew what he needed to do.

~

Erenemo was on his way to the war council when a servant stopped him. He scowled at the woman, eager to be moving on. He hadn't even gotten a chance to make it out of the compound and distractions were hindering him. The servant bowed, apologetic in all her movements.

"High Priest, the general of the Ega wishes to speak with you. The message just arrived."

She passed it over and Erenemo sneered as he saw the shaky scrawl of the south's language. Perhaps it was hard for the northern bastards to adapt to a proper mode of writing. He passed it back to the servant, thanking her, and leaving the family compound.

People bowed as he traveled. If they didn't know him by sight, the stark white of his robes and the purple and black sash at his waist told them exactly who he was. He nodded his head graciously back, inwardly pleased that they would be bowing to him not just as their high priest but as their dara soon enough. He wondered how they'd treat him. Surely there would be questions about his fitness for the role, but he would put them to rest in a short time.

Erenemo stopped at the headquarters for the Egan rule in the city since it was on his way to where he'd called the war council to assemble. It was a shame to see the home of the line of Inama come to this, with foreign squatters in their halls. The guards at the outer gate had the gall to bar his way with their spears. Erenemo looked these northern men up and down, the indignation plain on his face.

"Your general begged to speak with me," he said roughly. "Move out of my way."

The guards glanced to each other, assessing him before they stepped aside. "Take the right hall to the last room on the left. That's his office."

Erenemo didn't give them another word as he moved past. He took in the courtyard, cluttered with soldiers, and crinkled his nose. He thought that he'd been to a celebration here as a young man, before he'd risen to the rank of priest. Now it reeked of the Ega.

He walked into the general's office without a knock on the doorframe, wanting to invade this space as much as the Ega invaded his city. General Tutahmen didn't look up but continued writing in that child's scribble of a language they had. Erenemo glanced over and saw a woman standing, ready to serve. It took him a moment to take in her features before he recognized the lady of the house.

"My lady Olima," he said after composing himself. The woman stiffened at her name but gave him the barest of nods.

"So you know each other," Tutahmen said casually.

Erenemo realized that the man was looking at him now. This man, this foreign general, had a square jaw and hawklike eyes that seemed to take in every detail. There was white speckling the stubble on his chin and lines at the corner of his eyes. Erenemo frowned, his mind on Olima and the humiliations he must put her through. The priest took a quick breath before speaking.

"I received your message. What do you want?"

Tutahmen nodded. "I prefer bluntness. Good. From what I hear, you've been elected Great Dara. I'm glad the council finally came to a decision. With Ashaki dead, I wasn't sure who would be our liaison to your people."

Erenemo's jaw clenched. "The Great Dara is liaison to no one. What do you want?" A handful of statements and he was already tired of this man.

"I'm sure you're aware of the killings in the night. Several of my soldiers swept up, some of them even walking with friends, and slaughtered before anyone even realized it."

"Yes, of course."

"I need you to put an end to it. Find the culprit, execute him or whatever your people do, and report to me that it's done."

The priest stared at him incredulously. "Exactly how do you think I should find such a killer that no one has seen?" Of course no one had seen them. He'd had firsthand experience at how fast those monsters could move.

"We left you all with soldiers. Use them. Or do we have to instruct you how to properly protect a city as well?"

This bastard of the droppings from a baboon's ass. "You may have gotten away with speaking with my niece like this, but—."

"Stop the killings or I'll consider this an act of aggression against the empire and will deal with it as such."

Erenemo pressed his teeth together so hard he thought they might shatter. He slammed his hands down on this foreign maggot's desk. "Who do you think you speak to, foreigner? I am the Great Dara and—."

"And we're through here." Tutahmen turned back to his writings. "Leave or be removed."

The priest almost choked. This arrogant, smug, vile…. Erenemo checked his temper, swallowing his pride enough to think rationally. He turned and nodded to Lady Olima then left the compound.

The Ega had to go. Now. Nsongo, no the entire south, had endured humiliation after humiliation since the war's end. Now, a lowly general thought to speak to the Great Dara of the Golden City like that? Like he was another servant or soldier to be ordered about and he, Erenemo, would be eager to comply. He would see this man bleed for days. He would watch as all the smugness fell from his face and he begged for mercy he wouldn't receive. Erenemo smirked. Perhaps he'd even let Lady Olima deliver the final killing blow. She deserved revenge.

He didn't realize he'd arrived at the building for the war council until he pushed open the door to the room. Several members sat up, surprised at his entrance. Others stared at him, annoyed. His son sat in his appointed spot as fourth in line for war minister.

"Finally," the whelp muttered under his breath.

General Ngali stood up, her face a facade of calm. "Dara Erenemo," she said bowing and the others followed her. "We were afraid you weren't coming to this meeting that you called."

Erenemo came to the head of the table, a place that had sat empty for years, and took his rightful seat.

"We were going to war with the Ega." He was met with the sound of sucking teeth, gasps, and confused noises. "The boar fucked bastards have infested Nsongo long enough. It's time they were ousted."

Silence this time, but he did note a few faces held back their enthusiasm. Ngali steepled her fingers on the table.

"Priest—I'm sorry—Dara Erenemo, I'm sure that many of us would like to get revenge for our defeat at the hands of the Ega."

"Our surrender," said another commander.

Ngali cut her eyes at him. "Another conflict with them, as much as even I'd like it, would bring us even more casualties. So many warriors are gone. I shouldn't even be war minister." She gestured around the table. "So many of us shouldn't be where we are. But this is the situation that we're in. And if we fight against the Ega, they could bring the capital's army back down on us."

A young woman commander that Erenemo didn't recognize cleared her throat. "The capital's army . . . is occupied."

All eyes turned toward her. "Speak," Erenemo commanded.

"One of my lovers comes from a merchant family. From

what he's told me, talk along the trade route is that the netkoleh has declared war on Wiluru. Why, I don't know." She lounged on her stool; one elbow propped on the table. "But he trusts his traders. They bring as much news as they do goods."

Erenemo sat up on his stool. This was the most fortuitous news he'd heard in a long time. He glanced to Ngali who sat with her lips pressed.

"This would be the best time," he said, looking at the other members of the war council who seemed eager. He fixed his eyes on his son. Ofemu stared at him, trying his best to look indifferent, but he could tell his son was ready for revenge.

Ngali sighed, heavily. "Then is this your decree, Great Dara? That we go to war with the Ega again?"

"This is my decree. Nsongo is at war and we will not stop until the last warrior has fallen." He looked about the table, pleased that the majority were nodding their approval.

~

Another miserable night. Hotemkhar sat alone, as usual, in his own spot away from the rest of the soldiers. He tried to warm his hands and feet by the pathetic fire he'd managed to make but it wasn't doing much. It was unnaturally cold tonight. At least by the standards of this godsdamned jungle. A fine mist had risen by the time the sun set, causing a man to see things out of the corners of his eyes. An unease settled on the force as they set camp and Hotemkhar wasn't immune to it.

He chewed on his tough rations trying to keep the thought of death away. He tried to focus on all the amenities he'd enjoy when they returned triumphantly from this mission. He would take the longest bath and indulge in the pleasures of a dozen women. All his meals for weeks would be lavish although, at this point, even the simplest meal would be extravagant for him. And what he would give for a bath. These ruffians didn't even have the decency to pack his perfumes for him. He was forced to squat over a ditch to relieve himself, use salvaged rags or leaves to clean. Most of the few changes of clothes he had were dirty and he'd only gotten to rinse some of them out in a small creek they'd found. He was covered in insect bites. His nails were filthy. Surely he must look like the most wretched creature in the world.

Hotemkhar shook his head, trying to dispel the thoughts. He was stronger than this. He couldn't let these conditions break him. It was just what that damned general wanted. His face contorted in anger as he thought of Tutahmen. When he returned, he would have that man stripped of his rank and thrown in a cell for the kidnapping of an officer of the empire. He would be lucky if he didn't hang for this. In fact, he would have him dragged back to the capital to be punished. That man would learn his place. He swore it.

A man screamed in pain at a nearby campfire. At this point no one flinched. The sound had become so commonplace that no one was surprised. They'd buried three men who died from this mysterious sickness in the past few days. Only one had recovered but he was in no shape to fight for anyone.

Hotemkhar closed his eyes, praying to not get this disease. He would not die here. He would *not* die dirty and hungry in some southern jungle.

Another man joined in the screaming at another campfire. He was joined by a third then a fourth. Soldiers started moving, trying to calm down their brothers in arms. When two more started screaming, Hotemkhar covered his ears. He repeated his mantra against dying here until he realized the screaming had stopped.

He took his hands down hesitantly, looking about the encampment. Soldiers looked about, confused at the sudden silence. Some started shaking the ill men and by the desperation, Hotemkhar realized that they were dead.

Then he saw a shape move through the mist.

Just behind the farthest campfire he could see, a large shadow moved and then a soldier disappeared. Out of the corner of an eye, another man was pulled off into the darkness. A few soldiers jumped up when they realized one of their number was suddenly gone. The call that they were under attack went up as soldiers went for weapons.

Then the battle began in earnest and Hotemkhar was frozen with terror. All around him, giant creatures began running through the camp, pouncing on men before tearing them apart or dragging them off into the forest. He watched as a soldier at the campfire directly in front of him was bitten in the side. The creature held the man overhead and kept biting until he'd cut him in half. The soldier's screams couldn't be distinguished from the ones happening all around.

A severed arm fell with a thud at Hotemkhar's feet jolting something within him. He scrambled to his feet, running with all his might. A man fell, dying, in his way and one of these monsters turned its attention to him. It moved to attack but a soldier sliced it across the side with his sword. Hotemkhar nearly wet himself as the creature smiled and turned to attack the soldier. The magistrate wasted no time running again.

Something wet and heavy hit his face and he stumbled in panic. He frantically swatted the object to the ground, only then realizing it was half a tongue. His nausea kept him from screaming. A trio of soldiers fought with a beast, moving directly in his path and he changed directions. The only thought in his mind was to get away from this. He had to get away from this.

Hotemkhar was knocked over by a body flying through the air. He struggled to get up, realizing he was pushing himself off most of the bottom half of a man. Gagging and screaming fought again but his fear addled mind made his legs keep moving. He dodged more body parts and battles, turning this way and that, desperate to find a safe spot from the fighting.

He ran until he tripped over a root and fell into a creek. He fought the air until he opened his eyes, seeing the root entangled over his ankle. He freed himself, scrambling to the other side of the water. Around him, the forest was quiet. He couldn't hear any fighting, not even the sounds of screaming. He couldn't see anything for the thick growth overhead.

He waited. He waited some more. Nothing came. Nothing happened except night animals rustling, hooping, and mating in the trees. His breath eventually returned to normal, his heart not threatening to beat its way through his chest. He looked around the forest, even though his eyes could only make out the barest differences in the shadows.

Where was he? He knew he should head back across the creek, try to find what was left of the army. He gulped. If there was an army left. He tried to take a step forward, but his legs refused to move. He collapsed to a sitting position, disbelief sinking in. He was lost. He would die here.

~

Ofemu was ready. It was early morning in Nsongo and the sky was still painted the lavender of dawn. He was sitting in an alley of the merchant district, sword and shield in hand, braids tied back. He had on the quilted leather armor from his first war, each of the scratches telling the story of his many battles. Around him were five warriors, all perched low. In the surrounding alleyways, more of the squad he commanded waited. They wanted blood. They wanted revenge. But they had to hold it at bay until the right moment.

It pleased him to no ends that he was here, in the vanguard despite his father's advice against it. He was happy that war minister Ngali had insisted. She'd even insisted that Barabi be involved in planning it. That little twist of the knife had delighted Ofemu as well. Anything to vex his father.

The call to war had gone over quite well as he expected. How many people had been personally insulted when Ashaki had surrendered to the empire? Surrender was as good as a curse to an Nsongan. To any southerner. How many nights had he dreamed of slitting the throats of every strutting rooster that ran around his city in Egan armor? Now, they'd be putting an end to the occupation after all this time. The bloodlust in him jumped in glee.

He made the signal to be ready to his warriors as a group of Egan soldiers marched up the street to the building before them. The northerners had commandeered a number of the city's storehouses, guarding them like they were the most precious commodities in the city. Considering that they held much of the soldiers' food, it just may have been. And at this time, at the morning changing of the guard, when most of the city was asleep, when the guards were lax, they wouldn't be so interested in guarding their precious food so stringently.

The soldiers coming up the street met up with the guards in front of the storehouse. The old guard looked exhausted, despite their attempts at alertness. The new guard greeted them warmly, the kind of greeting of an old comrade understanding the plight of the other. They laughed and completely forgot about the fact that they were in an occupied city.

This was the moment.

Ofemu burst out from the side alley, his warriors in step behind him. One of the Egan guards saw him but he slashed out with his sword before the man could yell out. The beautiful arc of blood from his throat was caught in the dawn sun before spattering on the stones of the road. His other warriors were already out from their hiding places and attacking the other guards. Before his first opponent had finished bleeding out, the rest had been dispatched.

He assigned a trio of warriors to hold the storehouse while they continued on. Ofemu grinned broadly, running down the street to their next target. They reached the next storehouse that the enemy had turned into a sort of barracks. He and his men came up on the rear of it, creeping into the still dark walkway beside it. He peered into one of the skinny windows. Most of the men were still asleep or just starting about their day. He frowned. How had such a lazy force beat them so soundly?

He motioned for four of his warriors to head to the front, to take out the guards there, while the rest of them would come in through the back. He made his way to the door and just as he reached for the pull, an Egan soldier opened it, fumbling with his clothes. Ofemu froze just as the soldier did.

A breath passed and Ofemu stabbed the man in the gut. He slit his throat so he couldn't cry out, pulling him to the ground. His warriors followed him inside and then the slaughter began. The Egan soldiers scrambled to get weapons before the Nsongans attacked. Some managed to barely drag swords out just in time. Others weren't so lucky. The ones at the far end yelled out for the guards at the front but no answer came.

Ofemu was satisfied he'd managed to kill four of them before the end. He looked to his squad and nodded toward the back. They dragged the bodies to the refuse pile where they belonged and looked to their commander for orders.

There was only one more target in their part of Barabi's plan. A merchant's home that had been overrun. But Ofemu wanted more. He could do more. He gave his men their orders for now, but his mind was running over his knowledge of the city and where he could find more soldiers to kill. By the time they'd taken back the house, he knew where they could hit next.

There was a row of restaurants that rested on the edge of the merchant's district, just beyond the residences. Quite a few Egan had taken a liking to getting their breakfast there. More than a few people had come to him over the years to try and get him to persuade his cousin to do something about it. The soldiers were rowdy and many flat out refused to pay for anything. Today, he would see to it himself.

He called a halt right before they reached the street, motioning for them to fan out along the back streets until they could come up in the alleyways that led to the street. He waited with two others, watching the small group of Egans swaggering up to the outside stalls. He guessed they were too good to eat inside. He waited until they were good and settled, then gave a series of shrill, sharp whistles that echoed off the surrounding buildings. While they all looked his way, his warriors rushed out from their hiding spaces, weapons ready.

Ofemu ran out, freeing his sword, his heart singing at the prospect of battle. These men put up more fight than the just waking up soldiers they'd encountered before. His sword rang as it met Egan steel over and over. The man in front of him was determined and he had to commend him on that. But Ofemu hadn't risen so high on familial connections alone. He had years and years of training, grueling training by his uncle honed even further by skirmishes and then the final war with the Egan. What was a grunt getting breakfast to him?

A cut across the thigh stumbled the enemy soldier giving Ofemu a moment to run him through. A twist. A jerk outward. Next opponent. This one was wiry, fast on his feet and ready to fight. He tried to overtake Ofemu with a flurry of strikes, but Ofemu was just as fast despite his size and kept up. He used his greater strength to parry the man's sword so hard, his arm was thrown back. That was the moment the commander stepped in, head butting the other man in the nose. The crunch was music to his ears. A quick pair of slashes and this opponent was down too.

He jumped into help another warrior finish off one of the men. Ofemu hacked off one of his legs and the other warrior stabbed him in the neck. They turned to face other soldiers, both grinning at finally getting a chance to finally deal a blow to the Ega after three long years.

The street was red with blood, running in between the stones and trickling downhill when they killed the last of the soldiers. Store owners stared at them. The mid-morning sun illuminated everything. Then the store owners erupted into cheers and his warriors couldn't resist a cry of triumph. As they began singing a victory song, Ofemu counted the places in the merchant district where he knew the Ega gathered. This should be the majority. The other spots would hold just a handful that could be taken over easily. The merchant's district was theirs. And all over the city, other warriors were retaking vital spots.

He suddenly realized everyone was chanting his name. Ofemu smirked, never easy with accepting praise, then let loose a roar of triumph. Nsongo would be theirs again and everyone would know that he'd been at the forefront.

Chapter Twenty-Two

Izriamat was working in one of the temple gardens when Sami approached her with another of her followers in tow. The other priests and priestesses side eyed the pair as they worked, barely hiding their disapproval. Izriamat smiled at the pair, waving them over cheerfully.

Sami stopped and bowed, the young man with her following her example awkwardly.

"My princess, we have news from the wall," she said quietly. She looked around suggestively at the others around.

Izriamat raised an eyebrow but stood and led the group to a secluded nearby corner. "What is it?"

The young man bowed again. "Princess, I know you don't remember me, but you saved my life weeks ago. I just wanted to thank you," he gushed.

"Yazirim, the news," Sami chided softly.

"Yes. My princess, I've gotten work as a water runner for the soldiers at the gate. There was some kind of hubbub from the lookout station, then a messenger came riding up, full speed. Later I heard some of the soldiers saying that the Ega army was coming. They were maybe two or three days away."

Izriamat gasped. She knew Bakari would be back, but she didn't think it would be so soon. She made the sign of blessing over the young man.

"Thank you for bringing this to me. Yutuu smiles upon you."

He was an ear-to-ear grin as Sami bowed and ushered him away. Izriamat took a moment to compose herself. The moment she had been waiting, preparing, and praying for was finally here. Bakari would come and dare attack Wiluru, the favorite pearl of Yutuu, and he would pay dearly for it. *May he be dragged to the deepest depths where Yutuu's wrath awaited.*

She left the garden, heading for the innermost sanctuary of the temple. The priest at the door bowed to her with a wizened smile.

"If you wish to use the sanctuary, you'll have to hurry. High tide will be coming soon."

"Thank you, elder," she said returning the bow. "I'll keep it in mind."

They opened the door for her and she stepped inside. Waiting a moment for the door to close behind her. When it did, she slowly descended the few stairs leading down to the tiny underground beach. She disrobed with each step, leaving it behind her, and set foot on the cool sand. The moistness of it underfoot was comforting and she savored each step. When the water lapped at her ankles she took a deep breath, calling on the presence of Yutuu.

Izriamat waded into the waters until she was deep enough to float. She closed her eyes, letting the gentle pull of the weak tide push and pull her. Here, she was surrounded by his presence. Here there was nothing hindering her communion. She was bare to him, just as she was born, from water and blood.

She turned her thoughts to the upcoming battle, asking through her feelings how she should deal with the coming threat. Should she lead her people to war or should she leave that to others more capable of fighting? A deep, dark part of her wanted to plunge a spear into the emperor's chest herself. It would be satisfying to end his life for all the misery he'd caused. But if Yutuu had other uses for her during that time, she would bend to his will. She was his vessel, here to be filled with his presence and work his will on this land.

Then, she felt a movement in her spirit. Something divine permeated through her body. It gave her a feeling of calm and she sank into it. She saw herself leading her people, her army of those she'd healed going forth with the righteous might of Yutuu. She saw a sword in her hand and she glowed golden as she called them forward. She cut down the enemies of Wiluru, defending the gates and her faith.

More faceless Ega soldiers came against her but her sword was never slowed. She killed more of them. The killings became more brutal. Crueler. She saw her face, splattered with blood, contorted in a gleeful sneer. She delighted the ways she could make her enemy die a slow death. Izriamat grew drunk with the powerful feeling. A part of her protested the slaughter but the rest of her called out for more.

Suddenly, the vision stopped. Her feelings were conflicted, intertwined with the divinity inside her, calling for blood and calling for righteous wrath at the same time. It pulled back and forth until the feeling of wrath lessened and she was left with a calming peace. It stayed with her, that reassuring calm, and the image of her glowing and leading her people came back to mind.

Izriamat returned to complete consciousness when the water pushed her back to the sands. She opened her eyes, laying there, staring at the cave's ceiling. She was disturbed, the core of her being uneasy. Those feelings of feral rage and righteous anger, warring against each other left her. Izriamat crossed her arms over herself. Was that what Yutuu wanted or was that what she wanted? The rage had almost felt like a completely different presence within her.

She closed her eyes, reaching out with a prayer again. She would not leave here more confused than she'd come. The answer came sharp and quick.

Protect my people.

She jerked up and realized the tide had risen shin deep. The push of it lapped at her hips. She sat there, staring at the water. She said a quick prayer of thanks and went to fetch her clothes from the stairs. She redressed, focused on the finality of her deity's final statement to her. There was no mistaking the will of Yutuu in that decree, forceful like a wave rushing to the shore when trying to swim to sea. She was his chosen one and she would protect his chosen people. No matter the cost.

~

Umakaal stood on a hill of Wiluru near the temple of Lirtara, goddess of the wind. This was a point in the city that the sea winds could be felt the hardest and her priestesses had taken full advantage of that. The wind chimes played melodically in the breeze. This hill also gave the princess an unhindered view of the port and she could see every single boat docked.

She shaded her eyes from the sun and squinted to make which fleets ships had arrived. With the news of the Egan army arriving in just days, they needed every soldier they could get to fight. Hopefully, her brother and the rest of the main fleet were on their way back. She wasn't sure how they would fare if the Ega broke through the main gate. Umakaal looked down the orderly port. She could see ships from Yutina with their bright orange and gold flags. She could see Laatu, Falee's Bay, The Hook, and even little Geyarta. She stopped. That couldn't be it. She checked two more times. She figured that Tiiraza wouldn't be represented. Their ships were either protecting the border or away with Yutuuan. However, Asfara was distinctly absent.

Umakaal made her way down to the port, seeking out the ship of captain Netkala. Surely she would have some idea of what was going on. A nagging worry started in her gut. Asfara was the first major city that they'd secured the cooperation of for this war. Her brother had even promised to make the governor's daughter—that he detested—his queen. They couldn't have just forgotten their obligation. And if their governor had decided to renege then for the first time, she was going to lay hands on one of her elders.

Sailors greeted her with hearty salutes and she smiled and nodded as she walked along the docks. Captain Netkala was calling out orders as her sailors worked to move their supplies off ship. Worry put a crease between her brows and her voice sounded hoarse.

"Captain," Umakaal called, standing at attention.

The older woman looked over with a strained smile. "Princess," she said, clearing her throat. "I hope you fare well today. Did you have a message from the palace? I pray to Yutuu you don't."

Umakaal chuckled. "No, not right now. I have a question for you." She leaned in. "Have you seen any ships from Asfara? I don't see their banner."

Netkala looked left and right down the rows of ships. "Why no, no I haven't. When I didn't see them as the other fleets arrived, I just assumed they were delayed." She looked around again. "There's no reason they shouldn't be here by now."

"I'm worried that they might be forgetting their promises," she ground out.

Captain Netkala whistled. "That's a high accusation, princess. One I wouldn't throw about freely." She glanced about, lowering her voice. "But Asfara has always thought of itself as apart from the rest of the kingdom. However, I wouldn't think Governor Bergarmen so bold as to deny the rest of us aide." Umakaal nodded, taking in her elders' words. "There is one ship here from Asfara. Perhaps you should ask their captain if they know anything."

"I think I will." She nodded to the captain and headed off the ship looking around until she finally saw the red and gray of Asfara.

Far down, near the end of the docks, one solitary ship bobbed in the sea. It was a smaller navy vessel, one that would barely hold any more than thirty to fifty sailors. A pitiful number when you remembered that Asfara had the second largest portion of the kingdom's fleet behind the Wiluru. She walked up to one of the sailors unloading supplies. "I need to speak to your captain, please."

The sailor looked her over, questioningly. "Who's here to see her?"

Umakaal was a little insulted but made herself remember that this man had probably never seen her in his life.

"Princess Umakaal, daughter of King Taagreb, ninety-ninth of his line."

The sailor's eyes rounded as big as the jewels on her mother's best necklace. He managed an awkward combination of a salute and a bow.

"Right this way, my princess."

The sailor led her onto the ship where other sailors paused their work as they wondered about this newcomer on their decks. Umakaal felt the swaying of the ship underneath her and hoped that one day she would be able to still command the fleet. It didn't look like she'd be in charge of anything until her father passed away. She brushed the sorrowful thoughts away and focused on the now.

The Asfaran ship's captain was in his quarters, crossing items off a list, when the sailor knocked on the open door.

"Come," he said, not even looking up. Umakaal could tell, it wasn't out of callousness but concentration.

"Captain," began the sailor, giving a salute, "the princess Umakaal wants to speak to you."

The man looked up; his jaw slightly slack. He stood immediately, saluting her crisply. "Princess Umakaal, to what do I owe this honor?"

Umakaal stepped in. "I have a few questions for you, Captain. Privately, please."

He glanced and gestured with his chin toward the sailor. The sailor quickly left, closing the door behind him. "Can I offer you something to drink, princess. I have a little Tiirazan wine left."

"No thank you, Captain . . .," she trailed off, the question lingering.

"Nowari, princess."

"No, thank you, Captain Nowari." She paused, not wanting to start off with accusing the governor of light treason. "Have you heard anything from Asfara about more sailors for the conflict? Were they delayed?"

Nowari breathed in slowly. "I was . . . worried myself. No, princess, I haven't heard anything. It's strange. I thought I'd see more of my fellow Asfarans by now."

"Tell me what you know of Governor Begarmen."

"He's a distant relative on my father's side. A man that always sticks to his word. He views agreements between two parties as if they were blood oaths from ancient days."

Umakaal couldn't help the frown. "Your governor promised to send people to fight to help with the war and I don't see any others but you. With all that Asfara has, I know fifty men isn't it."

"I can write to him, princess, on your behalf." Captain Nowari tried to make himself seem as amicable as possible.

"I think that would be good. Tell him that Princess Umakaal wishes to know why he hasn't provided the forces agreed upon with his crown prince. War is very nearly on our heads." He nodded, face falling in worry.

She sighed then tried her best to seem like she wasn't angry at the captain, just the situation. "Thank you for your time, Captain, and may Yutuu lift your tides."

The captain bowed. "We'll be ready when the battle comes and I will get that letter together now."

Umakaal nodded and left the ship. Sailors gave her proper salutes as she departed. She walked back into the city, her mind a swirl of thoughts. The war was here, Yutuuan and the main fleet were gone, and here she was, in command of no one. Her mother would say it was her own fault. The princess frowned. How could they punish her for doing what was right? They were supposed to be teaching her the lessons of leadership. Did they want her to learn that you should show your belly to your enemy?

Her mind started to form the idea that her father was a coward, but she cut it off before it was fully formed. But they couldn't keep giving and giving and giving to the Ega every time they made a demand. One day, they would have nothing left to give.

Her feet took her on a winding path through Wiluru, roughly heading toward the palace. She looked up and realized she was near the great gate and turned to head to the guard station. Guards saluted her and the greeting pained her. She should be with them, commanding them in Yutuu's absence.

The on-duty commander jogged up, giving her a bow and salute. "Princess," he said. Was that relief in his voice? "Are you rejoining us?"

"No, I just want to climb the wall."

His face dropped just a fraction before he stepped aside. "Please, go ahead." As she passed, he said quietly, "Your presence is greatly missed in the palace guard from what we hear. We pray you'll be able to join us for the attack."

Umakaal gave him a smile and she begged Yutuu to hide how weak it was. "I pray so as well."

Without another word, lest she break out in tears, she took to the stairs that led to the guarded walls of Wiluru. It was from here that her sister had rebuked the netkoleh and it would be from here that her kingdom would be defended. It had been ages since the great gates were breached and she wouldn't see them breached again. But as she gazed out to the horizon, knowing the might of the Ega was somewhere just past it, her resolve wavered.

~

Izriamat walked proudly through the streets, people bowing to her and making the sign of Yutuu. The warm sea air moved through her braids. She no longer wore the long ribbons within the plaits; she was a priestess again. However, she missed the way it made her match the prayer flags in the city. But she was set apart, different from the other city dwellers. She couldn't indulge in such frivolities anymore.

Her path took her to the palace doors this afternoon. The guard before the grand stairs stopped her hesitantly.

"I'm . . . I'm sorry, princess. Your father's orders."

"Move aside," she commanded. There was power in her voice and the entire contingent of guards stood to the side. Izriamat climbed the stairs without any other protests.

She closed her eyes for a moment, taking in the coolness of the interior of the palace. She walked for the rear of the building, with purpose in her steps. At this time of day, her father would be in council deciding on the fate of the kingdom. She wondered if he was speaking on the coming army at all.

The guards at the council doors stared in disbelief as she walked up. They were in such shock, they only tried to stop her once it was too late. Izriamat pushed open the council room doors to their weak protests.

A weighted, shocked hush fell over the room as the banished princess strode in. She held her chin up, ignoring the stares from the councilmen. She kept her eyes on her father. He looked even frailer than the last time she'd seen him. His eyes held the sunken look of exhaustion. His cheeks were hollowing and his curls looked whiter than she remembered. But once his shock had worn off, he looked to her in anger.

"Izriamat, you were forbidden to return to the palace until I summoned you," he snarled at her although his bark held little force.

Izriamat paused at the sound of his voice. He was strained.

He was sick. She could heal him easily; he had only to ask.

"Daughter," her mother started in that warning tone of voice. "You should return to the temple where your father and *king* sent you. This is doing nothing to prove your true loyalty to the throne."

Loyalty to the throne sent me south be raped by the netkoleh. "I have only ever acted out of loyalty and love for my father, the king." She cast a smile at her mother before turning her attention back to her father. "This is why I am here. Father, mother, esteemed council members, the netkoleh and his army grow close, as I'm sure you know. With my brother and most of our forces caught up to the east, I and my army are ready to help with the defense of our great kingdom."

Her statement was met with silence, which she'd expected. What she didn't expect was the trio of chuckles coming from the councilmen. The others looked at her, either aghast or frowning their disapproval. The king's frown deepened.

"Did you really come here to waste our time? Izriamat, return to the temple and do not return until you're called for."

"I will not," she said taking a half step forward. "You will not disregard the will of the faithful," she looked over her shoulder in the direction the chuckling had come from. "And you will not laugh at the will of our god, Yutuu. These people are ready to fight, to lay down their lives for this battle, for their king and kingdom. I would call this brave. Far braver than those assembled here. We are ready to fight for Yutuu's chosen people if you permit it or not."

"This is foolishness," her father snapped.

"This is the path that our god has laid out for us. You would be wise to heed his message *and* his messenger."

Her father's face turned a deep brownish red. "How dare you come before this council and try to lecture *us* about bravery. War wouldn't be on us if you hadn't provoked the netkoleh at the wall."

Izriamat laughed, a deep sound that rumbled from her belly then up and out of her throat. "You still believe that peace can come from talking to that animal. Aren't you tired of bowing to the Ega and their foul ways?" She turned slowly to look every councilmember in the eyes. Her voice echoed off the walls. "Aren't you all tired? Do your knees not hurt from how low you must sink?"

"Leave this room," the king shouted behind her.

"They demand that we abandon our gods and you believe these people we can negotiate with."

"Leave!"

"The Ega and their blasphemous emperor are coming to destroy us, destroy Wiluru and all its cities. We all must be ready to fight, every single one of us. And if you all are too cowardly to lead in this time, then the one our god has chosen will." She concluded, turning back to her father.

Her father tried to speak but only a gasp came out. One hand gripped the arm rest of his throne until his nails were white. The other went to his chest just as he began to slump over. Her mother rushed to his side, calling her husband's name repeatedly but he couldn't respond.

Izriamat watched her father fall slowly to the floor, his reddening eyes locked on her until he couldn't anymore. She watched as the councilmembers flocked to their monarch, some of them calling for the guards to get a physician. It all happened around her as if she wasn't part of the chaos. She knew she should feel something. Anything. Her father might be dying, right in front of her. She searched herself, pulling from deep down within her being.

Nothing.

Her mother was crying. The council members were praying. And here she stood, empty of any emotion for the drama unfolding before her. The palace's physicians hurried by her, getting ready to use magic and all their medicinal knowledge to heal him. Izriamat looked at her father, prone on the floor, so terribly still, and walked out of the room. She had the work of her god to do.

Chapter Twenty-Three

Wiluru was in sight. As the army came to a stop Bakari couldn't take his eyes off the high cliff that made up the coastal city's walls. It stretched as far as one could see in each direction, a definitive barrier to almost the entire country. Wiluru had taken advantage of this spot that came so close to the coast and built here with easy access to the sea and to the rest of the land. Overhead gulls called out, flitting back and forth between the two areas of the empire with ease. Bakari looked onto the tall, carved gates that prevented his easy entrance. His hands flexed on his reins, his breath coming in a faster rhythm. He was almost there.

The sounds of chopping soon filled the late afternoon as every tree around the scrubby landscape was cut down and brought back to fashion into instruments of war. As Bakari waited for his tent to be set up, he took a walk around the encampment, watching the work. Incredibly tall ladders were fastened together with military efficiency. Logs were split and brought together to create towers that could be rolled on wheels up to the gates. The soldiers were so engaged in their work that many of them missed his passing. He didn't even mind the slight of protocol. They labored for Wiluru to be brought back in line. The sounds of their manufacturing could surely be heard on the wall and beyond. Bakari took a deep breath. There wasn't just the smell of cut timber in the air. There was fear and he relished in it.

The emperor made his way back to his now constructed tent in want for a way to occupy his time. The plan was already laid out. Once they'd breeched the gates, they would fight their way down the main street until they made their way to the palace and capture it. He gathered up a whet stone and sat down to sharpen his sword. Normally a servant would do this for him, but it gave him something to do with his ready hands and a task to focus his mind on.

He frowned as he ran his sword rhythmically along the stone. The plan was simple but carrying it out wouldn't be as easy. The gates of Wiluru were famous for repelling the invasions of the Ega for ages before his ancestor, Malukteht, forced them open. It had been a long-fought battle with forces sent to sneak their way around to other parts of the great cliffs and find another way in. Those forces then subdued the guards at the gate, opening the way for the ancient Egan leader. Since that time, Wiluru had closed off any possible other entrances leaving the great gates as the only way in. They would have to go through them if he wanted to recapture the city.

He listened to the music of the siege engine building for a moment. The ladders would be a risky way for his men to climb the wall. With such a distance that needed to be climbed, it gave the Wiluruans plenty of time to shoot them down. The towers would fare better but they had fewer of them. And then there were their magicians. Bakari's fingers slipped as he thought about the magical force he could have had if the Djelebans had only done what he asked. He winced at the cuts on his fingertips, the blood welling up bright red. Damn those cowardly scholars. But it was no matter. He still had the ex-priests from the capital and they would have to do. They'd better perform to the best of their abilities. Their lives depended on it.

Bakari pressed a cloth to his fingers just as his servants brought in dinner. He ate quickly, too quickly, his mind still focused on the imminent attack. Soon they would be in Wiluru and the destruction he'd sworn to enact would be happening. His uncut fingers tapped on the table he ate in an impatient rhythm. He knew his army would swarm over the Wiluruans like a cloud of locusts once inside the walls. These people were seafarers, used to combat on ships, not hand-to-hand fighting of an invasion. They couldn't possibly understand what was awaiting them.

As night fell, he tried to sleep. First light. That's what he and his commanders had agreed on. The noise of construction had stopped and the camp was finally quiet. Bakari lay in bed, eyes refusing to stay closed. First light was so far away. Before, in his last campaign, he would have spent a restless night praying over the next day's battle. He would have beseeched the gods for power and skill, for the enemy to fall before his sword. How odd yet right it felt to lay here in his own thoughts, to focus on the victory that would be won by his own hands. His ancestor had been the first to subdue the proud Wiluruans, turning their kingdom into a true empire. Now, he would be the one to bring them back to heel at the dawn of a new age. The thought didn't bring him sleep but brought him enough peace that his mind was restful for the remainder of the evening.

~

Bakari was up and ready for battle when the sky began to lighten in the east. He mounted his horse, his sword a welcome and familiar weight at his side. His commanders sat atop their steeds near him, watching as the army made the last adjustments to their formations. The soldiers with their ladders were ready, archers ready to cover them. The towers sat ready to be pushed forward. Bakari's fingers tapped on the pommel of his sword as he looked to the east. The deep blue black of night was slowly turning purple, then pink. On the wall he knew the Wiluruan soldiers were watching, feeling the same anticipation that ran through his own army. This was the moment before battle when everything was still and your courage tried to flee. It was then that you forced yourself to move on and destroy your enemy despite anything you might feel in your heart. Kill until that was all that you wanted from the day, to stand on the bloody heap of your enemy's bodies and know that you proved yourself better.

Bakari grabbed the pommel to keep his hand still. Just a little bit longer. Just an hour or two at most and he would begin the destruction of Wiluru. By the end of day, he may have Izriamat's throat in his hands.

The eastern sky grew lighter and the walls of Wiluru became clear in the strengthening illumination. Bakari stopped himself from fidgeting in his saddle as he watched the horizon. It was so near, he was nearly salivating. The brightness of the sky grew until, at last, the blinding light of the sun crested the horizon. Bakari raised his hand, then dropped it sharply. His nearest commander called out the order for attack. Horns blew, deep and rumbling, rippling through the ground and up through Bakari's chest. It echoed off the walls of Wiluru, filling the air. His men made a triumphant roar and the flag commanding the archers forward was raised. Rows of men marched toward the gates, taking high aim.

Bakari held his breath as a mass of arrows flew through the air, a cloud full of the promise of death. It sailed up and over the gate and the cries of alarm could be heard even from this distance. As the archers rearmed themselves, the former priests came forward. Groups of them clustered together and managed to produce balls of fire, some as tall as two men. Other groups gathered to make enough wind to feed the fire and launch it forth. Bakari's heart leaped when their attack hit the gates with a deafening boom. The priests had finally put their skills of tending the funeral pyres to effective use. More volleys of arrows flew over the gate. Fire balls pummeled the ancient gates. They groaned but didn't give under the assault. Then the Wiluruans began to retaliate.

A swarm of arrows, flying faster and harder than arrows should be able, arched over the gate, raining down on the closest of the Egan forces. The priests scattered, causing chaos on the front before they were forced back in line by the other soldiers. Priests sent more attacks at the gates and they finally caught fire. The small wisps of flame reached into the morning air weakly. If the gates were to burn, it wouldn't be quick.

Bakari gave the command for the towers and ladders to advance. The men carrying the ladders held their shields aloft to protect against arrows, looking like strange armored snakes parting the army. The towers rose above the forces, their many floors brimming with soldiers waiting to attack. On the side nearest the gates, men held tall shields to fend off arrow attacks. Bakari rode closer to the fighting, ignoring his commanders' pleas and warnings. It would only be moments now before the siege would begin in earnest. He wanted to get closer but he knew to stay well out of arrow range. He wouldn't fall to carelessness.

As he strained in his saddle to get a better look at the battle, the day began to dim. Bakari looked up and the sky above him darkened with clouds. More gathered and formed a swirling maelstrom. His horse took a nervous step and he tightened his hold on the reins of his faithful warhorse. He questioned whether it was his side or the Wiluruans who was doing this when he got his answer.

The air of the battlefield was rent by a bolt of lightning. The strike hit hard enough to be felt, the tingle from the electricity running up people's arms. Bakari watched, half deafened, as bodies and limbs were thrown in the air. Men on the battlefield stopped and stared. At the gates, more arrows were shot down on the gawking soldiers. Bakari narrowed his eyes, riding closer. He scanned the top of the walls, searching. At one point, he could just make out a Wiluruan soldier, arms outstretched. Their braids whipped in the wind. As they brought their hands down, the storm churned and another bolt struck the field.

Bakari searched until he found a field commander. "Bring her down," he shrieked. "Bring her down now!"

A handful of commands later and arrow fire was redirected in the storm magician's direction. Another lighting strike came close enough to Bakari for dirt and rocks to strike him across the face. He wiped his vision clear, fixing his angry stare at the enemy magician. Other Wiluruans had come to her aide, shielding her from attacks with gusts of wind. Another bolt landed across the army with a deafening blast. One of his commanders rode up, frantically.

"My emperor." His shout could barely be heard for the noise. "My emperor, you must get back to safety."

"Wait." Bakari watched as the first of the towers made it to the gates. Egan solders rushed to fight the guard at the top. Next, the ladders were raised. These were met with more resistance and as many soldiers made it over as were shot down. One ladder soon caught on fire. Men scrambled to climb up or down. Some, too close to the fire for either, chose to jump to escape.

"My emperor."

"Wait."

The second and third towers reached the gates, disgorging their masses on the Wiluruans. He could just make out the figures from the rocky walls rushing to help their comrades. The magical attacks dwindled in frequency. Bakari's fingers tapped along his sword handle. He made himself breath steadily. This was where the combat began. This was where his campaign won or lost.

The minutes dragged by like eons. The sounds of battle from behind the war started to drift over. They dare not send another volley of arrows lest they hit their own soldiers on the other side. They had nothing to do but wait.

The ground rumbled and Bakari braced himself for another lighting strike but none came. And all the soldiers around him watched in awe as, with a great groan, the gates of Wiluru began to open.

Bakari had to remind himself to breath. Utter elation coursed through him. This is what Malukteht must have felt when he forced Wiluru to open to him. He looked to the commander near him.

"Order the full attack. Hold nothing back but the reserve. I will take the Black Wing's command."

The older man lowered his head. "As you wish, emperor," he said and rode off to fulfill his sovereign's commands.

Bakari turned his steed, riding to the banner of the Black Wing. Its commander bowed from his saddle the moment he saw Bakari coming, moving his horse over to let the emperor take command position. Bakari surveyed the wall where no enemy soldier could bother with attacking the standing army; there were too many on the wall itself.

He held his sword high. "Black Wing, advance!" The command was relayed and his force moved forward. Bakari grinned wildly as the horns sounded again. He moved to a proper position at the front of the wing. Cavalry spread out to both sides of him, infantry backing them up. The emperor looked to the partially open gates, still wide enough for his regiment to pass through unhindered, and the chaotic battle within. He hadn't realized that he'd missed this rush. He hungered for it and soon that hunger would be satiated.

Bakari initiated his return to Wiluru by cutting down an enemy soldier about to spear an Egan fighter. All around fights had come together in small pockets of battle and the Black Wing surged forward to turn the tide. Just beyond the forces at the wall, he could see the next wave of soldiers holding off any advancement from the Ega. Bakari smiled. He would get to them soon enough.

The gates needed to be secured first. He was sure that was nearly done. Then they could make their way down their great road to the palace. He spared a glance to the white walled palace, sitting so haughtily on its hill. This time, the palace wouldn't be saved. It would burn just like its city. The royal family would be abolished and this kingdom would finally become fully integrated into the empire.

It was past time.

Bakari felt the growing heat just in time to move his steed out of the path of an arc of fire. He turned, urging his horse to ride the magician down. Another arc of fire snaked toward him making Bakari evade again. Two Wiluruan soldiers close in to attack him. Letting go of his reins and trusting in his steed, he caught the spear of one before it pierced his side. With his sword hand he parried the other's blow, retaliating with a deep slash down the chest. As he moved to deal with his other attacker, the magician's spell found its target.

Bakari was knocked from his horse, hitting the ground like a stone. He felt the rising heat and rolled to escape. He looked up just in time to see his spooked horse's hooves coming down. Bakari scrambled away, rolling to get on his hands and knees. After a moment, he caught sight of the magician. The northerner had a hand on his sword and breathed hard. Was he tired from all of his casting? Bakari was willing to take that chance.

He rushed to his feet, taking off for the Wiluruan. Another enemy soldier tried to get between him and the magician, but he quickly dispatched them. Bakari made himself run faster. The other man was starting to catch his second wind. The emperor held his sword to his side, ready for a horizontal strike. The magician was forced to draw his sword to defend himself. Beyond this man, the great road of Wiluru ran parallel to the wall. It was as if this lone magician was his last obstacle to the city. Bakari entered this sword fight, his heart singing. He slashed for the magician, hard strike after hard strike glancing off of Wiluruan steel. This man was no match for him. A winded, Wiluruan, magician sailor couldn't possibly keep up with the ruler of the empire.

Bakari heard the satisfying squelch of flesh being rent as he plunged his sword into the magician's belly. He savored the moment the man slumped against him, clutching his shirt like it was life. Bakari pulled his sword out and looked for his next opponent when he saw the most curious sight.

In the main road, stood another force. Not of warriors, but what looked like common people. A laugh bubbled up within him. Was this what the mighty Wiluru had been reduced to? Assembling an army of shopkeepers and artisans to fight its battles? They held makeshift weapons, knives, tools, and swords that had seen better days. None of them had the sense to be frightened.

"Are you going to fight your emperor?" he shouted, unable to keep the chuckle out of his voice. The people hesitated but some slowly moved forward. "Too nervous to start? Allow me to help you."

Bakari raced toward them, easily getting within the defenses of the first man he faced, cutting him across the stomach. He moved onto next before the first hit the ground. This one was an old man with a butcher's heavy knife. He soon bled out from his throat. Two women tried to stab him. He slashed the first from stomach to face and grabbed the other about the neck, pulling her close in a chokehold. He swung him around then used him as a shield from the next attack. He laughed when his next attacker stabbed her by accident. The man dropped his sword in horror right before Bakari struck him in the head.

A sudden tightness in his chest stopped his laughing. He looked down to see an arrow sticking out from near the bottom of his rib cage. He looked up confused. Near the middle of the crowd a solitary archer stood. She took out another arrow, the wind around her picking up. Bakari tried to move but his movements were sluggish. It was hard to breath.

The next shot took him off his feet.

~

Bakari was laying on the ground. He knew it. He felt the cold of the paving stones beneath his back. He saw the brightness of the morning sky. People were running around him, fighting slowly as if the air were honey. The noises of battle came to him, muffled. He couldn't move. Couldn't cry out. Did they even realize it was him lying on the ground?

His eyes searched around frantically trying to focus on . . . what, exactly? More feet ran past him. Then he heard footsteps coming near him. He searched around his limited vision until he could just make out a figure walking through the battle. They were dressed in white and their clothing rippled in an unfelt wind. As they came closer, he realized it was a woman, the most beautiful woman he'd ever seen. She was tall with a figure of alluring curves. But her eyes were cunning like a cat.

She stopped by his side, looking down on him with a loving smile. Bakari's eyes briefly slid from her to the flock of vultures circling high overhead but he brought them back to her. She stooped down and reached out a hand to gently caress his cheek.

"Well done, netkoleh."

Then the world fell away.

Chapter Twenty-Four

Umakaal could hardly sleep and could sleep forever. Her stomach cramped in painful anxiety, threatening to evict its contents at any moment. She paced back and forth in her bedroom, staying on the cliff bear rug to soften her footsteps. Ladawi slumbered peacefully in bed and Umakaal wanted desperately to join her but worry kept her body moving.

She'd rushed to her father's bedside the moment she'd gotten the message of his collapse. He hadn't risen or responded to them since. Her mother was already sitting beside him when she arrived, her face drawn into deep wrinkles of worry. Her father was breathing but it was so slight it barely moved the covers. Umakaal took his hand, tears trailing down her cheeks. It broke her heart to not have his hand immediately clasp around hers, his soft yet firm grasp reassuring her. There was no strength in it now. It was cool to the touch and she suddenly realized how thin his fingers were.

She'd lowered her head in a prayer, her grief too much to pray aloud. She'd never been staunchly religious and her visits to the temple had only been when mandatory, but it was all she could do. She needed her father.

Her mother had suggested she return to her rooms for food and rest after a time. The healers had done all they could for now. There wouldn't be any change until the morning. So, with a burdened heart she'd returned to her chambers to try to find some calm. Hours passed and she'd attempted to sleep, but her feet soon found the floor and her pacing began.

Umakaal breathed out in frustration, slipping on her sandals. The room suddenly felt like a cage, far too small for the emotions rolling through her. She left her room and soon found herself stalking the halls of the palace, too agitated to focus on a specific path. Guards on night duty saluted her as she passed and she murmured greetings in kind. She stopped herself from trying to give any orders. That wasn't her duty anymore and the thought plunged her into a deeper despair.

By the time the first whisper of light from dawn lit the halls, she'd wandered her way to the paths leading to the throne room. The area was empty and only the sound of her sandaled foot-steps brushed along the stone floors. Until she heard another set of steps.

Umakaal paused, not wanting to see another person, to have to muster a facade of strength when she felt anything but. She ducked behind a column, catching the barest glimpse of the other figure moving past the hall she was in, headed toward the throne room. The princess looked again as her mind recognized the figure and its priestess robes. *Izriamat?*

She moved silently from behind the column, taking up a pace that put her far enough behind her sister that it didn't look like she was following. Izriamat moved with purpose and that pricked Umakaal's suspicion. What was she even doing here? How could she even show her face when it was her petulance and disrespect that had caused their father's attack? She should be headed to his rooms to beg for forgiveness and pray over him.

Izriamat stopped before the doors of the throne room and the younger princess watched as she ran a hand over the carved wood, pausing on the center of the symbol of Yutuu. After a moment, Izriamat pushed one open, slipping inside. Umakaal rushed up as her sister closed them behind her, stopping it before it could close all the way and stop her from seeing inside. She watched through the tiniest sliver as Izriamat walked the an-cient carpet that led to the throne. The elder princess stopped be-fore the chair of their ancestors, getting down with her forehead to the floor in the deepest sign of reverence. Umakaal could only make out the barest sounds of her sister speaking. After a mo-ment Izriamat stood and came before the intricate driftwood chair.

Umakaal stifled her gasp as her sister took a seat on the throne of Wiluru.

-End-

275

Sarah A. Macklin is the author of The Royal Heretic series, Bride of the River God, and a number of short stories. She is also an avid comic creator who released her first graphic novel, The Violent Vixens Ride Again, in 2023. If she's not creating new worlds, you'll find her happily at her sewing machine or in the kitchen trying new recipes. She resides just outside Columbia, SC with her equally nerdy husband and youngest daughter.

For more exciting Sword and Soul stories visit the MVmedia, LLC website for the Best of the Black Fantastic!
www.mvmediaatl.com